BARBI AND THE VILLAIN

BARBI & THE VILLAIN TRILOGY
BOOK ONE

VERONICA LANCET

BARBI AND THE VILLAIN

VERONICA LANCET

PREFACE

Dear Reader,

Barbi and the Villain is the first book in a trilogy. This will end on a cliffhanger. Although there are many humorous and light instances throughout this book, it *is* a dark romance. As the title states, the main male character is a villain. He is a bad guy through and through, and whether he is redeemable of not is purely subjective.

Content Warnings: attempted sexual assault, blood (gore), blood play, death, derogatory terms, torture, violence, sexual situations, kidnapping, murder, mass murder, dubious consent.

I

Why are the best men fictional?

I stare dreamily at my wall-sized illustrated poster of Sir Damien and Lady Jocelyn, smiling like a fool. He's gazing down at her with such adoration that my insides turn to mush as I imagine someone looking at me like that.

One day! One day I'll have someone just like that!

Turning to the mirror, I add a bit more blush to my cheeks and some pink lipstick. Puckering my lips, I briefly close my eyes as I imagine a man with the face of an angel and the body of a Greek god swearing his undying love to me before he leans down to kiss me.

Ah! A shiver goes down my body at the delicious daydream.

PomPom releases a soft bark, grazing her fluffy body against my bare legs.

The spell is broken, my fantasy destroyed.

I sigh as I gaze down at my cute white Pomeranian wiggling her tail and looking up at me with those cute eyes of hers.

"If only you were a boy, PomPom," I whisper, picking her up in my arms.

She licks my lips, tasting my lipstick and making a disgusted face. A giggle escapes me at her antics.

I give her a treat to distract her for a moment while I finish dressing up and putting on my makeup—all pink and girly, of course. It's not only a costume for me, it's an empowering way of life. Dressing up as Lady Jocelyn always makes me think that the world is my oyster and that I can achieve everything I set out to do. She's a powerful pink princess who is the perfect mix of feminine *and* badass—everything I've always wanted to be, too.

I'm wearing a pink dress with a fluffy skirt and a fitted bodice that may or may not have an overly revealing cleavage. I might have to run out of the house before my mom sees me. The corset I added on top of it accentuates my waist. Finishing the outfit are, of course, Jocelyn's signature strawberry-blond hair—though I've resigned myself to wearing a wig since I almost burned my hair two years ago bleaching it —and her pink five-inch heels.

Satisfied with my outfit, I make sure to dress PomPom in a similar pink ensemble, topped with a cute pink bow. Taking her in my arms, I open the door to my room and poke my head out, listening for any noises downstairs. A voice echoes from the kitchen.

"Kang Min did? Oh, that is very nice," my mother says, though her tone lacks the necessary enthusiasm. She's probably on the phone with her pseudo-friend Ye Rim—I wouldn't call them friends when all they do is try to one-up each other. "What university did you say it was?" A pause. "Oh, Yale. My Babi is also thinking of applying there. They have one of the best law schools in the country..."

Squeezing my eyes shut, I take a deep breath. I still haven't told my mom that I didn't register for the LSAT—or that I likely will never do. Dad is supportive of my choice, but for some reason, Mom got it in her head that the only way to prove to her friends that I was *smart* was by getting into a top three law school. It doesn't matter that I don't want to become a lawyer, or that my dream is to work in the publishing industry. No, for her it's all about showing that her daughter is not just some ditzy pink-loving loser.

I square my shoulders in disappointment. PomPom releases a soft bark as she senses my distress.

"We need to change strategies," I whisper to her. I quickly take off my shoes. Carrying them in one hand and PomPom in the other, I dash out the door. I run down the stairs and go straight for the exit when I hear my mom calling my name from behind.

"Babi-ya! Where are you going dressed like that?"

My eyes widen. Of course the woman has superhuman hearing—she's been busting my attempts at sneaking out since I was sixteen.

PomPom barks at hearing her voice, so I increase my speed. Mom's thudding steps echo behind as she chases after me, her voice increasingly more irate.

"Babi-ya!"

The car is in the driveway, ready to go. When the driver sees me, he opens the door for me to slide in with PomPom and we quickly drive off.

One quick glance in the mirror and I see my mom gesturing furiously at us—no doubt promising retribution for both me and my dad for arranging my escape.

"To the Convention Center, Miss Bancroft?" Mr. Philips, the driver, asks a few moments later.

"Yes, please. The back entrance. I need to get there early to make sure everything is set for our scene."

"Sure thing, miss." Mr. Philips winks at me.

I nestle PomPom closer to me as I direct my thoughts to our scene.

Every year, my friends and I attend Comic Con and stage

a scene from *The Five Mages of Akkaya*, a popular fantasy book series with over a dozen installments. The Five Mages are a band of misfits, all from humble beginnings. They trained until they became some of the best mages on the continent of Akkaya and they protected its citizens by defeating a slew of villains.

The main character of the series is Sir Damien, an honorable and kind hero who rescues damsels in distress and who always puts the welfare of his people above his own. He is the epitome of a righteous hero, and it doesn't hurt that he is also handsome, with his golden locks, sparkling blue eyes, and muscular body.

A wistful sigh escapes me.

Lucky Lady Jocelyn! She gets to have him all to herself. As his love interest from book one, Lady Jocelyn has been by his side through thick and thin. He loves and cherishes her, admiring her strength and fortitude, and he always includes her in his decision-making. Despite being a pretty girl who loves pink, she is also a great fighter, and over the years, she's managed to achieve the rank of Mage all by herself.

Ah, they make such a good team! Where will I find my *own* Sir Damien who will see me as his equal and treat me like his queen?

Am I infatuated with a fictional character? Guilty. But real men just aren't the same. Maybe my standards are too high from years of daydreaming with my nose in a book instead of going out and experiencing the *real* world. But how can I go from heroic Sir Damien who saves the world and wins the girl, to Chad next door who is only a 'hero' in his video games, has seven girls weekly on rotation, and still lives in his mother's basement?

Of course, there's nothing wrong with living in your mother's basement—technically. I still live with my parents, too, although it's purely because my mom won't let me move out until I get married. But how could I date someone seriously if the only step further would be marrying him and moving in with him in his mother's basement?

Nope. I will pass, thank you very much.

Maybe my standards are a little too much. But I stand by them. So what if I am twenty-one and I still haven't had my first kiss? Lady Jocelyn saved her first kiss for Sir Damien. And if Lady Jocelyn could find her match, then maybe at some point I will be able, too.

The car draws to a stop and I'm wrenched out of my thoughts.

"We're here, miss," Mr. Philips announces.

I beam at him. I put on my heels and dig through my small purse for some cash.

"Here," I say as I hand the banknotes to Mr. Philips.

His eyes widen, and immediately, he shakes his head and waves his hands in denial.

"No, no. Your father pays me already."

"Come on, Mr. Philips. I know it's your wife's birthday soon, so you can get her something nice."

"You remember?" he asks incredulously.

"Of course. Mrs. Philips is a lovely woman. Please give her my best."

When he still doesn't want to receive the money, I leave it behind on the seat.

With a wink, I grab PomPom and head out.

"Thank you, miss. Have fun!" Mr. Philips calls out as he drives off.

Excited about the day ahead, I head to the entrance. Once security clears me, I'm allowed into the convention hall. PomPom is ever so curious as she yaps whenever she sees someone in costume—which is mostly everyone. But like her mama, she's also drawn to pink.

A good percentage of the people present is costumed in characters from *The Five Mages of Akkaya*. It's *that* popular, and not only for the main characters. There is a slew of secondary characters who get their story arc, all different species, with distinct appearances and abilities. It's what makes the series so much fun! There is representation for *everyone*. It's what attracted me to the series in the first place when I started reading it almost a decade ago. Lady Jocelyn is half Asian, too, which made my prepubescent struggles easier since I had someone to relate to—though admittedly, I was still a handful.

My smile grows as I spot some other renditions of Lady Jocelyn. Though we are all doing the same character, the girls have chosen different types of dresses to represent her, some longer, some shorter, some light pink, some deeper pink.

Ah, the magic of Lady Jocelyn! Anywhere else and I would have been ridiculed for my tastes in clothing. Not here, though. Everyone is so positive and accepting. I wish the rest of the world could learn more from this community.

"Barbi! You're here!"

I turn when I hear someone calling my name, my lips stretching into a wide smile the moment I see Sarah.

"You look gorgeous," I gush when I take a better look at her costume. She's dressed as a mermaid, with a blue tail and a small top that only covers her breasts. Her body looks amazingly toned, which is why there are currently at least three guys checking her out.

"Thank you so much. You too. And PomPom, of course." She smiles as she attempts to pet PomPom on the head. My cute baby lets out a loud bark and bares her teeth at her.

Sarah's eyes widen as she takes a step back.

"Just as vicious as ever," she mutters.

I give her an apologetic smile. PomPom doesn't like anyone but me—not that I'm complaining.

"She's my little bodyguard," I joke, though it's not entirely inaccurate. Once, I was out shopping with her and someone tried to steal my purse. PomPom might be small, but she's got the vigor of a dog double her size. She spotted the suspicious man the moment he had his hand on my bag. Before he could pull on it, she'd jumped on him, lodging her teeth in his crotch—not that *I* taught her that.

The irony of it? I'd had to take a trip to the police station because the man had accused *me* and my dog of assault. The gall on some people. I should have let PomPom tear out a testicle—would have served the asshole right.

"You're here early. The scene doesn't start until later, no?" Sarah asks.

"I want to make sure everything is in order. Did you hear *which* scene we're doing?" I add enthusiastically.

She shakes her head.

"It's from the sixth book, the battle between Sir Damien and the Dark One."

"Oh my. That's right before Sir Damien proposes to Lady Jocelyn, isn't it?"

I nod effusively.

"Who's playing Sir Damien this year?" she asks.

"His name is Brandon and he's one of Clarice's friends. I don't know him too well, but he looks the part."

Her eyes sparkle suggestively.

"Does that mean what I think it means?" She wiggles her brows.

My cheeks heat up.

"No. Of course not. It's just acting." I shrug.

"Hmm…" she hums, unconvinced. It's not unusual for scene partners to end up dating. It happened to her and her boyfriend last year. But just because she was lucky, doesn't mean I am, too.

"It is! Besides, there's only a hug at the end of the proposal. We're not doing the kiss."

"If you say so…" She smiles as she makes to leave. "I'll believe it when I see it." She winks at me.

"I swear! There's nothing more to it!" I call out, embarrassed.

People stare at me, which prompts PomPom to bare her teeth at them and hiss.

"Shh, baby. It's fine," I whisper. "Let's go to our corner."

I cross the distance to the spot we'd been assigned for the scene. A ruffle of pink catches my eye—anything that's pink usually does. But as I get a better look, I blink slowly.

Clarice is wearing the same outfit I am—Lady Jocelyn's costume. She's standing between Brandon's open legs as they're kissing passionately.

Someone clears their throat and they stop, spotting me.

"Barbara." She smiles sweetly at me.

"What's the meaning of this?" I ask as I point to her costume. I couldn't care less what she does with Brandon. But I do take an issue with her dress—even the shoes are the same!

"We've decided to change some things for the scene," she adds. Brandon wraps his arms around her in silent support.

"I don't remember being asked about any changes." I narrow my eyes at her.

"That's because we've all decided that I would make a better Lady Jocelyn."

I turn to look around. All the other people are silent, their heads bent low.

"Mona?" I ask my friend, who averts her gaze. "Lily?" She doesn't answer either.

"And of course, that means you're out of the scene. You can still watch, though." She shrugs.

"What?" I sputter. "But… I prepared the decor. I paid for everything…"

"And because you paid for everything you should *always* get Lady Jocelyn?" She raises a brow. "You didn't even agree to the kiss and it's in the book!"

"But—"

"You are the one who wanted it to be a faithful depiction of the scene in the book, but you changed the kiss to a hug," she continues.

"But that's not a reason to kick me out without even letting me know," I add in a small voice, doing my best to keep the tears at bay.

"Face it, *Barbi*. You know no one wants you around. You're a stuck-up bitch and no one even likes you."

I blink slowly.

"Do you think so too?" I address the other people.

Clarice crosses her arms over her chest as she comes closer to me.

"Of course they do. Everyone's friendly with you because you pay for everything." She rolls her eyes. "Who would ever want to listen to you blabber about your stupid-ass delusions for free?"

"W-what…" I croak.

Her lips tug up in a mocking smile as she points a finger at me.

"Don't make this worse than it has to be. We all know I'll make a better Lady Jocelyn than you," she adds smugly.

I stare at her unblinking. My throat clogs with emotion as tears stab at my eyes.

I don't understand. I really don't. What did I ever do to deserve to be treated like this? Publicly, too?

"Why?" I whisper. "Why would you do this to me?"

She leans in to whisper, "Because you're pathetic. Not even the expensive perfume you're wearing can hide the stench of desperation coming off you."

I inhale sharply, her words doing the intended damage.

My heart beats loudly in my chest, echoing in my ears. A tremor goes down my spine, my limbs shaking uncontrollably.

"I thought you were my friend. All of you." I look at my other two friends—correction, *former* friends.

"Another delusion." Clarice shakes her head, feigning a pitiful expression. "Maybe you should get that checked out, Barbara."

She takes a step back as she laughs.

The others join in, all laughing at me.

My corset suddenly feels too tight, my heels too tall. The makeup on my face is too heavy. I stick out like a sore thumb when all I want is to hide away and disappear from the world. My breathing intensifies. The seconds trickle by and I won't be able to keep the tears at bay much longer.

PomPom releases a loud howl as she senses my distress. She wiggles in my arms until I let her go. That little encouragement is enough for her to jump on Clarice. She bites onto the tips of her wig, pulling with enough force that the entire thing falls off her head.

She cries out loud.

"Get your goddamn dog off me," she yells, pulling on her wig.

PomPom hisses at her.

"Avenge me, PomPom," I tell her as I push my chin up.

My cute baby knows exactly what to do as she lets go of the wig just as Clarice pulls on it, the momentum making her lose her balance and fall to the ground. Once there, it's game over.

PomPom jumps on her, biting her dress and tearing the material into shreds.

"Brandon! Do something!" She shrieks. "Take it off me. Do something."

He moves toward my PomPom and I take a step forward, pinning him with my gaze.

"Don't you dare touch my PomPom," I grit my teeth.

They can insult me, but they won't get away if they do anything to PomPom.

His eyes widen in alarm and he freezes.

"That's enough, PomPom. We don't need to bother with these"—I wrinkle my nose in disgust—"*people*."

PomPom raises her head to look at me, giving a low bark. But before she comes to my side, she decides to debase Clarice further.

"W-what's that smell?" Clarice whines as PomPom jumps off her.

"Agh!" she yells when she pats her body, her hand coming into contact with PomPom's watery poop. In her attempt to wipe it off, she merely smears it more around the dress.

PomPom struts arrogantly to my side, swaying her hips from side to side.

I scoop her in my arms.

"Good girl," I murmur, kissing the top of her head.

I look up at my *former* friends and shake my head.

"May you have a…a…" I wet my lips as I try to think of something witty. "May you have poop-filled day," I say before I leave with a huff.

Okay, not the best line, but as long as I keep my head high, I can still make a good exit. After all, I'm not the one currently smelling of poop.

I manage to keep my composure long enough to get out of their sight. Tears roll down my cheeks, and not even PomPom's sweet barks can make them stop.

I was a goddamn fool to think I may have found my crowd. I was even more foolish to think we were *friends* because we had a common hobby and we hung out every now and then. The more I look at it from that perspective, the more I realize this was all my fault. I thought that if I was nice and generous, I could make people like me. Instead, they only saw me as an idiot—a pathetic idiot.

My makeup is further ruined as I rub at my eyes, and given the pity looks I get, I assume I look like a mess. The only goal I have right now is to get out of here with what little of my dignity I have left.

But as I round the corner for the exit, I almost bump into an elderly lady.

"I'm so sorry," I apologize.

"It's fine." She waves her hand at me. Her shrewd eyes

study me for a moment before she nods to herself. "Here. You seem to need it."

I look down at the book she's offering—a hardcover edition of *The Fate of Akkaya*.

"But…" I blink repeatedly to make sure I'm reading the title right. "It hasn't even been released," I mutter.

It's the much-anticipated thirteenth book and supposedly the last one in the series. Everyone has been going crazy trying to get any type of information about what to expect, but the author has been tight-lipped.

"A gift." She smiles. "For a lovely Lady."

"But… Is it okay to give it to someone? It's an early copy, isn't it? Aren't you under contract or something?"

"I am free to give it away, child. Please," she continues, placing it in my hand. "I hope it will give you some joy on a bad day."

"Wow. I don't know what to say."

"A thank you is enough." She grins.

"Thank you," I mumble in awe.

She nods, and without another word, gets lost in the crowd.

2

The book is beautiful. Thick and heavy.

PomPom is nestled by my side in the cab as we both admire the pink and gold design of the cover.

The Fate of Akkaya is written in pink foil.

I swallow hard, excitement bubbling inside of me. Someone pinch me! Is this real?

It's almost as if the entire incident with Clarice is forgotten as I stare at the book I've been waiting for over three years for.

With a deep breath, I pry it open, flipping through the pages.

Seven hundred ninety-eight pages.

My God!

I'm going to lock myself in my room and I won't resurface until I'm done with it. I just need a stash of Diet Coke and some chocolate, and I will have sustenance for the coming days.

But first, I must find a way to get to my room without running into my mother. After what happened at the convention, the last thing I need is to have someone else tear at me and my pathetic self.

I sniffle a sob. Just a bit longer and I'll get home where I can cry in peace and feel sorry for myself.

The cab drops me off a block away from my house, and heels in hand, I attempt to make a stealthy entrance through the back. I carefully pull the door open and run up the stairs. But as I'm halfway there, my parents' voices reach me and it soon becomes clear they're having an argument—again. About me—again.

I push PomPom up the stairs, signaling for her to go to my room while I plop myself down, listening with a lump in my throat.

"She's too spoiled, Victor, and it's all *your* fault. You need to put restrictions on her spending. She has one year of college left and she needs to do better if she's going to get into *any* law school, let alone a top ten one," Mom adds impatiently, and I can already picture her pacing around while gesticulating.

"Have you thought she might not want to go to law school?" Dad drawls in his relaxed and calm manner.

"What? Nonsense! Ye Rim's son got into Yale Law! She was just bragging about it this morning, and I didn't even have one good thing to say about Barbi. I'm sure if I mentioned that she *passed* her Econ course, she would have laughed in my face."

I frown. What's so wrong with a pass? It's not as if it goes as a bad grade on my transcript.

"An Econ course *you* forced her to enroll in," Dad adds.

"Because you're not strict enough with her!" Mom bursts out, and I physically cringe at her tone.

"She's fine, Mi Joo. She has hobbies and friends, and she's growing up to be a lovely young lady. You have to let her decide her future for herself."

"Have you *seen* her?" My mom's horrified cry echoes in the house. "She went out in a skimpy dress with all her assets hanging out in the open. Who knows what she's doing and who she's meeting."

I close my eyes as I sigh wearily.

Yes, Mom, I was sneaking out to prostitute myself to men with a pink fetish.

I glance down at my chest. Granted, the cut is a little low, but I don't really have *assets* that can hang out in the open. If anything, to reach Lady Jocelyn's level of voluptuousness, I may or may not have stuffed a few socks in my bra.

But Dad is wrong, too. I don't have friends—or, at least, now I realize that I don't. At school, I'm too weird and people judge me for my choice of clothing. At home, I'm not good enough and will likely *never* be enough. And when it comes to my hobbies…

I sigh.

Just when I thought I found somewhere to belong, turns out they don't like me either. And I can't figure out *why*. What is it that makes me pathetic in their eyes? I've never badmouthed anyone, nor done anything to warrant that behavior. I've always had a smile on my face, ready to help anyone.

I purse my lips.

Maybe I was *too* accommodating, too eager to help that it came across as pathetic.

But that's how I've always been. I like helping people and I like being…*needed*. Yet, turns out, I was never needed anyway, except perhaps for my money. But even that isn't good enough anymore.

Damn it!

"Mi Joo, you're exaggerating," my dad says in an exasperated voice.

Not in the mood to hear more jabs at my already battered self, I get up and quietly head to my room.

PomPom is already on her pink bed, probably tired from chewing Clarice out.

"You did well today," I murmur as I lay a kiss on her forehead.

Her eyes are closed, but she releases a soft sound of approval, which warms my heart. I may not have friends, but I have PomPom and she's the *best* friend in the entire world.

With PomPom asleep, I direct my attention to the beautiful book in my arms, and though I would like nothing more than to read it right away, I wouldn't want my sour mood to taint my experience of the story.

I turn to my bookshelf to put it away for now. But as I stare at my perfectly color-coded book spines, I realize it needs its own special place. I move a few books around, careful to keep the pastel aesthetic of the shelf intact.

I don't *always* buy pink books. Of course I care more about the contents than the cover. But I also prize my room aesthetic, so the non-pink books get a pink sleeve to fit the theme. This book, however, is perfect as it is. It's almost as if it was designed with me in mind, pink and glitter. And because of that, it deserves to be displayed in the middle of the shelf, with the cover facing forward.

Taking a step back, I nod in satisfaction at the pretty sight.

Now I can take my clothes off and go cry in the shower.

As soon as water streams down my body, the tears begin to fall. I let out all those feelings I'd kept bottled.

There's only the sound of water dripping to the ground and the echo of my sobs. There's only disappointment and hopelessness. There's only *me* who wishes I were a different me.

The water washes me, seeking to clean me of all these emotions, yet it's all in vain.

The stain of those words engrained in my mind is unwashable.

They're there, lying low and waiting for the moment I'm the most vulnerable to come out and whisper in my ear all the things I am *not*; all the things I should be but will never be.

The sad thing is that I happen to like who I am. But I am the only one…

Can I ever find someone who will accept the whole of me, not just the pieces that are convenient? Turning off the water, the echo of my harsh breaths drowned by residual sobs is all the answer I need.

I dry my hair and put on my comfortable fuchsia pajamas. Despite feeling like crap, I can't neglect my skincare—my old self will thank me. As I finish applying moisturizer, PomPom wakes up from her nap and comes to my side, wiggling her tail and signaling she needs cuddles. She's such a needy girl, though I can't fault her when she's learned those habits from me.

The crying session helped. My eyes may be swollen, but at least I feel better.

"Should I read the first chapter? What do you say, PomPom?"

She opens her mouth, her tongue hanging out as she smiles at me.

"I'll take that as a yes. Come, I'll read it to you."

It might be odd, but I always read aloud so PomPom can listen, too. She likes stories, and she likes listening to me as I tell them.

She's such a smart girl, she immediately dashes over to our little reading nook by the window. I grab the *Fate of Akkaya* from my shelf and make myself comfortable on the plush pillows. PomPom lays her head in my lap as she waits for me to crack open the book and start.

My hands are trembling. Excitement builds up inside of me, and despite my godawful day, I'm ready to find out what happened next.

"Ready, PomPom?" I murmur to my cute little baby. She lets out a small yap as she nestles closer to me.

I open the book to the first page, a map of the continent of Akkaya, followed by another map of the capital city, Kiya.

In the last book, the Five Mages had entered the Kiya Tournament, the most prestigious competition for mages in the entire continent. It had been their chance to prove themselves to the citizens who were still doubting them. Unfortunately, the book had ended with them entering their first battle as a group. Ever since then, I've been a nervous wreck thinking something might happen to them. But they're the protagonists. The author wouldn't be so heartless as to kill anyone off, right?

Although…

I bite my lip as anxiety ricochets through me.

There have been instances in which beloved side characters have been killed off. The fandom had been in uproar, with two camps coming out of it: one defending the author's decision and the other blaming it. The latter camp had taken to writing fan fictions in which the characters were still alive and well. But that shows the author doesn't shy away from drastic decisions.

"They'll be fine, right, PomPom? The author wouldn't kill a main character," I scoff aloud.

PomPom doesn't reply, which only makes my pulse thrum in my veins harder.

The urge to slip the book to the end to make sure all my babies are safe and sound is overwhelming. But I can't.

A deep breath.

I can do this. I can read in order, as intended.

Clammy fingers fight to turn the page. My breathing grows quick and shallow as I read the heading and the first lines.

Chapter One

The Continent of Akkaya is on the brink of extinction. A plague has ravaged the lands, killing almost half of the population. The disease presents as a red rash followed by bleeding from all orifices that ends with the death of the infected within hours. The rate of transmission is frightening, with only one scratch necessary for the infection to be passed from person to person.

Cities have been abandoned, looted, destroyed.

There is only one sanctuary left—Kiya. The capital city has become a fortress against the disease, and the last true mages its defenders.

They are the last hope Akkaya has for a cure.

If the disease doesn't get to them first.

I stop for a moment, my eyes wide with disbelief.

Wait, what?

Where is the continuation from the Kiya Tournament? How did we get from the middle of a competition to a plague that killed half of the population? Is there a time jump?

"This isn't right, PomPom." I frown. "It doesn't say anywhere that it's a time jump."

She shakes her head, agreeing.

Before I can stop myself, I flip through the book in search of answers.

PomPom suddenly becomes alert, barking at me.

"Down, PomPom. I need to figure this out," I tell her, trying to shush her with one hand while flipping the pages with the other.

PomPom becomes increasingly more distressed, her barks intensifying.

"Shh, baby girl. It's okay. What got into you?" I murmur with a frown.

But just as I press my palm on top of a page to keep the book from closing, an odd feeling envelops me. There's a deafening sound in my ears. The ground quakes, the walls of the house trembling. My eyes widen in shock.

An earthquake? Here? Now?

Before I can find a safe spot to hide, PomPom jumps on me, pushing me back.

In a matter of seconds, I'm falling, unable to keep myself upright. But it's the oddest thing as I was reclining on the wall in my nook.

My back hits something cold, and the breath is knocked out of me.

PomPom jumps off my chest, running around in circles.

Wait, circles?

I slowly open my eyes, squinting at the blinding light impairing my vision. Confusion swathes me. Feeling my way around the surface I'm currently lying on, I realize it's some sort of dewy grass. The moisture clings to my hand and clothes, giving the impression of cold where the sun is shining brightly.

"PomPom?" I croak, rolling to my stomach to avoid the direct sunlight.

She's busy exploring the surroundings while I'm moaning in pain, more confused than ever as I stare at a field. A green *empty* field.

Where the hell am I?

The first thought is that I'm dreaming, but as I pinch myself and yelp in pain, I have to begrudgingly agree that it's *not* a dream. What if I'm dead, then? Is this some sort of after-life? Maybe that earthquake killed me and now I'm somewhere in heaven.

But do dogs have the same heaven as humans? For some reason, I always thought there was a separate pet heaven. I'm not complaining, though. Heaven *with* PomPom by my side? I'd say that's a win.

Besides, if I *did* die, it was quite painless. Who wouldn't want to go that way?

As I ruminate over the state of my immortal soul, I slowly come to terms with the fact that I'm likely in the afterlife. It's not that hard to believe, after all. There's no other explanation for why I'm suddenly in a green field when moments ago I was in my house. And when logic fails you… Well, it's time to entertain the *illogical*.

Slowly getting up, I dust my clothes and note I'm still wearing my cute pajamas. Oh, well. That's another positive. Although I can think of ten other outfits I would have preferred to spend an eternity in.

PomPom comes running toward me, barking sweetly. She, at least, is enjoying this afterlife. But as I pick her up in my arms, a sliver of terror goes through me.

What if this afterlife doesn't have dog food or her favorite treats?

Do we even need food here?

A low, growly sound reverberates in the air—my confirmation that we do, indeed, need food. And my stomach would benefit from having some soon.

"Oh my God, PomPom, but this is a good thing," I exclaim after a moment's thought. "If we're dead but we can eat, then I doubt we'll gain weight. We can eat everything!"

Her ears prick at that and she looks at me curiously.

"Yes, you heard me right. You can eat all the treats in the world and I can have unlimited chocolate. How cool is that?"

PomPom emits a low sound of approval.

"Now we just have to find some food. Fingers crossed they *have* chocolate and dog treats. It should be organic, too. I'd be very mad if that wasn't the case. Do you think they also have dairy-free stuff?" I muse aloud. "I can do a *little* dairy, but too much and I will have stomach issues."

PomPom nods.

"And if they don't have nice toilets?" I pause as my eyes widen. "What if they don't have toilets *at all*? Will I have to poop in a field?"

PomPom growls.

"I know you're used to pooping out, PomPom, but I'm not," I tell her. "I've *never* pooped in a field. What if there are bugs and they bite my butt?"

PomPom doesn't seem too happy with my words.

"Fine, fine. I am getting ahead of myself. We should just explore this afterlife and get some food. Maybe meet other dead people. But I hope it's nice dead people, not bad dead people. If there are bad dead people, then maybe we're in hell, and I wouldn't want to be in hell. I don't think I've sinned that much to be in hell, right?"

I'm babbling at this point. Maybe I was too fast to declare this a good outcome. The more I think about it, the more questions come to mind—and I'm not sure I will like the answers.

With PomPom in my arms, I start walking. The green field stretches as far as I can see. There is not one soul in sight. We walk like that for minutes on end before I spot some houses in the distance.

"There, PomPom!" I exclaim, running toward those houses.

Good thing I was wearing socks and slippers when I died, otherwise my feet would have hated me for running barefoot across wet grass.

The village comes into view and my lips tug up into an optimistic smile. At this point, I'll take any type of food they have to offer. I'm sure PomPom will agree, too.

Yet a trail of smoke stops me in my tracks.

Now that I can get a better look, I see that some houses are damaged by fire. Some have been broken into, the windows and doors destroyed to get inside.

Worst of all, I don't see *any* movement.

"PomPom… Heaven shouldn't be this bleak," I whisper as dread envelops me.

I tentatively move forward, walking slowly into the village.

There's destruction right and left. The houses have been broken into and robbed. Some have already burned to the ground, and others are in the process of doing so.

But someone *must* have burned them. And if the fire is fresh, then someone must have been here recently.

As I continue, however, a sound comes from one of the buildings, so I stop, looking around.

"Help."

It's a voice—a human voice.

Immediately, I dash forward, looking for the source of that voice.

"Where are you?" I call out. "I don't see you."

PomPom slips from my arms, barking at me to follow her as she runs into one of the houses that's still standing. I'm right behind her when she stops in front of a door, sniffing at the ground and bumping her head against the wooden frame.

Taking her cue, I push the door open, but it doesn't budge. It's locked.

Yet right at that moment, the voice speaks again, another low cry for help.

"We need to get them out, PomPom," I murmur, wildly looking around for something to help me break the door.

I spot a chair by the side and grab it, throwing it with all my might at the door.

My strength is not the best, but a few attempts later, I manage to crack the wood. The chair breaks, too, and I keep hitting the door with pieces of wood.

Eventually, I manage to break the door enough that it slides open.

But as I see what's inside, my eyes widen in shock.

There are at least four people, all piled on top of one another. Blood is everywhere. Coming out of their mouths, their eyes, and ears—from all orifices.

A small movement grabs my attention. A woman is stuck under two men, her hand dangling as she tries to move but lacks the strength to do so. Her eyes are bloodshot, her pupils enlarged.

"My God," I mutter. "PomPom, step aside," I demand sternly. The last thing we need is for her to step into the pool of blood and stain her white coat.

She whines but does as told.

I jump over the first puddle, then the second, doing my best not to step into it either. By the time I reach the woman, she's no longer moving, her eyes dead.

"Hello?" I call out. Reaching with my hand to check her pulse, I'm not surprised to find that it's gone.

She's dead.

She…died right in front of me.

My heart is in my throat as I take a step back, staring in shock at the dead bodies in front of me. It looks like a scene out of a slasher movie, but it's quickly evident no killer has done this. The damage is internal, like a…plague.

I swallow hard.

The door had been locked. No, *someone* had locked the door, perhaps trying to control the infection. They left these people to die. That means they're either heartless, or they were protecting themselves and the rest of the village.

Good God!

These are people. *Dead* people. People who *can* die.

This is not an afterlife, and I am not dead.

But I *can* die, too.

"PomPom, we're leaving," I say, my voice wobbly.

I jump over the puddles of blood again and, picking PomPom up, I get out of the house.

Fear spears through me as my confusion mounts. Yet I don't have time to ponder on where I *really* am because soon, I see more and more dead bodies.

They're *everywhere.* On the street, by the side of the road. Some are stuck in windows, others in doorways, their body language suggesting they were mid-flight when death came upon them.

The stench of death is overwhelming. My mental state deteriorates the more I see the devastation around me.

I increase my pace, wanting to get out of this goddamn village before I catch whatever killed its inhabitants.

Thudding sounds echo in the air. I stop, tilting my head to the side and listening.

Hooves. Horses. Riders.

They're getting closer.

"Kill anyone still alive," someone declares. "Then burn everything to the ground."

I inhale sharply. Good Lord! What the hell is happening?

Looking right and left, I see a well in one of the yards. Without dwelling much on it, I dash over, looking down and assessing my chances. It's not very deep, but there *is* water.

Do I risk it?

The water will help us survive if there is a fire since I can submerge us until the danger passes. But PomPom will not like that.

The riders make it to the main road, the sound of hooves growing louder.

I gulp down in uncertainty.

Come on, Barbi! What would Lady Jocelyn do?

She would risk it.

I squeeze my eyes shut as I take a deep breath.

"We need to do this, PomPom," I whisper to her as I kiss her fluffy head. "Please don't be scared. And please, *please* don't make a sound. They can't find us."

She looks at me with confusion in her round, cute eyes.

Fear and anxiety grip me, not just for me, but for my baby, too.

It's now or never.

Holding on tightly to PomPom in my arms, I swing my legs

over the rim of the well and jump in. The water splashes all around, but luckily, my feet soon touch the bottom. The water only reaches my waist, so that leaves PomPom mostly dry.

I wait with bated breath, listening for the sounds outside. More voices. More orders of destruction.

No one is to be left alive for fear the plague might spread.

Seconds turn into minutes and into hours as the riders loot what's left to steal before torching the remaining buildings. The smoke travels down the well, and it takes everything in me not to cough. Poor PomPom struggles too, and I hold my hand over her snout to keep her from making a sound.

It seems like forever until there's no more noise around, not even the crackling of wood.

Though still slightly scared, I gather the courage to get out. First, I help PomPom jump out, after which I do my best to hold on to the slippery rocks and haul myself out of the well.

If I'd thought the village was the picture of devastation before, now I have no words to describe what I'm seeing.

Everything has been destroyed—leveled to the ground. The smell of burned flesh and wood permeates the atmosphere, almost making me gag. I'm wet, bedraggled, and smelly. My cute pajamas are destroyed. But hey, at least I'm still breathing. Yet no matter how much I'd like to wallow in self-pity, there is no time to dawdle around. I need to get out of here, and most of all, I need to figure out how the hell I can get back home.

"Shh, baby. It's fine. We're fine," I coo in PomPom's ear. "We're alive. That's all that matters."

As I make my way down the sinister road, the wind blows a small, half-burned piece of paper in my face. With a frown, I peel it off my skin and turn it over to study it.

It's a newspaper. And half a heading is still legible.

The plague has killed more than half of the population of Akkaya.

3

Disbelief fills my features.

Someone must be playing a prank on me.

Either that or...

I swallow hard.

"This can't be happening, PomPom," I whisper.

She looks up at me, her tongue out. She doesn't realize the panic that's forming in my chest or the fact that the *impossible* might have happened to us.

"This isn't funny!" I call out, looking around for any decor flaws.

Maybe I'm in a simulation. Or a highly modern Hollywood studio.

Yet even as I hope to explain my surroundings that way, the truth is staring me in the face.

This is real.

The village was real.

The dead people were real.

Somehow, I'm not home anymore.

"Okay," I take a deep breath. "If this is Akkaya by *any* chance, then it's not so bad, is it, PomPom? I know those books like the back of my hand. It shouldn't be too hard to figure out the rules and find a way out of here."

PomPom stares at me.

"Sometimes I forget you can't answer back." I sigh. "But I will get us out of here, PomPom. Even if this is just a bad dream, I'll get us back home safely. I promise you."

She releases a happy bark and settles nicely in my arms.

First, I need evidence that this is, in fact, the continent of Akkaya.

I continue walking as I think about my next steps. I can't deny that there is one part of me that wishes this *were* Akkaya. Haven't I always dreamed of living in that world? Of meeting my most beloved characters and telling them how much they mean to me?

Perhaps my love affair with the fantasy genre has made me go crazy. The rational side of me tells me that I need concrete evidence before I make any judgments. But the romantic, semi-delusional side of me is ready to embark on this adventure—sans plague and death, of course. Now that I think better, why did I have to be in *this* installment of the series? Why couldn't it be a previous book where the population of Akkaya was *not* on the brink of extinction?

But as that thought arises, I realize I have no idea what the rules are. If I catch the plague, will I die? And if I die here, will I die in the real world, too?

Lightning flashes across the sky, thunder making its appearance soon thereafter. And in a matter of seconds, cold, heavy rain pours down, drenching me.

I grumble something under my breath as I protect PomPom to the best of my ability.

It wasn't enough that I was already wet from before. Now I'm also chilled to the bone.

Starting in a sprint, I traverse yet another green field, wildly looking around for a shelter. PomPom whines in my arms, the terrifying sounds in the sky agitating her.

"Shh, baby," I try to comfort her, but it becomes harder to contain her as she moves wildly, letting out an agonizing sound that touches my heart.

The rain shows no signs of abating. I'm so wet, if the plague doesn't get to me first, pneumonia will.

A light shines in the distance, across a hill to my right. At first, it resembles a bolt of lightning. But as I get closer, I realize it's on the ground, not in the sky.

Hope blossoms in my chest. I change my direction, following the light. Mayhap I'll find a human establishment that can offer us shelter until the storm passes and more information about where the hell we are.

My lips tug up in a relieved smile as I see an inn, the windows blaring with light.

But my happiness is short-lived as I notice the horses tied around the barn, all of them garbed in military armor.

I stop in my tracks. Information from the fictional Akkaya is slowly coming to me. Only government officials or military personnel are allowed to use horses in full armor. That must mean they are sanctioned by the government.

Are these the same people who were looting and killing villagers? Now I am beating myself for not taking a good look at them.

I bite my lip in apprehension.

Do I risk it?

They could suspect me of being infected and kill me.

My feet move before I can come to a decision—seems like my self-preservation wins.

But just at that moment, a loud bang thunders across the sky.

PomPom releases a high-pitched screech that reaches the horses, making them even more restless than the storm.

The door to the inn is wrenched open, and two men with swords come into view.

"Damn it!" I curse, turning and running away from them.

"Catch her!" someone calls out.

It's a cacophony of noises. The rain splashes against my skin, the thunder a background melody meant to confuse my senses. The marauding steps behind me slam against the wet, slippery ground as they get closer. Horses neigh, the sound whispering past my ear and telling me I'm no match for armed riders.

PomPom struggles against me, my mood making her more agitated than the storm.

Tears stab at the corners of my eyes as my fate suddenly flashes before me.

"Get her!"

"Don't let her get away!"

Their voices are loud, but they are drowned by the beat of my heart drumming in my ears. Fear spurs me further. Fear also shows me another potential danger if they should catch me.

I get to the hill, but the ground is muddy and hard to maneuver. One glance behind me to check how far the men are is all it takes for me to lose my footing and fall, rolling down to the base of the hill.

And right at the feet of one of the soldiers.

"Kill her! We can't risk it!"

My eyes widen as I tighten my hold on PomPom, hiding her. I can't take any chances that they might harm her too.

"Please don't!" I shout. "I'm not infected, please."

"That's what they all say." He laughs, pushing a mask over his face.

The sky is downcast. But the sun, buried underneath a mountain of clouds, resurfaces enough to shine light upon the sword that is about to end me.

"Please! I just need to find Sir Damien and Lady Jocelyn," I say in hopes the names might be familiar to them. They're some of the most famous mages in Akkaya, and their names should carry some weight. I may still be conflicted about this being Akkaya, but at this point, I'd try anything as long as it saves my life.

The sword comes down with a swoosh. But it doesn't cut me. Instead, the soldier sheaths it, pulling his mask off his face and regarding me curiously.

"You know Sir Damien and Lady Jocelyn?" he asks as he narrows his eyes at me.

His other soldier buddies stop next to him, assessing me with skepticism.

"Uhm, yes." I nod, plastering a smile on my face. "We're *old* friends."

The soldier, I suppose he's the leader, tilts his head to the side.

"Good try. Everyone knows them." He guffaws, and his friends join him. "I doubt a nobody like you would be friends with our rulers."

My eyes widen. Rulers? When did *that* happen?

"No, no, I swear. I know them." I nod. "Ask me anything about them and I'll tell you."

The soldier frowns.

"Lady Jocelyn has a mole here." I point to the spot under my chin. "She also has one on her back, under her right shoulder blade. How could I know that if I hadn't seen her *in* person?"

"Lady Jocelyn does have a mole under her chin," one of the soldiers whispers from behind. "I've seen it. Swear I've seen it."

"When would you have seen that?" The boss rolls his eyes as he jabs his shoulder into the man's gut. He moans in pain.

"At the parade, sir. After the coronation. Her dog ran off and I caught it." He pushes his chin up, proud of his achievement.

A lightbulb goes on in my mind.

"Yes! Her dog! BonBon," I burst out, opening my arms to reveal PomPom. "If you've seen BonBon, then you should recognize my PomPom, too. They're the same breed." I hold up my pretty baby for his inspection.

Okay, so I may have gotten the same dog as Lady Jocelyn, in the same color. But BonBon is male, while my PomPom is female. I did intend to get a male and name it BonBon, too, but I fell in love with PomPom first, and she did *not* look like a BonBon.

He chews his lip as he assesses PomPom. She lets out a hiss before she bares her teeth at him.

"Oy, sir. It's the same!" he exclaims. "It even sounds the same." His eyes widen as he takes a step back. "He bit me, that dog. More than once," he mutters under his breath.

"Lady Jocelyn and I are the *best* of friends. Even our dogs are the same." I bat my lashes as I slowly get up, doing my best to assume a regal bearing. I can't very well look like a wet rat while I pretend to be pals with the queen.

"She might be telling the truth," the young soldier tells the leader in a not-so-low voice.

"She might also be infected." The leader grinds his teeth.

"But if Queen Jocelyn finds out we've killed her friend? She'll kill us too!" the young man exclaims, his face one of horror.

My brows go up in surprise at his vehemence and the pure expression of fear he's sporting. Lady Jocelyn isn't a killer. Even during her battles, she's never killed anyone, always offering them a way out. Why, she'd once declared that she would sooner kill herself than take another life. But this could all be part of some royal propaganda. After all, the continent is in a crisis if that newspaper clipping is to be believed—more than half the population has perished!

The leader studies me and PomPom, undecided.

"Sir!" the young one continues in a cajoling tone. "I have a feeling about this, sir. We're going to get in trouble with the Queen if we hurt her. Look, she's wearing the same colors as the Queen."

After another moment of deliberation, the leader finally speaks.

"Fine. We will take you to Kiya where the Queen will acknowledge you herself. But if I find that you've lied..." he trails off.

"And if you find that I didn't?" I retort with a huff. "Don't you worry. I'll make sure to tell Lady Jocelyn *everything* about your abysmal behavior," I tell him pointedly.

He stares at me. I stare back.

Okay, so maybe this small lie *could* technically get me in trouble. But it might also help me get back home. The Five, with their unparalleled magical knowledge, should be able to find a way to send me back home. After I get a tour of Akkaya, of course (the non-plague sites).

"Willy. Make sure she doesn't get away and she doesn't scratch anyone."

"I'm not infected," I interject.

"We will see," he adds skeptically, "if you make it alive to the capital."

With that, he turns and leaves me behind. The other soldiers follow the leader and go back to the inn.

Willy remains behind. He takes a step forward, wiping his clammy hands on his leather pants before offering me his hand.

I move past him. "I might be infected, remember? I should get my own horse."

"But..." Willy blinks.

"I am sure Lady Jocelyn will appreciate your contribution to my comfort, Willy."

"Yes, ma'am," he mumbles, confused. Poor lad.

"Call me Lady Barbi."

His mouth drops open in shock.

I hide a triumphant smile. Finally, I get to be my true self—*Lady* Barbi.

"Forgive me, your ladyship." He bends his head low. "Forgive all of us. We've been working all day and we couldn't recognize that you were a lady."

"It is fine. When are we leaving? I would like to bathe and change my clothes first. I also require some food for myself and for my dog."

He glances at PomPom in my arms. She barks at him.

"But… What is a lady like you doing here all alone? In a plague land, too?" he asks as he trails behind me.

I watch him from the corner of my eye. He's perhaps fifteen or sixteen, lanky and lean. He's also innocent enough to believe my lies. That should prove to be an advantage if I play my cards right.

"I was on my way to Kiya," I start in a dramatic tone. "But my entourage caught the plague and died. I was the only one who survived. Oh, Willy. It was *horrible*. They bled everywhere," I say, dabbing at my eyes for nonexistent tears. "PomPom and I were the only ones to survive."

"Oh, Lady Barbi. That's horrible!"

"Isn't it? Poor PomPom will be scarred for life. It was the first time she's seen a dead body, you know?"

"I can imagine." He nods sympathetically. "You are so lucky to be the only survivor."

I release a pointed sigh.

"Yes, the gods must be watching over me and PomPom. We have been praying daily and then you showed up," I continue. "I've made offerings to the Goddess and she has decided to take pity on me."

Invoking the Goddess should add to my convincing act, since she is one of the figures worshipped exclusively by the upper class of Akkaya. Those of lower ranks would not dare to utter her name, let alone pray to her.

As expected, Willy averts his gaze. Her name alone is too hallowed to acknowledge.

"You will have to excuse our leader, Lady Barbi. He did not mean to offend you in any way."

"It is all forgotten and forgiven."

"I cannot believe you did not catch the plague, Lady Barbi. We've been through tons of villages by now and we haven't found one person who wasn't infected. They were all either dead or dying," he explains, his expression sad.

Poor boy. He has a good heart, I can tell. So I take advantage of it some more.

"Do not tell anyone but"—I look right and left before I lean in to whisper—"I think I am immune to the plague."

His eyes widen.

I nod, my lips flattened.

"It is why I must reach Lady Jocelyn as soon as possible. She will help me make sense of this."

His eyes sparkle with hope after the shock wears off, and a small twinge of guilt stabs at my heart. Alas, the only way I can ensure that I survive until I reach Kiya is to make myself indispensable. With the way Willy is looking at me now, a mix of awe and adoration, I know he's not going to be able to keep this to himself, and the seed of the rumor will be officially planted. As long as they believe I might be useful, they aren't likely to hurt me, no?

A smile tips at my lips. Who needs *Econ* when I have my subterfuge skills and my doe-like eyes that work wonders on the unassuming—especially those of the male variety?

We head to the inn where all the soldiers are already back to their routine, eating, drinking, and being rowdy. It's then that I notice there is no staff around.

Of course there's no staff! They likely died from the plague.

The leader eyes me suspiciously as I enter, so I put on my best Lady Jocelyn act and push my chin up as I ignore him. I stop in the middle of the room as I address Willy.

"Is there a room where I may refresh myself?"

"Yes, of course. Come with me," he says, pointing me to the stairs in the back.

He shows me a small, unused room that is not the cleanest, but hey, I can't complain right now.

"I will bring you and your dog something to eat."

"Thank you, Willy."

He blushes and nods. I close the door in his face and put PomPom down, stretching my arms and body. She might not weigh much, but carrying her for the past few hours has caused my arms to go stiff.

True to his word, Willy comes back with a tray of food for me and PomPom. Not ten minutes after, he shows up again with a big bucket of hot water that almost slips from his hands.

"We shall leave tomorrow at first light. You have time to wash your clothes and take a nap. The door locks, but I will keep guard by the stairs so you don't have to worry about anything, Lady Barbi."

"You're a sweetheart, Willy." I smile at him.

His cheeks redden even more.

When he leaves, I lock the door and quickly undress, happy to be out of my soaked garments. I take my pajamas and my underwear off and use a rag to clean my body thoroughly and remove all the dirt. I use the same rag on PomPom, cleaning her paws and the tips of her coat that have become matted from mud.

When we're both clean, I let PomPom eat while I wash my clothes in the remaining water. There is some sparse furniture in the room aside from the single bed, and I manage to strew the clothes around to dry.

PomPom is satisfied with her modest meal, a bit of stew with some meat and bones.

I scowl.

As soon as we get back home, I'll have to brush her teeth and clean them properly, maybe schedule a visit to the vet to make sure this food didn't do any damage. Alas, beggars can't be choosers, and she needs to eat.

For me, Willy had added a chicken wing, a few slices of bread and cheese, and some of the same stew.

My stomach grumbles in hunger and as much as that food looks less than appetizing, I cannot say no either. I dig in, eating even the last crumb of bread.

I don't know when I fall asleep. But at some point, a banging noise startles me and I jump up. PomPom, too, starts barking, aggression rolling off her.

"Lady Barbi, it's me, Willy. We will be leaving soon."

"Oh." I sigh in relief. "I'll be right down."

The clothes are semi-dry, but I didn't expect anything better. I put my pajamas back on and, taking PomPom in my arms, I head downstairs.

All the soldiers are already outside, and as I get closer to the door, I hear the sound of conflict.

"She's a lady, sir," Willy whines.

"Are you ready to vouch for her with your life? You foolish kid…"

My eyes widen, and for some reason, Willy has endeared himself to me and I don't want to see him dead.

I open the door to the inn, step out, and meet the leader's gaze head-on.

"Willy is now my personal guard. You cannot speak to my guard like that."

"Personal guard?" The man laughs, the other soldiers joining in to mock Willy.

As I let my gaze roam around the crowd, I'm able to assess them better now that the sky is clear and the sun is shining brightly. They are all middle-aged, with the leader being somewhere in his forties. Willy is the youngest, and going by his subservient body language, it's something that the others hold against him.

"Yes. I assume you've heard of the Havilland family?" I ask in a haughty voice.

The leader's eyes widen.

I smile.

"I am the youngest child of the Marquis de Havilland. Should you mistreat me *or* Willy, it will not bode well for you."

PomPom barks, agreeing with me.

The de Havilland family is one of the wealthiest in Kiya. They were mentioned a few times in the books, and I vaguely recall them having ten or more daughters—the marquis could never get his much-desired male heir. With that many daughters, it's impossible that he would know all of them.

"If I remember correctly, the Marquis perished some ten years ago." The leader narrows his eyes.

"That does not take away *my* title, does it? Or the fact that my family owns half of Kiya." I stare him down. His nostrils flare in annoyance.

He doesn't trust me. Which, for good reason since I *am* spewing lie after lie. Luckily, his soldiers believe me as they one by one kneel in front of me and apologize for not giving me my due respect.

I smile.

God, my lies keep piling up. I don't want to imagine what will happen when I'm discovered. But I can't think about that. I just need to get to The Five and explain my situation to them. I'm sure they will forgive my small lies and help me get back home.

Willy gets me my own horse, and I thank the heavens I was inspired to take riding lessons when I was younger. But if Lady Jocelyn did something, I did it too.

Except magic.

Unfortunately, that is something I lack.

I easily slide into the saddle, ready to begin the journey to Kiya and hopefully see some plague-free sights on my way there. PomPom takes her place in front of me, and I hold on to her with one hand while gripping onto the reins with the other.

But just as we're about to leave, the sky blackens before it bleeds, drops of blood falling instead of rain.

I expect everyone to take shelter, but instead, they all rejoice, dancing up and down and hugging each other as if it's the most holy of events.

"What's happening?"

I look down at Willy. He's unmoving. His head is tipped back, his mouth open as he tastes the red blood drops on his tongue.

His eyes slowly open, for a moment shining a deep red.

"It is done," he says in a thick voice that echoes as the other soldiers repeat the same words, verbatim.

"What is done? What's happening?"

"The Dark One has been defeated," he states robotically, almost as if he were in a trance.

The other soldiers start chanting as they raise their swords to the sky.

"The Dark One has been defeated. The Dark One has been defeated."

In a matter of seconds, the sky clears.

Turning to me, Willy smiles brightly.

"Sir Damien has defeated the Dark One. It is done!"

I frown. This doesn't make sense.

"The plague will finally end," Willy gushes, tears of happiness falling down his cheeks.

"What do you mean?"

"You don't know?" he asks, surprised.

I shake my head.

"The Dark One caused the plague. And now Sir Damien will find a cure and save us all!"

But that is impossible. According to the books, Sir Damien defeated the Dark One long before the plague. That battle was in the sixth book, which we were supposed to enact for the convention.

The Dark One can't have caused the plague because he should already be dead.

4

We travel for half a day on horseback. My thighs hurt from being in the saddle too long. Despite my former training, I don't have the stamina for it.

Willy, seeing my struggle, calls out to the leader, who I now know is called Ivan.

"She's a lady, sir. She can't ride like us."

I give Willy a brilliant smile.

"That's what *she* says," Ivan grumbles, staring at me belligerently. "It still remains to be established if she is who she says she is."

What the hell is his deal? I am the most non-threatening person ever. I'm wearing *pink*, for God's sake, and I have a fluffy white dog that takes the word cute to a whole new level. What is more inoffensive than that?

"But, sir. Look how small and frail she is," Willy continues, pointing toward me.

I smile. Yes, look how small and frail I am. How could I be an impostor when I look so innocent? Perhaps I should have said I was a nun, something like *Saint* Barbi…

Ivan looks at me, and his expression says he doesn't buy

my innocent persona. Yep, even nuns would look suspicious to him.

Alas, eventually more soldiers suggest taking a break and he relents.

We find a pasture for our break—a welcome change of scenery from the plague-infested towns we've passed through. I don't think I've ever seen such a desolate landscape, not even in movies. Willy, ever the thoughtful lad, tried to shield me from the death around. We rode ahead while the soldiers remained to torch what was left behind—including any person who might have been alive.

A shudder goes down my back. I can't think of this right now. I need to stay focused on my task and find a way to get back home.

"We have a few more hours until we reach the Capital," Willy tells me as he helps me tie my horse to a tree. "We will get there before it gets dark."

I let PomPom out of my arms so she can stretch her legs and do her business in the bushes. She runs around, letting out a couple of excited barks.

"That's good." Okay, I can do a few more hours. But that also means only a few hours left until we reach the castle and meet the Five. With the lies I've told, I will need to be quick on my feet and make up even *more* lies.

From the corner of my eye, I note Ivan watching me suspiciously. He's hovering around Willy and me, pretending to stretch his legs, but I can tell he's eavesdropping on our conversation.

He's been awful to me the entire journey, at times insinuating what will happen to me once my lies are exposed. Of course, I merely smiled and pretended not to mind his comments, but inside I've been freaking out.

With how invested he is in my identity, I have no doubt he's going to need confirmation from Lady Jocelyn herself that I am her bosom friend as I implied.

"There will be a feast when we get back," Willy comments. "I can't wait to have some nice food again."

"A feast?"

He nods enthusiastically.

"The Queen organizes a feast for the return of the troops. That's when you'll meet her, too. She comes to address the soldiers in person. She's very nice," he says wistfully.

"I thought I would get a personal audience with her." I frown.

"No, no." Willy shakes his head. "The Queen and King have a very strict schedule. It's because of the plague." He sighs. "They're spending all their time trying to figure out a way to stop it. They do not even entertain their friends. The only way to meet the Queen is during the feast. Even with all this chaos, she finds a way to make time for her soldiers," he adds with a smile. He's *definitely* a Lady Jocelyn fanboy.

"I see," I murmur. So that's why Ivan has been so adamant about checking my claims. He knows I won't be able to see her by myself and he will be there to witness everything.

Damn it!

I must find a way to speak with her beforehand to consolidate my ruse. But how? She's *the* Queen.

Willy shares a drink with his fellow soldiers while I remain deep in thought.

Who knows what will happen to me if they realize I've lied about everything? They might think I'm some type of spy sent to infiltrate the Capital.

I purse my lips. This won't work. It's too dangerous. At the same time, it's imperative I see the Five if I want to get back home.

Hmm…

Maybe I can run away once we enter the Capital? I'm sure I could find my own way to the castle, but how would I get to the Five? The Queen and King are almost out of discussion, but what if I could meet the other three? They might not be as strong as Sir Damien, but surely they would have some insight…

I'm wrenched from my thoughts when I realize that PomPom is no longer in my line of sight. The breath is knocked from my lungs as panic overtakes me. I look around, my heart beating wildly in my chest.

But then I spot a flash of white in a sea of green. She's in the bushes!

"Don't eat the grass, PomPom!" I call out, running to her.

God, I hope she hasn't ingested anything. Who knows what the grass in this world can do to her? Fear grips me. One moment I was not paying attention and it could very well prove to be a fatal one.

Bad mom!

"PomPom," I cry out, raising her in my arms and prying her mouth open to check if she ate anything off the ground. I study her teeth and the color of her tongue, releasing a huge sigh of relief when I realize she didn't.

"Good girl," I praise softly. "You're my good girl, aren't you?" I coo, brushing my lips against her fluffy forehead.

She rumbles deep in her throat, a sound that suggests her pleasure.

As I turn to leave, however, my gaze becomes affixed to another drop of color at the base of the bushes, the contrast striking against the deep green of the foliage and the dark brown of the earth. (Okay, maybe it caught my attention because it's a light pink.)

I crouch down, brushing my hand over the small, bulbous root. A memory flashes in my head. Lady Jocelyn had described a plant like this in the third book when she'd been studying plants with magical properties. She'd noted the somniferous properties of the root. Even in the smallest doses, it had the power to knock over a horse.

Stealthily gazing to the side, I spot Ivan talking to someone in his troop and pointing at me, no doubt besmirching my name even further.

My eyes sparkle as an idea forms in my head.

We shall meet the Queen at the feast. But if Ivan and his goons are asleep during that time, they won't be able to accuse me of anything.

My lips curve in a sly smile as I quickly pull on a couple of roots and pocket them. Now I'll just need to find a way to add them to his food.

A comical, almost malefic laugh bubbles in my throat— finally I get some main character energy! Ivan won't even know what hit him.

"Come, PomPom," I say, taking her with me back to our horse. "Maybe the next book will be about us. Just imagine. Barbi and PomPom in Akkaya."

Instantly, I'm flooded with snapshots of our adventures, including defeating Ivan as a symbol of the oppressing patriarchy. It would be a victory for all pink lovers out there! He'd be on the ground, tapping his hand against the floor as a signal of forfeiture while PomPom and I would be standing victorious next to him.

PomPom releases a happy bark.

"Yes, baby. We'd be the next superhero duo," I coo in her ear. And the cherry on top, everyone would forget about Lady Jocelyn and her BonBon because me and PomPom would be the new *it* duo.

"Lady Barbi?" Willy's worried voice breaks the spell.

I open my eyes, blinking as I come face-to-face with Willy and about ten other soldiers behind him. A crowd has formed around me and PomPom.

"Don't move, sir. You'll hurt Lady Barbi and PomPom," another soldier adds, his eyes on the ground.

"Get this fucking bitch and her dog off me," a strangled voice calls out.

Oh God. I'm almost afraid to look down. But I have to.

Slowly, I direct my gaze to the ground where Ivan is currently on his belly, his hands gripping the grass. PomPom is biting his ear off while I'm holding him down with my foot.

Horrified, I quickly grab PomPom and jump back.

"I'm so sorry. I don't know how that happened," I stumble over my words.

"You're fucking dead!" Ivan yells, jumping at me. But the soldiers form a wall between us, keeping him away and telling him to calm down.

"Are you all right, Lady Barbi?" Willy comes to my side, looking mighty worried.

"I… I don't know what happened…" I stammer. It's almost as if I closed my eyes and then woke up in a different world—pun intended.

"We know it wasn't your fault. We all saw what happened," he starts and my eyes widen as he recounts how Ivan had come to me, demanding I show him my de Havilland birthmark—apparently, there is such a thing. PomPom had jumped out of my arms and tripped him. He'd lost his balance and fallen face-down in the grass, after which PomPom had attacked him—quite viciously going by the big scratch on Ivan's cheek and his bleeding ear.

"You bitch! I'm going to kill that fucking dog," Ivan continues to shout in the distance, but he's contained by four soldiers so he cannot come near us.

"PomPom was so brave," Willy adds as he turns his attention to my baby.

One by one, other soldiers come to tell me how much they admire PomPom.

"She's a fighter," Jerry, a soldier, mentions, nodding with respect.

"She might be small, but she's a worthy adversary," another compliments her.

"Yes, yes. That she is…" I smile awkwardly.

God, I need to stop daydreaming.

If before I might have had qualms about using the pink roots on Ivan, now I am convinced the man needs his comeuppance. Anyone threatening my baby is officially a *bad* person and they get a special spot in my big bad notebook (when I get back home so I can add the name in it).

Operation Pink Root is officially a go.

In an effort to keep the peace on the road, the soldiers asked Ivan to ride first so they could place themselves between us as a buffer zone. With the threats he continues to make, now targeting PomPom, too, no one wants to take a chance.

PomPom preens in my arms, happy that she's gained new acolytes.

As we continue onwards toward the Capital, I do my best to glean more information from the soldiers to know what to expect. They talk freely, sharing different anecdotes from their lives before the plague. But at some point, the discussion shifts to the Dark One. Curious, I pull on my reins and lead my horse next to them.

"I can finally sleep at night now that the Dark One has been defeated," a soldier jokes.

"Tell me about it." Another laughs. "Maybe my nightmares will finally stop."

I frown at their superlative language. In the books, the Dark One had been the villain in book six, but he had been far from the most frightening one the Five had been up against. If I were to make a top, he wouldn't make the top five of the most powerful opponents Sir Damien had faced.

Yet these people are talking about the Dark One as if he were the devil incarnate.

"Is the Dark One that scary?" I suddenly ask.

Their conversation dies as they all turn to stare at me as if I'd grown a second head. Fearing that I said something wrong, I simply add, "I grew up sheltered, so I am not that familiar with the outside world."

"That makes sense." Willy nods. "Your parents would not have wanted you to hear of the atrocities the Dark One committed."

"If he were still alive, we wouldn't be able to speak so casually about him. I still expect a dark cloud to appear and swallow me whole." Jerry laughs nervously.

I gawk at them.

"Could you explain, please?"

"He was a terrifying fellow, the Dark One. He established his own following in the eastern part of Akkaya, directly challenging the King. A lot of troops were dispatched to the east and they never came back, so it only reinforced the idea that he was invincible."

"Don't forget about Kuma," Willy quips.

"I am getting there, Willy." Jerry rolls his eyes. "As I was saying, when the Dark One gained more followers, he started attacking high officials at the King's court. He wanted to weaken the King as much as possible, and ultimately take the crown for himself. He even killed Kuma, one of the Five and the King's best friend."

My eyes widen in disbelief.

"Kuma? He's dead? But how… He was so strong…"

He was a master blacksmith who could craft any weapon out of metal. His skills were unparalleled in Akkaya, and not even Sir Damien could beat him in a battle with his magical weapons.

"You don't understand, Lady Barbi. The Dark One could destroy an entire army with the snap of a finger. He commanded a dark shadow cloud that would kill a target from miles away. Technically, he didn't even have to move and he could get rid of anyone he wished."

"That's why no one ever saw his face. He was a mystery."

"I heard he was heavily scarred," one soldier whispers. "He wore a mask and a black cloak to hide his features."

"Yes, I heard that too. Some said he had a scar this big

running down his face," one soldier says, trailing his finger down half of his face.

"I thought he was just ugly." Another laughs, and a mocking contest begins.

"Maybe he was afraid he'd be called the Ugly One instead."

The jokes run amok.

While they argue about how the Dark One looked like, how ugly or scarred he was, I'm left reeling from all this new information.

This is *not* the Dark One I read about. Hell, aside from the name, there's very little resemblance between the fictional run-of-the-mill evil dude in the books and this dangerous figure the soldiers are still terrified of.

Even his abilities are different.

The books only spoke of his ability to cast forbidden spells.

I've read the sixth book countless times, including recently for the play, and the main plot revolved around an ancient book of forbidden spells that the Dark One was searching for. The Five had teamed up to stop him since those spells could have serious implications for Akkaya. The Dark One had managed to get the book and was about to perform a spell that would grant him immortality when Sir Damien defeated him. Nowhere had it said anything about his ability to control shadows—or him being so powerful that the entire continent was terrified of him.

"King Damien must have seen him. He fought him face-to-face more than once. Remember when Kuma died?" Jerry asks, and the soldiers nod. "He couldn't kill the Dark One then, but he injured him badly."

"And then the devil started this damned plague," Willy curses in a low, somber tone.

"Wait." I frown. "What's the connection?"

"After the King injured the Dark One, the entire continent

was enveloped in a thick, dark fog. Soon after, people started dying. No one knew what it was for months, until the King discovered that the Dark One had been stealing the life force of Akkaya's citizens to heal himself and become more powerful. Anyone who died of the plague served as fuel for that damned devil," Jerry adds accusingly, visibly shuddering at the memory.

"He's been in hiding ever since, but the King had promised the people he would find and kill the Dark One once and for all. And now he's fulfilled that vow." Willy smiles.

"A worthy ruler, King Damien," another soldier chimes in. "No one will ever forget the dark days of Akkaya and how the King defeated the greatest evil to ever grace these lands."

There they go again about the Dark One being the most terrifying evil dude ever. Although I believe them when they say the Dark One is frightening and bad and just overall a supervillain, why is there a discrepancy between their account and the information from my books?

"What about Moloch? Or the Red Flame? Or…the Hybrid Witch?" I ask.

In the books, these three were the most frightening villains the Five ever faced. Moloch in particular, almost killed Lady Jocelyn in book eleven. He was so strong, the Five couldn't destroy him, so instead they merely locked him away in a mystical prison from which he could never escape.

Jerry, Willy, and all the soldiers who heard me turn to stare at me.

"Uhm, Lady Barbi… Who are those people?"

"You've never heard of Moloch?" I blink.

They shake their heads, their expressions downright confused.

"The big bad demon who could turn mages into his servants and have them do his bidding?"

"I have never heard of any Moloch," Willy adds tentatively, but the other soldiers back him up, a chorus of *me neither* erupting in the air.

I gawk at them.

How is this possible?

Moloch had been the Five's archnemesis for almost six books. *Six.* That's not just a passing villain like the book version of the Dark One, who only made an appearance in one installment. That's a super, mega, *ultra* villain.

Something is wrong.

Though this is the Akkaya I know from books, it also… isn't.

I swallow hard as I try to make sense of the conflicting information.

What if this *isn't* a book world, but instead it's a real world somewhere in the universe? What if whoever wrote the book series had some knowledge of the events but not enough to write an accurate account?

But that means that all the information I have is useless. I have no way of knowing what's true and what isn't anymore, and spouting nonsense will *not* gain me any favors at the court.

Until now, I've been betting on the fact that I have intimate knowledge of the Five—well, *four* now—that might make them more inclined to help me. But since I can no longer differentiate between fact and fiction, I need to reconsider my strategy.

"There it is!" Willy exclaims a while later.

Glancing at where he's pointing, I note an imposing fortress, the walls as high as the sky. Magical runes swirl around the perimeter in orange and blue flashes of light, creating a protective barrier. It's so powerful, even birds avoid it, flying parallel to the barrier.

I take a deep breath, a sliver of panic washing through me.

In less than half an hour, we will reach the gates of the fortress and enter the Capital. It won't be much longer until we reach the castle and attend the feast presided by Lady Jocelyn.

The clock is ticking, and I have to make up my mind fast regarding what version of events I'll present in front of the King and Queen.

Because if I mess up…

The plague is the last thing I'll have to worry about.

5

The grand hall is bustling with noise. The soldiers are raising their glasses and toasting to celebrate the defeat of the Dark One and the beginning of a new era.

Our welcome into the Capital was impressive. As soon as people saw our entourage, they threw flowers at us, chanting the hymn of Kiya and wishing us health for an eternity.

The streets had cleared so we could make our way to the palace where we had immediately been sent off to the grand dining hall. They even took our horses to feed and clean them.

I could not imagine a better welcome. It's evident that the people of Akkaya cherish the army and celebrate them for their brave deeds, especially after such a dark time.

But it's especially now that the Dark One is dead, everyone is ready to party and forget about all the death and gloom still existent beyond the Capital's walls.

"Let me get that." I smile at one of the servers as I pick up a large jug of mead. Big mistake. I almost topple it over as I wobble on my feet, seeking some balance. Damn it! This is too heavy.

I manage to haul it to the edge of the hall, where I put it down for a moment to seemingly—and accurately—get my bearings together. I pretend to breathe harshly as I fiddle with the pink root in my pocket, squishing it between my fingers before I stealthily drop it in the jug.

Everyone is too busy to pay attention to me, especially as some conflicts arise between soldiers. With so much testosterone in the room, it's no wonder they'd eventually do a dick measuring contest.

I linger around for a few more minutes to make sure the juice from the pink root has mixed with the mead before I grab it once more and head to our table.

"Thank you everyone for bringing me here. You have my undying gratitude," I address the soldiers as I pour each a cup, one by one. Luckily, each unit has its own table, so the damage will be localized. I do feel bad about the other soldiers who are innocent victims in all of this, but I also don't want to get myself killed anytime soon.

My lips are stretched in a perpetual smile as I hand Ivan his full glass. To my surprise, he barely glances at me. He's busy arguing with another soldier. He angrily downs the glass, and I'm quick to replenish it.

Now it's a waiting game.

I take my seat at the end of the table and sneak PomPom some food while I slowly pick at my own.

My stomach growls in protest.

I'm hungry. I really am. But how can I eat when my fate is currently hanging in balance? I won't be able to swallow anything until I see Ivan passed out.

The moments trickle by and my anxiety mounts.

A loud cheer erupts in the hall, followed by a chant.

"Long live the Queen! Long live the Queen!"

Fuck.

With a wave of a hand, Lady Jocelyn silences everyone.

Heels click against the pavement as she steps inside the hall.

She's wearing a light pink gown with frilly lace around the collar, sleeves, and hem. Her waist is accentuated by a thick belt with polka dots—*absolutely amazing!* I am, of course, taking mental notes of her outfit to go to my tailor and have a similar one done.

Her light hair flows down her back in perfect ringlets. She's even wearing a cute headband with a pink bow at the center. Oh my, I think I'm going to *die* of jealousy. I need that asap!

Bad moment, Barbi. You're in danger of being discovered and subsequently killed. It's not the time to admire Lady J's fashion choices— perfect as they are.

At that moment, Ivan's eyes find mine, a sly smile curving at his lips.

He stands up.

Oh no! Goddamn it! He's going to ruin everything!

I blink furiously as I will my brain to think of something. Quick.

He gets out of his seat.

"Your Majesty. I have…"

A loud, *loud* crack erupts in the air.

Ivan stills, his eyes wide.

More sounds follow before he doubles over, his expression strained.

My brows knit together in confusion. For a moment, I don't understand what's happening. But as a pungent smell wafts toward me, everything makes sense.

I gag.

He tries to take another step, only to fall to his knees in the middle of the aisle, right in front of the queen.

"Your… Majesty…" he stammers, his eyes bulging in his sockets. He opens his mouth to speak again, but no sound comes out—except from his butt.

Oh my!

My hand flies to my mouth in shock.

Not only does the smell intensify, but now it's accompanied by visuals too. The previously gray pavement is stained with a dark green, verging on brown, semi-liquid concoction.

Gasps erupt in the crowd before laughter follows. But it's not long before more people from our table start exhibiting the same symptoms, but luckily not as severe as Ivan—as in, they actually manage to leave the table and go to the bathroom.

"What is this repulsive creature doing at my feet?" Lady Jocelyn thunders, effectively silencing everyone.

She stares at Ivan's pitiful diarrhea-ridden self and makes an expression of disgust.

"I... I..." Ivan is still trying to speak, but each attempt only pushes more foul liquid from his butt.

Damn it! Of course the pink root wouldn't match the description from the books either. Oh, well. Better *something* than nothing.

Although... Somehow now I feel sorry for him, *and* the rest of the collateral victims of my little experiment—being stuck on a toilet is not fun.

Being so young, Willy was the only one who didn't drink any mead—thank God for that. I would have hated for this to happen to him, too.

"What is the meaning of this? Guards! Take him away this instant! Throw him in solitary for a month for his insolence," she commands in the most supercilious voice I've ever heard.

I gawk at her, unsure whether *this* is a dream—more like a nightmare—or not.

Yeah, this is gross. But surely this is not the way to deal with someone who is clearly suffering? Even *I* feel sorry for the pain evident in Ivan's features—and he threatened my baby, which in itself is unforgivable.

The Lady Jocelyn I know, however, would have asked for

help or offered him some relief with her powers—she is a healer, isn't she? Instead, she's sentencing him to a month in solitary?

My mouth hangs open in shock. Disbelief fills me to the core.

At the worst possible moment, however, PomPom jumps from under the table, sniffing the pavement and heading toward Ivan.

"PomPom, no!" I call out. I know what she's going to do and it breaks my heart I didn't think to hold her in my arms to stop her from sniffing that foul substance.

I catch her just in time, wrapping my arms around her. But as I slowly raise my gaze, I meet that of my idol, Lady Jocelyn, for the first time.

I have to control myself to not faint or fangirl too hard. But one look at her expression and I know neither would be welcomed.

She doesn't look happy.

Damn!

That is until her eyes take in the cute fluffiness that is PomPom and her expression softens—slightly.

"Oh, you pretty little thing," she coos, leaning down and patting PomPom on the head.

"Lady Jocelyn." I incline my head, keeping my eyes on the ground. "If I may have a word with you in private?"

"And who are you?" she asks in a disinterested tone.

One glance around and I note that everyone is staring at us with great interest, likely eavesdropping on our conversation.

"My name is Barbara Bancroft. This is my PomPom. We are from a world beyond Akkaya and we need your help to return there," I say succinctly.

As expected, my phrasing piques her interest.

"A world beyond Akkaya?" She lowers her voice so only I can hear her.

I nod.

"I have heard many things about your magical prowess and that of Sir Damien. It is why I have come to Kiya to meet you in hopes you may be able to help me return home," I whisper.

She assesses me with shrewd eyes.

"Follow me," she declares, turning on her heel and going out of the grand hall.

I trail closely behind her, praying she'll take pity on me. The Lady Jocelyn I know and admire would help me in a heartbeat. But I'm afraid my books may have been wrong on that count too.

As soon as we exit the grand hall, a dozen palace guards follow a few steps behind, their eyes trained on me in case I make any wrong moves. Their proximity stresses me out, but I suppose this is normal considering she's *the* Queen.

Lady Jocelyn leads me down a gilded hallway filled with statues of her and the King. Even the marble columns have their faces etched into them. And as we switch from the main hallway to a smaller one, the walls are littered with paintings of them. Few are with the other mages. Most are of Lady Jocelyn and Sir Damien, either together or by themselves.

A shudder goes down my back.

They wasted no time in filling every corner of the castle with their likeness.

"Uhm, where are we going?" I ask when we turn to yet another hallway.

This place is dizzyingly large. And I've been cursed with absolutely no spatial awareness, which means that if I tried to escape, I'd likely get lost.

Yeah, that's not at all assuring.

"There are ancient texts that speak of portals between worlds," she explains in a sharp tone.

"I am not lying. I promise," I hurry to say. "I truly am *not* from here. I was at home getting ready for bed and the next thing I know, I ended up in a field in Akkaya," I explain.

She stops in her tracks, pivoting to look at me.

"I believe you are not from here," she says, her words measured. "I can tell by your speech."

"My…speech?" I frown.

"There is a glamor around you."

She waves her hand, and shimmery particles surround me.

I blink repeatedly.

Suddenly, she closes her fist and the mist disappears.

"*Ibnfiorngorngrginrig…*" She opens her mouth to speak, but her words sound like gibberish.

"What?"

A smile curves her lips.

With a snap of a finger, the mist returns around me, dissipating until it can no longer be seen by the naked eye.

"We do not speak the same language," she notes. "Whoever sent you here must have also bespelled you to be able to speak and understand our language."

"You mean… *Someone* sent me here?"

She nods, pursing her lips.

"I do not recognize this magic signature, so I cannot say who could have done it. But if someone did this, it can be undone."

That sounds reassuring.

"We will need Damien's help, of course," she continues.

"Of course."

Without another word, she turns, continuing down the hallway.

"Thank you so much for helping." I feel compelled to add when the silence becomes overwhelming. "I've heard a lot about you. I'm a big fan."

She clicks her tongue, but she doesn't reply.

Awkward!

"I even got my PomPom because of you," I offer because I *hate* awkward silences.

PomPom, hearing her name, lets out a small sound of approval.

That seems to get her attention. Turning her head, she raises a brow as she glances at my dog.

"You have good taste."

That's all she says. Then she continues walking.

I swallow hard. Anxiety pierces through me as my illusions about this legendary meeting are slowly getting shattered.

In my dreams *before* Akkaya, we might have been BFFs. But now that I've interacted with her, I truly don't know how to feel.

There's only this slight disappointment that is taking root inside of me—this sense of feeling like a fish out of water.

From the first time I read about Lady Jocelyn, I've wanted to be like her. I've modeled my entire life to be like her. She was my role model and what I aspired to be. But now, meeting the real thing…

I briefly close my eyes, taking a deep breath.

She's a Queen now. She has an important position, so she cannot act casually with anyone. Yes, that must be it. I can't judge her based on a small interaction only.

We walk for a few more minutes before we reach a private wing of the castle that's teeming with guards.

She waves her hand around, and the servants open a wooden double door for her. I follow closely behind her, and the door closes with a loud thud after us.

My heart hammers in my chest as the moment I'll meet my second idol slowly approaches. Sir Damien has been my crush for as long as I remember and I am beyond curious to see what he looks like. But I'm also trembling from my nerves since he is an absolute legend—the most powerful mage Akkaya has *ever* seen.

"Put clothes on, Damien. There is something you need to hear," Lady Jocelyn calls out.

There's a ruffle of sheets and a few gasps and squeaks.

I raise my gaze, my eyes widening in shock.

Two naked girls jump from his bed, searching for their clothes. They giggle and joke around in hushed tones as they dash past us and out of the room. They never once acknowledge Lady Jocelyn or feel any shame for whatever they were doing with *her* husband.

Sir Damien is with his back to us as he tugs at his pants—*butt naked*. He turns as he puts on a shirt but leaves it unbuttoned.

His blond hair falls to his shoulders, curling slightly at the tips. His eyes are a deep blue shade, his features just as chiseled as I would have imagined.

Yet instead of butterflies in my stomach, all I feel is disgust and a deep-seated discomfort.

He has a bored expression on his face as he turns to his wife. But as his gaze flies past her to me, his eyes glint with interest.

"What do we have here, Jos? Don't tell me you brought me a gift." He lets out a laugh as he heads over to his table to pour himself a drink. "You could have at least waited until I was done with the other two, you know…"

"Cut it out, Damien. That's not why she's here." Lady Jocelyn rolls her eyes. "She's from *another* world," she adds pointedly—as if referencing a previous conversation.

Sir Damien stills.

"Is that so?" he asks as he swirls his drink in his glass, leaning lazily against the table and watching us.

"I believe she's speaking the truth," she continues, and their gazes connect. For a moment, neither says anything as they merely stare at each other.

Are they…communicating telepathically? Well, that's at least *one* thing the books got right.

"Barbara, is it?" He suddenly smiles. He is a handsome man. The descriptions in the books had not done him justice. But his smile is bleak. Instead of making me more comfortable, it does the opposite. The urge to squirm and leave right away is overwhelming, as is the fear that I might have gotten myself into something dangerous.

"You can call me Barbi," I add nervously.

"Barbi, then."

His smile widens.

My discomfort increases.

"Tell me about this world of yours."

"I'm not sure what you mean…"

"Describe it for me."

I look at Lady Jocelyn for confirmation and she nods, urging me to talk.

"We call it Earth. It's far larger than Akkaya and there are a lot of countries. We don't have magic, but we have technology. That sort of fulfills the same purpose. I come from the USA. It's one of the biggest countries and…"

I do my best to explain my country, our culture, economy, and anything else that might seem relevant. Lady Jocelyn and Sir Damien listen quietly, their expressions rapt with interest.

"And how many people did you say were on this Earth?" Sir Damien asks pensively.

"Around eight billion."

His eyes widen. Lady Jocelyn gasps.

"Eight *billion*?"

I nod.

"Akkaya has a few hundred million at best," he adds quietly.

"Damien, this is…" Lady Jocelyn's gaze connects with his.

"It is, indeed," he agrees.

"So, uhm, I was wondering if you might be able to help me get back there. I'm not exactly sure how I ended up here but—"

"Of course," Sir Damien cuts me off. "We would be honored to help you find a way to your world."

"So it is possible to go back?" I whisper in relief.

"There are portals that connect to other worlds across Akkaya. We will get you back," Sir Damien responds casually. "I will need to confer with my advisers. Until then, you shall, of course, be a guest at my court. It is not every day that we have an otherworldly guest." He chuckles.

I nod slowly, though a niggling feeling tells me this was far too…easy?

"Jocelyn will show you to a guest suite. Why don't we reunite for dinner so you can tell me more about this Earth?"

"I can do that." I offer a tentative smile. "Thank you."

"Don't even mention it." He waves his hand.

His gaze connects with that of Lady Jocelyn and something passes between them. After a moment, Lady Jocelyn nods and turns to me, plastering a smile on her face.

"I will show you to your suite now," she says, all but kicking me out of Sir Damien's room.

Not wanting to be ungrateful or rude, I follow her without protest.

The suite she assigns to me isn't far. It's at the end of the corridor, some six doors down from their own chambers. The room is a pleasant combination of brown and off-white. There is a king-sized bed in the middle of the room, an adjoining bathroom, and a sitting room with double doors that lead to a balcony.

I let PomPom out of my arms and she races across the suite to get familiar with the surroundings.

"A maid will come to bring you new clothes and food for you and PomPom." As usual, her voice softens as she mentions my baby. "Please have some rest and we will reconvene this evening for dinner."

With that, she turns to leave.

"Uhm," I call out.

She stops, turning her head to the side.

"Maybe I am overstepping my boundaries, but… I thought you and Sir Damien were married…"

"We are," she replies sharply.

"But then why was he—"

"Have a good rest," she declares before she's out of the room, the door closing with a resounding thud. It seems I *did* overstep my boundaries.

I gulp down as I stare at the closed doors, the disappointment I've been feeling for a while now finally sinking in.

For over a decade, Lady Jocelyn and Sir Damien had been couple goals for me. I'd never even entertained dating someone because my standards were too high and no real-life boy could possibly live up to them.

They had always been so in love, so devoted to one another. They had been a team—a pair of equals fighting for a common purpose.

But had any of that been real? Have I been living with an illusion all along?

Not only is Lady Jocelyn not the sweet, soft-spoken lady I thought her to be. But Sir Damien is a cheating scoundrel who doesn't even care if his wife sees him in the act. And it wasn't with just one woman. No, it was two. At the same time!

Disgust rolls in my stomach. I sink down on the bed, numb and utterly devastated by everything I've found out.

For more than half of my life, I've been worshipping a lie.

Tears of disappointment and frustration stab at my eyes, and I get the urge to scream my grievances at the top of my lungs. God, to think I was so happy I somehow ended up in Akkaya and so excited at the prospect of meeting my idols. Now? I just want to go home and forget all of this happened. Maybe even burn those damned books for making me entertain so many dreams only for them to be shattered in the end.

Yet more than anything… I guess I am mad at myself. I *let* myself buy into their story. Because my life was so damn bleak and lonely, I let myself get absorbed into their fantastical world, losing sight of what's real and what's not.

And now that the illusion has been destroyed…who am I?

I clench my hands into fists. Tears course down my cheeks.

If there's no Lady Jocelyn who loves pink, who has a white Pomeranian named BonBon, and who is utterly devoted to her beloved Sir Damien, then where does that leave me?

Who the hell am I?

PomPom rushes to me, whimpering and rubbing her head against my legs.

"It's okay, sweet girl," I murmur, petting her on the head. "Lady Jocelyn and Sir Damien are strangers. I shouldn't get so upset over this when they probably have no idea someone wrote a distorted account of their lives in another world." I sigh. "But that doesn't make this any less painful. I…" I swallow. "I just don't know anything anymore. Oh, PomPom, I feel so lost," I cry out.

She jumps in my lap and I hug her to my chest, rocking back and forth with her as I let my tears fall down.

A knock at the door startles me. I dry my tears and take a deep breath before opening the door. A servant comes in with clean clothes and a tray of food for both PomPom and me.

I thank her and lock the door after she leaves.

The dress is a beautiful pink—something Lady Jocelyn would wear, and by extension, me. As I stare at it laid out on the bed, I get the urge to rip it to shreds.

But as I grip the soft material in my hands, I can't bring myself to do it.

So what if Lady Jocelyn is not who I thought she was? So what if their love story is a fraud? That doesn't mean the characters I read about and loved don't exist—if only in my head? So what if the real people are shitty? I'll pretend they don't exist and keep the fictional ones in my mind.

With a deep sigh, I head over to the shower, washing

myself and PomPom. I'm not too hungry, but PomPom is, so I give her something to eat before we go to bed.

PomPom falls asleep right away. She must have been exhausted, poor baby. Unfortunately, for me sleep doesn't come too easily. I twist and turn, but my thoughts are too loud. I feel so silly for my obsession with Lady Jocelyn and maybe a little embarrassed of myself for trying to be something I was not for so long.

I sigh in frustration.

Eyes closed, I force myself to rest. But just as my body relaxes, a sudden noise makes me aware that I'm no longer alone in my room.

"She should be out by now," a feminine voice says—Lady Jocelyn.

My heart thuds in my chest, but I keep my eyes closed, feigning sleep.

"Do you think it's wise to do it now? We still don't have the last page," she continues.

"We don't need her alive. We just need to preserve her blood," Sir Damien adds, annoyed.

The cold metal of a blade slides against my skin. I freeze in fear.

What the hell is happening?

"But, Damien... I've been thinking. What if it doesn't work *because* it's not fresh blood? We can't afford to make any mistakes."

"It will be fine, Jo," he snaps, and the tip of the knife digs into my flesh, drawing blood.

I grit my teeth and clamp my mouth shut so I don't make any noise, but the pain echoes in my body.

"Will you take the chance? After what happened last time?" Lady Jocelyn counters. "We've worked too hard for this. I say we wait. She already thinks we're going to help her get back to her world. She won't suspect a thing."

He releases an annoyed sigh, removing the blade from my throat.

"Come on. Don't be impatient, darling. We're so close to our goal."

He utters a string of muttered curses, followed by more assurances from Lady Jocelyn. Eventually, they disappear from my room.

I count to one hundred before I finally dare to open my eyes, my entire being filled with terror.

What the hell did I get myself into?

6

"I still cannot believe how big your world is," Lady Jocelyn exclaims later that day at dinner. "Eight billion people is unfathomable."

I force a smile, though the fear from before hasn't subsided.

It is pure torture to sit at the same table as them for dinner and pretend to answer all their questions about my world. As if they didn't try to murder me just a few hours ago. But it is necessary if I want to escape unnoticed later tonight.

"You said your medicine is advanced?" Arisa asks.

The dinner is a small affair, and Arisa and Leoni, the other two mages from what once was the Five, join us. They're equally curious about my world, but their questions are few and far between due to their deference toward Jocelyn and Damien.

"Yes. People live longer and healthier lives," I murmur.

"That means they must have superior life force, no?" she asks, gazing hopefully at Damien.

He gives a tight nod but doesn't explain what that means.

I pretend to eat, stealthily stashing some bread in my

pocket to Hansel my way around this place. Luckily, the dining hall is on the ground level, and I managed to spot a few doors that might lead to the outside. Now it's only a matter of laying a breadcrumb trail to my room that I can follow later to trace my way back here.

The questions continue, and I give them the most outrageous and fake answers I can think of. I still don't know why they need to sacrifice me at some point—who knows what type of ritual they want to achieve with my blood—but I'm not about to stick around and find out.

My first red flag should have been the fact that so little of Akkaya is the same as what I read about. But I still harbored the hope that my idols were upstanding people—which clearly, they are *not*.

God, whoever wrote those books must have been heavily biased. How could someone describe Damien as a hero when he's nothing but a murderous psycho who also cheats on his wife?

Unacceptable.

I may not know how to get back home on my own, but I'd rather take my chances by myself far away from them.

"Thank you for this lovely dinner and for everything you've done for me so far," I murmur appreciatively as I get up from the table. "You have no idea how much I appreciate your help—"

"Nonsense," Damien cuts me off—he has a habit of doing that to women. "We are thrilled to meet someone from another world after having heard so much of their existence. Your tales alone are priceless."

I incline my head, forcing my lips in a deferent smile.

"The servant will see you to your room. Have a good night, Barbara," Jocelyn tells me dismissively.

The servant leads me back to my suite, and I drop little crumbs of bread on the way from the main hallway to my room. Now I just have to hope there's no nocturne cleaning going on at this castle. Otherwise, I'm screwed.

When I get back to my suite, PomPom is still out of it. Whatever they put in the food was too much for her small body. That sends a spark of anger through me.

How could they think to do this to a small, defenseless dog? I clench my fists in outrage, wishing I could retaliate against them in some way. But although I have yet to see evidence of their abilities, I've heard enough from the soldiers to know I am no match for them. The only recourse I have is to run away.

A few hours later, I fashion a carrier for PomPom out of a sheet and tie it across my torso. Opening the door to my room, I make my way out.

To my relief, the crumbs of bread are still on the floor, so I follow them to the main hallway. The castle is eerily quiet, not a soul in sight. Hope blossoms in my chest that I can, in fact, do this.

Now it's just a matter of finding the right door that leads to the outside.

A couple of failed tries and I manage to find the right one.

The cold air of the night brushes against my face and I take a deep breath to fill my lungs. I'll do this. I'll find a way out.

I step into the night, and a shiver goes down my back from the low temperature. The pink gown does not provide any warmth, and this might cause me to catch a cold…

That's the last thing I need to think about! This is about surviving and not being sacrificed to some pagan god, not catching a cold, which might I say, is not fatal.

I stealthily make my way across the main yard, but just as I think I've made it—that I've left the castle behind—I bump into the person I least wanted to see again.

"You…"

Ivan's face contorts in anger as he sees me. Especially as

his eyes scan my frame and he quickly deduces that I'm absconding in the middle of the night—which, he's not wrong.

"I knew it! You're a fucking impostor!" He grabs me by the arm and all but drags me back to the castle.

"Let go!" I scream. "They're all murderers. You'll get me killed," I say, hoping I might strike some human chord in him—though I doubt it.

The noise only serves to awaken more soldiers, and soon, we have an entire audience in front of the castle. Ivan takes great pride in telling all of them that I was trying to run away because I'm a spy.

"She probably tried to seduce our King and he wouldn't fall for it," he says further. A chorus of boos resounds in the air.

My eyes widen in shock.

"Seduce the King? He's a psycho murderer who wants to sacrifice me," I cry out as I struggle to get out of his grasp. I manage to push him away for a second before he lodges his fingers in my scalp, pulling on my hair and keeping me by his side.

I cry in pain.

"Harlot."

"Whore."

Oh my, these people take their King's virtue seriously. They don't seem to realize he has an entire harem at his disposal already.

"Our Queen won't stand for this," someone calls from the crowd, further getting the others worked up. The words they're spewing at me are not fit for any ears.

The windows of the castle light up. More people show up, curious about the commotion. At this point, instead of escaping silently, I'm doing the exact opposite.

And if I thought things couldn't get worse, well…they just got so much fucking worse.

The King and Queen make their appearance in a regal fashion. They teleport themselves in the middle of the crowd, merely a few steps away from me.

Oh. Shit.

"Your Majesty. I caught her sneaking out of the castle," Ivan speaks as he dangles me by the hair. "She must have been spying for the East."

"What?" I squeak. "I'm not a spy. I just want to leave with my life intact, all right? They"—I point to the King and Queen—"are the culty leaders trying to sacrifice me for whatever pagan god they're in cahoots with."

"What is your name, soldier?" The King takes a step forward, addressing Ivan without even acknowledging me.

"Ivan Rogers, Your Majesty."

"Ivan." He nods. "You shall be handsomely rewarded for catching her."

"I was right, was I not? She's bad news."

"You are, indeed, correct," Damien continues, sparing me a disdainful glance. "I have just found out that she is the Dark One's lover. She must have been trying to avenge her dead lover."

W-what?

"He's lying! I don't even *know* the Dark One," I hurry to say, though it falls on deaf ears.

"Kill her! Kill her!"

I blink, stupefied.

The crowd is asking for my death, cursing me for being related to the Dark One in any way.

With a wave of his hand, the King silences everyone.

"Ivan. Take her to the dungeon," he instructs my captor. Turning to the crowd, he continues. "She will be executed on the day of the new moon, as is our custom for anyone related to the Dark One."

People start clapping and praising the King—*and* wishing me a torturous death.

Great.

Just as Ivan drags me away from the crowd, Jocelyn suddenly stops him.

"Wait!"

With slow, dignified steps, she comes toward me. She wrenches the sheet from my torso and takes PomPom out of it.

"You may go," she says, cradling PomPom in her arms.

I'm too stunned to say anything but stare at my little baby as she gets farther and farther away from me.

Ivan purposefully digs his fingers painfully into my scalp, relishing hurting me. But I don't care. All I can see is PomPom and the fact that these evil people took her from me.

Tears stab at my eyes, and a rage unlike I've ever known overtakes me.

I thrash violently, screaming out for PomPom until Ivan has no choice but to slap me—so hard I see stars. Still, it's no match for the heart of a grieving mother as her child is taken away from her. So what if she's not human? She's my everything.

"PomPom!" I call for her, hoping she might wake up and run to me.

But she doesn't. She's still out of it.

"Let me go, you brute. Let me go," I continue to fight him, especially as we go down dark stairs that lead to an even darker corridor.

Fear creeps down my spine.

There are dirty cells on either side of the corridor. Some prisoners are still alive, but others have wasted away, only a pile of bones remaining in their wake.

Good Lord! I gulp down against the wave of terror that engulfs me.

He drags me to the darkest corner of the dungeon where there's barely any light. He only stops when he reaches the last cage—smaller and dirtier than the rest. Opening the latch, he throws me inside.

"Fucking bitch. I knew you were bad, but I didn't realize I was traveling with the Dark One's whore," he spits at me.

"Wait!" I call out, scrambling to my feet.

The door closes in my face, the latch back on.

Ivan smiles mockingly at me.

"I'm looking forward to your execution." He chuckles. "Until then, enjoy your stay in the most cursed cell."

Then he turns and leaves, his laughter echoing in the hallway.

For moments on end, I hold on to the rusty bars of the cell, staring into the darkness as my dire situation sinks in.

I'm in a different world. In a dirty prison. About to be sacrificed/executed. How the hell did my perfectly normal and pink life turn into dungeons and dragons—sans the dragons?

My breathing accelerates as panic overtakes me.

They took my baby from me, too. That stupid Lady Jocelyn, the fakest lady in the entire universe.

"I'll kill you if you do something to my PomPom," I yell, my voice traveling down the hallway and leaving an angry echo behind.

"Aghhhh!" I scream at the top of my lungs, pulling on the thick metal bars. Alas, it's in vain. Once my screaming session is done—merely because my throat hurts and I doubt anyone will bring me water in here—I release a frustrated sigh as I sink to the floor.

It's cold, damp, and dark.

"Why me?" I whisper, swallowing a sob.

The cell is so dark I can't even make out where the walls are and what parameters I'm being confined to, which makes it all the more claustrophobic.

"I've not done anything illegal in my life," I mumble to myself. "I've never even stolen anything, except if you count the chocolate my mother told me I was not allowed to have. But that was from my own fridge. It's not as if I stole someone else's chocolate. I would never do that. Not like that stupid, scheming Jocelyn who stole my PomPom."

At remembering my poor baby, I burst into tears again.

"Oh my God!" I cry out, nearly jumping out of my skin. "Stupid Jocelyn has BonBon, and he's a male. My PomPom is a female. What if he…" A strangled gasp escapes me. "What if he takes advantage of my PomPom? She's never been with a male in her life."

My sobs intensify as I think of my PomPom being assaulted by BonBon. And it's all my damn fault.

"He's going to take my PomPom's virginity and I can't do anything to stop it." I continue crying. Big, fat tears stream down my face as I imagine my sweet angel being debased by that woman's dog.

"Wait for me, PomPom. Mommy will come for you. I'll save you, baby!"

Except I have no idea how I'm going to get out of here. Alive.

Minutes trickle by, turning into hours. My body is tired, but my mind is wide awake, trying to solve this conundrum.

The sun is up, some light streaming into the dungeon, but not enough to reach my cell. Ivan wasn't kidding that this is the worst one.

I mutter a string of curses that are not at all ladylike. But you know what? To hell with being a lady. I've had a first-hand experience of what it means to be a lady—*cough, cough, stupid Jocelyn*—and I don't want to have anything to do with it.

I get to my feet and pace around my cell, keeping an eye out for any soldiers patrolling the premises—anyone other than Ivan, that is. If I play my cards right, maybe I can charm them into opening the door for me.

A ray of light dances between the metal bars and illuminates the corner of my cell. I wouldn't have paid it much attention if I didn't catch the glint of something red and shiny.

I blink and the light is almost gone. But I'm sure of what I saw.

It was a precious stone, mayhap attached to a ring.

A bulb lights up in my head.

Maybe I can bribe a guard with it and he will let me go!

I clasp my hands together in excitement and take one step at a time until I reach the other end of the cell. I slide to the floor, and slowly, I inch closer to the area where I saw the jewel. My poor pink gown will likely become black from all the dust I'm collecting. If my execution truly comes to pass—which, fingers crossed it won't—I hope stupid Jocelyn will at least let me have what's left of my dignity and give me a clean pink gown.

Another ray of light makes its way into the cell, and I spot the stone. It's a ruby ring, I think. Before the light can go out again, I move swiftly and grab onto it.

But just as it gets dark in the cell once more, a cry is wrenched from my lips when I realize that it's not *just* a ring.

It's attached to a hand.

A mummified hand.

"Holy Mother of God!" I cry out, falling on my ass.

I gulp down as the first wave of shock passes.

"It's okay, Barbi. It's just a dead guy. He can't do anything to you. In fact, maybe he'll be happy to know his ring helped you avoid the same fate as him." I try to give myself a pep talk. "It's not stealing if they're dead, right? I'm not committing a felony. I'm just…surviving. Yes, that's right. I'm doing this for my PomPom. If the dead guy will be mad at me for stealing his ring, he should at least consider it's for a good cause. I'm saving my dog. And who hates dogs? No one!"

I nod to myself, satisfied with my line of thinking.

"It's for PomPom. Who can say no to my PomPom?"

Getting on my hands and knees, I once more slowly get closer.

"Sorry, dead guy. I promise I'll write you a dedication in

my pink notebook for special people," I say as I pat his mummified arm in my search for his hand. He's still clothed, though the material is tattered. To my surprise, though, he doesn't smell like a dead person—not that I'm an expert in what dead people smell like, but I've seen a few since coming to Akkaya.

"I have two notebooks, you see. A pink one for the good people that I like, and a black one for the bad people. Oh my." I gasp. "That reminds me. When I get home, I need to transfer stupid Jocelyn and psycho Damien's names from the pink one to the black one. They're worse than bad, actually. Maybe I should start a new notebook just for them," I muse to myself.

I find the end of the sleeve and slowly touch the mummified hand, afraid I might break it if I'm too rough.

"Don't worry. I won't desecrate your body. I'm just borrowing your ring. I promise you, PomPom and I will be forever grateful," I tell him as I find the ring and slowly pull it off his finger.

"Will you stop yapping about, female? You are ruining my restful sleep."

"Oh, I'm sorry. I didn't mean to—"

My eyes widen as my brain slowly processes what I heard.

A voice. A deep, manly voice. Talking to me.

A voice coming from the mummy. As in, the mummy is talking to me!

"Ahhhhhhh!" I scream, falling backward.

The sound of a rip follows the echo of my scream.

My fingers close around the ring, but to my renewed horror, it's not *just* the ring. It's attached to something. A finger. The mummy's finger.

Oh my God! I just broke a mummy's finger.

Another scream pierces the air until my throat is too sore to make another sound. My chest rises and falls, my breath ragged as I stare at the dark spot where the mummy is—the *talking* mummy.

"Can I have my finger back now?" he asks in a dry, bored tone.

For the first time since arriving in Akkaya, I've had enough.

My eyes roll in the back of my head and I slump to the floor.

7

"**G**ood. You are finally awake," a manly voice drawls. It's deep and lyrical, and quite pleasant.

"Five more minutes," I grumble.

I stretch, yawning as I slowly awaken. God, I had the most terrible dream. Not only was I trapped in a fictional world with no idea how to get back home, but all my role models turned out to be assholes. To top it off, I also annoyed some talking mummy who was just about to jump on me for stealing its finger.

Good thing this nice voice woke me up, or I would have experienced the wrath of the mummy in my dream. A shudder goes down my body. Why am I even dreaming about talking mummies? Do I have some unresolved trauma or something?

I smack my lips together, a little thirsty.

"Can I have a glass of water?"

Why am I so thirsty? I always hydrate well before bed, but now it's like I haven't had a sip of water in ages.

"Wake up, female!" the same voice commands.

My eyes flash open.

It's dark. Too dark for this to be my room.

I'm also holding on to something.

I gulp down in apprehension.

The ridges of the ring are familiar. But there's something else clinging to the ring. Something…

Oh. My. God.

Everything comes back to me, together with the realization that this is *not* a dream.

"Stay away from me!" I cry out, jumping up and scrambling as far away from the talking mummy. I hold the finger with the ring in front of me as some kind of crucifix, hoping it might save me from its wrath. After all, if it wants to hurt me, it might accidentally hurt its finger first. Awful logic, I know. But at this point, my brain is as mushy as the mummy's insides.

"Cease your hysterics, female," he decrees. But his imperial tone only makes my anxiety skyrocket.

"Don't come closer. You'll regret it," I tell him, backing away until I hit the other wall of the cell. "I… I'm not someone you want to mess with," I mumble, wildly looking around. It's too dark to make sense of anything around me, and my heart is beating too loudly in my ears to be able to hear anything else.

Oh, God! I won't even get to my execution because I will be killed by a mummy. Damn Ivan! He did this on purpose, that blasted man.

"Is that so?" he mocks me.

"Y-yes." I raise my voice. "I…" *Come on, Barbi, think of something. What could a mummy be afraid of? It's already dead!*

"You may not be aware, b-but I…" I swallow. "I was locked in here because the Dark One is my boyfriend."

"Your boyfriend?" A low chuckle echoes in the cell.

"Y-yes. He is my boyfriend. He… He is *very* bad and dangerous and he can summon dark clouds and kill anyone with the snap of a finger," I enumerate the things Jerry had told me about him. "He also loves me *very* much. I am the apple of his eye, his most beloved treasure, the beat of his heart—not that you would know since you're a mummy and your heart is likely not beating—" I stammer as I try to think of more descriptors. "I'm the reason he wakes up in the morning, the light to his dark, dark soul—emphasis on *dark*," I add, proud of my quick thinking.

"He would burn the world for me, you know, and you might be dead, but mummies can catch fire, too. In fact, you'll probably be easier to incinerate than a non-mummified body, so you'll die faster." I clear my throat. "So you see, if you do anything to me, you'll be the first one to pay the price."

Silence greets me.

"Are you done?" he eventually asks in the same lazy voice.

"Uhm, no? He's bad. Very, very bad."

"So you have said," he drawls.

I frown. I may not be able to see him, but I have the vague impression he's laughing at me. And I can't have that. He needs to understand I am off-limits.

"Well, he's the worst villain Akkaya has *ever* seen. He's so scary, people are afraid to even say his name because he might kill them."

"You do not seem too afraid to say his name," he notes drily.

"Everyone *but* me. I am his heart," I repeat the lie.

Although wouldn't that be nice? I release a wistful sigh as I let my foolish self dream once more about true love; the eternal kind that would withstand any test—as if I haven't already been disappointed enough by my own delusions.

"I see. So you are the exception to the rule," he utters, his tone skeptical.

"Of course. I told you. So don't even think of trying something with me because he's going to come and get me out of here and if I tell him you've been bad to me, he's going to make sure you never see the light of day. Not that you *see* the light of day here since it's a little too dark. But you know what

I mean," I snap, pushing my chin up. "He's going to turn you into mummy dust."

He doesn't reply, and a smile pulls at my lips.

Aha! My ruse worked. Since everyone is so afraid of the Dark One, and psycho Damien already declared me his lover, why shouldn't I make use of his reputation?

"And here I thought he was dead," the mummy murmurs.

I blink. How the hell does *he* know that?

"Oh, that is…he…he faked his death, but he's going to save me," I huff aloud.

Seconds stretch into minutes and no sound comes from him.

"I just want my finger back," he eventually says.

My lips flatten as I consider his words. I did steal his finger —and his ring. Now a pang of guilt stabs at my chest. He's probably a poor enemy of psycho Damien and he's been wasting away in this cell for God knows how long.

"If I give it to you, you won't hurt me?" I ask tentatively. Just to make sure.

"No."

"Really?"

"You have my word," he promises.

"Okay. I guess I can do that. I'm sorry I took it when it wasn't mine to take," I add apologetically.

I dangle the finger with the ring, waiting for him to come get it.

"You will need to come to me," he decrees.

"W-what?" I squeak.

"Come to me, female. I gave you my word I will not hurt you."

"But… But…"

"Your big, bad, and dangerous boyfriend will make sure I never see the light of day if I do anything to you."

"Are you making fun of me?" I ask in outrage.

He sighs.

"My finger, female. I would like to have it back."

I stare at the darkness for a few moments as I debate what to do.

"Fine," I mutter under my breath.

Mustering all the courage I can get, I get to my feet. I make my way toward the other end of the cell, but due to the darkness, I can't see where I'm walking.

I take small, careful steps. Yet it only takes one wrong move for me to lose my balance. I wobble on my feet, a strangled cry escaping me as I flail my arms around.

"Ahhhh," I whimper as my foot catches onto something solid and I fall.

Against all odds, though, I don't hit the pavement.

I hit the mummy.

"Uhm, I'm sorry?" I whisper as I realize my fingers are pulling on the already tattered material of his clothes.

He grunts but makes no effort to help me up.

I hold on to him to raise myself up, only to fall once more, this time flat *on top* of the mummy.

"You can have your finger back," I say as I search in the darkness to give it to him. Up close, there's an inviting scent coming off him—not at all what I would have imagined death and gloom to smell like. It's a mix of tobacco, musk, and ash with the lightest hint of coffee.

I find his hand and I put the finger where it belongs. That's also when I realize why he could not move. He's chained to the wall. There's a heavy metal chain around his wrist, holding him in place.

"Do you need any glue? Or clay?" I ask innocently. "I can try to put it back together for you, but—"

"It will mend itself just fine," he strains a reply.

"Oh. Okay," I murmur.

It hasn't escaped me that I should have moved ten seconds ago. But he's comfortable. And warm. Surprisingly warm. And I'm so damn cold and shivery.

"I'm really sorry about your finger. I promise I'm not a thief, especially not a body part thief," I add nervously, just so I can buy myself a few more moments with his body heat.

"It is fine," he replies.

His warm breath brushes against my skin. Goose bumps erupt all over my body, accompanied by a light ticklish sensation.

"You're surprisingly big," I murmur appreciatively as I shamelessly feel up his shoulders. Hmm, they are quite broad. "I thought mummies were shriveled up, but you don't seem to be all that dry…"

A blush stains my cheeks as my thoughts go in a different direction.

God, Barbi! You're having dirty thoughts about a mummy of all things. You should be ashamed of yourself!

"Do you always talk this much?" he suddenly asks.

I blink.

"Only when I'm nervous."

"Why are you nervous?" he counters.

"Uhm." I swallow. Why does it have to be so dark? Why can't I see him? And why does he have to smell nice *and* feel nice. This is too deceiving for my poor, already messed up mind. "Because you might hurt me?"

"Strange creature." He tsks at me, and if it weren't so dark, I would imagine him shaking his head at me. "I have already given you my word that you are safe with me."

"Hey, I am not a creature, nor am I strange." I push against his chest, belatedly stopping when I realize I might cause more damage.

"Sorry," I mumble.

I am hopeless. I'll destroy this poor mummy in no time if I keep this up. But as I continue to feel my way around his body, I encounter more chains. One is around his neck, the other at his waist. A pang of sadness pierces my heart at his situation.

He's chained to this wall like an animal, barely allowed any movement.

"You *are* strange. But I welcome it," he adds in a wistful tone. "It has been a long time since I have talked to someone."

"H-how long?" I ask on a whisper.

"Years? Maybe more? I no longer know at this point."

"How could you be here *that* long?"

"Does that surprise you? I am a *mummy*, after all," he mentions drily.

Oh, my. Did I offend him by calling him a mummy?

"If it makes you feel better, you're a *toned* mummy," I say as I pat his chest. Yes, that's quite nice. Not shriveled up, nor dry. "Of course, I am not an expert on mummies. I've only watched a couple of movies, and those mummies looked pretty disgusting before they did some magic to get back their looks—not that *you* look disgusting," I hurry to add. "I don't know what you look like since it's so dark. But you don't feel disgusting," I say as I touch him some more. Yes, very nice and warm, snuggly too if I were to lean closer. "Those mummies had holes and tears in their flesh, and bugs were crawling through their orifices, but you seem quite whole to me—except for the finger I broke. Did I apologize about that?" I laugh nervously. "Oh, my. I hope you don't have bugs crawling through your skin or something like that. I can't imagine feeling them move on your skin and inside your body…"

A sudden, deep laugh erupts in the air.

I stop mid-sentence, my lips parted as I feel the vibrations coming from *his* chest.

"Where did you come from, female? I have never met someone like you before."

"What do you mean?" I demand in indignation.

"You are…interesting," he murmurs in a low, barely audible voice.

"Oh." I nod. "Interesting good or interesting bad?" I ask, just to make sure.

He doesn't answer.

"Come on. You can't say something like that and not qualify it," I complain. I've often been told I am too curious for my own good, but I prefer to call it inquisitive. I merely like to have all the facts before me.

Once more, he doesn't reply.

"Hey!" I jab my finger in his hard, not quite mummy-like chest. "I'm talking to you."

He releases a deep sigh.

"Interesting good or interesting bad?" I repeat. "Please don't say bad, though. Maybe choose another word. I'd rather not have that hanging over my head while I'm already in such a precarious situation with all this death and gloom. But if it's interesting good then you can say so. Maybe use another adjective as well, as long as it's complimentary," I yap happily. It's been far too long since anyone's said anything kind to me, so any compliment would go a long way considering I've been told all my life what a disappointment I am.

I await anxiously his next words. I am not sure why the validation of a stranger—of *this* stranger that I haven't even seen—matters so much. But it does. My heart is in my throat, beating loudly and making me choke on absurd anxiety.

"You talk too much. Be a good girl and go back to your corner of the cell. I would like to have my peace back," he drawls, effectively ending the conversation.

I blink in the dark, swallowing hard at being dismissed like that. To make matters worse, he turns his face away, the sudden absence of his warm breath on my cheek making me feel rather bereft.

I grit my teeth. I am not one to let myself be intimidated by a rough, manly voice, so I feel compelled to continue making my case.

"Psycho Damien and stupid Jocelyn also think I am interesting. Well, not in a good way, seeing that they want to sacrifice me for some nefarious purpose, but not in a bad way either since they *need* me. So you see, I am quite important." I sulk. "And, of course, I am the Dark One's heart," I add grumpily when no reply is forthcoming.

With a loud huff, I get up to leave, stumbling again on my way and almost falling a few times. As I reach *my* corner of the cell, I slump my shoulders and I drag my knees to my chest, finally able to let out the weary breath I've been holding in.

My lips tremble and tears gather at the corners of my eyes. My awful situation is dawning on me, as well as the fact that there is little I can do to save myself and my PomPom. I can put on all the bravado in the world, but in the end, I have to face my fate. I'm going to die in a goddamn fictional world —one that I, ironically, worshiped for half of my life.

I stare at the darkness, coldness seeping into my bones once more. My arms tighten around my knees in an attempt to preserve what little body heat I have left.

He's there. In the dark. I can't even make out his shape, but if I focus hard enough, I can hear his quiet breaths. They're short and clipped, just like him. There are other sounds in the dungeon. Moans and whines of other prisoners still alive. But they're all a low, muted sound. Removed from my reality, or perhaps, I have yet to accept that *this* is my reality.

A deep sense of shame envelops me as I realize I've been taking out my anger on the wrong person—a poor mummy who is also Damien's victim.

But just as I'm about to apologize for my abysmal behavior—I did steal his finger first—more sounds erupt from deep within the dungeon. My head whirls around as I drag myself closer to the bars. There is a source of light at the end of the tunnel—one that's becoming stronger with each passing moment.

I smack my lips together. I'm so thirsty. Do prisoners get water benefits? Somehow, I doubt that. But that still doesn't stop me from asking.

"Excuse me. Is anyone there?" I call out to the flickering light.

The only response I get is the piercing moan of pain from a random prisoner.

I feel for you, buddy.

"Can I speak with someone, please? Someone higher, preferably?" I stop myself short of asking to speak with the manager. Gosh, am I becoming a Karen? But I suppose these are completely different circumstances. I'm not complaining about a perfectly rendered service, nor am I calling the cops about the kids loitering around the neighborhood. I am merely asking for some human decency, although I doubt that's a concern here.

Akkaya has no human rights council, though I now see it is in dire need of one. Take my mummy friend for example— not that he's *my* friend, but he's the only one around. He's been left to rot here. In my world, that constitutes about a hundred human rights violations.

My voice echoes in the dungeon, but there is no reply forthcoming.

Why is everyone ignoring me today?

"Someone? Anyone? I would like a glass of water, please," I call out. No response. "In case you haven't heard, I am to be executed on the new moon. I doubt your mighty King will like it if I'm dehydrated and weak. What's the joy in killing someone who's already down, no?" I ask hopefully. Executions are supposed to be a spectacle (not that I want to die anytime soon).

The light flickers and comes closer and closer.

My lips slowly spread into a smile as I dab at the errant tears falling down my cheeks. Maybe someone heard my plea.

I blink repeatedly, shielding my eyes as the source of light stops right in front of my cell. But as my eyes get accustomed to the light, I realize that I might be in more trouble than before.

Ivan looks down at me with malice in his eyes.

"Not so high and mighty now, are you?" He laughs at me.

I yelp as he gives me a kick, falling to my ass a distance away from the bars. He opens the lock and enters the cell. He's carrying with him a torch that lights up the entire room.

"I'm surprised you're still so cheery after spending the night with this freak," he sneers. Right at that moment, I gaze back as the torch lights up even the darkest corners of the cell.

My mouth parts in an O as I stare at my cellmate. His long, dark hair is draped over his face, reaching his waist. I cannot make out his features, but it's clear he's *not* a mummy. He's not in the best shape, that's for sure, but he's human and alive. His skin has a sickly hue, an ashy brown color. His body is big and broad, his chest just as large as I'd felt with my hands.

My eyes immediately go to his hand, and I note that the ring finger had attached itself to his hand—just as he'd said.

I swallow hard.

There are over a dozen chains keeping him tied to the wall —around his neck, chest, arms, and legs. He is thoroughly immobilized.

A pang of hurt echoes in my chest as I take him in. He can't even move, can he? But why go to such extremes? Why so many chains when one would have done the job?

As the light shines over him, he turns his head to the side, avoiding looking at Ivan. The nasty man takes a step forward.

"Leave my friend alone," I burst out before I can stop myself.

He turns to me, a sick smile on his face.

"Friend?" He chuckles at me. "What do you have to say for yourself, freak? You have a pretty young woman in your cell and you can't even move," he mocks him, using his foot to kick at the man's leg. The chains rattle, but his leg doesn't move—it is too tightly secured. "Can your cock even get hard after so long?"

My cheeks burn with embarrassment at his crass words, and I scurry backward.

Ivan moves his torch back and forth over the man's body, stopping above his crotch.

"Why don't we put it to the test." He guffaws as he flings the torch.

My eyes widen as I realize what he means to do, and before I know it, I throw myself against him, kicking him off balance and causing him to miss. But instead of helping the poor man, I make everything worse.

My breath hitches as I see the torch fall on his chest, the fire engulfing his hair. The scraps of material on his body catch fire, spreading further and burning his skin.

"No," I whisper in shock.

Ivan laughs maliciously as he admires his handiwork.

The fire engulfs the man, but he doesn't make a sound. Not one whisper of pain. He bears it all in silence, letting the flames lick at his body.

The pain must be unbearable, yet he withstands it all.

How? How can he not make a sound when his flesh must be aflame and blistering?

Tears course down my cheeks as I turn my gaze to Ivan. Hate unlike I've ever known fills me.

"You evil man," I cry out. I curl my hands into fists and hit at him. "How could you do that? How could you—"

I don't get to complete my sentence before his palm connects with my cheek, the blow hard enough to send me flying backward.

"Did I give you permission to speak?" he bites out at me.

I bring my hand to my cheek, rubbing at it while I give him a mutinous look.

"I *hate* you," I grit out.

But that makes him laugh harder.

"Do you think I care?"

He takes a step toward me, his lips pulling into a lascivious smile as he regards me.

"Tell you what. His cock might not get hard, but mine can."

At the same time, his hands go to his belt and panic flares in my chest, as well as the realization that no matter what world I might be in, women will always be targets for this type of violence.

I blink wildly as I crawl back, shaking my head at him. He comes slowly toward me, almost as if he's enjoying this cat-and-mouse game, and he wants to make sure my fear is at its peak before he reaches for me.

I try to think of *anything* that might help me, but my mind blanks on me, fear echoing in my ears under the guise of an erratic pulse.

He's a few steps away from me when the light goes out in the cell.

8

The fire goes out.

Darkness surrounds us.

An eerie silence envelops the room before Ivan's bloodcurdling screams erupt in the air. A flash of light fills my vision. Ivan's entire body has been set ablaze, the fire consuming him from the inside.

His screams continue, making me press my palms to my ears to block the merciless sound.

As the fire burns him alive, my eyes skitter past him to my cellmate. If I expected to find a charred corpse, I am sadly mistaken. His clothes are mostly burned and sticking to his skin. But his flesh is unmarred. There are no blisters, no burn wounds. There isn't even a little bit of redness.

"Stop this!" Ivan screams, falling to his knees and turning to the man to ask for help. "Please, stop!"

His pleas go unanswered.

Slowly, the man turns his head. His hair is half burned, but it still reaches his shoulders. It's a pure black, with the barest hint of ash from the fire.

I swallow hard as I get my first glimpse of the mysterious man.

His face is ashy, sickly. But it doesn't detract from the sheer beauty of his features. His jaw is strong and defined. His cheekbones so sharp they could cut through steel. His piercing eyes are big and round. I cannot make out the color of his irises, but there's a mesmerizing quality to them—so much so I cannot look away.

His face is expressionless as he watches Ivan succumb to his death. He falls to the ground, his screams a muted echo. His body continues to burn long after he dies, what's left of his remains feeding the fire.

"H-how…" I whisper as I stare at my cellmate.

He shifts his gaze from the fire to me, his eyes narrowing.

"What are you?" I whisper.

Only someone with immense power could have done something like that. But it doesn't make sense. If he is so powerful, how come he's still chained in this dungeon? How has he not escaped yet?

He stares at me for a few moments, his expression unchanging. It's dry, emotionless. There is no reaction. No joy at vanquishing an enemy, or at least annoyance at me for getting him set on fire. Nothing.

I lick my lips as I take a step toward him, crawling on my hands and knees.

"Don't," he rasps in a rough voice. "Do not move."

"What?"

He winces. Squeezing his eyes shut, he slumps forward. His mouth opens and closes as his breathing becomes labored. Whereas before his skin had looked almost translucent, now it's enveloped in a reddish hue. The veins on his neck and forehead protrude as he grinds his teeth. It's almost as if he's fighting an invisible force. His body angles forward, his chains rattling. He can barely move, and that serves to intensify his pain.

"Are you all right?" I ask, concerned.

"Do not," he grits out, "move."

"But…you're in pain," I whimper.

He shoots me a grave look before he lets out an agonizing groan.

Good Lord, what's happening? Is he suffering from some secondary effects because he killed Ivan?

His body spasms uncontrollably, his muscles straining against his chains. A cacophony of sounds erupts in the air as his chains rattle increasingly louder.

I wet my lips as I drag myself forward, ignoring his decree.

"Please. Tell me how I can help," I whisper as I reach his side.

The light is already dimming in the room as the fire from Ivan dies out.

I feel my way around his chains, trying to find a way to take them off him since he's so obviously in pain. But the moment I pull on one, a zap of energy thrusts me back.

"Agh." I gasp, rubbing at my hand.

His body spasms some more as he moves wildly against his chains, and that's when I realize that every time he tries to force the chains, currents of energy zap him, too.

"All…your…fault," he wheezes.

I blink in confusion.

"What? What do you mean?"

He opens his mouth to speak, but his eyes roll to the back of his head. He bites hard on his lower lip. Tension reverberates through him, his veins visible all over his face.

"He…knows. He…saw," he mumbles incoherently. "Need…out…"

"Please tell me how to help you," I repeat. Watching him in so much pain causes me physical discomfort.

He doesn't answer me.

Steps echo down the hallway of the dungeon, together with muffled voices.

Someone's coming!

He releases a shallow breath, slowly coming out of his trance.

"You want to help?" he asks, craning his neck to look at me. Up close, his eyes are a grayish silver hue—cold, icy.

I nod eagerly. He did save me. If there's anything I can do for him, I will.

"Come here," he demands in a curt voice.

"Here?"

I slide closer to him until I'm right by his side.

"Closer," he murmurs.

"W-what?"

"I cannot move, female. You will have to move for me," he bites out. "Now come closer."

"I don't understand…"

"Sit on my lap."

My eyes widen and I release a scandalized gasp.

He shakes his head wearily.

"Do I look like I am fit to do anything to you?" he asks drily.

I have to concede that he has a point. Besides, I was on his lap not too long ago when I stumbled over his body. It's not as if this is any different.

But that was when you didn't know what he looked like; when you thought he was a mummy.

So what if he's *not* a mummy? Or that he happens to have a stunning face that models would kill for? He's chained to a wall and he can barely move. It's impossible for him to take advantage of me. If anything, *I* could take advantage of him —not that I would. I pride myself on being a law-abiding citizen—most days. And though I might borrow his face for my dreams where I might or might not indulge in *some* fantasies, it's not as if I'm directly doing anything to him. Right…?

I shake my head at my foolishness. This is a life and death

situation—where a man actually died, though good riddance. I need to get a grip on myself.

Slowly, I take a seat on his lap, holding on to his shoulders. The heat of his body penetrates mine, and instinctively, I want to wrap myself in it. I am too traumatized right now to think straight, and he's my only tether. So I hold on, soaking in his warmth and that tantalizing scent that's now even more intoxicating.

I blink slowly as I raise my gaze to his. Our eyes lock, and a tremor goes down my back.

"And now?" I bite my lip as I glance coyly at him.

"You agree to help me?" he asks again, the vibrations from his voice traveling straight through me.

"Yes. What do you need?"

He nods at me with his chin to come closer.

I do, and his hot breath brushes against my ear, making me shiver.

"We do not have much time. The rest of the guards are on their way here."

I gulp down.

"I need to feed to regain my strength and get out of here. If you help me, I will get you out of here too."

"You want to eat *me*?" I ask breathlessly. Images dance in my brain, very much *non* PG-13 images. "Isn't that too soon? I mean, we haven't even been on a date and frankly, I wouldn't let you do that even after a third date. Maybe I will allow you a peck on the cheek. But—"

"What are you rambling about, female?"

My lashes flutter in confusion.

"Didn't you say you wanted to eat…me? I don't know how that will help you regain your strength, but—"

"Your blood. I require your blood."

"Oh," I whisper. Heat blooms across my cheeks as embarrassment overtakes me.

I clear my throat.

Okay, so maybe he's a vampire. That would make sense. I've read about some vampiric species residing in Akkaya. Maybe he's just one of them.

"It won't kill me?" I ask, just in case.

I can't believe I'm even entertaining this, but I do need to get out of here, and I kind of owe him too. A bit of blood won't hurt me.

"No. I will not take enough to hurt you."

"Okay. You can feed on me with one condition. You must help me get my PomPom back too," I tell him. That is non-negotiable.

"Fine. I give you my word," he murmurs against my skin. Somehow, his lips have gotten surprisingly close to my flesh.

Goose bumps spread all over my body.

He brushes his lips against my neck. Once, twice. The anticipation increases as my breathing grows shallow.

His mouth parts over my flesh to reveal sharp teeth that softly graze my skin.

I squeeze my eyes shut and wait for the pain.

But even as his razor-sharp incisors penetrate my flesh, there's only a dull hum that slowly blossoms into a warm sensation. His mouth is hot against me, his tongue lapping at my skin as he sucks in the blood flowing from the puncture wounds.

I hold tightly onto his shoulders to ground myself, and I can't help but feel the way his muscles slowly inflate, his body seemingly growing larger with each passing moment, each drop of my blood.

I gasp as I dig my teeth into my bottom lip to keep myself from releasing an embarrassing moan as the heat from the puncture site continues to increase, traveling down my body and making me shamelessly rub myself against him.

Yet just as it starts, it's over.

He pulls back, a few drops of blood glistening on his plump lips.

I lick my own in response.

Feeling for the puncture wounds, I realize they have already healed, the skin smooth as if nothing had happened.

"Thank you," he inclines his head.

The color has returned to his cheeks. His complexion is no longer pale and sickly. There's renewed vigor in his features. His skin is now a bronzed, healthy hue and his eyes a swirling silver where before they were just a dull gray. His body, too, is far larger than before, his muscles rippling with strength.

He moves one arm, then the other and the chains snap in two. He moves his neck forward, and that chain breaks as well.

One by one, he destroys every chain that was holding him in place. When he's done, he pulls me in his arms as he stands up.

"We will get your PomPom now," he decrees.

"Oh. Okay." I nod dazedly.

With a snap of his finger, the door to the cell bursts open.

The moment we step into the hallway, tens of guards line up in the narrow corridor of the dungeon, their swords raised and ready to fight.

"Good Lord," I mutter in shock. "We're going to die."

He doesn't answer me, nor does he seem particularly impressed by the guards' show of force.

Holding me with one arm, he uses the other to move the soldiers aside, parting the crowd as if he were Moses himself. But the guards don't just move to the side. They turn to dust as they hit the wall, leaving the path clear for us to go forward.

I blink in distress that slowly turns to awe.

Did that… Did that just happen? Did he turn people into dust?

It's like I'm in a fantasy movie! My excitement rises and I squeak giddily. Of course, this is *not* a good thing, nor do I condone violence. But these people were about to commit violence against us—never mind the fact that I was going to be sacrificed for whatever pagan ritual psycho Damian had in mind. I believe this constitutes extenuating circumstances.

My savior continues to turn every guard into dust and I cheer him on, pointing right and left as I see another head our way. The other prisoners clamor as they see us leave the dungeon, and this guy proves that he's not all good looks, he has a heart too as he opens all the cages and lets the rest of the prisoners go.

"My, you're so strong," I murmur as I pat his biceps appreciatively. I guess I should thank Ivan now for putting me in the same cell as my mysterious savior.

As we exit the dungeon, the sun shines brightly in the sky.

I take a big gulp of fresh air. Ah, this feels good.

My good-looking friend does the same, looking up at the sky and closing his eyes, enjoying the light breeze and the way the sunlight streams down his face.

I release a dreamy sigh as I watch his perfect profile. His jaw is so sharp, I could see him on the cover of a romance novel. And with that straight, aristocratic nose, he looks both royal and domineering at the same time.

And he's been nice. To me.

Agh! I'm too giddy for my own good. I need to remember this is a life and death situation and not one of my dreams where I meet my Prince Charming. Going by the way he so easily turns people to dust, he's not exactly a paragon of virtue. But hey, all's fair in war and love.

"Stupid Jocelyn stole my PomPom. We need to go to her quarters," I instruct him before my mind can cook up some more ludicrous scenarios. This is a time for *war*. Maybe we can save the *love* aspect for later. I certainly wouldn't mind going on a date with Mr. Turns Everything Into Dust—if he asks, of course.

He grunts an acknowledgment and continues walking.

Anyone coming toward him is rendered to dust.

A black cloud surrounds us, spreading left and right as if it has a life of its own. Dark tentacles tackle the magic users that attack us, shielding us at the same time. Nothing seems to penetrate his dark shield, not the power of the elements nor the blasts of energy coming from the mages.

A few moments later, we're in the castle.

I do my best to instruct him where to turn and which wing might be the right one, but my spatial awareness sucks and we end up getting lost—and getting surrounded by yet another horde of royal guards.

He grits his teeth, growing annoyed with these pesky soldiers. I can't blame him. Even the magic users are no match for his elevated skills—all of which makes me perpetually sigh in wonder at my new friend.

Once he's done killing the rest of the guards, we head to the west wing. It doesn't escape me that he avoids harming women and children, and my admiration for him rises exponentially.

"There, I remember the stairs." I point to the gilded marble stairs Jocelyn and I had taken when we'd gone to the royal quarters.

He nods—he's not a man of many words, but I happen to like the silent, brooding ones—and he takes the gilded stairs.

"What if Damien and Jocelyn are there? They're strong," I say as the thought crosses my mind. They aren't the rulers of Kiya for nothing. They're the strongest mages Akkaya has ever seen. Despite how strong he is, I wouldn't want my savior to get hurt or anything.

My good-looking friend grinds his teeth, a sign he doesn't approve of my assessment. But he doesn't give me a reply, his eyes taking in everything around us.

"I think it was that room." I point to one at the end of the hall. "Oh, no, wait. I think that one." I change my mind, pointing to the opposite. "Or was it that one…"

He doesn't listen to me, striding to a hidden hallway before taking a few more turns and stopping in front of a door.

"What are you…" I trail off. My eyes widen as he wrenches the door from its hinges with the wave of a finger. Going inside, he looks right and left before traversing to yet another room. It's luxurious as I've come to expect from Damien and Jocelyn. There are fluffy chaises everywhere, as well as dog toys and other accessories.

It's at that moment that a cute, familiar sound reaches my ears.

"PomPom!" I exclaim, all but jumping out of his arms as I run toward my poor baby. She sees me too and lets out a sharp bark, running toward me. Her tongue is out, her eyes sparkling with happiness—and maybe a few unshed tears. I know I have plenty.

We meet in the middle. I open my arms and she jumps to my chest, her short legs doing their job for once. She smells so good and she's so fluffy. Jocelyn must have had her bathed. Well, it's the least she could do after stealing my baby, that wretched woman.

PomPom licks my cheek and releases a series of consecutive barks—her way of telling me she missed me.

"Aw, baby girl. Mommy is here," I tell her, hugging her to my chest and letting her warmth sink into my skin.

Another bark echoes in the room, but this time it's not from my PomPom. From under the covers, a head of dark brown fur peeks out, jumping out and running toward us.

Is that…

PomPom whines as she turns her head to the other dog, trying to escape my arms to go to him.

"BonBon, no!" A feminine gasp follows. She rushes forward, stopping in her tracks as she sees my friend behind me. Her eyes widen and she falls to the ground.

"Please don't hurt me. Please…"

She must be BonBon's caretaker. But if that's BonBon… I blink as I look at his fluffy fur that is a mix of black and cream, so different than his description in the books. Yet he's not any less adorable, and my heart melts at his cute expression.

"We need to leave," my good-looking friend says as he spares my PomPom a glance.

As I turn, PomPom's whines become louder just as BonBon barks and attacks me.

Oh no! Did my PomPom fall for him? Did she…

"Tell me you didn't, PomPom," I murmur worriedly.

Her only reply is a whine and a longing glance toward BonBon.

My gaze moves back and forth between the two and I realize I need to make a last-minute decision.

The other woman is still on the floor, mumbling a series of pleas to spare her life but not daring to look at us. I take advantage of that to swipe BonBon in my arms, cuddling him next to PomPom before I go back to my friend.

God, I'm now turning into stupid Jocelyn, the dog stealer. But I have no doubt BonBon will have a better life with me and PomPom—why, they seem to be in love already! I may not have been ready to share my love with another baby, but at the same time, I can't say no to my sweet PomPom.

My good-looking friend takes a look at the extra dog in my arms and rolls his eyes. But as I stop in front of him, he lifts me up in his strong, manly arms, with my two dogs in tow, and proceeds toward the exit.

He's no longer walking. The dark cloud surrounds us, carrying him with it. He hovers over the ground, his posture straight, his face expressionless—and handsome, oh, so handsome.

My, but look what a bit of blood can do to a person. No wonder that vampire face treatment is all the rage in Hollywood. I gaze wistfully at his perfectly sculpted cheeks while he turns some more people into dust. PomPom does the same with BonBon—after all, I taught her well.

He not only saved *my* life. He saved my PomPom too!

If that's not the definition of *swoon*, I don't know what is.

As we walk out of the castle, I'm surprised to realize that the only ones who'd put up any fight had been low-level mages. There is no trace of Damien, Jocelyn, Arisa, or Leoni. Not even the King's guard of specialized mages is present. No wonder it was so easy for us to get in and out of the castle.

"Uhm, why is psycho Damien letting us leave just like this? Not that I'm complaining, but he was quite adamant about sacrificing me. It's odd that he would let me go now. You, too. He's been keeping you in those godawful chains for who knows how long and now he's simply letting you escape?"

His lips pull in a thin line. His eyes shrewdly move around the place as he takes inventory of everything. His nostrils flare, the only sign that this bothers him.

"I am not surprised he is not here," he eventually says. "He finally got what he needed from me."

"Huh? What do you mean?" I frown.

"You do not need to concern yourself with that," he replies in a brisk voice, opening one of the windows and flying us out. On his dark cloud, we leave the castle grounds and the fortress of Kiya.

I release a surprised squeak as I realize I am *flying*—as in, floating in the air over the spectacular buildings of Kiya. Not only do I get to experience my favorite fictional world—okay, granted, it might not be as nice as I thought it would be—but I also get to experience magic.

I. Am. Flying.

I throw my head back and release a bunch of unintelligible noises. PomPom and BonBon do the same. The three of us create a chorus of gibberish as we enjoy this new experience.

Unfortunately, our journey in the clouds is soon over as we touch the ground. We're somewhere in a forest, with tall trees and rich bushes surrounding us. It's sometime in the afternoon based on the position of the sun.

He puts us down before he takes a step back. He stares at me for a moment, his icy gray eyes affixed to mine. My, but in direct sunlight, he's even more good-looking. His bone structure is simply divine, combined with his height, broad shoulders, tapered waist, and long legs. I almost want to fan myself. He's still wearing the tattered clothes from before, so there's not much to be left to the imagination. I might not have been able to see him before, but even then I could feel the hardness of his chest and the dormant muscles that are now rippling with strength—due to my blood, of course.

I bite on my lip. He has my blood! How cool is that? Not that it's cool that he feeds on blood, although I've always had a bit of a soft spot for vampires—not the Edward type, the Lestat one. But he has *my* blood running through his veins and giving him power. There's something rather wicked and erotic about that and I can't help but release a sigh as I continue to admire him.

No wonder Damien locked him up for years in that cell. He must have been jealous of his god-level good looks. I don't think I've ever seen a man as beautiful as him, and I've watched a lot of TV shows. Why, even K-pop stars don't come anywhere close.

I swallow hard, unable to take my eyes off him. Of course I wouldn't ever notice the guys back home when someone like this was awaiting me somewhere in the universe. Who cares that it's in a fictional world, or that I might have initially mistaken him for a mummy?

It was all *fate*.

My lashes flutter as a blush climbs up my cheeks. Putting my dogs down, I tuck a lock of hair behind my ear and give him a coy smile.

This is it. This is the moment that happens in every book where the male lead takes one look at the heroine and says *mine*. He will claim me for his own and we will live happily ever after with PomPom and BonBon, going on double dates and hopping around worlds. I don't have a preference for where we live, as long as it's not here. Not that I don't like it, but I'd rather not live in a plague-ridden land. I'm sure he will agree.

I wait breathlessly as he opens his mouth to speak.

"You are safe now," he starts.

"Yes." I give him a smile as I move closer to him. "I am safe thanks to *you*."

He nods.

"Farewell then." With that, he turns to leave.

W-what?

9

I stare at his retreating figure in shock.

Did he…

Did he just…

PomPom and BonBon bark happily as they circle around me, oblivious to the way my heart just plummeted to the ground.

He didn't even tell me his name.

I blink repeatedly, somehow thinking this is all just a bad dream.

I finally find a man who I consider worth pursuing and he does what? He leaves without sparing me a glance!

Worse still is the fact that I'm back to ground zero—sans the execution debacle. How the hell am I going to get back to my world now? How am I even going to survive long enough to figure that out considering there is a deadly plague raging in Akkaya?

The answer is clear.

I cannot do it on my own, therefore I need to stick by my good-looking friend and hope he will find it in the kindness of his heart to help me. Of course, there's the fact that he didn't seem to consider me his friend, given how easily he abandoned me. But the only way for me and my babies to make it out of here alive is to stick by his side—whether he wants it or not. In fact, I must find a way to show him I'm indispensable, maybe even offer him some more blood.

I nod to myself, satisfied with my train of thought.

The blood taking wasn't nearly as scary as I would have thought, maybe even a little pleasant. It will not be a hardship to keep him well-fed as long as he keeps us plague-free, no? I think that's a rather good deal. But I must convince him of that too.

I purse my lips.

He's getting farther and farther away from me. In no time I'll lose track of him, so I must act fast.

Getting to my knees in front of PomPom and BonBon, I address them firmly.

"The moment has come. I need your help. We're going to follow that nice and good-looking man, but we must not make a sound, okay? We need to be like ghosts. He can't find out we're following him." At least not until I find a way to make my case and convince him I can be his food bank. It's a win-win. I bet there aren't too many healthy—and pretty—girls he can feed from, not with the plague having killed nearly everyone.

But the moment I imagine him finding another pretty girl to sink his teeth into and brush his lips over her skin and hold her that close, I see red.

No, he will not do that!

I will feed him—exclusively. And he can protect me and my babies, and maybe along the way realize that this is all fate and we are meant to be.

I don't believe in coincidences.

The mere fact that I'm in this weird—not so fictional—world is testament enough.

This is fate. And I can only embrace it.

I sigh dreamily at the thought. Ah, the romantic in me is

coming out in full force after lying dormant for so long. Well, not exactly dormant, merely relegated to my dreams. But now I've found the perfect man!

He's handsome—always a requirement. He's strong and steadfast. But most of all he's kind!

He saved my PomPom—and me, but my baby is more important in this equation. He also killed that annoying Ivan and though I don't necessarily condone murder, I say good riddance.

I blink slowly. Damn it! I almost got lost in my thoughts again and my good-looking friend is getting farther away from me!

"PomPom," I whisper to my pretty baby. She has her tongue out as she smiles at me with her eyes. "I must count on you to make sure BonBon is quiet. Can you do that for me?"

She releases a low whine as she brushes her head against my legs. Immediately after, she turns to BonBon, her expression one of savage feminine authority. She barks a few times and BonBon lowers his head in submission.

"Good girl." I pat her head. And since I don't want to play favorites, I turn to BonBon and pat him too. "Good boy."

They both preen, happy at the praise.

Nodding at them, I get up and signal for them to follow me in silence.

He's already out of sight, damn it! I walk briskly in the direction he went, making sure to avoid areas with high foliage that might give away our presence.

He's strong. I wouldn't put it past him to have super senses.

But as we cover more distance and get closer to him, he doesn't turn to chastise me for following him. He continues on, oblivious.

A satisfied smile pulls at my lips. We'll manage to do this.

He walks slowly. His clothes are so tattered, there are only a few strands covering his torso and the semblance of a pair of shorts on his lower body. His skin is flawless, but black soot from the fire mars that perfection.

He needs a shower.

I need a shower too, I realize as I raise my arm to sniff myself.

God! One day in a cell and I already stink. And he held me close to him.

Oh my! Is that why he left me behind? Did my smell bother him? He had his lips on my neck. Could he detect the cell stench then too?

This isn't fair! The man smelled divine after years left to rot in that cell and I stink like a sewer after only a day.

Now another thought crosses my mind. What if he cannot hear us, but he can smell *me*?

Even PomPom smells better because she had royal treatment. BonBon too.

"Do you think I smell, too?" I ask the dogs in a low voice. They have better noses. They would tell me if I stank, no?

I stop for a moment, letting PomPom sniff me.

She makes a disgusted face that BonBon emulates and my confidence officially plummets.

Shaking my head at my predicament, I decide to find a river and bathe before I go anywhere near him again. Yes, that might help.

We continue following—*stalking*—him. PomPom and BonBon are surprisingly well-behaved. They don't make a noise as they walk stealthily behind me. Every now and then I give them a smile and an airy kiss to incentivize them to keep up the good work.

But as we get to a river, he suddenly stops.

I do, too, putting my hand up for the dogs to stop as well. We hide behind a clump of trees, lying low behind the bushes.

I part a few branches to peek through.

He gets to his knees in front of the river, staring at his reflection for what seems like an eternity.

Of course he would. He's probably making sure his god-tier looks are still intact.

Putting his hands together, he scoops some water and washes his face. He proceeds to do the same with his neck and armpits, removing some of the more visible soot.

After he's done, he stands up.

He's tall. So much taller than my five-three frame. He must be over six feet tall and that only makes me giddy as I release a dreamy sigh.

We'll look perfect together. I'm already imagining all the pictures we will take together and how those so-called friends of mine will swallow their insults when they see my beau.

Take that, Clarice!

He turns to leave, and I get out of the bushes, telling my dogs to follow me.

The river is a little too alluring after my burst of panic over my scent.

"Just a little. Stay here, PomPom, and don't let BonBon wander, okay?"

She nods as if she understands. Sometimes I'm sure she does.

I run to the river and wash my face and armpits too. If only I had some soap… But beggars can't be choosers.

Alas, feeling a bit refreshed, I beckon my dogs to follow me as we resume our stalking activities. They are the perfect partners in crime, and I couldn't be prouder of them for being so silent as they follow me.

We quickly catch up to my good-looking friend. Leaving a bit of distance between us, we continue to follow him around as he goes deeper into the forest.

It's a couple of hours later that my feet start killing me and my stomach starts rumbling with hunger. I haven't eaten in… over a day! That's just criminal.

And to make matters worse, my brain decides to introduce images of all types of delicacies into my mind, making me drool at the thought of having a bite of juicy meat or at least some chocolate—I'm not picky.

PomPom and BonBon are good sport. They haven't complained so far, but I know they must be hungry and tired too.

What is his itinerary? And why does he have to walk—though I'm not complaining since that allows me to follow him. But he has that dark cloud of his. Why isn't he using it? If I had one of those, I wouldn't walk even to get a glass of water. But then again, he's been locked inside that prison for a long time. Maybe he needs to stretch his legs.

The forest scenery is all the same. We walk and walk and there are only tall trees, thick shrubs, bushes, and the sound of bothersome insects. I'm not a hater, I swear. But I have sensitive skin, and insect bites make me break out into hives. That's the last thing I need right now when I'm already stinky enough. How will I get this man to notice me with red welts on my face and a fetid stench? Then again, maybe the stench will also keep the insects away…

He stops.

He makes camp in a small clearance under the canopy of trees.

I put my hand up to stop PomPom and BonBon as I study his next movements.

He's humming a melody to himself as he gathers some tree branches and places them on the ground, forming a firepit before using his magic to light it up.

That's when I realize that the sky has already darkened. He's probably stopping here for the night.

That means we're stopping too.

I sigh. If only we had some food. Glancing back at PomPom and BonBon, I notice they're huddled together, almost embracing. They're tired, the poor babies. But at least they have love to keep them warm.

Ah, to be young and in love. I admire them wistfully for a

few moments, happy at my baby's new relationship before I turn my attention to my own prospective love interest.

My eyes immediately widen when I don't see him there anymore.

The fire is blazing up, smoke traveling in the sky, but there's no sign of him.

For a moment, panic takes hold of me.

What if he realized I was following him and he used the fire as a distraction so he could slip away and evade me?

I look right and left, my heart thudding in my chest as I cannot find him anywhere.

But just as my chest is about to explode with worry, the bushes at the other end of the clearing rattle and he resurfaces.

He's holding a dead bird in his hand. The feathers have already been removed and it's only the skin and the meat now.

My mouth instantly waters as he carefully builds a rotisserie on top of the fire. He places the bird over the flames, slowly rotating it and roasting it on all sides.

The smell of food reaches the dogs too and they release soft noises.

"Shh," I tell them. We can't have him hear us now.

But as I stare at that glorious bird being roasted, I can't help the way my body angles forward, my mind blanking on me until that juicy bird is all I see.

This is torture. Pure torture.

Even with the light dimming in the sky, I can see the golden hue of the bird's skin and the way the juices fall down onto the flames, fanning them even more.

It's even more painful as I watch him tear out a leg and bring that crispy meat to his lips.

I swallow. Hard. I have to bite my lip from crying out for mercy, and maybe some leftovers.

Digging my fingers into my thighs, I stare at his plump lips as they wrap themselves over the meat, biting into it before chewing slowly.

His Adam's apple bobs up and down as he swallows.

The flames cast a shadow over his neck, emphasizing his muscles and tendons, and now I'm not only salivating for the meat, but for his perfectly sculpted body too.

God! What have I done to deserve this?

He eats the leg before he throws the bone to the ground, and I have to physically hold on to PomPom and BonBon so they don't fly from my side in search of that mesmerizing scent of food.

"We're all in this, guys," I whisper. "I feel your pain. I promise I'll give you lots of treats once we're out of this, okay?"

They don't seem too happy with me at the moment. I guess food is where they draw the line. But at the same time, I can't let them blow my cover, so I pull both of them into my arms—they're small enough to fit comfortably—and I try to get them not to bark or make too much noise.

My good-looking friend is enjoying himself as he tears out a breast piece, all meat and crispy skin. God, how will I resist this?

His mouth movements alone will get me into trouble.

My stomach rumbles again.

He eats that piece before he suddenly gets up. He looks around for a moment, holding his hands apart from his body, and I realize he's searching for something to wipe the juice off his fingers. With a shake of his head, he teleports himself out of the clearing.

Based on his body language, I'm assuming he went to the river to clean himself. I wait a couple of minutes to make sure he's not coming back before I decide that this is my chance. Surely he won't miss a bit of meat, right?

"Easy, guys. I'll get some for you too, okay?" I tell my dogs.

They're growing rather impatient with me, but PomPom knows how to obey, and in turn, she gets BonBon to follow my instructions, too.

I leave them hidden in the bushes while I run across the clearing to the still roasting bird. Knowing time is of the essence, I quickly tear out the hind legs, a bit of breast meat, and the thighs. Okay, maybe he will miss this much meat, but there are wild beasts roaming around in the forest at night. Any one of them could have been lured by this tantalizing scent and stolen a piece, no?

Once my arms are full of juicy meat, I steal away into the bushes with my loot.

PomPom and BonBon dance around me as they see the food and they make low sounds of approval.

"Here, this is for you," I say as I give PomPom one of the hind legs. "And this is for you." I do the same with BonBon.

While they munch away on their food, I take my first bite of the meat.

A divine sigh escapes me as I lick my lips, not wanting to let any of that tasty juice go to waste.

My, but this is divine.

He cooked it to perfection.

Another added perk that makes him the perfect love interest.

Ah, but I'm finally in my main character era! I don't have to read about others getting their forever love when mine is just within grasp—as soon as I make my good-looking friend realize that we're perfect for each other.

For now, I'll settle for this wonderful meat.

Hidden in the bushes as I am and with my only audience of the four-legged variety, I don't even have to mind my manners. I quickly finish my portion and give the bones to the dogs while I suck on my fingers for all the residual juice—we can't have it go to waste now, can we?

"Have some more."

More pieces of meat dangle in front of my eyes.

My hunger must be more potent than I realize since I'm now seeing things.

"Thank you," I say as I take the holy offering, my eyes affixed to it as I smack my lips together, my eyes sparkling with want.

But as I reach for the meat, my hands still and I slowly look up.

I blink repeatedly, hoping this is all a bad dream.

He's clean and dressed in new clothes—a dark shirt and a pair of loose pants. His hair has been tied back, away from his face, emphasizing that striking cut of his jaw and those ungodly cheekbones that would have nuns go into heat.

He looks down at me with amusement in his features—the first expression I've seen on his face that isn't a scowl or that attractive brood he usually has going. His brow is raised, his mouth curled in a lopsided smile that makes my insides go all gooey.

I gulp down.

Good Lord, how is he more striking than before?

Is it the moonlight? Or is it my starved pitiful self that now sees *him* as food.

PomPom and BonBon are so busy with their food they don't even realize I'm having the most embarrassing moment of my life—one I'll likely *never* live down for the rest of my life. Main character energy my ass. More like class clown energy by the way things are going.

I wipe my mouth with my sleeve before I give him a guilty smile.

Seconds pass as I think of a proper reply, but my poor starved brain decides on the least appropriate thing to say.

"The dogs stole the food!"

IO

"The dogs, huh?" He raises a brow at me.

"Yes."

"Was it also the dogs that prompted you to follow me?" he questions.

"Uhm, yes? They only met you briefly, but they're big fans. Very, very big fans."

"I see." He nods. He still has the meat in his hands, and while he's distracted by my poor excuse for stalking him, I grab the rest of the meat and stuff it in my mouth. At least this way, even if he kicks me to the curb, my stomach will at least be full.

He blinks in surprise.

I chew fast, my arms already searching for PomPom and BonBon to dash out if need be—not that it would help. He has a dark cloud! I'm sure he'll catch up to me. But maybe he'll give me bonus points for the lousy attempt.

"There is more meat. You do not have to hide in the bushes."

I swallow the last of the food before I give him my best puppy-eyed look.

"You will give me more?"

I add some eyelash flutter, too, just in case.

He shakes his head at me and turns his back.

"Come," he calls out as he heads back to the fire.

Not one to lose this important chance, I get PomPom and BonBon and follow after him. I let the two play around within eyesight as I take a seat next to him by the fire.

Without waiting for his approval, I dive in, pulling some more meat from the bird carcass.

"I thought your big, bad boyfriend would have come for you by now," he adds in a lazy voice, leaning back to study me.

It's at that moment that I slow down my eating, remembering my manners. I cannot have him shun me because I behave like a pig, now, can I?

"He's...busy." I make up the excuse. "He's somewhere around doing some evil things. You know how it is with those villains," I add nervously, waving my hand around. "They're always looking for the next morally questionable thing to do."

My nervous ramble has made an appearance. Not good.

"So you decided to follow me instead?" he asks, amused.

PomPom has found her way to his side, sniffing his hands before plopping herself on his lap. He doesn't seem to mind it. In fact, he's petting her absentmindedly as he continues to stare at me with those wicked eyes of his.

"Ah, well..." I murmur.

Damn it! Why does he have to be nice to PomPom? Now that makes him a thousand times more attractive.

My eyes dip to his hands. Big, manly hands.

I gulp down.

"I didn't properly thank you for saving me. You did. Save me, that is. And I thank you."

Idiot!

"You have now thanked me. Consider us even."

He places PomPom to his side as he prepares to get up—and presumably leave. Again.

I panic.

"Wait! Wait! That's not the only reason."

He stops. He tilts his head to the side, waiting for my explanation.

"I don't know anyone here. Well, aside from stupid Jocelyn and psycho Damien, but we've all seen how that turned out. I thought they could help me get back home, but instead, they decided to sacrifice me for whatever pagan ritual they had going."

"Home?" he inquires.

I nod fervently as I slide closer to him.

"You might not believe me, but I'm not from this world. I don't even know how I got here. One moment I was in my room, the next I was in a field in Akkaya, and then I came across a plagued village and I almost died, and then those pesky soldiers captured me and I almost died again." I let out a big sigh. "I've had no rest from *almost dying* in two days!"

"Another world, you say?" He narrows his eyes at me. "Hmm…" He taps his finger against his chin pensively. "That makes sense."

"What makes sense?" I suddenly ask.

"Your strange manner." He chuckles. "You are a strange one, indeed," he muses, almost to himself.

"So you believe me?"

"Akkaya is a pseudo-intermediary realm. It is home to a myriad of portals that lead to other worlds," he mentions.

"Oh. Why wouldn't they just help me get back home if it's so easy? Why try to kill me *and* steal my dog? Just who does that?" I ask angrily, shaking my head as my ire is awakened once more.

"Did you not steal that dog, too?" He inclines his head toward BonBon, who's currently chasing after my PomPom.

"I *saved* him. There's a difference," I huff. "He's happier with me and PomPom. Plus, they're *in love*," I declare proudly.

"If you say so." He laughs.

I blink.

"Are you mocking me?"

Again?

"Far be it from me to mock you. I am merely pointing out the facts."

I narrow my eyes at him.

"You are not, by any chance, taking stupid Jocelyn's side, are you?"

"Of course not. I happen to dislike that female as much as you do. Perhaps more." He shrugs. "You may have saved the dog from her clutches, but the truth remains that you did the very same thing you accuse her of doing, which is hypo-critical."

I frown at him.

"Are you always so…pedantic?"

"It allows for a more comprehensive perspective." He nods politely.

I mutter a few unladylike obscenities under my breath that prompt him to release a chuckle.

"Anyhow." I clear my throat. "The truth remains that they tried to kill me. And when I tried to escape and tell everyone what sadistic psychotic bastards they were, they tried to spin it on *me* and accuse me of God knows what. I mean, have you looked at me? I couldn't hurt a fly!" I exclaim, rather annoyed.

"You did steal that dog," he points out, rather cheekily. "And my ring."

I give him a harsh stare.

He laughs.

"I only *tried* to steal your ring. I gave it back."

"And my finger."

"I gave back your finger too!"

Noticing my raised voice, PomPom dashes to my side and resumes her stance, growling at him. BonBon follows her cue and does the same.

Aw, my little army!

He stares at us for moments on end before he bursts out laughing.

"You are a breath of fresh air, female."

"I have a name, you know." I cross my arms over my chest. "It's Barbi."

"Well, Barbi. I am pleased I allowed you to follow me. I have not laughed this much in…eons."

"You…*allowed* me?" I repeat, scandalized.

"You were not exactly quiet." He smiles.

"What? I was *very* quiet."

"Has anyone else told you that you think out loud? Because you do. It was quite entertaining to listen to it."

I gawk at him and it slowly dawns on me. He stopped at the river because I worried about my stinky hide. He got food because I was starving. He *let* me steal the food.

My anger melts away as my heart grows larger in my chest. My cheeks warm up, and it's not due to the proximity to the fire. No, it's all because of him.

I suddenly look away.

"Oh," I murmur. "Thank you."

He nods at me, and instead of saying anything, he just places another piece of meat in my hand.

My heart. It's so big it's about to burst.

I turn my eyes to him as I munch on the piece of meat, attempting to show him my gratitude.

"What is your name? You never told me."

"You never asked." An amused smile plays at his lips.

When he smiles like that, he's even more breathtaking, and not as intimidating as before. God, I could watch him for days on end.

I slide closer.

"So? What is your name?" I ask, taking another bite of meat.

He turns, his face mere inches away from mine.

His gaze meets mine, and I forget to breathe. As in, I actually *forget* to breathe—so much so I have to take a big gulp of air to not suffocate. Which ultimately causes me to choke on my food. If I was embarrassed then, I'm about to bury my head in the sand when uncontrollable hiccups overtake me.

My eyes widen, and I slap my hand over my mouth.

It's in vain, though, as the sounds are rather loud and distracting.

"I'm not a pig, I swear." *Hiccup.* "I was just hungry and…" *Hiccup.* "I think I ate too fast." *Hiccup.* "But I promise you I have better manners than this." *Hiccup.* "If you took me out to eat, I wouldn't embarrass you and—"

"Nykander," he interrupts me. "My name is Nykander."

And to make me swoon even more, he materializes a jug of water in front of him and hands it to me.

"This should help."

Oh, Nykander. If you only knew… You just got yourself a lifelong stalker.

"Thank you," I murmur before I take big gulps until the hiccups calm down. Maybe I should slow down with the eating. The last thing I need is to get sick on this poor man and totally turn him off me.

"What world are you from?" he inquires after I've calmed down.

"Hmm. We call it Earth, though I'm not sure you would recognize the name."

"Earth?" he muses. "Oh, I see. Anthropa. I should have known. You are human, after all."

"Anthropa?"

"That is what your world is called by outsiders. I have been there a few times. Beautiful sights. Awful people." He shakes his head.

"You've been to my world?" I blink.

He nods.

"It's been a long time, though. I will assume things have changed," he adds diplomatically.

"Not that much." I shrug. "The people are still awful."

His brows go up before a smile touches his lips that my own lips mirror.

"Was there anything in particular that Damien asked you about your world?"

"He wanted me to describe it to him. Although he seemed awfully fascinated by the population, which I don't fault him. We have almost eight billion people, and the numbers keep climbing."

He freezes, his eyes glinting dangerously.

"I see," he murmurs softly, looking pensively in the distance.

"They were also surprised by our healthcare," I add.

"Huh?"

"I mean, we do have state-of-the-art technology and we can cure almost every disease," I continue rambling. "Considering that half the population of Akkaya has died from this plague, I can see why they'd be interested in it. Maybe they were curious if the healthcare in my world could help cure the plague."

"This is the second time you mention a plague. What are you talking about?"

I stop, turning to look at him in shock.

"You don't know?"

He shakes his head.

"But… Didn't you just admit you have super senses? And you can teleport around? Surely you know about the state of things."

He frowns.

"I am asking because I do not know what you're talking about. During my time in that cell, I only used enough energy to keep myself alive. I did not hear anything about the outside world."

"A plague swept through Akkaya a few years back. From what I heard, it was caused by the Dark One. Damian injured him and now he's using the energy of the souls to heal."

A harsh expression crosses his face.

He curses under his breath as he takes himself away from me. Dark mist surrounds him. It bleeds from his skin, creating a protective cocoon around him. The mist almost has a life of its own as it moves wildly around, almost like the untamed flames of the fire, seeking to burn everything in their path.

"Nykander? Are you all right?" I ask tentatively.

The darkness suddenly dissipates.

He blinks once. Twice.

"You mean *your* Dark One?" He raises a brow, the dark atmosphere from before all but gone.

"Ah…yes…" My eyes widen. "The evil dude everyone's afraid of. But you see, he's evil but *not* that evil. He's a nice guy once you get to know him. He wouldn't cause a mass plague. Only if people threatened me, of course…"

"Because you are the light to his darkness," he says, a smile playing at his lips.

"Exactly. I am his heart," I proclaim proudly. "If anyone hurts me, then of course he *will* cause a plague. But other than that, he's chill. If anything, I bet it's that psycho Damien who had something to do with it."

He sports an amused smile as he stares at me, resting his chin on his palm.

"You speak very highly of the Dark One," he notes.

"Yes, he…" I close my mouth as it dawns on me I just made myself *very* unavailable in front of my love interest. Damn it! This little lie might have worked when I thought he was a mummy who might harm me, but now that I realize he's my soulmate, I need to come up with a *new* lie.

"Unfortunately, he broke up with me." I clear my throat, feigning a sigh.

"Did he now?"

I nod.

"He broke up with me after we escaped the cell. Telepathically. Because he's a strong villain who has lots of powers, you know."

"I can imagine." He nods sympathetically. "But didn't you say you were his heart?"

"That's exactly *why*!" I burst out, my imagination dripping with new ideas. "He knows he's a big, bad villain who is hunted left and right by everyone. He doesn't want to put me in danger, so he decided to let me go." I feign a sigh. "He told me to find my happiness somewhere else, even if it won't be with him. Because he's nice like that—but only with me. Now he's off on his next villainous adventure."

"Hm." He clicks his tongue against his teeth. "He is not much of a villain if he would let go of his heart, no? If it were me, and I were such a villain, I would not let anything stand between me and my female," he notes, a wicked gleam entering his eyes.

Did it suddenly get hot in here? He said *'my female'* in that deep voice of his.

S.W.O.O.N.

"He's a different type of villain," I scramble for an explanation, praying he doesn't notice the blush climbing my cheeks. He's making me scatterbrained—not that I already wasn't a little before. But now I can barely function, let alone come up with a thousand more lies! "He's the misunderstood type that may seem evil to everyone else but actually has a heart of gold. Because he does," I stammer. "He is bad but not *that* bad. Why, he sometimes volunteers at a pet shelter. It's because of me and PomPom, you see. We converted him and now he's on a path of self-improvement…"

"You are doing that thing again," he says in a low voice as he gets closer to me.

I blink rapidly.

"W-what thing?" I whisper, suddenly aware that the distance between us is shrinking by the second. My heart cannot take this much tension. The drum of every heartbeat is a loud echo in my ears. Sweat gathers over my forehead, dripping down my temples.

He's so close.

Oh my God! He's *so* close.

"Talking too much." The corner of his mouth pulls up.

My eyes move up slowly, from that irresistible curve of his lips to those mesmerizing eyes that have me in a chokehold.

I gulp down. Hard.

"Are you nervous, Barbi?" he drawls, his deep voice washing over me and causing my skin to erupt in goose bumps.

"Nervous? Me? Why would I be nervous? I'm calm—*very* calm," I mumble.

"Hm," he muses, biting on his lower lip.

Oh Lord! Please take me *right* now!

His teeth are straight, white, and absolutely perfect.

And I'm a sucker for good teeth.

"Are you sure about that?"

"Perfectly straight—sure. I'm sure."

I squeeze my eyes shut in embarrassment as I mentally chastise myself. Blunder after blunder. I am *not* fit to be out in society. No wonder everyone laughs at me. I'm a walking disaster.

His laughter reaches my ears and as I slowly open my eyes, I see that he has resumed his place—away from me.

I release a disappointed sigh.

"You need to learn how to lie better, Barbi."

I blink at the sudden shift in his tone.

He gets up and straightens his clothes.

"You can have the rest of the food. If you go straight up the mountain, you will find a portal that should take you back to Anthropa."

He's dismissing me.

Just like that.

"B-but—"

"It will not be hard to recognize it. It should be a blue…" he continues to explain how to get to the portal, and whereas twenty-four hours ago that's all I would have needed, that is no longer the case. How can I go back when I'm finally about to embark on the adventure of a lifetime? I no longer have to *read* about quests and magic and true love. I'll get to *live* it.

Besides, it's not as if anything out of the ordinary awaits me at home.

"I don't want to go home," I state firmly as I get up to be on eye level with him. Okay, that might be a reach considering I'm half his size. But I place my hands on my hips and look him straight in the eye as I say. "I am coming with you."

The amusement drains from his face.

Silence envelops us for moments on end. There's only the crackling of the fire and the dogs' barking.

"And where do you think I am going?" he asks in a low, measured tone.

"I don't know. But wherever you're going is far safer for me than setting out on my own. You're strong. You can protect me," I admit shamelessly. "There's the plague to worry about, but also psycho Damien and his entourage. Since we both escaped, I have no doubt the entire continent is already looking for us. So I am not going to take any chances."

"I have my own mission that requires my immediate attention," he adds tensely. "I cannot be responsible for a human."

My heart plummets. Again.

I stare at him, my shoulders squaring. Disappointment ricochets through me, though I am not sure what I was expecting. My illusions slowly shatter and I'm mad at myself for having those illusions in the first place.

"More important than me?" I whisper, not intending for him to hear me.

Foolish, foolish girl.

Books and real life do not mix.

His countenance suddenly changes. No longer the playful, somewhat roguish man from before, the one in front of me exudes dark energy. His dark mist doesn't have to materialize for me to feel the shift in the air. It's in the way his face becomes expressionless again, his lips set in a grim line just as his eyes regard me with chilling coldness.

"You *are* young and foolish, Barbi. You have no idea what the world can do to a girl like you," he rumbles, taking a step forward. I wobble backward, but I keep my ground—the last thing I want is for him to see me as weak. "You might have stumbled here by chance, but you should thank all your gods, holy and unholy, that you have a chance to go back to your quiet little home and live a quiet little life."

"You… You're just trying to scare me," I mumble.

A cynical smile tips at his lips. It doesn't reach his eyes.

"Is it working?"

I slowly shake my head, though a tremor claims my body. My heart races in my chest, but I tell myself it's just his proximity, not his intense demeanor that *does* scare me.

"It should, Barbi. It should." He smirks. "It seems I made a mistake indulging you." His form a thin, foreboding line.

"No, I—"

"You will go to that portal, and you will go back to Anthropa. Is that clear?" His voice has a mesmerizing quality to it, but one that's tinged with threat and the promise of punishment.

I shake my head again.

"If you leave me, I will just follow you again," I say in defiance.

He takes a step forward.

My back hits the hard trunk of a tree, leaving me no route of escape. I slowly look up to find him watching me with a mocking smile on his lips.

"That is where you are wrong. I *allowed* you to follow me. It will not happen again," he notes wryly.

"So that's it? You'll just leave me by myself? What if something happens to me on the way to the portal? What if I never make it to the portal because psycho Damien decides to show up and kill me? You'll have my death on your conscience…"

He raises an amused brow as he places his palm against the trunk, right by my face. He leans in, his breath a razor's edge away.

"Do you think I *have* a conscience?"

"W-what?" I blink rapidly.

"Let me put it this way, *Barbi*. You were my brief distraction after eons of nothing to entertain myself with. Nothing more, nothing less. Although I realize now that was a mistake."

"You… You're wrong." I gulp down. "You're nice. You were nice to *me*. You killed that terrible Ivan. You saved my PomPom, and you gave me food and water and—"

"Nice…" he repeats, suddenly bursting into laughter. "Nice. You say I am *nice*…"

"To *me*. You were nice to me. So you can continue being nice by letting me tag along and then I can entertain you some more. Maybe even give you more blood," I stammer as I pull on the collar of my gown to reveal my neck. "You like my blood, no? I can give you more."

"Hm, and what else will you give me?"

"What?" I blink.

"You will give me your blood and what else?"

"I—" I lick my lips. "What else do you want? I can sing, but not terribly well. You may not like it much, but it might prove entertaining. I can also do a dance routine with my PomPom, but I suppose I should instruct BonBon too so he doesn't feel left out, and that might take some time, but I promise you that's *very* entertaining. We've won awards for it and—"

"Let me get this straight," he interrupts me. "You will sing and dance for me?"

"And give you blood," I whisper.

"And give me blood," he repeats, his tone marred by irony. "What else?"

"Uhm, what else do you want?"

His lips curve up in a dangerous smile.

"Do you have to ask?"

I gulp down uncomfortably. This is going all wrong and for so many reasons. Good Lord, was I actually wrong about him? Is he just another Ivan?

"What you are insinuating is inappropriate," I choke out, averting my gaze.

My chest feels suddenly *too* tight, my breathing constricted.

"Is it? Why?" he inquires lazily, leaning in until his warm breath fans my cheek.

I squeeze my eyes shut.

"My ex-boyfriend, the Dark One, would mind it *very* much. He doesn't like to share, you see. We might be broken up, but he doesn't want these lips to go anywhere near another man. If you try anything, he might show up and turn you into mummy dust—even though you're technically not a mummy. But he's *that* strong," I speak breathlessly, word vomiting in my panic.

He doesn't reply for a few seconds. Seconds that feel like an eternity.

Then he laughs.

He rests his forehead on my left shoulder and laughs. The vibrations spread through my body, creating a paradoxical mix of yearning and fear.

When he's finally done laughing at my expense—since let's be honest, he's *not* laughing *with* me—he pulls back.

He takes a step away from me, and his expression strikes a new fear in my breast.

It's empty.

Dark.

The shadows from the fire play ominously on one side of his face, leaving the other shrouded in mystery. One corner of his mouth is raised sardonically—a wolfish smile that threatens to swallow me whole.

"I am sorry to break it to you, sweetheart, but I am not a misunderstood villain, nor do I have a *heart*," he drawls mockingly. "I may not have caused the plague you speak of, but I have done everything else they accuse me of."

My eyes widen as I stare at him in shock.

"Y-you… B-but… You can't be… He's dead…" I stutter. Embarrassment, shame, and mortification prevent me from uttering even one proper word.

"Oh, but I am very much alive." He smirks.

I may have mentally swooned plenty of times before in his presence, but at his proclamation that he is, in fact, my *fake boyfriend*, the Dark One, my spirit decides to leave my body.

For the first time—or maybe the second, since it did happen before when I stole his finger—I swoon. And I fall limp to the ground.

I waver in and out of consciousness to the point I no longer know what is real and what is not.

On the ground, my head rests against Nykander's thigh as he gazes down at me pensively.

My lashes flutter against a flicker of awareness.

"You silly girl," he mutters to himself.

His hand cups my cheek, his thumb caressing my skin in circular motions.

A shiver goes down my back and I try to move.

"Do not," he commands, and for some reason my body obeys him.

My eyes are wide open now, feeling returning to my limbs. Pain echoes from the back of my head, and something wet sticks to my hair.

"You are ruining all my plans, aren't you, Barbi?" He muses to himself.

I stare at him unblinking.

His fangs elongate, and bringing his wrist to his mouth, he bites hard into his flesh. I don't have time to wonder what he means to do for he presses his bloody wrist against my lips. His blood floods my mouth, the taste metallic but oddly sweet.

My body hums in response, and a pleasant calm settles over me.

"Sleep now," he whispers. "Sleep until I am the only thing you can think about…"

His last words are fuzzy. I don't know whether he truly spoke them or they are merely a figment of my imagination.

Heat erupts across my chest, concentrated in the area just above my heart.

I thrash against him, a fire building inside of me—one that makes me want to pull the skin off my bones. The pain builds to an unbearable crescendo until I can no longer bear it.

"Damnation!" His thundering voice echoes in the stillness of the forest. Dark, shadowy tendrils surround us, moving wildly around in a primitive dance. They flame in and out of focus, curling around my body and seeping into my flesh.

But I am too weak to react.

I sleep.

II

A startled gasp flies past my lips as I shoot up straight, panic overtaking me.

It was a nightmare, wasn't it? I couldn't have possibly developed a one-sided crush on *the* Dark One. And I couldn't have possibly thrown myself at him and offered him *my* blood so he can go back to being a bad guy and terrorize more people. No, I could have *never* done that.

To my everlasting disappointment, it was *not* a nightmare.

A shudder goes down my back as flashbacks inundate my mind.

Gray icy eyes. Sharp cheekbones. Strong jaw. Big, manly hands.

My breathing intensifies.

His name… He said his name was Nykander.

I squeeze my eyes shut as I remember begging him to take me with him, telling him everything I could do to *entertain* him. God… How could I allow myself to become such a clown?

My ex-boyfriend the Dark One doesn't like to share.

He doesn't want these lips to go anywhere near another man.

Meanwhile, the actual Dark One was secretly laughing at

me while I made a cake of myself with all those silly proclamations.

Even now, my stomach rebels at the thought. My cheeks burn with shame as I remember all the nonsense I spouted.

I am the reason he wakes up in the morning.

The light to his dark, dark soul…

Those words mock me, echoing in my mind until all I want to do is melt onto the floor and become a tiny dust particle invisible to the naked eye. Only then will I be able to escape the mocking laughter accompanying those thoughts.

"Aghhhhh!" I scream, flailing my arms and legs back and forth. The plushness of the mattress allows for my rather violent and uncivilized outburst. But as I stretch even more and bang my head on the wooden headboard, I'm brought back to reality.

"Ouch," I murmur as I rub the back of my head, a modicum of calm settling over me.

If it wasn't enough that I told him I would perform a dance routine with my PomPom for him, he had to make me a lewd proposition that shattered all my romantic dreams.

He wanted me to *entertain* him in a completely different way than I had in mind. And I thought he was a better man because he had been nice to me and my dogs.

"Stupid," I mutter to myself. "So damn stupid!"

That's what I get for mistaking the least amount of attention for interest. I deserve that embarrassment and more since it was all my fault for envisioning myself as the main character in a romance novel. Thinking back, a shudder racks my body as I remember all my foolish romantic notions.

And for what? Because he was tall, dark, and handsome? So are a billion other people—though admittedly, not *as* handsome.

I take a few calming breaths. Once I have a better grasp on myself, I study my surroundings. Wooden panels fill my vision. There is a door a few feet away, and two windows on each side, allowing for light to stream inside.

I frown. The location is unfamiliar.

Where am I?

I swing my legs over the bed.

The room is small. Maybe two hundred square feet at best.

The floor is heated, and my toes curl in satisfaction as I tread barefoot across the room. That's also when I realize I am not wearing my shoes. Glancing down at myself, I note that I'm wearing a clean pink dress instead of the stinky gown from before. And just for good measure, I sniff my armpits, nodding to myself.

Not bad. I am clean.

But that also begs the question. *How* am I clean? And who the hell changed my clothes?

A scowl pulls at my face.

That Dark One should better hope he wasn't the one to undress me or he will feel the full power of my wrath. Hell hath no fury like a Barbi scorned!

I continue to look around. There is a wardrobe to the side and a small table with one chair next to it. Behind me is the bed I was sleeping in and a small nightstand by the side. There are no personal items around or anything to suggest that anyone inhabits this cabin.

In the back, there is a semi-open door that leads to a small bathroom, equipped with a shower, sink, and toilet.

But something is missing.

Where are PomPom and BonBon?

Panic swells in my chest and I run toward the front door, wrenching it open and ready to go searching for my dogs.

"What the…" I squeak as I grab onto the doorframe to keep myself from falling. My feet dangle over a precipice, teetering back and forth as I attempt to haul myself back up.

This damn tiny house was built on a cliff that feeds directly into a ditch.

Good Lord! I can't even see the bottom.

Mist slithers through every crevice of the valley, obscuring much of the landscape. A few mountain peaks in the distance are entirely covered in snow and ice—not at all comforting since that only occurs at *very* high altitudes.

"Help," I whimper. My hands are slowly slipping, gravity pulling me down.

Seconds trickle by. My life flashes before my eyes as I say a small prayer.

This is it.

This is the end.

I squeeze my eyes shut just as my grip on the wood fails me, my nails chafed to the bone and bleeding.

The next moment, I fall.

A whooshing sound explodes in my ears from the pressure of the fall.

Mom, Dad, I'm sorry. I've been a bad daughter. I'm sorry I never met your expectations and always disappointed you.

PomPom, forgive me for not taking care of you better. You, too, BonBon—even if our acquaintance was brief.

A scream is wrenched out of my throat, my arms flailing all around me as my heart threatens to explode in my chest.

There is no more time for regrets as I fall through the mist, heading straight for the ground.

But there is one certainty above all.

There is no Prince Charming to save me.

There is no Dark One to torch the world in his search for me.

The books *lied*.

A green patch of land appears in sight, but I have no time to process the visual stimuli before I hit the ground.

I blink against the wave of pain that assails me. I am flat on my back, my gaze toward the blue sky with a tint of gray.

My limbs are in an awkward position, one leg beneath me, the other bent the wrong way. My shoulders are bent at an angle, and based on the blood I note as I glance down, I assume the bone has broken through flesh.

Deep breaths.

I am not dead.

How? I don't know.

But my body is absolutely wrecked.

I try to move my hands. The pain is astounding, and I cannot stop myself from crying aloud as I pull my arms into a normal position. There are, indeed, quite a few broken bones that are protruding through my skin.

Despite the pain, I manage to pull myself into a sitting position.

Confusion swirls in my mind, but at the same time, there's an odd calm that settles over me as I jolt my arm with enough strength, the bones align into position. I do the same for the other one, not surprised to see that they easily go back into place. Even better, the skin slowly mends until no blemish remains.

Odd. But I'm not complaining.

I move my attention to my legs. If my arms could mend, then my legs should as well.

I pull my right leg from under me, placing it straight on the ground as I push my weight onto my bones so they realign. Somehow, that happens seamlessly.

What sorcery is this?

The left leg is a bit more tricky. My tibia is broken in two, one side sticking out of my skin. I punch the protruding side down until it meets the other one. Like a puzzle, I put my body back together until I'm back to normal again—or as much as I can be.

Once the pain has subsided, I get up, feeling my limbs whole again but also feeling them…foreign. As if they're mine but not mine anymore.

A deep sense of disappointment envelops me—something akin to having my heart torn out of my chest. There's longing. A bleeding hole inside my chest that's hemorrhaging invisible blood.

Where am I? *What* am I?

And how the hell am I alive?

I fell from a distance of over a thousand feet. By all accounts, I should not only be dead, but there should be little left of me intact. Instead, here I am. Alive. Healed.

How?

Did I catch something from the Dark One? He healed himself before, didn't he? When I gave him back his finger, it immediately attached itself to his hand. The puncture wounds on my neck healed too when he bit me. Did he have anything to do with this?

But as I think about him, a pang of pain stabs at my heart. Why is the memory of him so poignant? Whereas before I was mortified of my actions, willing myself to forget all those silly interactions, now I replay them in my mind continuously—almost as if searching for something but not knowing *what.*

He is a hateful man. *He is a beguiling man.*

I shake my head at myself. Stop it, Barbi! You deserve better!

You deserve an *actual* villain to burn the world for you, not one who'd let you fall from a cliff.

That's it! Mr. Nykander the Dark One is *not* the villain for me.

I trudge my way forward, wandering aimlessly and thinking of more silly things—like how to find and train my own villain.

I chuckle at my own expense as I continue walking.

Am I still in Akkaya? I wonder.

There was no accessible entrance to that cabin, so the only reasonable explanation is that a certain someone must have taken me there.

But why?

If he was so hard-pressed about me remaining in Akkaya, why did he not take me to the portal and haul me back into my world?

Or am I already *in* my world, and the cabin is where the portal took me?

Then what about my dogs? Where are PomPom and BonBon?

I release a ragged breath. So many questions, so few answers.

My dress is stained with blood. My skin, too.

I look like a walking nightmare.

"At least there's no one around to see how low I've fallen," I murmur to myself, self-deprecation my only remaining friend.

Once upon a time, I was pink. Now I am bloody red…

The landscape is as I imagined during my fall. A lush, green valley between mountains, with massive forests stretching in front of me. It's also devoid of life. There aren't people around, but more surprisingly, there aren't any animals either.

I suddenly stop.

A prickling sensation builds just under my skin—a hum that makes all my cells vibrate in unison. The skin over my heart burns. I rub the spot with my fingers to alleviate the discomfort, but the burn becomes increasingly more pronounced.

That's when I hear it.

"Barbi!"

His thundering voice echoes through the valley, the bass reverberating through my body—a soft caress that makes me betray my previous conviction.

The burn intensifies, pulsating to life and dictating the tempo of my heart.

Thump. Thump. Thump.

It echoes in my ear, seemingly echoing in the valley, too.

It echoes in the distance, washing over me, over the landscape, over the world.

Thump. Thump. Thump.

I bang my fist over my heart. It will not stop.

Nykander comes into sight just as his voice becomes louder. He travels down from the sky, his body floating effortlessly.

He flies, but he has no wings. Just as my heart sings, but it has no strings.

My mouth is dry, my pulse drumming in my ears.

He's bloody red too. Head to toe, he is covered in blood.

"Barbi!" he calls out as his feet touch the ground in front of me.

His eyes are wide with shock as he regards my red-stained dress. He peruses my body for injuries, circling around me and regarding me with an unusual worry in his gaze.

"What happened to you?" he demands in a rough voice.

His hand circles my arm, pulling me toward him.

"How did you get here? Are you hurt?"

"Let go," I grit out, pushing him out of my personal space. His mere presence does things to my heart, making that heartburn choke the life out of me.

He doesn't budge.

"Where are you hurt?" He grinds his teeth, his hands moving up and down my body.

"Let. Go!"

"Stop moving."

"I am fine. You do not need to fake worry about me, oh you dangerous Dark One." I roll my eyes. "Go back to terrorizing poor villagers and forget about me," I mutter drily.

He purses his lips.

"Start talking, Barbi. What happened? How did you get down here?"

"I fell. Seems I am fall-proof, though." I laugh.

He doesn't find it funny, his eyes dipping to my chest.

"Eyes here, mister," I snap, using one finger to push up his jaw—or attempting to since he's quite a bit taller than me.

"You fell and you are fine. You are *not* injured…" he muses to himself. "I see."

"What? What do you see?"

Does he know anything? Was I right and he infected me somehow? Maybe with his saliva when he bit my neck?

Ugh. Only I would have the luck to let a guy's lips close to me for the first time and get infected.

"It does not matter. Let us go back." He shakes his head, pulling on my arm and dragging me with him.

I stand my ground.

"I am not going anywhere with you, mister," I tell him.

He half-turns, raising a brow at me.

"Not too long ago you were begging me to take you with me."

"A lapse of judgment on my part." I push my chin up. "I have since seen the error of my ways."

An amused glint enters his eyes.

"Is it because you found out who I am?"

"As if," I huff aloud. "It's because of your abysmal behavior. It seems there has been a misunderstanding between us." I clear my throat. "I was merely being grateful for your help. There will not be anything inappropriate going on between us. In fact, we can each go our separate ways now."

"Is that so?"

He doesn't sound convinced.

"Yes. We clearly do not suit. And regarding my previous claims," I swallow hard, embarrassment once more filling me to the brim. "Please disregard all I have said about the Dark One. It was merely a defense mechanism, you know. I am, after all, a defenseless girl in a foreign world. My innocent lies were only meant to deter bad guys from doing bad things."

His lips tip up in an amused smile—one that makes my insides flutter.

No! I cannot let myself be lured by his handsomeness. Get your hormones under control, Barbi!

"Innocent lies? One could say those were devastating lies," he drawls.

"W-what?" I blink.

He takes a step closer. His shoes meet my bare feet.

I tip my head up to look at him as I nibble on my bottom lip.

"I have a reputation to maintain. What would people say if they found out I have a *heart*?"

My lashes flutter. A flush spreads up my neck.

"Well." I lick my lips. "You should take that up with psycho Damien," I stammer. "He's the one who told everyone I was the Dark One's lover. I merely capitalized on it."

He laughs.

"I think I might allow you to entertain me, Barbi." He nods to himself.

My eyes widen.

"The hell I will," I burst out. "You…" I jab my finger in his chest. "You…"

"Yes?"

"You are a *bad* guy, and I don't entertain bad guys," I add with a huff. "Now tell me where my dogs are and we can part ways."

Once I get my babies back, I can put this entire thing behind me. No more embarrassment and no more making a clown of myself. It doesn't matter how handsome or how attractive this *villain* might be, he is clearly not for me. And I will not beg for scraps, nor will I swallow my dignity for one moment of attention.

"They are at the cabin," he slowly answers, his icy eyes half-melted by a hint of warmth.

"Good. Take me to them and tell me how to get to the portal. I will make my way home."

I move past him in the direction of the mountain where the cabin is. It takes me only a few steps to realize he hasn't moved from his place, his gaze clouded and conflicted.

"I am afraid that is no longer possible," he speaks slowly.

"What do you mean?" I ask, scandalized.

His lips morph into a thin line.

"You fell from a mountain, Barbi. Are you not curious why you are still in one piece?" he inquires lazily.

I stop.

Meeting his eyes, I hold his gaze, unsure how to answer his question.

I *am* curious. I am also terrified of the answer.

"I must have caught a bug or something from you," I mumble.

Placing his palm up, he materializes a small knife and offers it to me.

"Cut yourself," he instructs.

"What? Are you crazy?"

"Cut yourself, Barbi," he repeats, coming closer. He takes my hand and wraps it around the handle of the knife, placing the blade against my open palm.

"Uhm, Mr. Dark One, erm, Nykander... Maybe we can discuss this without sharp objects around... I'm sure we can come to an understanding and..." I mumble nervously.

He doesn't listen. Instead, he forces the blade down my skin, cutting a straight line on the inside of my left palm.

I yelp in pain. He releases me and I stumble back, my expression a mix of shock and hurt that he would do something like that.

But then he raises his own left palm.

The same line appeared on his flesh, mirroring my own.

But just as it appears, it starts closing. The blood stops and the flesh mends together. And as his wound heals, so does mine.

I stare in shock at my palm. Only stains of blood remain, but no wound.

"How? What's happening to me…" I whisper.

My cut appeared on his palm, and when his healed, mine healed too.

I grab the knife and cut again, this time somewhere less coincidental—my face. The blade digs into my cheek and I grit my teeth as I drag it down. My eyes are affixed to his face. The same cut appears on his cheek. As I cut my skin, his gets cut, too—even though there is no blade to cause the damage.

Whatever I do to my body is duplicated on his.

My body freezes in shock. The blade falls to the ground as I watch dumbstruck as his cut heals completely, and with it mine too.

We stare at each other. He has a grave look on his face; mine is one of disbelief.

"When you hurt, I hurt," he speaks in a haunting voice as he comes toward me. "When you fell, I fell too, despite having my feet firmly planted on the ground."

My eyes scan his bloody clothes, the patterns of bleeding unusually similar to the ones on my dress.

"I don't understand. You're saying that if I get hurt, you get hurt too? But how? Why? We're nothing to each other."

A sad smile tugs at his lips.

"As much as I would like to agree with your statement, I am afraid I cannot."

"What do you mean?" I frown.

He takes a step toward me.

I gulp down, watching him warily.

He holds my gaze as he raises his hand.

I squeeze my eyes shut, thinking he's going to hurt me again to prove a point.

But there is no pain. There is only the sound of material ripping as he pulls on the top of my gown until it tears.

I gasp, instinctively wrapping my arms around myself to keep my top from falling and leaving me naked from the waist up.

"What the hell do you think you're doing?" I demand sharply.

He doesn't answer me. Instead, he pulls on his own shirt, buttons flying everywhere as he tears it open to reveal his naked chest.

There, over his heart, is a dark mark that looks as if it has been carved into his flesh with a hot iron. It's an intricate design comprised mostly of straight lines and sharp angles.

I don't know what prompts me to lower my arms and look down at my own chest. An identical mark is over my heart, right above my breast. It has the same patterns and the same dark color as if it had been burned into my skin.

And it had, hadn't it?

The site of the mark has been burning viciously for some time now, but I'd been too caught up in my feelings to investigate.

"What is this?" I whisper, swaying on my feet and feeling a little lightheaded.

"A mating mark," he responds slowly, angrily.

"A what?"

"It means you are my mate, Barbi. Whether I want it or not, we are bound together now."

12

"Say that again?" I gawk at him.

"We are—"

"Stop." I put my hand up. "You're not making sense. How would we be mated? *Why*? I don't understand. In books, people had to at least sleep together for a mating bond to be triggered, or they had to say some magic words that bound them to someone forever. We did neither. So how the hell are we *mated*, Nykander?" I demand, throwing my hands in the air.

He grinds his teeth.

"I can assure you this is not what I would have willingly chosen for myself," he mutters drily.

"Gee, thank you, Nykander. Glad to hear I wasn't even on your radar."

"You do not need to take offense. It is simply the truth." He shrugs.

"But *how*? How did this happen then?"

"Blood bond." He purses his lips.

I frown.

"I fed from you in the dungeon, and after you passed out yesterday, you injured yourself, so I gave you a few drops of my blood to heal you. The blood exchange must have triggered the bond," he explains.

"And does this regularly happen when you exchange blood with someone?"

"No," he answers darkly. "As a matter of fact, it only happens *once* in a lifetime, and it is supposed to be a joyous event since very few people are fortunate to find their mate in this vast universe."

"I am not feeling overly joyous," I mumble drily.

"Oh, trust me. I am far from joyous either."

"What do we do then? How can we…unbond?"

He takes a deep breath.

"I do not know," he eventually replies.

Conflicting emotions war on his face.

"For my kind, a true mating is a blessing from the fates. It is supposedly fulfilled when two people have exchanged blood *and* consummated their relationship. I assume that since we have not done the latter and we will *not* do it, the bond remains only half fulfilled, and as such, it stands a chance to be annulled."

He certainly needs to reiterate how much he does *not* want me. And here I thought I met my rejection quota for the year —perhaps my entire life.

"You don't seem too certain," I remark.

"As I said, very few of my kind have found their true mates," he adds wryly.

"And what's this kind you're talking about?" I narrow my eyes at him.

He meets my gaze but remains silent.

"I'm well aware you're not *human*. But what are you?"

"Are you certain you want to know?" he asks dangerously.

"We're mated, no? I think I deserve to know what you are."

"Only by necessity," he mutters under his breath.

"If you want to be rude, suit yourself." I shake my head at

him. "I'll go back to my world with my dogs and you can forget about me and this so-called blood bond."

"I'm afraid it is not that easy." He releases a ragged breath. "You are now my weakness. Should my enemies find out about our bond, they will target you to get to me."

"Of course," I mumble. "So what do you suggest we do then?"

"You will accompany me, of course. I will allow the dogs, too."

"You will *allow*?" I ask incredulously.

"I will also require you to tone down your excitement. I understand you tend to ramble when you are nervous, but I hope you will keep that to yourself from now on," he continues.

I stare at him unblinking.

He… Who the hell does he think he is?

"Right. Thank you, but no. I am going home," I say as I turn my back to him and head back to the mountain.

To think that just yesterday I was ready to beg him to take me with him… I shake my head at my own foolishness.

Mated.

He says we're mated.

And considering the evidence I've seen so far, I'm inclined to say he's right.

Under any other circumstances, I would have thought this the epitome of romanticism. Not only are two people chosen to be together by the fates, but they actually become *one*! How cool is that?

Except not in my case because not only do we not know each other, I'm not very certain we like each other very much.

I take a step forward, but he appears in front of me, blocking my path.

"That was not a suggestion, Barbi. You *will* come with me."

"Or else?" I push my chin up defiantly.

"I will *take* you with me," he says casually, though that dangerous glint in his eyes tells me he knows exactly what he's doing—he's threatening me.

The cad!

"So I have no choice in this?"

"No," he answers glibly.

"For how long?"

"Until we find a way to void our bond."

"*If*. We don't even know if that's possible."

He shrugs again.

"So you just expect me to follow you around for the rest of my life?"

He tilts his head to the side.

"Technically, the rest of your life is an eternity seeing that you have now borrowed my life-force and my power to regenerate. You are welcome."

I blink slowly. I have been stunned into silence. Not just because he just told me I may have turned into an immortal, but because immortality comes with a binding clause—*him*.

"Y-You don't actually mean that I'm stuck with you for *an eternity*." I gasp.

"If we do not find a way to void our bond, that is exactly what I mean." He gives me a pointed look.

"But… That's kidnapping. I do not consent! I didn't consent when you gave me your blood and I do not consent to this sham mating or blood bond or whatever you call it," I burst out. "I. Do. Not. Consent."

His features darken.

Grabbing a piece of material hanging from my dress, he pulls me brusquely toward him. His breath brushes against my face as he stares me down with those icy eyes of his.

"Do you think I wanted this?" he asks in a low, ominous voice. "Do you think I wanted a goddamn mate when I vowed to never look upon a female again?"

My lashes flutter in confusion at his vicious tone.

"I was doing fine rotting away in that cell until *you* showed up and caused nothing but trouble."

"Wait a moment. What are you—"

"Do you know the price I paid for using my powers to kill that man?"

I slowly shake my head.

"I let down my guard long enough for Damien to pry into my mind and get the clue to the location of a precious item. All because I decided to help *you* instead of fortifying my mental barriers."

A tremor goes down my body.

"I-I'm sorry," I whimper.

"Sorry does not cut it. Not when Damien might get to that location first. So save your silly complaints for another day, Barbi. You are coming with me and this is final," he states harshly. "We may not have had a choice in this farce that the fates orchestrated for us, but we will damn well make the best out of an awful situation."

I bite my lower lip.

"Do you understand what I am saying, Barbi?"

I nod.

"Good. You will be a good girl and follow me. You will do what I say and you will *not* get into trouble. Is that clear?"

"It's not like I have another choice," I mutter.

"Precisely. You do *not* have a choice," he comments. "You wanted to come with me. Congratulations. You are never getting rid of me now," he adds in a mocking tone. The corners of his mouth curl up, but the smile doesn't reach his eyes.

He doesn't like me very much, does he?

Yet before I can let him have the last word, I pick up the knife I discarded earlier and stab him in the chest.

He stares at me wide-eyed as if he hadn't expected me to do that.

I grind my teeth, waiting for the pain to come to me too.

"I'm not getting hurt," I murmur as I search for the stab wound on my body.

"It only works one way. You can thank the fates for that one. Males of my kind are built to protect their females."

He plucks the knife from his chest and his wound closes.

"Oh, and one last thing," he mentions as he regards the bloody tip of the knife. "I will take you up on your offer."

My brows go up in question.

"What offer?"

"I will require to feed every day to be at optimal strength. I will accept your blood offering," he says shamelessly.

My mouth hangs open in shock as I stare at him.

"Absolutely *not*. That offer has expired, mister," I tell him, jabbing my finger in his chest to make my point.

Hear that! Now he wants my blood? After he already refused it once and made me that inappropriate proposition that still makes my cheeks burn.

"What did we just agree on, Barbi?" He tsks at me, his tongue clicking against his teeth and drawing my attention once more to his straight, white, *beautiful* teeth.

"I did not agree to *feed* you!"

"You agreed to do as I say, and I am informing you that you will be feeding me every day."

I gawk at him.

"Next you will tell me that I am required to sleep with you, too."

"Do not get your hopes up, sweetheart. That I shall not do. Not only will I not risk fulfilling our bond, but I made a vow, and I have no intention of breaking it."

"Get my hopes up? I wouldn't sleep with you for anything in the world," I point out, scandalized. "And stop calling me that. I am not your sweetheart, you blackguard!"

He cannot help himself from being a rude, pompous bastard, can he? Yet with every word, he makes it clear what he thinks of me—our bond was an unfortunate accident and I am only an accessory for him.

"I am sure," he drawls as his mouth curls up in a lopsided smile.

I take a deep, steadying breath.

"I do not care what you think. I do not want to sleep with you, nor do I want to feed you. Find yourself another blood bank. My veins are closed for business—indefinitely."

"I cannot do that. Since we are blood bonded, your blood is the only one that can feed me. Should you fail to feed me, I will slowly waste away as I was when you first met me. But the difference this time is that we share the same life force. If I waste away, so will you."

Suddenly, it dawns on me.

"Oh my God! You are a vampire, aren't you?"

He throws his head back and laughs.

"A vampire," he repeats, shaking his head. "I have heard of those beings, but I am sorry to tell you I am not one."

"Then what are you? Why won't you just tell me?" I sigh in annoyance.

"I come from a realm called Tartareia," he replies. "We used to be called the Sons of Tenebreis, but a lot has changed since the old days. To some, we are gods. To others..." he trails off, his eyes blackening as dark mist surrounds his body. "We are demons."

"Oh," I murmur, slowly taking in the new information.

I am mated. Quite accidentally, if not forcibly. To a god/demon.

You wanted adventure, Barbi. There's nothing more adventurous than being stuck with a god/demon for an eternity.

Lucky fucking *me*.

"If I satisfied your curiosity, we can now return to the cabin and prepare for the journey ahead of us," he says as he grabs my hand.

The black mist envelops us, raising us off the ground and propelling us in the air.

"I have one more question," I add after a moment's thought.

"Hm?" He hums as he spares me a glance.

"Are you…gay?" I ask on a whisper. "Not judging or anything, just curious."

"Am I…gay?" he repeats, chuckling. "And how did you reach that conclusion, Barbi?"

"You are, aren't you? I knew it," I muse quietly. Now it makes more sense why he hates being mated to me. The fates really did a number on him.

"Is this because I will not consummate our bond?"

"Oh, of course not," I mutter awkwardly, waving my hand around. "But you mentioned a vow and…"

"You do not have to concern yourself with that. Our partnership will work just fine as long as you do not get yourself in trouble. Is that clear?"

I wet my lips as I consider arguing with him again. But what am I going to gain from that?

"Right. Until we find a way to void the bond."

"Precisely." He nods.

And I'm still left wondering if he is into women or not. I guess it doesn't matter now, does it? It's not as if our relationship will become…more. He has his weird vow and I have… well, I have standards.

We fly up the mountain and we reach the entrance of the cabin. From this perspective, I can see that the house has been built into the rock itself, with some of it jutting out to allow for his aerial entrance. A smart way to ensure no one would trespass.

We get in and he locks the door behind. Two loud barks erupt in the small house. PomPom and BonBon rush toward me, happiness etched on their faces as they see me.

"My babies!" I call out, extricating myself from Nykander's hold and opening my arms to receive my two fluffy angels. They whine and lick my face, and I cuddle them in my arms, murmuring sweet endearments.

Nykander grimaces and heads to the closet. He opens it to reveal a few outfits, as well as a couple of dresses similar to the one I'm wearing.

"Take a shower and change. We will leave in a few hours."

I give him a reluctant nod as I pretend to lavish all my attention on the dogs. But my mind still cannot help but focus on the fact that he'd changed my clothes and cleaned my body. As in, he'd likely seen me naked. And based on his vehemence that he wouldn't touch me… Maybe he really isn't into women and I have nothing to worry about. But why do I feel a small seed of disappointment?

"Where did you take the dogs? They weren't here when I woke up."

I give them something to eat while I brush their coats to make sure they don't get any matting. I spotted a toothbrush in the bathroom…

I sneak a glance at Nykander. It's likely his. But he's my mate now so he will have to share, which implicitly means he needs to share with PomPom and BonBon since they need to have their teeth brushed.

"You were sleeping. They were loud," he answers matter-of-factly from the bathroom.

My hand stills on PomPom's beautiful white coat as I churn his words in my mind. He took them somewhere else because they were loud and I was sleeping?

That sounds awfully…nice.

The sound of the water running from the shower fills the small cabin. I glance at the closed door, my cheeks heating up as I imagine him inside…

I need to purge these thoughts out of my head. Especially now that we find ourselves in this predicament.

We're mated.

I thought that only happened in my romance books where a strong male claims his reluctant mate and woos her until she gives in.

My situation, unfortunately, is far removed from that. Nykander is too good-looking for his own good, but he is in no hurry to claim me. And no matter how reluctant I'd like to be, the truth is that I'm yearning for a deep connection like that far too much to not give in under the right circumstances.

All my life I've wanted to belong somewhere.

I never fit my mother's culture and always underperformed for her standards. My father's side of the family wasn't much better, since he married my mother against his family's wishes, which meant that my relationship with my paternal grandparents was always strained.

At school, things weren't different, and making friends became more and more difficult as I grew up. And based on my track record with friends, I'd say it's another failure to add to my résumé.

I was always the odd one out.

The one chance I get at seemingly belonging somewhere turns out to be nothing but a sham—an accidental one at that.

Mated.

I scoff aloud.

In less than a week, I have gone from pink Barbi who did role-play with her PomPom to red-blood Barbi who is stranded in a not-so-fictional world and accidentally mated to a rude and domineering god/demon. But hey, at least now I have not one but *two* dogs. I should look at the bright side.

The door to the bathroom opens and Nykander strides out. I don't think he realizes his own appeal because he's only wearing a towel draped around his waist. His bare chest is on display, as well as that mark that we now share over our hearts. The striations of his abdomen and protruding biceps make me swallow hard and avert my gaze.

This is not fair! Why couldn't he be an actual ogre so I didn't have to actively lust after him? I wonder if this is a side effect of the mating—the fact that I see him as the most appetizing food.

Yes, this must be it. I can't be that foolish to still want someone who clearly doesn't want me if not for supernatural influences.

"You may have the bathroom. Do not take long," he says as he throws a towel at me.

I barely catch it, sputtering some nonsense. As I walk to the bathroom, I stop to grab one of the dresses too, and I can't stop my mind from going places.

"Whose dresses are these?" I ask as I half turn to watch him.

He's leaning against the wooden wall, the dogs chasing each other playfully at his feet—perhaps hoping for some attention from him. He watches me intently with those icy eyes of his and goose bumps erupt on my body.

"They are yours," he replies.

"Now. But what about before? I don't want to wear another woman's dresses," I say as I cross my arms over my chest.

The corner of his mouth curls up.

"They are new, bought just for you."

"Oh," I murmur. "That is kind of you."

His smile vanishes.

"I am not kind, Barbi. I am practical. Do not mistake my actions for anything but self-interest. You are tied to me now, so I must ensure you are taken care of."

"Right. How foolish of me to have forgotten that." I roll my eyes. "Yet that doesn't explain why you were nice to me *before* we were bonded. You can't deny that—"

In a split second, he's in front of me. His scent drifts to my nostrils, soap and that specific scent of his. It gets under my skin as nothing else has ever done. Since I smelled it for the first time in that cell, I haven't been able to take my mind off it.

I gulp down as I slowly raise my gaze to meet his.

"You were a distraction. Nothing more," he enunciates each word. "Your manner reminded me of…someone," he says as he brings a hand to my face, brushing a strand of hair out of my eyes. "I merely allowed myself to live in an illusion for a few moments."

"Who?" I whisper.

A sad smile forms on his lips.

"It does not concern you. Now go."

I stare at him for a moment longer before I slowly retreat, closing the door to the bathroom.

13

"**Y**ou still haven't told me where we're going," I grumble as I wipe the sweat off my forehead. We've been walking in this forest for *hours*. "And why we have to *walk* and not teleport like you always do."

PomPom and BonBon are walking by my side, wiggling their tails. Their faces are the epitome of happiness as they explore their new surroundings. Surprisingly, they haven't made a sound of protest at the long distance.

The forest is thick, the canopy obscuring the sky. There is a myriad of sounds around, all pointing to different creatures that might pop out and bite me.

So what if I'm technically immortal now thanks to this annoying bond to Mister Grumpy Pants? I still wouldn't appreciate being bitten by a giant anaconda or whatever prowls in the forests of Akkaya.

And since I'm wearing a dress that only reaches past my knees, my calves are fair game for the tall grass and plants that brush against me. There is no beaten path where we're going —nothing to indicate anyone's been around for years.

I scratch my ankle, the spot red from the bite of an insect.

It itches, and I'm getting annoyed. But I take consolation in the fact that he's itching too.

Nykander stops, raising a brow at me as he studies me from head to toe.

"You will know when we get there," he answers cryptically.

"See, now, Mr. Dark One. I don't appreciate being kept in the dark, no matter how much you might like it there," I tell him pointedly. "I get that I'm basically your portable food bank, but I would appreciate some information."

His lips tremble with mirth at my description of *portable food bank*.

"I cannot teleport us to a place I have never been," he answers slowly. "My powers only work with familiar places."

"Oh," I murmur.

"It is getting dark. We should camp here for the night," he mentions, ignoring my *actual* questions.

He studies the area, settling on a remote spot between two giant trees. He leaves me alone as he teleports back and forth to bring supplies—fresh water, food, and a makeshift tent that he ties on the branch of each tree to provide a modicum of cover. When he's done, he builds a fire and disappears again.

I'm staying by the sidelines, staring at him as he moves at the speed of light arranging everything. But it's when he teleports back for the last time that my heart explodes in my chest.

He quietly carries two dog beds and lays them in the tent. PomPom and BonBon give him a happy bark each and a lick as they hurry to their beds, exhausted after a day of walking.

"That was thoughtful of you." I take a seat by the fire.

He grunts, turning his attention to setting up the rest of the tent while I heat up some food.

When he's done, he joins me, though a distance away.

"I'm still waiting, you know," I mention as I hand him a small bowl of meat and roast potatoes.

He gives me a deadly look and mutters something under his breath.

"I'm not going to stop. I will continue to ask and annoy you. So you'd better tell me," I warn.

He doesn't answer, taking a small bite of his meat.

"Dark One?"

No reply.

"Nykander?"

Nope, he continues to ignore me.

"Nyk?"

"Do not call me that," he growls.

Finally! A reaction.

"Then you'd better answer me. I'm waiting." I lean back and give him an innocent smile.

He shakes his head at me. After a moment, though, he speaks.

"I am looking for an artifact. The same one that Damien is searching for."

"What artifact?" I ask, curious.

I slide closer to him.

He scowls at me.

I flutter my lashes at him.

"The realm I am from, Tartareia, was sealed off thousands of years ago by a goddess. It is impossible to go in or out of it now. The artifact in question would allow me to enter the realm."

I blink, surprised by his answer.

"So you want to go home?"

"In a manner of speaking," he notes, his expression shrouded in mystery.

"What type of artifact is it?"

"You ask a lot of questions," he grumbles.

"Of course. Wouldn't you if you were in my shoes?"

He narrows his eyes at me. With a sigh, he continues.

"There are two realms that have always been in opposition, Aperion and Tartareia. To some, the former was the home of the gods while the latter was the home of the demons. To others, it was the reverse. We are all products of the Source, but the universe thrives on balance—where there is darkness, there will be light."

"Okay… I get it, you're the *Dark* One."

"You asked me to explain. I am," he fires back at me. Clearing his throat, he goes on. "These artifacts are items infused with the essence of The Primordials—the first gods. There are fourteen of them, housed securely in Aperion."

"So we're going to Aperion?"

"No." He chuckles. "I would never be allowed to step foot in Aperion. But a few thousand years ago, I heard rumors of one artifact being hidden in a different part of the universe." He pauses. "In Akkaya."

"Oh." I blink.

"There are fifteen royal Houses in Aperion. Each House has a Temple and a High Priestess who is in charge of the protection of its artifact, except for the House of Moirai and the House of Psyche who share one artifact. Soon after Tartareia was sealed off, the High Priestess from the House of Ananke disappeared, together with the artifact."

"So we're looking for this High Priestess?"

He nods.

"I don't have the exact location, but I have a few clues. The problem now is that Damien has those clues, too," he adds, his expression tense.

"Wait. Is Damien from Tartareia, too?"

"In a manner of speaking. He is not the same kind as me, but he is…similar."

"I don't understand." I frown.

"My kind is born this way, with these abilities and increased lifespan. We require blood to keep our energy flow constant. But there is another way to gain similar abilities."

He pauses as he takes a deep breath. "The blood bond between two mates is not the only type of bond there is."

"What do you mean?" I frown.

"A Son of Tenebreis may use his blood to turn a person into his thrall. This usually happens with corrupted spirits that have the capacity for destruction but no guidance for it. Damien was such a spirit at one point, before a Son of Tenebreis converted him into what he is now—a high-level demon. Although our abilities are similar, there is also a difference. High-level demons do not feed on blood. They only feed on energy. Souls," he adds grimly.

"He eats souls?" I repeat in a low voice.

A shiver goes down my back.

Damien was a demon. I sat and ate at the same table as a demon.

Good Lord! I was almost sacrificed by a demon!

"Souls are the purest energy in the universe. Why do you think there is a rumor about me causing that plague to use the energy of the souls to heal?" He raises a brow.

"But..." I falter as I put two and two together. "Oh my God! Does that mean that Damien caused the plague? And he is the one consuming the souls?"

He nods.

"It is the most plausible explanation."

"But a plague? Couldn't he just, I don't know, eat one or two souls? Why does he need so many? Half the population of Akkaya is *gone*!"

His mouth pulls into a tight grimace.

"Because that is the nature of a thrall demon. In the beginning, one soul can provide nourishment for a long time. But as these demons use their powers more and more, they need to feed constantly. By my calculations, Damien should be close in age to me, which suggests he needs a high volume of souls to operate at an optimal capacity."

"How old are we talking about?" I dare to ask.

"Time flows differently here, but in Tartareian age, I am thirteen thousand five hundred and nine years."

I gawk at him.

Thirteen thousand…

"I am twenty-one," I whisper.

"I did not ask for your age, human, nor do I care about it."

"But don't you see?" I burst out, grabbing onto the material of his shirt and dragging myself closer to him. "I am twenty-one and I am mated to a thirteen-thousand-year-old god/demon, whatever you are! I'm getting lightheaded," I add dramatically.

"I do not see the need for histrionics, Barbi," he mumbles drily. "It is what it is."

"How could it be? Do you know there are hundreds of forums making fun of books where the heroine is a young and innocent human and the hero is a hundred-year-old supernatural baddie? In our case, you're thirteen *thousand* years old—even worse. You're basically robbing the cradle, Nykander." I shake my head at him.

He plucks my hands off his person and deposits me away from him.

"You are not a heroine and I am not a hero, Barbi," he speaks slowly, his eyes trained on me.

I release a heavy sigh.

"Of course you would say that," I mumble.

He gives me a warning look.

I return my attention to my food, chewing slowly as I think of painful ways to make him regret his words.

"Wait a moment!" I suddenly say, my eyes widening at the realization. "If Damien is consuming souls at such an alarming speed, then…" I gulp down. "Is that why he was so interested in how many people are in my world? Because he wants to eat them too?"

Nykander nods.

"Precisely. It is also why he would need to sacrifice you," he explains matter-of-factly. "Demons can only travel from one world to another in their physical form by using the blood of someone from the target world. Your blood functions like a key to open the portal for him to go to Anthropa."

I stare in shock at him.

"Does that mean I saved my world? By not dying, I mean?"

"Well," he muses thoughtfully. "Technically, you did."

"Ha!" I point my finger at him as I jump to my feet.

He blinks in surprise.

"I *am* a heroine. I saved Earth from psycho Damien!" I jump up and down ecstatically. "I knew I was meant for greater things," I add in a wistful tone. "Ever since I was young, I knew I had a bigger fate than just going to school and becoming a boring lawyer—which I was never going to do anyway, and my mother would have probably disowned me."

"Barbi, you are doing that thing again," Nykander mentions wryly.

"So what! I am a *heroine*. You should thank me, you know. Now, by extension, you are a hero too since you are my mate. I know you would have never imagined such a thing, with your villainous reputation and all."

"Your logic does not make sense," he murmurs, though he's fighting a smile.

"Come on, Nykander. I know you secretly like it," I say as I drop down next to him. "Admit it." I wiggle my brows at him suggestively.

"I will admit no such thing." He chuckles.

My lips slowly stretch into a smile as I regard him. He looks like a different man when he's laid-back like this, laughing instead of scowling at me and telling me all the things I *can't* do.

"There is one thing I am not clear about, though," I start. "Why is it that you have such a bad reputation in Akkaya?

Everyone was telling me that you were after Damien because you wanted to steal his crown."

He scoffs.

"As if. I was after him because he happens to be the thrall of a man I abhor. He heard the rumor that the artifact might be located in Akkaya and he sent Damien here to get it for him. But you have met him. He is a narcissistic bastard who thrives on adulation."

"A cheating bastard too," I quip. "When I met him, he was in bed with two naked girls. *Two*, Nykander. And his wife was standing right there!"

"She is his wife only in name," he mentions. "She is also a thrall, and they use their marriage as a cover."

"It doesn't matter! A marriage is a marriage," I declare proudly.

The corner of his mouth pulls up.

"That is the least of Damien's sins. I have been trying to create a resistance against him, which worked for some time while I searched for clues about the artifact's location." He purses his lips. "Someone in my camp must have betrayed me because not only did he know I found new clues about the artifact, but he also knew when I would be at my weakest. I hadn't fed in months when he ambushed me and locked me in his dungeon, hoping to pry the clues from my mind," he explains.

I frown.

"Why hadn't you fed in so long? You said you need to feed daily to operate at optimal strength."

A rueful smile tips at his lips.

"I used to only feed out of necessity and never from a live donor. You could say you were the exception." He laughs. "And look where it got me," he mutters in a low, barely audible voice.

"Why? If you're such a baddie, why would you *not* feed from people? You're the Dark One! Surely you could get away with killing a few people—not that I'm instigating murder." I quickly put my hands up. "I would never do that," I whisper. "But what do villains care about murder, no? You killed those guards at the palace with ease."

"Killing and feeding are two different things," he muses as he leans back, closing his eyes and tipping his head toward the sky. "I vowed to someone I would never personally feed from another. Although now I have broken that vow…"

"Out of *necessity*," I point out.

Why do I feel the need to comfort him? Especially when it reinforces the fact that I'm nothing but a tool to him.

But there's something about his body language that tugs at my heartstrings. The wind blows his dark locks into his face, but he makes no effort to move them aside. He simply stays like that, face oriented to the sky, eyes closed, and lips parted. It's almost as if he's not here anymore—as if his mind has traveled to another location.

I stare at him for moments on end as silence descends between us. All I hear is his breath, complemented by the whoosh of the wind and the sound of the wild animals roaming through the woods.

There's a tinge of sadness emanating from him, and I have the sudden urge to move to his side and give him a hug —wrap him in my arms and murmur that it's okay.

But I don't. I just look at him while he looks at his past.

I draw my knees to my chest and place my head on top of them.

We might not be talking in this moment, but we share something.

Loneliness.

We might be together, but we are each lonely in our own way.

I know my demons well. But what about his?

What haunts him when he closes his eyes?

Bringing the back of my hand to my eyes, I wipe away the moisture coating my lashes.

"I'm going to sleep," I speak as I get up.

He doesn't hear me. He remains in his trance.

I take my place in the tent next to the dogs, and I bring their little bodies closer to me, borrowing their warmth.

Nykander doesn't move.

My lids become heavier and heavier, but until the moment I fall asleep, my eyes are on him.

A deep rumble wakes me up from my sleep. The sound is insistent, preventing me from going back to sleep. My babies stretch around me, whimpering but not waking up. I lay a kiss on top of their heads as I groggily get up to investigate the source of the noise.

It's pitch-black out.

The fire has almost burned out. Only a few pieces of wood retain a spark, enough to illuminate the outline of a sleeping Nykander caught under the weight of his nightmares.

"Nykander?" I whisper as I tread carefully toward him.

He's on his back with one hand under his head. His long body is stretched on the ground, with nothing to cushion him from the abrasive soil.

Why hadn't he come to the tent? We'd set it up for this exact reason, so we would be comfortable lying down. The stubborn man had gone through the trouble of getting special beds for the dogs but had paid no mind to his own comfort.

I shake my head.

He releases another low moan, his lips half parted, his face marred by a scowl.

He must be having a nightmare. And after being imprisoned for so long in that dungeon, I don't blame him. He probably has all types of PTSD related to it.

Reaching his side, I get to my knees and carefully touch his shoulder.

"Nykander? Wake up and come to the tent. You'll be more comfortable there."

Of course I don't expect him to easily acquiesce. In fact, he might put up a fight for the mere fact that *I* am in the tent too. He sometimes behaves as if I were a leper—which is not great for my confidence. Alas, hopefully, he will make an exception this time so we can all go back to sleep.

"Nykander?" I push gently against his shoulder.

He murmurs something, his brows bunched up together, his body rocking softly from side to side.

I lean in closer to his mouth and strain to hear what he's saying.

"Mo…"

Mo?

"More what?" I ask, but he doesn't seem to hear me.

Drops of sweat are gathered on his forehead and dripping down his face. I place the back of my hand to his skin. He's burning! Is this normal? Shouldn't he self-heal?

"Don't," he rasps. "Mo… Don't… Please…"

He's not making any sense.

"Nykander." I shake him gently. "You're having a bad dream. Wake up!"

He doesn't react.

He's trapped in his nightmare, trying to claw his way out of it but being unable to do so. And I don't know how to help him.

"Nyk, please…" I whisper.

His eyes snap open.

Despite the darkness of the night, his eyes shine brightly, a molten silver that lights up as he sets his gaze on me.

"You're awake." I release a sigh of relief. "I was worried for a moment since you weren't answering and…"

My relief is short-lived as I find myself on my back with him looming on top of me, his hand wrapped around my neck. It's not a bruising hold. In fact, it's almost gentle as he swipes his thumb over my skin in circular motions. His warmth transfers to my skin, infiltrating my pores and consuming me like a raging inferno.

My heart thuds in my chest.

Thump. Thump. Thump.

The sound echoes in my ears, complemented by his harsh breaths as he stops a breath away from my face. A low tremor starts from the base of my skull, traveling all the way to my toes, making them curl and do a weird dance of excitement.

I lick my lips, staring into his beautiful face.

His eyes are on mine, his stare boring into me.

There's an intensity to his gaze that renders me speechless —a mess of sensations, all foreign yet familiar at the same time.

My breath hitches.

There's heat. Searing, insufferable heat. Yet the last thing I want is to cool off. No, I want to plunge myself into this inferno and never resurface—at least not whole.

The mark on my chest burns, lighting up under my dress, almost as if it can sense the proximity of his own mark. I bring my hand to his chest, draping it down his unbuttoned shirt and searching for that spot. As my palm makes contact with his mark, a zap of energy shocks me. His mark becomes alive as it twirls and slithers on his chest. Like a serpent, it curls over my palm, pulling me closer almost as if it wants to tie us together through an invisible threat.

He doesn't look away.

I can't either.

My hand against his naked skin, I feel every beat of his heart as he regards me.

Thump. Thump. Thump.

There's an eerie exactitude to the rhythm of his heart, one that emulates mine to the beat.

He moves sinuously on top of me, placing his arm under

me so he won't squish me with his weight. His hard body blankets my own, his hips cradled between my legs.

He's…hard.

"Nyk…"

"Mo," he murmurs, lowering his head and breathing me in. "Mine. Mo. Mine."

His lips hover over my face as he slowly slides lower and lower until he reaches my neck. His tongue peeks out to lick the spot right under my jaw.

My mind blanks on me as goose bumps cover my skin, thrills of pleasure shooting through me.

He wraps his lips around my skin, drawing it into his mouth and nibbling at it with his teeth. At first, it's playful bites. But as his fangs protrude and sink into my skin, I feel a sharp pain that is quickly replaced by sheer pleasure.

"Nyk." I gasp, arching my back against him, holding him close and willing him to never stop.

The blood leaves my body, transferring into his, and the connection between us strengthens. His mark pulses under my palm. My mark burns as it seeks more of his touch.

"Mine," he whispers sensually, making me blush uncontrollably.

He licks the wound on my neck languidly as it heals and he drags his fangs across my skin, more blood pooling to the surface. His own skin breaks, too, in response.

"Drink," he commands in a rough voice.

I blink, disconcerted for a moment. But as his big hand cups my nape and pulls me closer to his neck, my mouth automatically opens to taste his blood. But as I run my lips over his neck, his wounds close too quickly for me to get more than a small taste.

"Bite me," he commands.

His voice is deep and alluring, speaking to a hidden side of me that wants nothing else but to please him. My body is no longer my own as I move and writhe to rub myself all over him, bathe in his essence while he feeds on my own.

I wrap my lips around his flesh, feeling the blood pump in his veins under his skin, hearing the beat of his heart as if it were my own.

Yet how can I bite him with my blunt teeth?

"Bite me," he repeats. The command booms inside of me, the bass of his voice reverberating through my entire being until all I can do is obey him.

I was born for this. I was made *just* for this.

To be here, in this moment. To be…*his*.

I bring my teeth down on his skin, my canines lengthening until they're buried deep in his flesh. Fresh blood flows into my mouth and I gulp it down greedily, feeding as if I've done this my entire life.

"That's my girl," he rasps against my ear, the praise feeding my ego like his blood feeds my essence. "Drink me up. Every drop. Every fucking drop, Mo."

Mo.

Mo.

Mo.

The word echoes in my mind, a thousand warning bells going off at once.

When he was mumbling it before, I thought it was merely an incoherent word.

But it's not, is it?

My body goes slack under him.

It's not what I think it is…right?

He peppers kisses all along my jaw, his fangs grazing my flesh as he licks his way toward my lips.

"My girl," he whispers. "My Mo."

I freeze.

My stomach plummets, a wave of nausea rolling over me.

Before his lips can touch my own and steal my first kiss, I muster up all my strength and push him off me, moving my head out of the way so I can drag a deep breath into my battered lungs.

My lashes are damp and tears burn behind my retina.

Inhale. Exhale.

The sky is closing in on me as the burn in my chest becomes an unbearable inferno. But not one of pleasure. It's one of pain.

He rolls away from me.

He blinks slowly, clarity entering his gaze, and with it, a harsh look that speaks more than a thousand words. His cheek twitches. His mouth is set in a grim line as he sets his deadly glare on me.

Then he proceeds to kill me with five words.

"You are not my Mo."

We stare at each other in silence, both breathing hard.

He wipes the blood from his mouth with the back of his hand, the gesture one of disgust. A feral expression claims his features as his nostrils flare.

"I—" I open my mouth to speak, but he cuts me off.

"Go to sleep, Barbi," he orders, his voice vibrating in the air.

I lick my lips, tasting his residual blood, and I falter.

"Go to sleep. Tomorrow we will leave at first light."

"We should talk about this. About—"

"There is nothing to talk about. Go. To. Sleep."

His eyes flash at me and I scurry away from him, running back to the tent.

He stands up, looking up at the sky for a few moments before he disappears.

I know he's not far. I can still sense him—or, this wretched mark over my heart can sense him. But his absence cuts a hole inside my chest.

I lie down, hugging PomPom and BonBon, but sleep proves elusive.

There is only one pervasive thought.

Who is Mo?

14

We don't speak in the morning.

I brush my dogs' hair while Nykander is studying some ancient map a distance away. If he won't make an effort to discuss what happened last night, then why would I try to do it? He's made it perfectly clear that I am just his portable food source, so what happened last night can be successfully written off as him feeding off me.

My lips curl in a scowl.

Damn you, Nykander! Damn you and your sleepwalking tendencies and damn you for making me lose my mind with one touch.

How is this fair?

I wonder if our accidental mating has anything to do with why I am so drawn to him—why I crave his touch and presence more than anything. If only I knew more about his kind and what mating means for them. So far, I only have what Nykander has told me, and he could very well spin the information to suit his nefarious purposes. As in, he might be aware that there is no way out of this and I am basically tied for all eternity to his grouchy-ass self.

Ugh!

Why am I so unlucky?

I only wanted a taste of adventure and maybe an epic love story along the way. Instead, what do I get? A domineering asshole who can't stop reminding me that he would have never been with me had it not been for those pesky fates.

And if that wasn't enough, he also had to feed from me and touch me and kiss my neck while calling me by a different name. If our lives weren't technically tied together, I would be busy figuring out a way to dispatch him to his next life.

The audacity of this man to not even explain himself.

I get angry the more I think about it, and to make him feel my silent wrath, I glare at him every now and then.

Too bad he has no eyes for me—literally *and* figuratively.

I mutter a string of curses under my breath, making my own incantation of bad luck aimed straight at his dark hide.

Even then, he ignores me.

PomPom whines as she comes closer, brushing her head against my leg. She can sense my annoyance and wants to make it better, bless her fluffy heart. BonBon is still getting to know me, but he takes his cues from PomPom, so he inundates me with love too. I may not have my epic love, but I have the undying affection of these cute babies.

"You two are the cutest couple I've ever seen," I coo at them as I give them a small treat.

Nykander might be an asshole, but he is an *acceptable* asshole. Whenever he teleports himself to God knows where, he always comes back with some food and treats for the dogs. That is the only reason why I have not attempted bodily harm yet, or maybe some type of castration (though he would deserve that after the stunt he pulled last night). But I have a policy of being nice to whoever is nice to my dogs. So for as long as he keeps PomPom and BonBon happy, I will not do anything…extreme in his sleep.

If he offends my babies, then all bets are off.

I turn my head and give him another glare that is once more ignored.

"Yo, Dark One," I call out.

He slowly turns, raising a brow at me.

"I have already told you, human. We will not discuss what happened last night again," he adds in a stern voice.

My nostrils flare. Why does it seem like he's chiding a child?

"Whoa, easy there. You don't even know what I was about to say. You're not all that, you know?" I mutter under my breath, annoyed.

He tilts his head to the side, pursing his lips. Disbelief is written all over his maddeningly handsome face.

Damn you, Nykander! Why do you have to make my heart flutter even when I'm mad at you?

"In fact"—I clear my throat as I push my chin up—"I have had better."

He narrows his eyes at me.

"And what is it that you have had better?"

"Oh, you know." I shrug. "Those kisses on my neck. They were rather sloppy. I would think a man of your age would have more flair."

"Is that so?" he asks in a grave voice.

"Yes, indeed." I nod. "You could use more practice. Not that I'm offering. But just so you know, they were rather subpar. Guys my age do it better."

The lie burns on my tongue, but the last thing I would want him to know is how much those *sloppy* kisses affected me, or the fact that I was about to let him have his way with me— well, not *all* the way, I still have standards—if he hadn't messed it all up.

I'm still bitter about that *Mo*, whoever she is.

"Guys your age," he repeats, unconvinced. "And you have been with many guys your age?"

"Tons," I hurry to reply. "So many I have lost count."

"Hmm."

"They were all *much* better," I continue, needing to convince him somehow, as if that would lessen my mortification in any way. "One did this tongue trick that had me in a puddle on the floor," I say with a sigh.

God, I sound like the biggest player for someone who's never held a boy's hand before—well, except for his.

"Really? And this male wouldn't happen to be the same as your Dark One boyfriend?"

"Of course," I say without realizing. My eyes widen as I slap a hand over my mouth.

He smirks.

"Hey!" I get up and point at him. "You tricked me!"

"Me? When did I do that?" he asks, amused.

"I'll have you know I am *very* popular in my world. Guys line up to date me. Why, you should see my social media. It's full of hot guys sliding in my DMs."

Well, technically, that is not a lie—or, not a full lie. My DMs are full, but it's not hot guys. It's creeps and incels who think sending a dick pic is the way to get a girl.

He stares intently at me.

I swallow.

He takes a step forward.

"Sliding in what?" he asks in a low, gravelly voice.

"Uhm… DMs? You wouldn't know since you don't have social media in your world and all that," I add, forcing a smile.

He takes another step forward.

"There will be no sliding of anyone *anywhere*. Is that clear?"

"You don't get to dictate—"

Before I can finish my sentence, he's in front of me.

I wobble back, slowly raising my eyes to meet his.

"There is one thing I forgot to mention," he starts in a dangerous voice. "Mated males are…territorial."

I blink rapidly as I try to process his words.

"Uhm…"

"There will be no mention of males your age, hot males, or any other males for that matter. Do you understand me?"

"I don't think I do. You don't even like me—"

"Do you understand me, Barbi?" he repeats, his hand coming to rest on my neck.

I gulp down as I try to keep my composure.

"I—"

"Yes. You will say yes."

"But—"

"Yes, Barbi. You will say yes."

His hold on my neck tightens as he pulls me closer. His fangs elongate, his features darkening as he stares down at me.

A sliver of fear goes down my back.

"Y-yes," I stammer.

His eyes don't leave mine for moments on end.

"Good." He nods, taking a step back.

I release a deep breath, my body trembling lightly.

What… What was that?

I don't get to ponder on it, though, as he suddenly stops, his jaw tensing.

"We have visitors," he notes.

"What?"

"Stay behind me and do not speak unless I tell you to."

Although my first instinct is to argue, I also have a pretty strong self-preservation instinct, so I grab my dogs and hurry behind him.

It's a few minutes before the bushes in our proximity start rattling and footsteps echo in the forest.

"How many?" I whisper.

"Ten."

"Do you think Damien sent them?"

He grunts.

"Will they want to hurt us? But you're strong, right?" I say as I lightly pat his arm. "You will not let them harm my babies," I mention as I glance at PomPom and BonBon looking around in confusion.

"You do not know how to listen to commands, do you?" he mutters dryly.

The thick foliage parts to reveal a group of men, all carrying heavy bags on their backs. Their expressions are haggard, their skin sallow and marred by lines. The clothes on their bodies are dirty and worn, holes poking through the material.

When they see us, they stop in shock.

"Mika, look! More people!" the one in the front exclaims as he points to us.

Nykander stares them down. He extends his arm protectively around us.

"Who are you?" Nykander grinds his teeth. He resembles a feral dog protecting his master, and my heart flutters in my chest—unwittingly, of course. I am still angry that out of all the men in the universe, my body decided to react to *this* one.

The men take a step back, fear clouding their features as they look from Nykander to me. They scramble away, ready to run in the other direction before they catch sight of our food, and hunger fills their gazes.

"I don't think they're the enemy," I whisper to Nykander.

He doesn't listen to me as he commands his dark cloud to envelop us. His expression turns murderous as he gets ready for attack.

"Who are you and who sent you?" he demands in that scary voice of his. Black tendrils slither from him, making their way toward the men.

"Oh…we…" one of the men, the leader, stammers, fear echoing in his voice.

"We mean no harm. We are merely passing through," another one says as he comes forward. He's older, his hair mostly grayed. "We have heard of a village that is free of the plague and we are searching for it."

"See, they're not bad guys," I whisper again.

Nykander doesn't move.

The men stumble over their words in an attempt to explain that they've barely escaped alive from the plague, but Nykander isn't convinced. The dark cloud around him grows in size, and if this continues, I fear he might turn these men into dust before they've even had a chance to defend themselves.

His dark tendrils are almost upon the men. They step back, huddling together in fear.

No, this won't work. Nykander may be the Dark One and all that, but even he shouldn't stoop so low as to harm some innocent passersby. It seems he needs saving from himself. Otherwise, his dark soul will become even more blemished—not that I worry about his soul. He can go to the deepest pits of hell for all I care, but that would mean I need to follow right behind because we're tied together now and I don't do well with extreme heat. My babies would hate that too since they like a temperate climate. No, hell isn't an option.

"You must be hungry," I quip loudly. I let PomPom and BonBon down, and I grab Nykander's arm. "Stop it, Nykander! You will *not* hurt them," I tell him and surprisingly, the dark mist immediately recedes.

"We have spare food if you would like some," I offer with a kind smile.

Nykander stares at me in disbelief. His nostrils flare as his body tenses.

I ignore him as I give the men a reassuring smile.

Heading to our tent, I take out the rest of our food and hand it out to the strangers, making small talk and inquiring about their families. Nykander stands there, still as a stone, staring at our interactions. His shadows might have disappeared, but his murderous intent did not. If looks could kill, I would already be in my grave.

Moments pass and he finally snaps from his brooding. He

comes closer, his lips curled in a snarl. If I expected him to suddenly turn into a great host, I am sadly mistaken. As the men are wolfing down our leftovers, he yanks my arm and pulls me by his side.

"My female is *very* generous. You will do well not to abuse that generosity," he growls, his voice a dangerous warning.

A chorus of thank yous erupts in the air, and Nykander leans in to whisper in my ear.

"What do you think you are doing, Barbi?"

"They're starving." I point to the group as they're ravenously eating everything I laid out for them. "We have enough food. Besides, you can catch more game later."

"And you think a group of ten males cannot catch game for themselves?" He raises a brow. "The forest is teeming with creatures."

"Look at them! Do they look capable of anything to you? The poor men must have been walking for days to escape the plague."

"Oh, Barbi." He shakes his head at me. He rakes his eyes over my face, seemingly deep in thought. Eventually, he releases a deep sigh as he steps away from me. "Fine. I will leave it to you to learn the hard way that not everyone is deserving of kindness."

I frown.

"What are you talking about?"

He merely smiles.

When the men finish eating, the leader of the group comes to us to thank us for the food.

"You have been most welcoming when others would not have done so. If we could return the favor, please let us know," he says with a smile.

The older man nods.

"Where are you heading to? You could join us in our search for the plague-free village."

"Oh, no, thank you…" I bite my lip. Even *I* don't know where we're going.

"My *female* and I are enjoying some personal time away from the capital. I trust that you can now be on your way?" Nykander interrupts, emphasizing our relationship in a strange way.

Just what is wrong with him? He has told me repeatedly how displeased he is with our *situation*, but now he's publicly claiming me? Not that I mind it. In fact, the words *my female* sound rather delicious coming from his mouth. But the sad reality is that I can't trust them.

I release a disappointed sigh.

"We thank you for your kindness." The man inclines his head. "If we shall ever meet again, we will return the favor."

"Don't worry about it," I tell them with a smile, ignoring the way Nykander is sending them death glares.

I wave at them as they leave, and when we are finally alone, I turn toward Nykander.

"What is wrong with you?" I grit out. "Are you so heartless you wouldn't help people so clearly in need?"

He merely turns to pack our equipment.

"Now you're ignoring me," I huff aloud.

PomPom barks at him, echoing my displeasure with him, while BonBon follows her lead.

Take that, Nykander. You might have your dark mist, but I have my two faithful companions that will not stand for any disrespect!

It's moments later that he deigns to speak.

"Did it not cross your mind that they did not even check to see if we had the plague?"

I frown.

"What do you mean?"

"They ran away from the plague but did not even ask us if we were infected or checked for any signs of the disease."

"Well." I wet my lips. "The plague is fast acting. We

wouldn't have been alive if we were infected. You're just trying to find reasons to hate them."

"And why would I do that?"

"Because they're males." I cross my arms over my chest. "You're jealous," I point out, smiling in satisfaction.

He might not like me, but he said it himself that the mating bond is making him territorial. And although it might be for all the wrong reasons, my cheeks heat up at the thought that someone would be jealous over *me*! How many times had I imagined that while reading all those romance novels where the men are growly and possessive and they always say mine this, mine that? How many times had I wished I were the object of someone's possessiveness? Of someone's utter attention and obsession. Okay, it might not be *really* healthy given how it's portrayed in those books, but I'll settle even for a smidge of possessiveness.

Unfortunately, Nykander's is the *wrong* kind.

Nykander chuckles.

"Oh, Barbi, Barbi." He shakes his head. "What am I going to do with you?"

I take my time as I consider a witty reply that won't have him mocking me again. But it seems I am too slow as he drops the tent to the ground and teleports himself in front of me.

His hand shoots out, his palm unfurling in front of me just as an arrow pierces his flesh.

An arrow meant for me.

My eyes widen in shock.

"They were some poor people in need of help, huh?" he asks slowly as he plucks the arrow from his hand. But just as I wait for his wound to mend, it doesn't.

There is a blue substance clinging to the arrowhead, and particles of it are now embedded in his flesh.

"Damnation," he mutters, squeezing his eyes shut and taking a deep breath.

When he opens his eyes again, they're a different shade of gray. A tumultuous one that's frayed by pain.

Dark mist surrounds us like a shield as more arrows descend upon us. But it's not before he pulls PomPom and BonBon next to us inside the protective shell.

His hand still does not heal.

"What's happening? Who are they?" I ask as I hug my babies to my chest.

"*What*, not who. They are demons."

"Demons… But… Why didn't you say so before? You let me give them our food!"

His lips pull up in a smile.

"Would it have mattered?"

I blink.

"You do not listen, Barbi. You are brash and impulsive, and you throw yourself head first into danger without considering the consequences."

"It was just this once," I whisper. "I didn't know…"

"Oh, but it was not just this once, was it? We are here, are we not? This would have not happened if you were a good girl and returned to your world when I told you so. It would not have happened if you did not stubbornly decide to follow me."

Just when I thought we had made a little progress, he throws this in my face again. As if I wanted to be mated to him. The gall on this man! Who asked him to give me his blood? If anything, it's on *him*. He knew about the potential danger of exchanging blood. I didn't even know what kind of creature he was before all this.

So how am I, who was wholly ignorant, the guilty one?

"Nykander…" I stop myself when I see the look of pure hatred crossing his face as he regards me. His dark mist envelops us in a cocoon that repels all the arrows coming our way. And there are many, each one emitting a loud bang as it touches the mist and falls to the ground, nearly obliterated.

"This is one of many lessons I will have to teach you. Because you are my mate and I am responsible for you, whether I want it or not."

I avert my gaze as a sliver of guilt washes through me.

His words *hurt*. Not just because he is right about my impulsivity, but also because it's clear how much he dislikes me.

I am sure if he could, he would have turned me into dust too—a long time ago.

I take a deep breath. This is not the moment to dwell on this wretched situation and the fact that the person I have the silliest crush on absolutely abhors me.

"Your hand…" I grab his hand, my eyes widening as I note the blue substance is spreading through his flesh and impeding his healing. "What's wrong with it?"

"We can worry about that later," he strains out a reply.

"Tell me to kill them."

"W-what?"

"Tell me, Barbi. Now."

"K-kill them. Please…"

He gives me a brisk nod.

Turning his attention to the incoming attacks, his expression changes.

His dark mist transforms into tendrils that reach out and take out the men from their hiding places. The mist surrounds each one of their bodies, and before I can blink, they turn into dust.

One after another, what little is left of the men drops to the ground, only to be swept away by the wind. Nykander barely moves a muscle as he watches his dark cloud consume the men.

In a matter of seconds, they're gone. He dispatched them so easily, it makes me wonder *why* he waited until they shot their arrows at us.

"If you knew they were demons, why didn't you kill them

before?" I ask in a small voice as I take out a cloth, wetting it and dabbing it around his wound.

He closes his eyes and exhales through his nose.

"Do not, *ever*, tell me to stop again."

I shrink back at his biting tone. But as I look at his hand, it's no wonder he's mad at me. He got that trying to protect me and for some reason, it's not healing.

"I'm sorry," I whisper.

He does not reply.

Glancing at his hand, he scrapes the remaining blue stuff away, and his flesh slowly starts to heal.

"What is this blue substance?"

"A toxic powder that can neutralize my healing abilities," he answers blithely.

"But *what* is it? Where does it come from?"

He gives me a warning look, a sign he does not like my line of questioning.

"You ask too many questions, Barbi."

"Am I not entitled to know this if it puts you—*us*—in danger? You're always berating me, but you forget that I'm a stranger to your world. I know next to nothing about…well, everything. Why are you always blaming me? It's not as if I'm doing things on purpose! I just saw some men in need and I wanted to help them. What's so bad about that? And just because I followed you doesn't mean I wanted to end up tied to you like this! You may dislike me, but you forget that I may dislike you back! You've certainly been a grumpy, rude, nasty man ever since we got roped into this situation."

"Are you done?" he drawls lazily as he leans back to look at me.

"I am *far* from done! You are awful to me and I will not stand for it. So you either change your behavior or this will not work. And we might be trapped together until we figure out how to get out of this *binding* situation, but that doesn't mean I have to be pleasant. You already dislike me. I will make you absolutely detest me, and I will not let you have one moment of peace if you continue like this," I tell him firmly.

"So let me get this straight. Are you threatening me with more of your incessant talking?"

"Damn right I am."

He stares at me. The corners of his mouth tremble before he bursts out into laughter.

"All right, Barbi. You win," he mentions as he shakes his head.

"What?" I blink. "What do I win?"

"I will be more considerate of your…delicate sensibilities. Will that work?"

"I will have to see it first. You can start by telling me things. I hate being kept in the dark, no matter how much you may like it," I add pointedly.

His smile widens.

"So what's this blue stuff and why does it neutralize your healing abilities?" I ask as I dab the cloth more carefully around his wound. Removing the particles allows him to heal once more, so we have to make sure the wound is completely clean.

"The deadliest weapon against a Son of Tenebreis is one dipped in the blood of his sire," he speaks slowly, his eyes affixed to mine. "It is a well-guarded secret that only a Son of Tenebreis would know."

"But…" I frown. "That would mean…"

"You are correct. They were sent by a Son of Tenebreis— someone who could have access to the blood of my sire."

"Who?"

His lips pull into a sad smile.

"Baine. My brother. The one who controls Damien and an army of thrall demons. The man I am going to kill once I get back to Tartareia."

15

"**D**amien also used the blood of my sire to subdue and capture me," he continues.

"But why would your sire allow that? Wouldn't he know what the blood was being used for?"

He purses his lips.

"My sire has been dead for thousands of years. Long before I left Tartareia."

"Then how?"

"My brother must have kept some of his blood before his death. It is the only plausible explanation, but it is also the one that cuts the most because it means he must have been planning to kill me from the beginning."

"But he's your brother! How could he kill his own blood?"

"I am sorry to break it to you, Barbi, but my world is nothing like your human one. There are no fraternal bonds, nor are there paternal or maternal. Marriages are alliances and children are a way to gain power. Every single Son of Tenebreis is on his own, selfishly killing, scheming, and betraying. It is why Tartareia was sealed off so easily in the past because we are not capable of working together. Everyone wants power. But no one wants to share that power."

"That sounds…bleak."

"It is." He nods. "For all intents and purposes, the universe is better off with Tartareia sealed off."

"Yet you're searching for an artifact to break the seal," I note, regarding him thoughtfully.

"I never said I was not selfish," he remarks.

I bite my lip in worry.

"What will happen once the seal breaks?"

He tips his head back, his eyes closing.

"Mayhem. There are not that many Sons of Tenebreis surviving since the war with Aperion decimated our ranks. Within our royal houses, there are perhaps a few hundred purebloods remaining. But they are all hungry for power and vengeance. They will not rest until Aperion, and the whole universe for that matter, is theirs."

"And you want to unleash that into the universe? Knowing what a danger they are?"

"If not me, then someone else will."

"Then why all this trouble? Why not let Damien get to the artifact first and just go after him when the seal is broken?" I ask, confused.

"Because that artifact does not only break the seal." His lips quirk up. "It also gives its owner an advantage."

"I'm not following."

"The Sons of Tenebreis are dangerous, do not get me wrong. But they are not the *worst* danger in the universe. Eons ago, there were three types of beings created from the Source—of light, of darkness, and of nether. Seven beings of light, seven beings of darkness, and seven beings in between. They were the Primordial gods, and together, they created all mortals—of the human kind or the super-natural."

I listen to his words, entranced. I have never heard of anything like it, and for some reason, excitement unfurls in my chest the more he recounts about these ancient powers. For someone who's been consuming fantastical fiction from a young age, this is a dream come true!

"But conflict soon arose among the three factions of Primordials. Each wanted to control the mortals in a way, some for good, others for evil. The first war was started over the fate of mortals. It raged for millennia. All factions were equally matched in strength, so all the battles would end in a draw. That is until the light Primordials struck a deal with the nether Primordials to share power. And the only way for them to do so unbothered was by getting rid of the dark Primordials. Together, they created Tartarstasis, a prison realm that could hold the seven dark Primordials."

"Okay, and what happened next?" I ask eagerly.

"The Seven were trapped in Tartarstasis, and the fourteen Primordials created Aperion, a joint realm that would allow them to control the universe as they saw fit. And as a reactionary movement, the descendants of the Seven created Tartareia, a realm directly opposite to Aperion in every way and meant to continue the fight in the name of the Seven. Except... Something happened. No one knows why, but after some time, the Primordials simply disappeared. It was as if they washed their hands of the fate of the universe."

"What?" My eyes widen.

"But they left something behind." He smiles. "Fourteen artifacts that contain their essence—should the universe ever need their power again. And since the fourteen imprisoned the Seven with their essence, only their essence can free them once more."

"So while this artifact we're looking for can break the seal of Tartareia, the fourteen of them combined can open Tartarstasis? Do I have that right? And the Sons of Tenebreis want to release the Seven into the universe and control them?"

"Yes. That is the short version."

I stare at him wide-eyed.

"So who are the good guys?"

He chuckles.

"Are there *any* good guys? I doubt it."

"Of course you'd say that," I grumble. "You're a Son of Tenebreis. You're literally a descendant of the Seven."

"I never claimed to be a good guy."

"But…" I blink furiously, my mind trying to make sense of all of this. "Is that why you want the artifact? Because you want to free the Seven into the world? You want to…" I choke on my words. "You want to unleash those evil beings into the universe? And you want me to go along with that? Are you absolutely mad?"

He scoffs.

"Do not be so dramatic, dear. Unfortunately, my goals are not so lofty. I do not care about the Seven. But my brother does. And if I get the artifact first, that means *he* will not get it. The only reason I wish to return to Tartareia is to eliminate my brother once and for all."

"Why? Because he tried to kill you? I'm sure if you talked, maybe you could find some common ground. Why, maybe it was all a misunderstanding and—"

"You are far too innocent, Barbi." He laughs. "There will be no talking. There will only be blood spilled and screams of pain. It is the least he deserves after everything he's done to me."

"But you're still alive. It can't be that bad. Brothers shouldn't kill each other," I whisper softly.

"I may be alive. But Mo is not. And it is all because of him," he grits out, the color of his irises shifting to reflect his rage.

I freeze.

There it is, that name again.

Mo.

"Who…" I take a deep breath, unsure whether I am ready for his answer. "Who is Mo?"

He spares me a bored glance.

"The female who should have been my mate."

The words aren't spoken with malice or a hint of accusation. It's just an observation, and that makes it all the more painful to hear.

My heart slams against my ribcage as I stare at him. I gulp down against the wave of emotions threatening to spill over.

Pain strikes in my breast, leaving me gasping for air as I try to maintain my composure lest he sees how much those words affected me.

So Mo was a woman.

I suspected as much, but to have it confirmed feels like a thousand bullets have pierced my body all at once.

It's just a silly crush, Barbi! You'll get over it.

I try to convince myself of that, but the truth is, the more time I spend in his presence, the less it feels like a silly crush and more like…

My lips tremble as I stretch them in a nonchalant smile.

"So you're not gay?" I ask jokingly in an attempt to hide my hurt.

"No." A smile pulls at his lips.

"So when we get to Tartareia, someone should be able to help us sever our bond?"

He nods.

Hope blooms in my chest. I will nurture this crush until then and enjoy this adventure for however long it lasts. And when it's time to say goodbye… I will just have to be strong enough to be able to utter the words aloud.

"The elders should know what to do."

"Good. Then let's get this artifact! The faster we get it, the sooner we can go our separate ways."

"You are eager to get rid of me now?" He raises an amused brow.

I smile as I flutter my lashes.

"I might have liked you a tiny bit before I realized you

would condemn the universe to a wretched fate just to get revenge against your brother. Now…" I shake my head.

"It is better we reach an understanding before we move forward," he starts in a stern voice. "My only purpose is to avenge Mo. I do not care about the world or what happens after I have killed my brother." He pauses, his gaze finding mine. "I am not a good person, Barbi, nor do I desire to be one."

Lucky you, Mo. Nykander would literally bring about the apocalypse for you. Maybe it's a tad bit extreme, but I can't deny that the romantic in me is ready to swoon at his declaration.

The rational part of me, though?

Dear Lord, I got accidentally mated to a goddamn psycho!

"Oh, don't worry about me." I wave my hand around dismissively. "I'll just tag along until we break our bond and then we'll never see each other again," I quip happily, though the pretense is costly.

Why does my chest feel so tight?

Why does it feel as if I swallowed pieces of broken glass, the sharp edges stuck in my throat, clogging it and making it bleed until I'm overflowing with blood on the inside?

I do not have an answer for why I feel that way, but I fear I may know the cause.

It is a plague. The most widespread plague.

And I have finally caught it.

Unfortunately, my demise will not be swift. It will be slow and torturous, each minute creating a new wound on my poor heart.

"Right," he mutters, his eyes narrowed at me.

I force my smile to be wider, happier.

"What's next then? Where are we going?"

A pensive look descends on his face as he releases a deep breath.

"I have a clue. But I have yet to figure out what it means."

"So what's the clue? Maybe I can help."

He gives me a pointed look that says *as if*. But he shares it anyway.

"All I got is a riddle, but I cannot seem to solve it. It goes as follows: *the vinerelle will lead the way east of the Gyral Mountains*. We are in the Gyral Mountains. But I do not know what *vinerelle* is supposed to mean," he adds in a gruff voice.

I stare at him in wonder.

"You don't?" I ask in surprise. "How long did you say you have been in Akkaya?"

"Some thousand years," he grumbles.

"And you don't know? How can you *not* know?" I squeak.

He narrows his eyes at me.

"What are you talking about?"

"Give me a piece of paper and something to write with," I tell him.

He doesn't move as he regards me skeptically.

"Come on! Do it!"

Shaking his head at me, he disappears for a second before he returns with a piece of paper and a pencil. He hands them to me and I get to work.

My drawing skills might not be the best, but they get the job done.

"Here," I say as I thrust the paper in front of him. "This is a vinerelle. I can't believe you would not know this, Nykander. It's the ancient emblem of Akkaya."

On the paper, I drew a white and pink flower with a long, thorny stem. Not only do the thorns hurt anyone who dares to pluck it from its home, but the petals are poisonous to everyone, human or mage alike. The books had spoken at length about its history. Because it was such a wild and untamable flower, it had been left unbothered. No one dared touch it, so it had grown in an odd pattern across Akkaya—almost as if it had a mind of its own. The vinerelle is so important in the history of Akkaya that a special edition of the hardbacks had been commissioned with an illustrated vinerelle on the cover.

I, of course, own all of them. I had to pay a pretty penny for them, considering only a limited number of sets were printed.

"No, it is not. There is no such thing as the ancient emblem of Akkaya." He immediately dismisses my drawing.

"Yes, it is! You've lived here for so long and you don't know this? It's like the heart of Akkaya! While every other flower and plant has been used in spells and rituals throughout the years, the vinerelle alone has been left unbothered."

He tilts his head, regarding me with a raised brow.

"And how would you know that? You have been here for a few days only."

"Because… Erm…" How do I explain where my knowledge of Akkaya comes from? Especially since most of it has proven to be rather…false. "In my world, there is a series of books revolving around Akkaya. I know everything by heart and I'm telling you, the vinerelle is a flower. This flower." I point to the piece of paper.

Maybe I shouldn't be so overly confident considering this might very well be another false piece of information. But my gut tells me it's not. This is it. This is his damn clue.

He doesn't speak as he considers my words.

"A book series centered around Akkaya?"

"It's how I know about Damien and Jocelyn, and Kuma and the other mages. It's how I know about everything here. Well, *almost* everything. But I swear the books are real, and this is vinerelle."

Once more, silence descends between us as he stares thoughtfully at my drawing.

"I suppose we could look for this flower," he eventually says.

"Yes. Good call, my friend. See, I am not useless after all," I say as I get closer to him and flutter my lashes.

His only reaction is a roll of his eyes before he takes BonBon in his arms. My brows shoot up in surprise as he motions for me to get PomPom so we can embark on our journey. He must have realized walking too much is strenuous on their tiny bodies and they need to be carried.

Before I can help myself, a huge smile spreads across my face.

He might be bringing about the apocalypse, but he's nice to dogs!

A dreamy sigh escapes me as I hurry to follow after him.

We head east and we keep our eyes open for vinerelle. Fortunately, it's not long before we spot it. Almost like a path, the cluster of flowers leads us uphill into the mountain. There is no walking path, and we do our best to avoid coming into contact with the poisonous petals.

Almost like they had been intentionally planted, the flowers lead farther into a thick forest. The canopy blocks the sunlight. Tall trees surround us from all sides, all covered in thick vines that curl around the branches, some drooping low and creating a swinging haven for the many tree-dwelling creatures. Some monkeys swing from tree to tree, taking great interest in us as they spot us encroaching on their territory.

PomPom, not used to having her authority questioned as the only cute and tiny creature around—save for BonBon, but love does wonders—starts barking incessantly at them.

A couple of monkeys congregate in the tree right above us, watching us with great interest.

"Nykander! Look how cute they are!" Their tails are intertwined, their bodies forming a heart, making the romantic in me swoon. The two monkeys have brown, luxurious fur, their little faces so cute and cuddly.

PomPom, sensing my appreciation for them, lets me know that she will not allow anyone to replace her in my affections as she barks at me.

"Easy, baby. You're still my favorite girl," I coo as I kiss the top of her hair.

Nykander shakes his head at me, and without sparing a glance at the monkeys, he walks ahead. Too bad PomPom is not the only one with attention issues. The monkeys, seeing that Nykander ignores them, decide to teach him a lesson. Something falls from the tree and lands on top of his head.

"What…" He blinks as he brings his hand to his hair, feeling for the object.

My lips tremble with laughter as I watch him scoop a small piece of poop from his hair. And once he realizes that the monkey must have pooped on him, his expression turns thunderous, while mine breaks into laughter.

"Oh my, Nykander!"

The monkeys express their excitement as they jump around and squeal. But just as I'm about to make more fun of Nykander—he deserves it after being such a grump—another little clump of poop falls from the trees.

This time, on my head.

Seeing this, Nykander throws his head back and laughs as he points at me.

I give him my best deadly glare as I take out the little poop and throw it to the ground.

"You…" I point to the monkeys. "I thought we were friends!"

They don't respond to my words, merely releasing more noises that sound an awful lot like laughing.

"Not every creature is your friend, Barbi," Nykander murmurs in amusement.

I walk past him.

"And now we shall move on. We need to get to that artifact, no?" I mutter under my breath.

We continue our journey, following the flowers for another hour or so before Nykander suddenly stops.

"Do you feel this?" He looks around, his nostrils flaring.

"What?" I ask, worried we might be set upon by more demons, or God forbid, more monkeys.

He sets BonBon down and comes closer.

My heart flutters as he stops in front of me. He lowers his head, his breath fanning my cheek.

Breathe, Barbi, breathe!

"What? What is it?" I stammer.

"What is this smell?" He feigns ignorance as he sniffs my hair.

My mouth drops open in shock as I realize what he's doing. The wretched man!

"Oh, do be quiet. If I smell of poop, you do too," I tell him pointedly, hitting him lightly.

"So? I do not mind it. I have smelled far worse. But you…" His eyes crinkle with amusement.

"I what?"

"You strike me as a spoiled little girl who has been pampered her entire life. I doubt you have experienced much hardship." He smirks.

"I will have you know back home I scoop PomPom's poop every time we go out. I am not a stranger to poop!"

"Is that so?" he drawls.

"It is *exactly* so. I've had her since she was a little babe. I trained her how to go potty and there's been quite a few times she's had an accident while we were home. Once even on my lap. Poop does not scare me!"

"Understood. You are a poop master."

"What—" I stare at him in shock for a moment before I realize he's just making fun of me.

Nykander is making fun of me instead of scowling at me.

My lashes flutter, emulating the beats of my heart.

A deep blush stains my cheeks as I avert my gaze.

"I was joking, Barbi." He chuckles. "You are surprisingly easy to rile up."

"Well…" I wet my lips. "I suppose being a poop master is better than being a master of nothing," I murmur, my lips quirking up.

He shares the smile, and for a moment, we just gaze at each other.

Did it suddenly get warm in here? I fan my face with my hand.

BonBon's bark breaks the spell as he begs Nykander to swoop him in his arms.

And so we continue our journey.

Yet that moment becomes a precious memory that I tuck away in that part of my brain that will likely never forget him.

As it gets dark, we come across a dead end. The path of the flowers suddenly stops, but there is nothing else around us except an open field.

Nykander's lips snarl in disapproval as he looks around.

"Maybe we missed a path?" I offer.

He grunts.

PomPom struggles in my arms, releasing a loud bark as she jumps to the ground, running around us in a circle. BonBon does, too, and at first, I think they just want to play since they've been in our arms for too long.

A blinding light appears in front of us, making me stumble back.

Nykander is behind me, his arms coming around me so I don't fall.

I don't even get to romanticize the gesture in my mind as four men appear in front of us. They're fully garbed in armor, with two or more weapons sheathed at each of their waists.

"W-what…"

"Welcome to The Sanctuary." One of the men takes a step forward to address us. "My name is Elijah and I am the head guard. What is your purpose for coming here?"

Nykander's cheek twitches as he scans the men from head to toe.

"We're here to meet the High Priestess," I reply.

Elijah nods thoughtfully.

"The Sanctuary is closed to outsiders. You may only enter inside if you have the blessing of the High Priestess."

"And how are we to get it if we can't meet her?" I ask.

He smiles.

"Stay by my side, Barbi," Nykander whispers.

"If you have the blessing of the High Priestess, you will be able to correctly answer three questions. If you answer correctly, you may proceed inside. If you answer incorrectly, you will be turned away and the location of the Sanctuary will change so that you may not find it again."

"What are the questions?" Nykander demands.

"The first question." Another man steps forward as he speaks. "What is long, hard, and covered in ridges?"

My eyes widen at the question.

Nykander tenses by my side.

"I know!" I blurt out.

"Barbi…" he calls my name in a warning tone. "This is not the time for your dirty thoughts."

"What?" I frown at him. "*You* are the one with the dirty thoughts. I happen to know the answer to the question."

"I will have the answer, female," the man speaks.

I clear my throat.

"The *loza*."

Nykander's hand tightens over my arm.

"That is correct." With a nod, the man steps back, and the second man comes forward.

"What is the middle, the beginning, and the end?"

"The river Mazu," I answer immediately.

"That is correct."

"Yes!" I jump up in excitement.

Nykander turns to me, his expression one of shock.

The third man steps forward for the last question.

"What is the way of the soul?"

"P'asala!" I say eagerly.

"That is correct."

"Oh my! I did it, Nykander! See, I am not useless," I cry out, jumping up and down around him. PomPom and BonBon emulate my movements until we're all circling around Nykander, dancing and squealing with joy.

He's frozen on the spot—perhaps unable to believe that *I* got all of them right. Yet how could I not when they were the same questions Lady Jocelyn got on her initiation as a mage in the books? At least some things are not too different from the books and I can't contain my excitement.

The man retreats, leaving Elijah to address us once more.

"Well done." He inclines his head. "Please, welcome to the Sanctuary." He extends his arm, and a portal appears.

We grab the dogs and walk inside the portal, and in no time, we find ourselves in a different time and space.

The village is full of life, with kids running around and people going about their days. It's almost as if we're in a different world altogether—one that's not plagued by disease or strife.

"When can we meet the High Priestess?" Nykander turns to Elijah to ask.

"The High Priestess will call on you when she is ready to receive you. Until then, please make yourselves at home. My lieutenant will see you to your accommodation," he explains as he introduces us to Jeya, his lieutenant. And with that, the other men disappear from sight.

Nykander makes a sound of disapproval, but he doesn't probe further, probably realizing that we are mere guests in the Sanctuary.

As we walk deeper into the village, the locals glance at us with curiosity, all stopping what they're doing to stare at us.

"I guess you don't get too many newcomers," I joke to Jeya.

"Indeed. We have not had a newcomer in thousands of years."

"Oh," I murmur, surprised.

Nykander is for some reason grumpier than before as he places himself between Jeya and me and gives the poor man a deadly look. His chest rumbles with an unspoken warning, and I have to elbow him to get him to behave.

"Right." Jeya clears his throat. "This is the village plaza, where all the events take place. Over there is the healer's hut. And this way is—"

"And the High Priestess?" Nykander interrupts him.

"She resides in the valley. But it is prohibited to go there without being called upon first."

"Nykander, be nice," I hiss at him. These people have been so polite and he's being rude.

He glares at me and continues to sulk in that manly, too handsome for his own good way of his.

Jeya continues to tell us more about the village, but I only listen with half an ear as I stare at Nykander's handsome profile. My, but he would be the perfect model for a romance cover. I would buy all the copies in the world and stare at him all day. And if the story in the book had two protagonists named Barbi and Nykander, even better. I could read *and* stare at him while imagining our happily ever after.

"Here it is. Your accommodation. Please make use of our facilities and consider the village your home for the time being."

Jeya opens the door to a small cabin and invites us to step inside, after which he takes his leave.

The door closes behind us with a thud and we're suddenly alone—plus the dogs.

All I can do is stare at the small space that only has one bed, a desk, two chairs, and a small shelf with a few books. In the back, there is an even smaller toilet and washing basin. There isn't even a shower!

Yet that's not the most glaring thing.

"Nykander… There is only one bed," I mutter in shock as I point toward the bed. It's small, too. "Oh my God!"

All the scenarios I've read about flash into my head and my heart starts beating uncontrollably fast.

"Yes, so?" he asks in a bored tone as he puts down BonBon and his bag with our supplies.

"There is *only one* bed, Nykander. Don't you know what that means?"

He frowns, staring at me as if I've grown two heads. "No?"

"Oh my God!" I burst out. PomPom jumps out of my arms, joining BonBon on the floor, while I run around the small room, squeaking in excitement. "It's just like in the books. There is only one bed and we will have to squeeze in it together, which *will* be a tight squeeze since you are not exactly small. But we will then cuddle and—"

"You can take the bed. I will take the floor," he interrupts, squashing all my dreams.

"What?"

"I do not…cuddle," he states in a firm tone.

My excitement deflates. "But—"

"There will be no cuddling, Barbi." He sighs.

"But what if I am cold at night?" I ask, turning to him and making puppy eyes.

"PomPom can warm you up. And if she's not enough, BonBon can join you, too."

"But what if that's not enough either? Will you let me freeze to death?"

He stares at me.

"I do not cuddle," he repeats in a deadpan voice.

I pout.

That's when he shakes his head and turns his back to me.

Damn you, romance novels! You've skewed my standards for love. Finally, I have the opportunity to experience the one-bed trope, and my not-quite-love-interest vehemently disavows cuddling.

Maybe he thinks cuddling will make him less villainous?

"You know, cuddling will not decrease your villainous reputation. Besides, my lips are sealed. I won't tell if you won't," I tell him, motioning with two fingers across my lips to let him know I will keep his secret.

"Barbi," he groans.

"Fine, Mr. Grumpy Pants. I will cuddle with my dogs and you will *not* be invited. Not even if you are cold. You can freeze to death for all I care, you cuddle-adverse demon!" I say as I stomp to the bed, pulling my dogs next to me and giving him the cold shoulder treatment.

"I will take my chances," his amused voice echoes.

16

I wake up in the middle of the night. The room is dark and foreign, and for a moment, panic swells in my breast. I immediately reach for my baby, but the place next to me is empty.

"PomPom?" I ask in a low voice.

She doesn't answer me. BonBon doesn't either.

I strain to look around the room. Nykander is not here either. He'd gone to sleep on the floor as he declared, but the blankets where he slept are an empty mess.

Where did he go? Where did the dogs go?

I swing my legs over the bed, carefully making my way around the cabin without hitting anything. But I don't need to go outside to search for them. Not when the small window leads directly to a backyard where Nykander is hanging out with the dogs.

"No. It is not the time to play around, PomPom," he says in a low voice as he waves his finger at PomPom. She runs around him excitedly while BonBon is going potty a small distance away. "Come on. It is your turn, PomPom," he instructs her, but she doesn't seem to listen.

BonBon finishes his business and joins her as they both run around him. I expect him to get annoyed. PomPom doesn't listen to anyone but me. Yet as I silently continue to watch them, Nykander drops to his knees to pet the two dogs. A genuine smile appears on his face as he tentatively tries to play with them.

The dim light from the moon illuminates his face and makes my heart still in my chest.

The dogs jump on him at the same time, making him lose his balance and fall on his back. His laughter fills my ears as he lets them lick him and sniff his face. Every now and then he encourages them, giving them a light pat or scratching their bellies.

Eventually, with enough coaxing, he gets PomPom to potty, all the while giving her words of praise.

"That's a good girl," he murmurs, scratching her behind her ears. BonBon jumps around, wanting to be praised too, so Nykander gives him attention and calls him a good boy.

Moisture clings to my lashes as I stare at them.

I want to be a good girl too—*his* good girl.

Damn it. Why does he have to be so awfully attractive? And why is he so kind to my dogs, making my heart leap in my chest at the smallest interaction?

Once the dogs have done their business, he takes them back to the cabin.

When he opens the door, he doesn't seem surprised to see me—of course he doesn't. He has super hearing.

He gives me a tentative smile. "They wanted to go out."

"You should have woken me up."

He shakes his head. "You were sleeping."

That's all he says as he resumes his place between the covers on the floor, but somehow it's enough to make me ache like crazy for the same attention my dogs got.

Isn't that pathetic? I am now jealous of my dogs!

I muster a smile.

"Good night, then."

He grunts a reply, but it's clear he's not inclined to make conversation with me.

With a heavy heart, I join my babies on the bed and will myself to sleep. Mentally, I count down the days until we can get that artifact and find someone to break our bond. Because until then…I fear my heart is in too much danger in his presence.

The following day, we wake up in the morning and make our way to the village. Jeya appears by our side and tells us the village works as a commune, which means that everyone must participate in an activity. Every morning, there is an event called the *drawing*, in which every member of the commune draws a ticket that lists an activity. Since Nykander and I are considered a pair, we only get one draw.

Nykander mutters something under his breath about meeting the High Priestess sooner, which I would normally agree with, but in this instance, I don't want us to be seen as ungrateful or rude.

I elbow him and tell him to cut it out while I plaster a smile on my face for Jeya. Alas, that seems to get Nykander even *more* rude.

"I know you have been imprisoned for a long time, but you need to mind your manners. These people have graciously allowed us to stay here. You won't help our cause by being rude."

He glares at me.

I roll my eyes.

"We are here to speak with the High Priestess, not engage in frivolous activities," he declares, rather loudly.

People stop what they're doing to stare at him, some even muttering a few admonishments under their breaths.

"You do realize that by being a boor you won't get the

High Priestess's favor. You *need* her to tell you where the artifact is."

A mutinous expression appears on Nykander's face.

"I know you don't want to do this. I don't either. I mean, there's nothing in it for me except getting rid of this bond faster."

"Fine," he grumbles.

The entire village is gathered together in front of a bucket holding a multitude of pieces of paper. Families and couples form one group while children over the age of twelve are on their own. One by one, they go and pick one, which designates their activity for the day. Since Nykander doesn't seem inclined to play by their rules, I head forward and stick my hand in the bucket, rummaging through the pieces of paper and drawing one.

I read the text.

"We are on laundry duty," I tell Nykander.

He scoffs.

Jeya appears by my side as he peeks at my note.

"I will show you to the laundry room to pick up the garments."

"You don't have washing machines by any chance?" I ask as he leads us to one of the main buildings in the village.

"What?" He frowns.

"Yeah, I figured," I mutter. "So how are we supposed to wash them?"

"By hand, of course. The river is at the edge of the village. Since this is a daily task, there will not be that many clothes to wash. Do not worry," he assures me.

"Not so happy about this now, are you?" Nykander murmurs in amusement as he sees me scowl.

"I can wash by hand," I fire back at him. "Can you?" I raise a brow at him. "*Without* using your powers."

His eyes narrow at me.

"Are you sure you want to turn this into a competition?"

"Bring it on, oh Dark One," I mock him.

"It is on," he declares confidently as he crosses his arms across his chest.

"You need to be done by noon," Jeya tells us as we enter the laundry room. He gives us a few instructions before he leaves to take care of his own tasks.

Nykander and I stare at all the clothes we have to wash. Jeya said there wouldn't be much, but this room is full from floor to ceiling with dirty clothes.

But just as we think we're going to have our work cut out for us, more villagers come to the laundry room to deposit their dirty clothes. One after another, it's almost like the entire village suddenly decided they have clothes in need of washing.

"They did this on purpose, didn't they?" I mutter numbly.

Nykander purses his lips and nods.

"Maybe I can allow for your abilities just once—to transport the clothes to the river."

He slowly turns to look at me, his brow raised, his lips curved in a lopsided smile.

"We shall have to locate the river first. I will then bring all the items."

For the first journey, we both get an armful of clothes as we traverse the village. PomPom and BonBon are following behind, getting the first dose of exercise of the day.

Despite the fact that it feels as if the villagers had purposefully given us a heavy workload, everyone is hard at work. There are people cooking, cleaning, and tending to small children. Every task required for the optimal working of the village is accounted for, and I can't help but admire how well they do it.

"Where do you think these people are from?" I ask Nykander as we pass around families doing their tasks together.

He shakes his head.

"I am not sure. But most people here have abilities."

I frown.

"What do you mean?"

"I can feel the energy simmering around. It is strong and heavy, but it does not come from one individual in particular, which leads me to believe it is the energy of the collective."

"Oh. I wonder why they would choose to live so cut off from the world."

His smile turns sad.

"Because it might be the only way they can be at peace," he says. I glance at him curiously as I wait for him to continue. "I have traveled to many worlds since I left Tartareia seven thousand years ago. And while some realms celebrate those who exhibit strong spiritual energy and extraordinary abilities, most do not. The number of human mortals far outweighs the number of supernatural ones, and that establishes a norm within a population. To deviate from that norm means to be ostracized. Sometimes hunted…killed. The world is not a safe place when you are different."

"But why is the number of supernaturals so low? Wouldn't it be the reverse? I would assume that humans can die far more easily than supernaturals, no? That would decrease their numbers while those of supernaturals would keep on climbing."

"In theory, yes." He nods pensively. "But there are those factors I mentioned. Supernaturals are hunted, sometimes even seen as prizes. But that is not the only reason for their scarcity. It is also the fact that the stronger the spiritual energy of a species, the lower the birth rate. For example, my kind is considered mature at three thousand years old. It is very rare for a female to bear a second child before the first one has reached at least one thousand years old."

I stare at him in wonder.

"Wow. That is so interesting. I guess it's similar to apes in my world," I mention thoughtfully. "Gorillas are endangered because of their low birth rates. They only bear one child at a time and it is very rare to have a second one before the first is weaned. And because humans keep encroaching on their territories, they are now susceptible to some of our diseases too."

"Yes." He nods. "That is, indeed, a good analogy. I have noticed this in the realms I have visited, too. Some diseases that were previously only encountered in humans have now spread to supernaturals, too. But due to a different biology, the effects are far more dire," he adds. "It makes me wonder how the plague in Akkaya manifests in humans and supernaturals alike."

"I can't say about supernaturals, but I saw how it manifested in humans. It was grotesque." A shiver goes down my back as I remember the first time I came face-to-face with death. I recount my experience and what I witnessed in the village the soldiers burned down.

He listens thoughtfully to my explanation, and before I know it, we have reached the river.

"This is…beautiful," I whisper as I take in the landscape.

The water of the river is a see-through crystalline blue. A few feet away, there is a waterfall coming from the mountain that feeds into the river, the water splashing onto the river bank.

I drop the load of clothes to the ground as I dash toward the water, taking off my slippers as I run. Plopping myself on the lush grass, I dip my fingers into the cold water and release a loud squeak of excitement.

"Come try it, Nykander! It's so cool and refreshing!"

He regards me with an amused expression as he shakes his head. Instead, he drops his load to the ground before he teleports to the laundry room to bring the remaining clothes. PomPom and BonBon run around and play, and it seems I won't have to worry about them for the time being—except watching to make sure they don't eat some weird plant.

It takes Nykander a couple of trips to get everything.

What's even worse is that these people don't even have liquid soap. They only have a lye-based solid soap that people in my world used long ago—and some might still use in the countryside. But that means we will have to scrub the clothes by hand with the soap.

My expression falls as I look at the mountain of clothes. It will take us the entire day! Maybe more!

As Nykander comes toward me, I look up at him, batting my lashes.

"Can't you use your powers and you know, do some magic?"

He chuckles.

"We convened I would not use my powers."

"That was before I saw how many clothes there were! We're never going to finish this!"

"Then we might as well start."

He surprises me when he unbuttons his shirt and throws it aside. His naked torso greets my eyes, our bonding mark there in the open for anyone to see. Somehow, knowing that I have a claim on him—a visible one—makes my insides all restless. I cannot wrench my eyes away from his hard chest and even harder abs.

"Barbi!" Nykander calls my name, shaking me from my reverie.

"W-what?" I stumble over my words as I bring my hand to my mouth, wiping it. I'm pretty sure I was drooling. And the devil knows it, going by his smirk.

"Get to work." He winks at me.

Stooping down, he folds his pants to his knees. He grabs an armful of clothes and places them on the bank next to him before he steps into the river. He visibly shudders at the contact with the cold water, but he wastes no time in starting on his task. The soap is in his right hand while he holds the garments in his left one, scrubbing intently.

I'm still frozen to the spot, unable to look away from him.

Minutes pass and the sunlight shines on his skin. Drops of water splash onto his torso, slowly dripping down his hard abs.

I bite my lip.

What I wouldn't give to be one of those drops. She's so lucky, damn her!

"Barbi, I am almost done with my first load and you have not even started," he mentions, once more catching me staring.

My cheeks heat up and I feel like the biggest fool.

"Right. I'll get to it now," I mumble.

My dress is long, but I can't roll it up like Nykander did with his pants. Instead, I knot a corner and make it shorter. Grabbing an armful of clothes, I place them next to me and get to work.

By the time I'm halfway through my load, Nykander is already done with his and moving to the next.

I grumble something under my breath and push myself harder. My competitive side rears its ugly head as I see the ease with which Nykander washes the clothes while I'm out of breath after one scrub and a half.

I narrow my eyes at him.

"You are cheating. You're using your powers, aren't you?"

He turns to me, a bored look on his face. He gazes at the load I've done so far and sniggers.

"You wanted a competition."

Then he's back to work.

My nostrils flare as I think of all the possible ways I can catch up to him. I glance back at the remaining clothes and an idea comes into my mind. Well, it might not be a *great* idea, but it is an idea.

I unknot my dress and step farther into the river until the water reaches past my knees. I fold the skirt around the corners into a makeshift basin and let water creep inside. Taking all the clothes, I plop them inside my skirt and I add soap, spending a few minutes scrubbing it against the material.

The water in my skirt is all soapy and it helps to wash all the clothes at once.

This speeds up my process and my excitement soars as I get my first load done. I quickly go on to the next.

Nykander looks at me, his lips quirking up in amusement.

"You are inventive, I will give you that."

"Of course," I huff, scrubbing some more. "I will *not* lose."

"I did not realize you had such a competitive streak, Barbi," he mentions, his eyes twinkling.

The light hits his eyes at the perfect angle to emphasize that beautiful shade of gray.

Thump. Thump. Thump.

Damn my treacherous heart! Why does it have to be so weak in front of a pair of beautiful eyes?

"Why enter a competition at all if not to win?" I raise a brow at him as I try to divert my attention from his other-worldly appeal.

"Some might say the journey in itself is worth it."

"I don't see how washing clothes might be a worthy endeavor," I grumble.

"Because patience is not your strongest suit, is it, Barbi?"

"Well… I suppose so," I mutter under my breath.

He smiles, and we're both silent for a moment before he speaks again.

"How did you know the answer to those riddles?" His voice is no longer playful or teasing, a dangerous gleam entering his gaze as he stops what he's doing and turns to me.

"The same way I knew about the flower. From my books."

"Those books again?" He frowns.

"Maybe now you will believe me. I really did read books about Akkaya and they contained all those riddles, together with the answers. It was all part of the lore of Akkaya. The *loza* is an ancient traditional Akkayan weapon. Mazu is the mythological river that surrounds the whole of Akkaya, and P'asala is—"

"The intermediary realm all souls cross to reach the afterlife."

"You know about that?" I blink.

"I did not know about the first two, nor have I ever heard about them, which is odd considering I have been in Akkaya for long enough to know its entire history. As far as P'asala goes, that is the intermediary realm under the control of Aperion. It is a long road all souls must cross before their merits are weighed and they are sent to the appropriate level of the House of Psyche in Aperion."

"What?" I blurt out. Either I am dumb or he's speaking in terms I've never heard about. "I did not understand anything of what you were saying."

"Your concept of hell and heaven. The House of Psyche houses levels that would technically qualify as your understanding of heaven or hell."

"Oh." I nod. "But why would hell belong to Aperion? Shouldn't it be in Tartareia? After all, you said the Sons of Tenebreis were the descendants of the Seven Primordial dark gods."

Nykander smiles.

"You're clever."

My eyes widen at his compliment just as a deep blush stains my cheeks.

"Oh, thank you—"

"That was the initial design of the afterlife according to the treaty between the light, nether, and dark gods. There was heaven, where the souls of good mortals went; purgatory, where the stained souls went, and lastly there was hell, where sinful souls went. Each one of the Primordial triad had control over one. But after the war, the light and nether gods fully took control of the afterlife. Tartareia was built in response to that. While Aperion is, indeed, the most common destination for souls, it is not the only one. The Sons of Tenebreis search for corrupted souls and turn them into their thralls before Aperion can send their messengers after them."

"You mean you turn them into demons."

"Correct." He nods.

"Have you ever turned a soul into a demon?"

He shakes his head ruefully.

"I was not concerned with it. I had my *kiyrayà* and my vocation. That was enough for me."

My brows furrow at the foreign term. But I have one more pressing curiosity.

"How come you were not in Tartareia when it got sealed off?"

His body freezes. A look of pure horror descends upon his face before he averts his gaze.

"Perhaps it was a blessing that I was not present," he murmurs, his voice far away.

I take note of his body language and I don't probe more. It seems to be a painful memory, perhaps because he was separated from his family for thousands of years—well, except his awful brother, whom PomPom, BonBon, and I have decided that we don't like.

"Tell me more about those books of yours. It is intriguing that stories about Akkaya would reach your world," he adds thoughtfully.

"No one knows who the author is. They've chosen to publish the books anonymously. But they are super popular. Even more popular than Naruto and that says something since it was a global phenomenon." I lean in closer to whisper, "Don't tell anyone, but I did have a Naruto phase, too. I imagined myself as Sakura, of course, since she eventually ends up with Sasuke and he was the hottest illustrated character to ever grace my world." My mouth widens in an O. "Sorry for the spoiler."

Nykander looks thoroughly confused.

"But that was around a decade ago." I wave my hand.

"Since I first read the books on Akkaya, I became an immediate fan. I've been attending conventions and I even lead a discord based on the mage system in Akkaya where we do more role-play," I explain. I don't, however, tell him about the fact that Lady Jocelyn and Sir Damien were the main characters since I am still nursing the wound of finding out just how foul they are in real life. He doesn't need to know that Lady Jocelyn has been my role model my entire life, or that I modeled everything after her.

As soon as the thought crosses my mind, I berate myself again for being so foolish as to make a fictional character my entire personality. Yet despite what I know now, fictional Jocelyn did help me get through some rough patches in my life. She was there when no one else was.

"I see." He nods.

"Yes! It's the best book series! If you ever come to my world, I'll lend you my special editions to read. You should be honored, you know. I've never lent those babies to anyone, but for you, I will make an exception."

His lips tip into a smile.

"But only for you…" I trail off.

In my excitement to tell him all about my favorite book series, some garments escaped from the makeshift net I'd made with my skirt. I startle as I see them being carried away by the river, and before I can think it through, I throw myself after them, losing the others too.

"Barbi!" Nykander calls out after me.

But as I step farther into the river, my foot catches on a rock and I trip forward. But as I try to find my footing again, I realize there's a steep incline and the water is much deeper.

I fall, water flooding my mouth and nose.

But before I can panic, strong arms lift me up.

I splutter as I draw a deep breath into my lungs.

Nykander holds me in his arms, pulling me out of the water and onto the shore.

"You mad, mad creature," he mutters as he lays me on the grass.

I am drenched from head to toe. Moisture clings to my lashes, some of it dripping down my face and neck. Yet all I can do is stare at the handsome face above me. He blocks the sun with his body, looming over me.

I gulp down as I watch drops of water dance on his skin, hypnotizing me with their odd movements as they traverse those hard and delicious planes. My tongue peeks out to lick my lips.

"Are you all right, Barbi?" he asks, a hint of worry in his voice.

It takes me a moment to get my bearings together and meet his concerned gaze.

My lips strain into a smile that quickly dies as I note the grave look on his face.

He's staring at me intently, his pupils growing in size as his fangs elongate, pricking his bottom lip and causing drops of blood to fall onto my body.

"I am fine. Just a small accident." I make light of the situation.

But he doesn't reply.

His Adam's apple bobs up and down as he bites his lip hard, more blood pouring out of the new wound.

"Nykander?" I whisper.

His gaze is fixed on me, or rather, on a point on my body. I look down, following the path of his eyes, and a gasp leaves my lips as I realize what he's looking at.

My light pink dress is completely drenched. The material is a thin cotton that has become see-through.

And I'm not wearing a bra.

My nipples are hard from the coldness of the water, and they're poking through the material, leaving nothing to the imagination.

He still has not said a word, nor has he looked away from

my rather nude form. And it's not just his fangs that are having a reaction to my breasts. Eyes wide, my mouth forms a shocked *O* as I stare at the dent in his pants. They are entirely wet, clinging to his muscular legs and emphasizing the outline of his hardness.

Oh my!

That is quite…something. A big something.

I nibble at my lips as I continue to shamelessly stare at that part of him, committing it to memory.

I've watched porn. Who hasn't? But those men weren't quite as…gifted as him in that department. And supposedly porn stars are quite well-endowed. I mean, it's a requirement for the job, no?

And if he's bigger than a porn star… Just how big is he?

I lean forward, trying to get a better look and gauge his size—for research purposes, of course. And for my dreams. Girls have wet dreams too, after all. They're just a little more…romantic? And dirty. Let's be honest. My dreams about Nykander have been dirty as hell. The amount of times he told me what a good girl I am while he's deep inside me, claiming me fully and branding me as his…

I sigh.

In my dreams only.

Unfortunately, in real life, he only tells my dog what a good girl she is.

Up close, I can make out the outline of his shaft. It's thick. I glance at my forearm. Good Lord! Those old-school romances were right! It is the size of my forearm.

A shiver of alarm goes through me.

You're a big girl, Barbi. You can take it.

The pep talk is rather useless, though, since I doubt that would happen—he's made it clear that there will be no skinship between us. But that monster in his pants certainly has other plans.

I slowly drag my gaze up, meeting his hungry one.

We stare at each other, both unmoving.

My breathing grows labored as I see the signs of desire become more pronounced on his features. He's breathing equally hard.

He leans forward, and the intensity in his gaze should scare me. The darkness of his pupils eclipse his light irises, lust and longing echoing in those beautiful depths.

He's close. So close.

His hand moves from my shoulder to my neck, then slowly descending down my collarbone until he reaches the valley of my breasts. His touch is intoxicating, so much so, my mind becomes a blank mess. He's the only thing I see. The only thing I feel. The only thing that matters right now.

He spreads his big palm over my breasts, the breadth of it almost covering my chest.

My heart thunders against my ribcage, seizing this moment as she wants to make herself known and show him just how fast she can beat. She wants him to know how hard at work she is, pumping my blood and getting me ready for him to sink his teeth into me.

Taste me.

Consume me.

Get drunk on me and let me get drunk on him in return.

His breath fans my face, a cool breeze that makes me shiver with want.

I lick my lips. This is it. Oh, God! This is it. The moment I have waited for all my life.

My *first kiss.*

My eyes squeeze shut as I pucker my lips, waiting for that magical moment when his lips will touch mine and fireworks will explode.

I wait.

And I wait.

But as I slowly open my eyes, I realize he's no longer on top of me.

He's a distance away, scrubbing his face with his hands as he mutters a string of curses.

"Nykander?" I tentatively call out his name.

"Do not come closer, Barbi!" he grits out, his tone harsh and full of anguish.

"Are you all right?"

"Stop!" He puts his hand up, but he doesn't look at me. He keeps his eyes closed. His chest expands as he drags a long breath into his lungs.

Bringing his hand to his mouth, he bites into it.

Hard.

He's feeding on his own blood.

Worry flutters in my chest and I take a step forward.

"I can give you blood. Here," I say, extending my arm.

"Do. Not," he rasps.

"But—"

"Blood is not the only thing I will take, Barbi. Stay. Back."

Confusion swirls inside my mind as I watch him struggle with himself. Yet as the seconds trickle by, it seems the animal within is winning over the man.

He swivels.

His eyes are wholly black, his fangs long and daunting.

Blood dribbles down his chin as he comes toward me.

And if it's possible, he's even harder than before…

"Barbi…" he groans, as if with each step he takes, his pain intensifies.

I open myself wider to him, tilting my head and offering him my neck.

His eyes flash with desire. So much desire I want to drown in it and never resurface again. But I want him to drown with me. Because my own eyes echo the same desire. So much so, it burns my insides until I become a slave to these foreign and all-encompassing sensations.

Only a few steps separate us. A few steps, but they feel like worlds apart.

"Come," I whisper, beckoning him to me.

He stares at me hungrily. He's like a ravenous wild bear coming out of hibernation.

"Come to me," I whisper again.

He grinds his jaw, his fists clenching by his sides.

"Fuck," he curses before teleporting himself out of sight.

17

"Here, taste it," I say as I scoop a spoonful of the stew I made.

Nykander leans forward, opening his mouth and wrapping his lips around the spoon.

I do my best to remain unaffected, though it's been harder and harder to do, considering we are together every waking hour of the day—and we sleep in the same small cabin, despite him continuously choosing the floor.

It's been close to three weeks since the river incident, and just like before, it has become a taboo subject between us. We don't speak about it. We don't reference it. We simply pretend it never happened.

Well, he can pretend all he wants, since I've developed insomnia from overthinking every little interaction we had as I wondered if I did something wrong.

I can't even ask the man what happened because he will simply disappear on me.

Yet despite that, our relationship has changed for the better. We've become…friends—if I can even call us that considering I have a one-sided crush on him.

Our days are filled with doing tasks of the commune, and since we're always together, we've found ways to get along and have fun with each other. Of course, Nykander being Nykander, he asks the guards every day when we can see the High Priestess. And every day he gets the same reply—she will call on us.

But when my good-looking friend isn't scowling or telling me I talk too much, he's actually pleasant to be around. Bonus, PomPom and BonBon already consider him a part of the family.

He is the first to wake up in the mornings to exercise the dogs, and he's also the one stealing meat from the kitchens to surreptitiously feed them. He doesn't know I know that, but he forgets I am the one who folds his clothes and takes them to the laundry room. And every time I search his pockets, I find little pieces of meat stuck to the material.

That silly man.

He is the most thoughtful villain I've ever met—not that I've met others. But I've read about them, and they don't usually go around stealing meat for dogs or sourcing pink clothes for me. Because he's done that too.

I would randomly come back to our little cabin and find a new pink dress on the bed. When I asked about it, he would always shrug and say someone had thrown it away and he'd salvaged it.

He doesn't seem to realize that no one throws things away here. What they do is trade.

And for a while now, Nykander has been without his precious ring.

My heart clenches with longing the more I think of those hidden gestures for which he never wants to claim any credit. And despite knowing what's in store for us, I can't help but hope that maybe, *maybe* it doesn't have to be that way.

Maybe there is still hope.

"This is good," Nykander exclaims, surprised. He licks the spoon and dips it in the pot to get some more.

"Really?" I blink.

"Taste it. It's the best one you've cooked so far," he praises, his words genuine.

I taste the stew, smacking my lips together to analyze the taste.

"It *is* good. Oh my God, Nykander! I did it!" I exclaim as I jump up and down, throwing myself at him.

He catches me in his arms, hugging me to his chest.

"You did it," he murmurs in my hair.

"I can't believe it," I cry out, my emotions getting the best of me.

This is the third time I have been on cooking duty, and the only time I have managed to make something edible. The previous times, Nykander had to swoop in and save the day but now, for the first time, I did it all by myself.

And it's rather delicious, if I do say so myself.

"Here, let me get you a bowl. You deserve the first one after all your patience." I smile. Turning to where the dishes are, I select one of the bigger bowls for him and fill it up with stew.

"Thank you. I am deeply honored." He inclines his head.

I chuckle, pushing the plate in front of him.

He takes a spoon, but I stop him as I get a sudden idea.

"Wait."

Grabbing a knife, I prick my finger and let a few drops of blood fall into the soup.

His eyes widen in surprise, but he doesn't stop me.

"Now it's personalized, too." I wink.

"Hmm," he murmurs as he takes a few sips. "It is good. But I think I prefer it straight from the source."

My cheeks redden and I look away.

"I suppose you have earned that," I murmur, extending my wrist toward him.

Since that night when he bit my neck, he's never attempted to do so again. He only feeds from my wrist, keeping me a distance away.

He takes my hand, turning it palm up as his mouth hovers over my wrist.

I watch anxiously as I wait for the moment his teeth will sink into my skin—for the pain that is always shadowed by immense pleasure.

His lips skim my skin, making me break out in goose bumps.

I bite my lip, my heart slamming against my ribcage.

But just as his fangs graze my skin, the door to the kitchen opens and Jeya strides in.

Nykander doesn't move. He keeps my arm next to his face as he regards Jeya with annoyance.

"Can you not see we are busy?" he asks dryly.

Jeya rolls his eyes.

"Oh, I can see. So can everyone else." He points to the big windows that lead into the courtyard. There are some twenty-thirty kids and youths crowding the windows as they stare curiously at us.

Mortification swallows me whole and I pull my arm away from him.

"Why are you here, Jeya?" Nykander straightens his back, giving him a deadly stare.

"Aside from the fact that you are corrupting the minds of our youths?"

"W-what? We were not doing anything bad," I sputter. "I was only giving him some stew."

"Yes, I noticed that. He was really eyeing that stew," Jeya says with a wiggle of his brows.

"What did I tell you before, Jeya?" Nykander narrows his eyes at him. "Mayhap you remember our conversation from three weeks ago."

"And what if I decided not to…heed your words?" He tilts

his head, amusement playing at his lips as he regards Nykander.

I look between the two of them, wondering what the hell they're talking about. When had Nykander and Jeya spoken? *What* had they spoken about?

Nykander's dark shadows emanate from his body, tendrils of darkness reaching toward Jeya. His irises turn black and the mood inside the kitchen suddenly shifts. There's pure murderous intent coming from Nykander, and I can't understand why.

"Nykander?" I ask, pulling on his sleeve. "There are children watching."

That seems to momentarily stop him from going berserk.

Jeya smirks.

"Four weeks from now, there will be a festivity in the village. It is our annual moon festival. The High Priestess will not personally attend, but she will be watching. Based on your performance that night, she will decide whether to allow you to meet with her."

I frown.

"Our performance? What do you mean?"

His eyes move from me to Nykander.

"There is a celebration, of course. But each year, there is a competition to crown the King and Queen of the Moon. It is a silly custom, of course. The High Priestess has not specifically expressed that she wishes you to attain those titles, but it would not hurt to try. The winners are always invited to spend an evening with her."

"And how would we go about winning?"

Jeya smiles.

"That you will find out during the festival. Each year, the High Priestess comes up with different tasks."

With that, he turns to leave. But not before he scolds the youths hanging by the window and telling them to go do their chores.

Nykander is silent as he mulls over Jeya's words.

"I'm sure it can't be anything too hard," I say in an attempt to alleviate his worries.

His lips flatten.

"Or it might be intentionally hard. A test. And if we do not pass…"

"Don't be so pessimistic." I hit him playfully in the shoulder. "The villagers might have powers, but I doubt anyone is as strong as you."

In our time in the village, we've witnessed some of the abilities of the people around. They ranged from control over the elements, to the manipulation of metals and enhanced senses. Yet despite their abilities, they are all mortals, which makes Nykander the only god/demon around.

"I appreciate your trust in me, but this trial might not measure strength, or abilities. And do not forget it is King *and* Queen, which means you will need to win as well."

"And you think I won't?" I raise a brow at him. "I was *born* to win. You should see the trophies I got at all the dance competitions I attended with PomPom. One might say I revolutionized tandem dancing with dogs."

He shakes his head at me.

"I doubt you are going to be asked to dance with your dog."

"You never know," I fire back. "It might be a secret talent show. And that *is* my secret talent. Not only is my routine with PomPom flawless, but it also shows how well I trained her."

"And here I thought your secret talent was to talk someone's ear off," he mutters.

"Hey!" My eyes widen. "What did you say?" I narrow my eyes at him, picking up the spoon and pointing it at him, splashing him with a few drops of stew in the process.

And here I thought things were going too good between us since we have not squabbled in a full day.

Alas, it proved to be too good to be true.

"Do not even try to deny it, Barbi." He shakes his head in amusement.

"I never—"

"Barbi." He sighs, though a smile pulls at his lips. "You speak an average of two hundred and five words per minute when you are excited."

"Two hundred and five?" My lashes flutter. "That is a very exact number…"

"Of course." He nods. "I counted."

"You…counted?"

He proudly nods again.

"You…" My nostrils flare as I take the spoon and hit him lightly. "Instead of listening to me, you were counting my words? How dare you!" I cry out.

"I am sure the color of PomPom's poop is very interesting, but not when I am trying to sleep after an entire day's worth of work," he adds, slowly walking away from me.

My eyes widen and I start after him.

His lips are tipped up in amusement as he watches me chase after him, seemingly deriving great pleasure from making fun of me.

"It's her health! I need to be mindful of her poop."

"As you say, poop master." He inclines his head in a mocking gesture.

"Nykander…" I grit out, not seeing the fun in this. "Pom-Pom's stomach has been upset lately. Of course I need to make sure there is nothing wrong with her."

"I never said otherwise." He chuckles.

"Oh you…you sneaky demon! I will catch you and—"

"Lecture me on more poop?" he asks with a raised brow.

"Ugh!" I stomp my feet as I continue to chase him.

He stops, and I almost collide with him. He steadies me, placing his hands on my shoulders and keeping me in place.

"Her poop is fine, Barbi. I asked around. Mr. Foerie from

two cabins down from ours worked as a healer, and I asked him if there was anything wrong."

"You…did?" I glance up at him. "So you did listen?"

"You are very hard not to listen to." He chuckles. "But although there is no problem with her poop, there is something else…"

Panic flares inside of me.

I grab his hands, sliding closer.

"What? Please don't tell me she's sick. Not here, away from modern medicine and—"

"She is not sick," he assures me. "She is just breeding."

"She is…" I repeat numbly. "Did you say breeding?"

"She is carrying younglings. Mr. Foerie suspects she will give birth sometime next month."

"My… My PomPom is pregnant? As in… BonBon and her mated?" I ask, my voice trembling.

"That is how younglings come about, Barbi," he says with a deep sigh.

"Oh my God! How could I not know this? How could I have not seen it coming? Nykander! My PomPom is going to have babies," I exclaim, freaking out.

"It is what dogs do. It is not that shocking."

"It is! Oh Lord! She needs to be more pampered and she needs better nutrition."

Right as I say that, it dawns on me that I am in the kitchen. I have access to the food.

Leaving Nykander's side, I ransack the meat pantry and pull aside some raw chicken.

"This is what you usually get for them, no?" I turn back to ask Nykander.

A guilty look flashes across his face.

"You…knew?" he asks as he scratches the back of his head.

"It wasn't that hard to figure out."

"It is that one." He steps forward and grabs it for me.

Taking it to the table, he chops it in small bites and he adds them to some boiling water.

"PomPom and BonBon have grown on you, haven't they?"

"You could say so." He shrugs. But I don't miss the smile that tips his lips.

We fill a small pouch with pieces of meat and abscond away. Well, technically, our shift at the kitchen is done since I finished cooking.

PomPom and BonBon are chasing each other around, playing together, and immediately, worry grips me. Shouldn't PomPom be more careful? For the first time since this adventure, I wish we were home since a vet could run tests on her and ensure she's doing fine. But I guess we have to make do with Mr. Foerie's advice.

The door closes behind us, and PomPom and BonBon notice us. To my surprise, it's not me they hurry toward.

It's Nykander.

"Aha." I narrow my eyes at him. "This is why you've been feeding them all this time. You wanted to gain their favor."

He doesn't answer, a hidden smile playing at his lips. He takes out the pouch with meat from his pocket. The dogs immediately jump up and down, spinning to express their joy. He lures them with the food to the corner where we'd placed their feeding bowls, and he splits the meat between the two.

They do another happy dance in front of him—one that PomPom used to do only for me.

I stand on the sidelines and glare at him.

He stole my heart, and now he's stealing my dogs.

After the dogs eat, Nykander takes them out for a walk, and again I can do nothing but follow behind, feeling like a damn forth wheel. Especially as he continuously praises PomPom and calls her his *good girl.*

"Such a good girl," he murmurs as he scratches her ears after she poops. BonBon, wanting to be praised too, starts running in circles around him. He raises himself on his hind legs and dabs Nykander with his little paws.

"You too, BonBon. You are a good, good boy," he says with an easygoing laugh.

I sulk.

Despite the routine we've established with our chores around the village, he's never once been this relaxed with me. There's always tension between us, as if he holds himself back.

I am a few steps behind them as I watch their interactions green with envy. It's not that I'm actually jealous of my dogs—they deserve the world. I just wish he gave me the same love and attention, too.

PomPom barks as she jumps on him, yapping back and forth.

"You like that, do you not?" He laughs as he pets her gently. "Yes. Good girl." She responds to the praise, pushing her snout into his palm and asking for more.

"You are the *best* girl," he says with a chuckle.

"What about me?" I blurt out, crossing my arms over my chest.

He turns to regard me with a raised brow.

"What about you?"

"Am I not a good girl too?"

PomPom and BonBon also look at me questioningly.

Nykander tilts his head and stares at me, his gaze deep and penetrating.

"What are you asking, Barbi?"

"You always tell PomPom good girl this, good girl that, but what about me?" I push my chin up. "I am also a good girl. I do my chores. I learned how to cook. I even put in more work to make up for the clothes I lost at the river. How come I never get a praise?"

"They are dogs, Barbi," he says, straightening his back. "There are different expectations with dogs."

"How so? I have worked my ass off and deserve some praise, too. Is it so hard to call me good girl every now and then too?"

My cheeks heat up in mortification as it dawns on me I'm begging at this point.

"And will you get on your knees in front of me to receive it as well?"

My eyes widen.

He doesn't blink, watching me and awaiting my reaction.

"Is that what you want?" I speak slowly. "For me to get on my knees in front of you?"

"Will you?" He smirks.

"Well." I clear my throat, suddenly out of my depth. "I am not sure what exactly you want me to do."

"I think you know exactly what I want you to do," he drawls.

The dogs have already wandered off, playing around. They are oblivious to the thick tension simmering between us.

"You are a cad, Nykander. Has anyone told you that before?" I throw the words at him when I realize he is messing with me.

"Maybe not in so many words."

"Then take this! You are an insufferable cad and I am sick of your games! You are an asshole and a player. A villainous fuckboy!"

"When have I played any games?"

Pure rage grips me at seeing him so nonchalant about this.

"You're always hot and cold. One moment you behave as if you care about me, the next you ignore me as if I'm not even there. Like today. You were so nice to me, but then you had to ruin everything by being an ass just now."

A bored expression appears on his face.

"So?"

"What do you mean *so*? Don't you see that you're sending me mixed signals? Like what happened at the river a few weeks ago. We never talked about that because you always disappear when I bring it up."

His expression hardens.

"Nothing happened, Barbi."

"See? That's exactly what I'm talking about! Something *did* happen. We almost kissed, Nykander. Perhaps even more than that. I am not dumb, no matter what you may think of me. I saw the way you looked at me. I saw that you were… hard." I swallow hard, fighting the flush that envelops my entire face.

He takes a step forward. His eyes flash dangerously.

"Nothing. Happened. Barbi."

"Ugh, you insufferable man!" I stomp my feet. "Is it so hard to admit that you're attracted to me? That you *wanted* to kiss me?"

Before I know what's happening, my back hits a hard surface—the wall of the cabin behind us. The impact is enough to rattle me, but not enough to hurt. He's in front of me, caging me in as he leans forward.

His silver eyes shift under my gaze, a mix of light and dark as if both essences were fighting for supremacy inside him.

"You really do not know when to shut up, do you, Barbi?"

"Uhm…" I bite my lip. "I prefer to be straightforward. If something bothers me, then I will talk about it. If we don't talk about it, then how are we going to resolve the issue?"

"I was not aware there was any issue to be resolved."

"There clearly *is* one since—"

"Since I will not call you a good girl, and I will not kiss you or do more. Is that it?"

My lashes flutter as my chin tips in a small, barely perceptible nod.

"Should I do it then? Kiss you now? Will that satisfy you?" he asks, a mocking smile pulling at his lips.

My lips part as I stare at him.

He is absolutely breathtaking up close. But all that beauty

is marred by the way he looks at me—the way he seemingly has no consideration for me or my feelings.

He comes closer, and I feel his erection against my belly. Bringing his hand to my throat, he tips my chin up with his thumb until our lips are a mere breath apart.

"But no. You will not be satisfied with one kiss. You will want more, won't you? Because you are a greedy bitch begging for cock every time you look at me with those fucking doe eyes of yours. So what is next? Will a fuck do? Will that satisfy you so that you will leave me the fuck alone and stop with your goddamn incessant yapping?"

A pang of hurt goes through me at his words.

"W-what…"

"I can't fuck your cunt—that would fulfill our bond. But I will fuck your ass. What do you say?"

I gulp down, but it feels as if I'm swallowing glass.

"One kiss. One fuck. Will that suffice?"

"You're being mean," I whisper.

"I am not being mean, Barbi. I am being real. I do not want you. I may desire you, but I suppose it is to be expected since we are blood bonded. But I will not do anything that may risk us becoming permanently attached."

"Yes, you are." My voice trembles. "You are being crude and vulgar and—"

"One kiss. One fuck. Take it or leave it," he grits out.

His hand caresses my neck, circling it like a necklace. His mouth hovers over mine, his breath hot against my cold skin and even colder heart.

I have never had anyone speak to me like this. What's worse is that it's not only his words that are like an arrow to my heart, but also his gaze. He looks at me as if he's disgusted by me. Perhaps I have misjudged the situation once more because of my silly dreams and ideas. Perhaps his attraction to me is just a byproduct of our bond and nothing else.

But why does this hurt so much?

Why am I so caught up in this maddening crush that I would allow myself to be humiliated in such a way? Because this *is* humiliation. I wanted praise. He gave me degradation —and it's not even the sexy kind.

"One kiss. One fuck," I repeat. His brows shoot up, surprised I would actually consider this. "You will give that to me. Now?"

"Say the word, and I will."

A dry smile pulls at my lips.

"But I am a greedy bitch begging for cock. How can you be sure I will be satisfied with that?" I raise a brow at him.

My heart hardens in my chest. All the hopes from before are dashed again, and I can't help but wonder. Just how long will I continue like this? How long will I hope for a modicum of attention from a man who, at best, tolerates me?

"I reckon it will only whet my appetite for more," I add with a shrug. "But I suppose it is all right. There are plenty of available men in this village. I was talking to Jeya just yesterday and he seemed interested. I guess I will have to fill the void somehow, no?"

"When did you talk to Jeya?" he suddenly rasps, his hold tightening against my neck.

"Wouldn't you want to know?" I smirk. "I was curious to see if his kisses are as sloppy as yours. Just for comparison's sake, you know. And I am happy to inform you that—"

He snarls. A loud, grating noise that makes me squeeze my eyes shut in alarm.

"Did he touch you?" He growls in my ear—an animalistic sound that makes me shake with alarm. "Did he fucking touch you?"

"Maybe. Maybe not." I give a careless shrug as I stare at him right in the eyes. "Tell me something, Nykander. If another man fucks me, will you feel that too? Will you feel him deep inside of me, stroking me and filling me with his cock?

Will you feel every time he gives me an earth-shattering orgasm?"

I've always known I was petty, but not to this degree. And damn if it doesn't feel good.

"Barbi…" he grits out, his voice barely controlled.

"What? I am a greedy bitch begging for cock. You said it yourself."

"If any male lays a finger on you, I will raze this entire village to the fucking ground. Do not test me, Barbi," he rasps, his voice a dangerous warning.

I frown.

"You called me a villain. Then for you, a villain I will become. One finger, Barbi. One finger, and all those lives will be forfeited."

"Even the children?"

His smile widens.

"One finger, Barbi. That is all. You so much as smile at another male, and he will be dead. You have my word on that."

"You are awful," I mutter in shock. "How… How could I have believed there was anything nice about you when—"

"Because you are a silly little girl with stupid romantic dreams who thinks she is living some type of epic romance. I am sorry to break it to you, sweetheart, but—"

I don't let him finish as I bring my knee up and hit him right between his legs with as much force as I can muster.

"Take that from a silly little girl, you nasty old man," I tell him.

His hand falls from my neck, and a look of pure shock descends on his features. He takes a step back, reeling from the pain.

I stand my ground as I stare him in the eye.

This is all my fault. Once more, I fell for his little tricks, which I now see were only meant to keep me pliable and by his side.

Squeezing my right hand into a fist, I rotate my shoulder and make contact with his nose, gleefully watching the blood pour out of his nostrils.

"Good luck winning that competition by yourself," I tell him before I stomp away.

As I walk, I straighten my back. For the first time since… forever, I am proud of myself.

Even though my heart is in pieces at my feet, I am damn proud of myself.

18

"He is the most attractive male I have ever seen!"

"I cannot believe he is staying in our village. Do you think he will be at the moon festival tonight?" A girl around my age gushes about Nykander.

"He will! And he might even enter the competition," her friend says with a conspiratorial grin.

"He is? But what about that female he is with? Won't she be with him?"

"I have not seen them together in weeks. In the beginning, they were doing all their chores together, but now they are on their own. I think something must have happened," the girl whispers.

"That means you have a chance. And if you both win—"

I stop listening as I slowly back away, more annoyed than anything. Of course Nykander would gain an army of admirers the moment people think he is available. And what do I get? Nothing!

Despite my big proclamations, I have not seen nor spoken with Jeya or any male since then—and not for lack of trying.

If I so much as try to talk to someone, they ignore me and

pretend I am not there. With the women, it's even worse. There's no such thing as female solidarity—not even in Akkaya. They are all too enamored with Nykander, and that means I am the competition in their minds.

"Ugh!" I grit aloud as I kick a pebble on my way back to the cabin. "What the hell is so great about him anyway?"

Well, everything *but* his shining personality.

I continue to mutter obscenities under my breath and curse him for being a wretched man, when I suddenly stop.

A tremor goes down my back, accompanied by a sliver of awareness—almost as if I were being watched. I turn, but I don't see anything.

I shake my head in annoyance.

It's not the first time I've felt like this—as if I had eyes trained on my back. Yet who could it be other than some of those girls in the village who seemingly pity me and hate me at the same time? Although my foolishly romantic heart would wish it were Nykander, it better not be him!

I don't want to see him, talk to him, or otherwise have anything to do with his nasty ass.

He can keep himself away from me until the end, thank you very much.

Since our row weeks ago, Nykander and I have not spoken.

Not even a hello. He has not been sleeping at the cabin either.

As a matter of fact, I have no idea where he is sleeping or what he has been up to.

I sometimes spot him in the village doing his chores, but the moment he notices me around, he drops everything to just stare at me—no doubt to reinforce how much he hates me. I wonder if that's his way to shoo me away, and if it is, it works. I just have to notice those icy eyes of his trained on me and I turn my back and leave.

He has not fed from me since then either, and I do not know how that affects him.

I shake my head as my thoughts threaten to stray in that direction. I no longer care about him. He can be the most handsome man in the entire universe—which he, arguably, is—but that doesn't excuse his abysmal behavior. I never believed someone would be so goddamn mean to my face. I am aware he was trying to drive home the point that he doesn't want me—his body might, but his mind does not. That doesn't mean he needed to be so crude about it.

Yet I have now finally gotten the hint. And in the last few weeks, I have come to terms with the fact that I may always have a weakness about it, but that may very well be because of our bond. Maybe it is not real, just as he implied. As long as we get the artifact from the High Priestess, we will break our bond and we will each go our separate ways. Although, to be honest, I do not know how I will go on with my life after experiencing Akkaya.

I release a deep sigh.

Opening the door to the cabin, I am greeted by PomPom and BonBon and their beaming expressions. My eyes make contact with their feeding bowls and I note the scraps of food there.

I haven't fed them yet today. I just managed to smuggle some chicken. So that means *he* must have fed them.

Why is he so awful to me but so nice to my dogs?

"Here, babies," I murmur, waving the pieces of chicken around. They follow me to their bowls and watch me as I divide the food equally. They sniff it for a couple of minutes before they relent and dive in.

I slowly step back, plopping down on the bed. The festival is tonight and while I have no reason to attend, I do not want to be rude to the villagers.

I open my small trunk and peruse my options. I don't have

many dresses. But I do have the pink one Nykander got for me.

The material is silky and luxurious. Considering I have been on laundry duty a few times now, I can attest that the villagers don't have clothing this nice. I don't know where he got it, but while I appreciated it before, now that feeling has been marred by his behavior toward me. What was his intention? To keep me in good spirits so I would go along with his plan?

Yet no matter how much I'd like to burn this dress for the mere fact that it's from him, I can't.

It's too pretty. The prettiest thing I have here.

"What should I do, PomPom?" I ask my favorite fashion buddy. She hears her name and looks up at me, but she just gives me a shrug before she continues eating.

I guess I will be wearing it after all.

Going to the bathroom, I take off my sweaty work clothes and take a quick shower before I don the pink dress. It has an empire waist and puffed sleeves, with buttons running down the middle. Reaching my ankles, it has a small opening on each leg, the cut making me seem taller.

Glancing at myself in the mirror, I brush my hair and put it up in a messy bun atop my head.

"Your loss, Nykander," I say with a satisfied jerk of my shoulder.

I take a deep breath and charge myself with new confidence.

The festivities are about to begin once the sun sets, which will be any moment now.

The dogs have finished eating, so I take them to potty before I leave them behind at the cabin and make my way toward the village square.

Music is already playing. Someone is singing a beautiful ballad accompanied by a string instrument and what sounds like a trumpet. As I near the square, I note a big bonfire and a crowd of people gathered around it. Drinks and food are being passed around. A girl hands me a glass of ale, and I quickly down it. It's not too strong, but it should help me get through the night—and seeing Nykander again.

More questions flood my mind, the most pervasive being where he slept. I've barely seen him around, which seems rather impossible considering the size of the village. Then again, maybe he is so disgusted by me that he actively avoided me. With his superior senses, that was probably piece of cake.

For a while, nothing happens.

People drink, eat, and dance.

The music is very pleasant, and I tap my foot to the beat, watching from the sidelines as men and women flirt openly, while couples kiss unabashedly. It is surprising, however, to note there are no children. The youngest people are my age. That makes me wonder about the nature of that competition to crown the King and Queen of the Moon and what it might entail.

The moon is full, shining brightly over the raucous crowd and climbing higher into the sky.

"The competition will start soon," a voice speaks from behind.

I turn to see Jeya stop next to me, his eyes on the bonfire.

"What is it?"

"You will have to see. But to enter it, you will have to join the females on the other side." He motions to the right where a bunch of women my age formed a line.

I frown.

"Why?"

"The titles are not dependent upon one another. There is one competition for the King and one for the Queen. At the end, however, there will be a union of the two reigning monarchs of the night."

My eyes widen. If another female wins, she will be paired with Nykander.

"What type of union?"

The word *union* sounds…suggestive. And if it means what I think it means…

My features darken.

He may not like me, but that does not give him leave to like anyone else. Nor is he allowed to touch anyone else, either. Anger slowly builds inside of me as I think of him being crowned with one of those pretty girls who were whispering about him this morning.

No. He will not get that. I will win this damn competition just so I can publicly reject him and this…union.

I have already reached peak pettiness. What's a little more?

Jeya's lips slowly tip up.

"I have said too much."

"Please explain," I persist.

"This is my cue to leave," he mutters under his breath, disappearing into the crowd.

I stare after him, flabbergasted. What the hell?

The music suddenly stops and the mood shifts. The men gather to the left, while the women are on the right. Those participating in the contest are forming a line and I spot Nykander in the men's section.

Our eyes connect, his gaze harsh and unyielding.

He stares me down, almost as if he wanted to communicate something with his gaze.

Maybe he's pissed—not that he wouldn't have reason. I may or may not have stabbed my hand daily so he can feel the pain too. Petty? Yes. Painful? Another yes, but worth it.

I walk to the right, joining the line of girls at the end. I might not know what this competition entails, but I would love to win just to see Nykander's shocked expression at the fact that this silly little girl could achieve something by herself, without his help. Even more so when I tell him in front of everyone that he is the last man I would have by my side.

My mind is made and I push my chin up, wearing my confidence like I'm wearing this pretty dress—as if it were made for me.

But despite my bravado, awareness pricks at my back, and without even looking back, I know he is staring at me. Or, rather, he is staring a hole through me.

There are ten women in my line and an equal number of men in the line parallel to us.

The bonfire illuminates a circle around where the other villagers take their positions as spectators, their beady eyes following everything closely.

"The Moon Festival will commence shortly," Elijah appears in the middle of the crowd. "Each side will be allowed to vote after every trial. The male side will decide which females remain in the contest and vice versa until we have narrowed down our winners. There will be a total of four trials."

The villagers clap. Murmurs and whispers abound at this change of rules, but it seems it is rather well received.

"The first trial will test skill. The other three will test the senses."

Another round of applause. These people are very eager to see the competition unfold.

"Before I ring the bell for the beginning of the first trial, let us welcome our participants. Females, please state your names."

One by one, the women introduce themselves with a pretty smile, surreptitiously glancing at the male side and batting their lashes. Since everyone is introducing themselves with their full name, when it is my turn, I step forward and state monotonely, "Barbara Bancroft."

A low hum reverberates through the crowd, as well as some less than happy people voicing their displeasure at the fact that I am not smiling or preening around like I should.

I glare at them.

The boos intensify.

Well, I don't think I will be winning any popularity contests.

Alas, I am not in this game because I *want* to win. I only want to spite that wretched Dark One, maybe even sabotage him a little on the way. God knows he needs someone to take him down a peg.

I step back in the line. It's the men's turn now.

A few of the village men are first, introducing themselves and rolling their shoulders to emphasize their muscles.

I blink.

There is something very specific about these introductions and I feel as though I am not in on the joke.

Nykander's turn comes. His eyes are on me as he steps forward. His hands are behind his back, his back straight as he gazes around as if everyone is beneath him. He has an air of superiority that aggravates me even more. Especially as I note the subtle smirk pulling at his lips.

"Nykander v'Kyró."

My eyes flash.

It's my first time hearing his full name.

Nykander v'Kyró. Somehow it suits him. I wonder what it means…

Cut it out, Barbi! You are not interested in him. You hate him, remember?

I school my features into a dismissive scowl.

He raises a brow at me.

Damn you, you insufferable oaf!

I don't say it aloud, of course. But I do mouth it to him, and with his sensitive senses, he gets it, because that arrogant smile of his widens.

The rest of the males step forward to state their names.

"Wonderful! Welcome, everyone!" Elijah exclaims, and all attention returns to him. "I wish you all luck in this competition and may you find what you seek."

A round of applause ensues.

"For the first trial, you will show off your skills. Choose one skill that recommends you and show it in front of everyone. You have ten minutes to prepare. It is permissible to use your abilities. For this round, one female and one male will be voted off the game!"

The villagers go crazy, and I hear some murmurs about how this is one of their favorite trials.

"Ten minutes start now. Do your best!"

The girls immediately disperse as they run toward their family members for support. They must have known what this trial involved because all are ready. Meanwhile, though, I am the only one left next to the bonfire.

I glance up. The men, too, are getting ready to show off their skill. But while I am slowly freaking out because I don't know what I will do within such a short time frame, Nykander looks wholly relaxed as he leans back against the trunk of a tree and observes the madness around.

Damn it! What am I going to do? I don't want to look like a complete fool and give Nykander more reasons to laugh in my face.

My first thought is to get PomPom and do our dance routine. But she is trained on specific music and I doubt these musicians can play Cardi B. I am sure our number would be well received, but I don't want to take any chances. No matter how smart my baby is, she is still a dog and she can only do as good as her training.

What other skills do I have?

I suppose I could try singing, but there is a fifty-fifty chance I will be booed and dismissed from the competition immediately. Other than that…

I sigh.

My skills run more to the introverted type—the ones I do alone, in the intimacy of my home.

Like writing. But no one will want to listen to me drone about that.

As my mind goes through the list of potential skills I can display, a bulb lights up in my brain.

I slowly search Nykander with my gaze, a little unsettled when I find him staring at me intently—again. I wonder if he's mentally planning how to get me to lose the competition or how to embarrass me further since he seems to derive great pleasure from that.

And that solidifies it for me.

If there is a skill I excel at, it's being petty. And I aim to show him just *how* petty I can be.

"Ten minutes have passed. Please line up again," Elijah calls out. "We will have one female contestant and one male at a time. Audee, you may commence." He motions to the first girl in line. "Please tell us your skill and demonstrate your talent."

She steps forward, placing herself in front of the bonfire. The fire illuminates her features and her pretty white dress.

"My skill is that I can create a garment out of any piece of material. For that, I have brought here a plain white cloth that I will fashion into an item of clothing." She turns to the males. "Please tell me what you would like me to make."

Somehow, her hopeful gaze lands on Nykander, but he is not even paying attention. No, he is just staring me down with those icy eyes of his.

My lip twitches in annoyance, so I do the only thing a petty person would do. I stick my tongue out at him and look away.

The men propose different items of clothing, and one of them is louder as he says, "Drawers."

I frown at the unfamiliar term.

Audee smiles. She produces a pair of scissors and she begins working, cutting the plain cloth in record time. She then sews a few corners, plaits another few, and in less than five minutes, she waves around the finished product.

A pair of underwear. Male underwear.

Whistles and applauses resound from the audience. The man who'd suggested the item nods appreciatively and gives her a nod of acknowledgment. Audee blushes.

"Well done, Audee. Please return to your place. The next one is Flin."

Audee takes her place back in the line and Flin comes froward, the first in the men's line.

I watch curiously to see what he will come up with.

But just as he rips his shirt from his body to reveal his nicely sculpted muscles, a growl slithers past my ears.

I blink, looking around.

Shrugging, I glance back at Flin, who is now showing off his strength by cutting a block of wood with one strike—half-naked. His performance has the intended effect as the girls in front of me nearly swoon. They talk amongst themselves and praise his looks and strength and deem him the protective type—whatever that is.

Yet I don't get to enjoy the show as every time my gaze lands on his marbled abs, a warning sound blares in my ears. My brows bunch in a frown, turning around to search for the source of the sound, but nothing catches my eye.

What the…

Flin ends his routine and from the girls' side, Loraine is next.

She demonstrates her prowess with a blowing musical instrument, and the men all give her nods of approval.

All but Nykander, who is not even looking at her.

No, he's holding his arms crossed over his body as he glares at me as if I'd done something wrong when he's the asshat in this situation.

My nostrils flare. I narrow my eyes at him and barely

refrain from giving him the finger. He wouldn't even know what it means.

The trial continues as the men show off their manly skills while the women focus on their feminine assets—not that there's anything wrong with it. But as I notice a theme arising, I wonder if my idea will work. If I were to lose this contest from the first trial, I doubt I will ever live it down. Nykander will forever mock me for it.

Nykander's turn comes before mine.

He leisurely moves to the center. He's sporting a bored look as he gazes around lazily until his eyes find mine. He doesn't even put in the effort as he allows his black tendrils to slither in the air, a halo of dark mist forming around his body.

His tendrils reach for the wood left behind by Flin, enveloping it in his darkness before turning it into dust.

A chorus of cheers erupts, and for some reason, the girls seem to find that utterly charming. They swoon and praise and make gooey eyes at him.

"He is the most handsome male I have ever laid eyes on," the girl in front of me says—the same one who was singing his praises this morning.

I scoff under my breath.

"He's also rotten to the core."

She turns to glare at me.

"You are just bitter that he dropped you," she sneers at me. "But do not worry. I will be happy to replace you."

"I'd love to see you try."

She huffs aloud, getting ready for her turn.

She walks in front of the bonfire and states that her skill is polishing swords.

My brows go up.

She gets a sword from one of the people on the sidelines, but instead of showing off how she cleans it, she brings the hilt to her mouth. She hollows her cheeks and slides the entire hilt to the back of her throat.

My eyes widen and it dawns on me what type of sword polishing she's hinting at.

The men shout expletives as they stare intently at her performance, clearly imaging it's something else she's polishing.

When she's done, she comes back to the line, giving me a smirk.

"At least you will never be out of a job. Everyone there carries a sword." I point to the other side.

Her lips twitch in annoyance, but she holds her tongue as the next male steps forward to display his talent.

I can't pay attention, though, as I go over my own performance in my mind. In a little while, it's going to be my turn.

Can I do it? *Should* I do it?

The doubts eat at me. But as I glance at Nykander and his smug look, I decide that screw it.

The man goes back and I am called forward.

"Hello. I am Barbara Bancroft and my skill is being petty."

Silence descends among the villagers.

"Can you explain?" Elijah asks.

"I can withstand any type of pain as long as my enemy feels the same." I smile prettily.

People are still confused.

Removing a small knife from the pocket of my dress, I pull up the sleeve to my shoulder. With the sharp edge of the knife, I carve out letters in my arm, gritting my teeth at the pain.

ASSHOLE—that is what the final word says.

When I'm done, everyone stares at me in shock.

Blood pours to the ground from the gnarly wounds, but I continue to maintain my composure. Especially as my gaze collides with Nykander's thunderous one.

Blood pours down his arm, too, dripping to the ground.

His eyes slowly turn entirely black, his fangs elongating before my eyes.

So this is what weeks of not feeding is doing to him—it's destroying all his self-control.

My wounds heal. A little slower than before since I derive this particular power from the man himself—who is currently salivating for my blood.

"Uhm, Miss Barbara." Elijah blinks. "That is…uhm… impressive?"

I force a smile.

With a swift maneuver of the blade, I slash at my throat. I raise a brow at Nykander just as a slash appears on his own neck.

His jaw is ground tight and he takes a step forward.

I reach to my already closing wound and swipe some of the blood, bringing it to my lips.

I stare at him.

"Delicious," I murmur.

He growls in anger.

I shrug in satisfaction.

Revenge feels good.

He takes another step forward, his hunger bleeding through. The handsome man from before is slowly transforming into a beast.

Yet if I hoped that this would make the other girls dislike him, it has the opposite effect.

They positively *drool* after him.

I release a deep sigh.

It doesn't matter what world I am in. A tall, dark, and dangerous man is always going to have women fall over themselves. And Nykander is the true definition of that.

With my last wound healed, I bow out and head back to my spot.

The last man goes through his performance and then it's time to vote.

The girls all gather together to debate while the guys do the same. Of course, they all want Nykander to continue.

"Mino should go," one whispers. "His act was the weakest."

"I agree. I've been with him before and his performance is not the best," another agrees.

I'm silent as this goes back and forth since I know my opinion would not be welcomed—especially since it's an unpopular one.

After a few minutes, the girls decide that Mino will be voted out.

On the men's side, they decide that Aida should go, a girl who'd done a demonstration of cooking a dish. To be honest, I am quite surprised it wasn't me, since Aida's skills were more on point than mine.

But I guess no man can resist a little blood.

"Aida, Mino, please make your way to the crowd," Elijah intones.

Once the two eliminated are out of the way, he continues, "The next trial will be based on scent. Females, please follow Greta. Males, please follow me."

The request is strange, but the nine of us follow the elderly woman called Greta to one of the cabins in front. When we get there, the door closes behind us and she voices her request.

"Each of you, hand me your underthings."

No one protests as they raise their skirts to take off their underwear.

"W-what?" I blink in shock.

"Miss Barbara, please remove your underthings."

"I don't—"

"Miss Barbara?" She raises a brow, her tone unyielding.

Maybe I should quit now. Yes, that would be the most optimal solution.

So why is it that I am actually complying and removing my underwear?

God, I am even pettier than I realized if I'm willing to go this far.

19

As she collects the underwear, she tags each one of them with a number. Mine is number six.

"You will remain here until I shall return." And with that, she's out the door.

I am still dumbfounded. The other girls, however, are not.

They giggle around as they make bets on who's going to be voted out. Apparently, this round three girls will be eliminated.

When Greta returns, she is carrying a bag full of numbered underwear—the men's.

"You have ten minutes to deliberate which men you will vote out," she instructs.

"What? How?" I blurt out.

"By smelling these, of course. It is a scent test. You must decide which ones are the most appealing."

I stare at her, flabbergasted. Did she just say that we must smell the men's underwear?

Ewwww.

Greta leaves the room and we are all left alone with the men's pairs of underwear. The other girls, however, don't seem in the least put out as they go, one by one, and they start sniffing the underwear.

"This one has a pleasant musk," one notes, inhaling deeply. She behaves almost like my dog, and that is concerning.

More girls come forward to smell the piece.

They do the same with the others, complimenting some while placing others aside. Yet it's all very personal, so it comes down to a majority vote. What is pleasant to one, may not be pleasant to the other. If a pair is not chosen by three or more girls, it is set aside.

"This one has no smell at all," Loraine frowns. "Do you sense anything?" she asks her friend, who shakes her head.

"Barbara, you have not smelled any," one of the girls calls out.

My lips tremble as I stare at the underwear in her hands.

"I don't have the same olfactory senses as you do," I say as an excuse. "I'm human."

"Human? But how so? We all saw you heal from those cuts."

"Well, it's complicated. But I cannot tell one smell from the other, so whatever you guys choose, I'll go along," I mention.

They don't seem to mind. But as they continue to classify each pair, I can't help but wonder which one is Nykander's and what *that* would smell like. My lips draw into a tight line. A hole forms in my stomach as I regard the other girls sniff away at the underwear, somehow uncomfortable with the thought that they must be smelling *him*.

You're not supposed to care, Barbi! Get a grip.

Yet it's easier said than done. Even though weeks have passed—enough for me to get over the incident—I haven't managed to forget him. And that is the most infuriating thing.

It's the bond. It *must* be the bond. Because who's sadistic enough to drool after an entitled asshole? Not me! Well, technically not me. I would not *normally* do that. But I will accede that this time there might be extenuating circumstances and I *might* be drooling over him.

Ugh! Goddamn it, Barbi! You're the worst, you know that? You're like those doormat heroines you hate to love in romance novels who swoon at the very sight of a tall, dark, and handsome hero.

My nose wrinkles in disgust at myself.

It's the bond. It must be the bond.

YES. And *because* it's the bond, which is instinctual, I must use my brain to combat it. Which is where my pettiness comes into play. I will win this competition and I will show Nykander who the silly little girl is.

But while the girls are chatting merrily on the subject of the men's underwear, it dawns on me that the men must be doing the same over our panties.

Oh my God!

My cheeks flame up.

I only put on those panties today, so I doubt there is much to smell, but still. Even when my parents threatened to cut me off and I briefly considered resorting to selling my used underwear or feet pics to feed my book addiction, I realized I could not do it. Not because I have anything against those who do, but because I couldn't imagine anyone getting aroused at *my* stuff without my express permission—and presence. But now it's happening. And like a fool, I allowed it to happen because I am the queen of pettiness who would rather put up with that to continue in this cursed competition.

I'm suddenly startled out of my thoughts when the time is up.

The girls have piled up the pairs they are voting out, and Greta comes to take them with her. We are instructed to follow her back to the location of the bonfire where the men are also back in their line.

"Welcome back!" Elijah intones. "You have decided which people to eliminate for this round. I will now call them out," he says before he proceeds to recite a few names.

The girls whimper when they hear theirs, and I am entirely surprised that I do *not* hear mine.

So I'm still here.

And Nykander is still here, too, judging by the fact that his name doesn't get called.

I give him a deadly glare.

He returns it with a wicked smile that's half grin, half smirk, which infuriates me further.

You panty-smelling pervert!

I don't know whether I'm more mad at the fact that the girls smelled *his* underwear, or that he smelled the girls' panties. Never mind, I should be angry that someone else smelled *my* underwear.

Ugh! Such a dilemma.

Maybe I should be mad at all instances equally.

"Congratulations, everyone. We can now move to the third trial. After smell, the second sense we will entertain tonight will be sight."

Entertain… That is an odd way of putting it. I wonder who came up with these tests because they're all a bit wonky if you ask me.

"For the trial of sight, you will all be required to shed all your clothing. As before, three males and three females will be voted out via the consensus of the opposite party. The goal is to ensure that the remaining contestants find each other's form pleasing, which will ultimately culminate in the fourth trial, that of touch. You have ten minutes to deliberate."

I frown. I did not understand anything of what he said except that I need to undress.

Hell no!

I stare around, noticing that both the men and the women are already pulling at their clothes. Panic swells inside of me.

I've never been naked in front of anyone before! I would never want the first time I do it to be in front of tens of strangers.

My voice is trapped in my throat as my limbs tremble with fear.

What the hell is with these trials? These people are fucking perverts! First the sniffing of underwear and now the nakey-nakey stuff? No, thank you. My wide eyes crash with Nykander's icy ones.

The men's shirts are flying, but he doesn't move a muscle. And before I can blink, he teleports in front of me.

His dark mist emanates from his body, solidifying and surrounding us in an opaque cocoon, away from everyone else's gaze.

I slowly look up.

He is…pissed.

His jaw is clenched tight as he stares down at me.

Screams and shouts resound from the other side of the mist as people try to get him to lower his shield or they will remove both of us from the competition.

"What are you doing?" I whisper.

"You will not look," he rasps.

"W-what?"

"You. Will. Not. Look," he repeats roughly, his nostrils flaring.

"Nykander…"

"This competition ends here," he declares, not even bothering to ask me what I want or think.

Loud noises erupt and the shield becomes translucent enough that I spot others using their powers against us. There are some fire balls and even shards of glass, all thrown against his dark mist.

"Stop it," I say. "Stop it, Nykander."

His eyes flash for a moment before his dark mist recedes

back in his body. The action is forceful, not at all the graceful way it used to undulate around his body.

He stares at me with a combination of awe and outrage, as if he doesn't know whether to kiss me or strangle me.

I mentally scoff at my train of thought.

He'd never kiss *me*. Where the hell do these ideas even come from?

See, Barbi, this is what happens when you live too long in fictional worlds. You start waxing poetic about undeserving assholes.

"This is not permitted." Elijah steps forward. "You two are disqualified."

The other contestants agree, though some of the girls are put out that Nykander will not be in the competition anymore.

Nykander grunts absentmindedly and we are told to leave or go back to the crowd.

I turn to leave, but he stops me. He grabs me by the hand and pulls me in front of him, covering my entire line of sight with his body.

"Do not move," he says in a low voice.

"What the hell is wrong with you?" I frown and try to bypass him.

"Do not push me, Barbi. Not now. I have not fed in weeks and you have flaunted your blood in front of me all night. I am close to my breaking point and if you do not want to see people die, do *not* push me to my breaking point."

"Well, you should have thought about that before you behaved like a raging asshole. You have now lost all feeding privileges, so I would appreciate it if you could unhand me and let me go. I wish to see the end of this competition."

"No."

One word. Just one word. His body is tense, his entire aura murderous despite seemingly being in control of his shadows.

"What?"

"We are leaving," he says and pulls me toward the end of the crowd.

With our ongoing dispute, I miss the rest of the trial. Elijah announces three men and women as the finalists moving to the last round, and I strain to catch sight of who they are.

Nykander, though, pulls me back, once more blocking my view.

"Let me go, you beast," I mutter under my breath.

"Stop. Squirming," he grits out.

A tremor goes down his body. He closes his eyes briefly before he pulls me toward him again.

I stumble forward, and I instinctually reach for him to stabilize myself. He's there, though, catching me. His hands find my ribcage, keeping me in place so I don't fall. His body is frozen to the spot and taut with tension.

Is he going to snap at me? I wonder.

He's so tightly wound up and I don't know what triggered this awful mood of his. Then again, he *is* an asshole, so he doesn't need much to go off on me. I only need to exist and he scowls at me every second.

I wrap my fingers in his clothing to pull myself up when a flash of pink material catches my eye.

There. In his pocket.

I slowly look up. His eyes widen, and I could swear his cheeks redden.

We stare at each other for moments on end.

Voices blare in the distance as the competition continues. Shouts, grunts, and other indescribable noises echo in my ear. But they all fade away as my focus becomes wrapped up in him.

"Why do you have that?" I whisper.

He blinks, his Adam's apple bobbing up and down.

"Why do you have that, Nykander? Why do you have my panties? Did you steal them?" I squeak.

He takes a deep, shuddering breath.

"Because you are a little fool. You gave them away with

little to no coaxing. What were you thinking, Barbi? Giving strange men your underwear to sniff at?" He scowls at me, his expression dangerous.

"You're calling *me* a fool? You gave yours as well!"

"No. I did not."

"What?"

"Good thing I was there to stop this from happening before some misguided lad got his hands on your underwear. I doubt I would have been able to control myself then."

I blink as I stare at him, flabbergasted.

"I don't understand you," I whisper.

"It is better that you do not." He sighs. "If you only knew…" He scrubs his hand over his weary features.

"You were the one who wanted to enter this competition in the first place. Now you're blaming me for playing by the rules? You're a hypocrite, Nykander!" I tell him sternly.

"Do you even know what this competition is about, Barbi?" He raises a brow at me.

"To crown the King and Queen of the Moon, of course."

"And what do you think happens once the king and queen are crowned?"

"That…" My brows draw together. "I don't know."

"They fuck," he states blankly. "They fuck in front of everyone."

My lips part in shock.

"W-what?" I mumble. "What do you mean?"

"This is not a competition per se. It is a mating ritual. The king and queen will mate and receive special treatment from the village. Why do you think scent plays such an important part? Why do you think people removed their clothes and are now touching and caressing each other?"

"I—"

"It is all part of a scheme to match a compatible male with a compatible female."

Right at that moment, Elijah announces the winners: Flin and Loraine.

The crowd cheers for them, and the celebrations resume with more vigor.

I peek through the gap of his elbow, straining to see what's happening.

There is a bed in front of the bonfire that wasn't there before. The spectators are loud and boisterous as they give pointers to the winners. I catch sight of movement on the bed and a few flashes of naked limbs tangled together before a loud moan pierces through the air.

That's all I can see, however, before Nykander once more blocks my view.

"They're… They're having sex. Right there," I stammer, my eyes wide.

"That is enough, Barbi. We are leaving," Nykander states tightly.

"But if you knew… Why would you participate? Why would you let *me* participate?" I ask on a whimper.

"Because I just found out," he grunts. "That fucking Jeya tricked us both."

"But…" I don't get to say anything else as Nykander envelops me in his arms and teleports us back to the cabin.

PomPom and BonBon startle awake at our presence, rushing to greet us.

I push him away from me, my expression one of pure disdain.

"Don't touch me," I grit out.

I take a step back, and surprisingly he allows me.

His features are still tense, his breathing labored.

He stares at me with a pensive look on his face.

"You can see yourself out now," I mutter as I walk deeper into the cabin and take a seat on the bed.

PomPom and BonBon jump in with me and I pet them both while ignoring Nykander.

He doesn't leave, though.

He stands there, unmoving.

PomPom turns on her back, exposing her little pregnant belly and begging for belly rubs. I, of course, indulge her—everything in an attempt to ignore Nykander in hopes that he will leave. There is slight movement in her stomach, and I swear I can almost feel the babies move. Tears poke at my eyes as my whole being fills with an ineffable description.

My PomPom will have babies. And she's so close to giving birth. By my estimates, it's been around fifty-five days since she and BonBon met, and her gestation period should be around sixty-three days. That's just a week away.

Worry gnaws at me.

I've never seen a dog give birth. I don't know what she will need and if I will be able to accommodate her needs from here. That healer Nykander had suggested hadn't been of much use. He specializes in people, not dogs.

"You're going to be a daddy soon." I scratch BonBon's ears. "Are you excited?"

He lets out a loud bark before he turns to PomPom, licking her on the stomach and sniffing her privates.

I blink, then I blush.

Why do I feel like I'm intruding on an intimate moment of my dogs?

From the corner of my eye, I see Nykander is still there. He's balancing himself on his heels as he stares at us intently.

"Why are you still here?"

He purses his lips.

"Are you going to blame me for failing the competition now?" I raise a brow.

"No," he mutters.

"Really? Because this was your chance to meet the High Priestess if you won."

He shrugs. "She will call on us eventually."

It doesn't escape me that he said *us* not *me*.

I narrow my eyes at him.

"So that's it? No insults? No more calling me a fool?"

"What you did was foolish." He sighs as he steps closer. "Were you going to take off your clothes?" He surprises me by asking.

"Of course not," I reply immediately. "I thought it was weird with the whole panty-smelling thing. I mean, who does that? But because I didn't know what it was for, I sort of went along."

"Why? You didn't have to enter the competition."

"Because I am petty," I tell him as I cross my arms over my chest. "And I planned to humiliate you once you won."

A smile pokes at his lips.

"I see. You certainly displayed your pettiness in the skill trial."

"Damn right. It happens to be a true talent, so you'd better watch your back from now on. I have downgraded you from my pink notebook to my black one to suit your dark, dark soul."

"But I thought *you* were the light to that dark, dark soul?" he adds with a smile.

"Careful, Dark One," I tell him in a warning tone. "You might unlock my other talent. And it will not bode well for you, especially seeing as how we're trapped together for now."

"And what is that talent?" He takes another step forward.

I smirk and get up. "I am as petty as I am obsessive."

His features light up in surprise.

"But whereas you might have earned my good type of obsessiveness while you were a member of the pink notebook crew, since you are now on my black list, the level of obsessiveness will be adjusted accordingly."

"And what does that…obsessiveness entail?"

"I'll make your life a living hell," I say without missing a beat. "I might not have any of those fancy powers of yours, but I do have something that's even better."

He raises his brows.

"Perseverance," I continue. "I do not forget, nor do I forgive."

"Not even if you receive a sincere apology?"

His words startle me.

"What?"

He takes one more step. We're now in front of each other, which does me little good since he's even more good-looking than I remembered. But I will not let his godly tier looks rattle me. Not when I am in full vengeance mode.

"I apologize." He brings a hand to my face, tucking a stray strand of hair behind my ear.

His eyes are on mine, and I am surprised to see his words are genuine.

"What are you saying?" I swallow.

"I am sorry for how I behaved. I should not have spoken to you in that way." He takes a deep breath. "You did not deserve any of it, Barbi. It was my own frustration that got the best of me and I lashed out at you."

"Did you just..." My lashes flutter in absolute shock. "You're saying you were wrong? You're taking accountability for your words and actions?"

He nods solemnly.

"Dear God, I truly must be in a fictional world," I mutter to myself, which prompts him to frown in confusion.

"I am sorry if my words hurt you," he repeats, his voice grave and unsure.

His entire countenance screams uncertainty for someone whose natural confidence oozes at any moment.

I tilt my head as I study him.

"You don't apologize often, do you?"

He shakes his head.

"It is my first time."

I stare at him, dumbfounded.

"First time since you escaped, or first time in your thirteen thousand whatever years?"

He mutters something under his breath.

"What?"

"First time in thirteen thousand years," he eventually admits.

"That's why you're so bad at it." I nod pensively.

He's taken aback by my words.

"Whatever do you mean?" he demands.

"Well, first of all. It's been *weeks*, Nykander. You don't apologize now because it's convenient. You apologize after you mess up and realize you hurt the other person."

He glances away, looking thoroughly chastised.

"I did not realize how much I hurt you until weeks after," he murmurs guiltily. "I have been…watching you. Trying to decipher you. But the more I learned, the more confused I became about how to approach you. And there was no manual for this at the village library."

"You… You searched the library for a manual?" I ask, flabbergasted.

"I am not the best when it comes to feminine sensibilities. I did not want to mess it up even more than before."

"Oh, wow." My eyes widen. "So you decided avoiding me for almost a month was better?" I ask.

He sheepishly nods.

"You, my dear Dark One, are quite emotionally stunted for one so old." I shake my head at him.

He blinks. Then smiles.

"You called me my dear," he says, pleased with himself.

"Is that all you got out of this? Good Lord, you're hopeless."

"Will you forgive me?" He bats his lashes at me as I used to do and for the first time, I'm on the receiving end of this tactic. Horror grips me as I realize *how* effective it is.

"No," I reply firmly. "You treated me badly. A verbal

apology will not change anything. You will have to prove that you are apologetic."

"And how do I do that?" He blinks.

"That, my dear Dark One, is your job to figure out. Now you can see yourself out. I need a shower." I turn to leave. "Oh, but first, give me back my panties," I say as I reach for his pocket.

He sidesteps me and moves my hand aside.

"You gave them freely. I took them, therefore I will keep them."

"You pervert!" I accuse. "Give me my panties back!"

He backs away, a devilish smile pulling at his lips.

"Nykander! I don't have that many pairs as it is and I have to wash them daily. Please give me back my panties," I say with a sigh.

"I will get you more," he replies, evading me further.

I consider his words for a moment.

"Pink?" I raise a brow.

"*Very* pink."

I purse my lips as I regard him. Then I shake my head.

This man is odd. And that is saying something since I am quite odd too.

"Fine. Whatever. Now go."

Just when I think he's finally going to leave me alone, he does something that surprises me. He catches my hand, twirling me back to him. My breasts brush against his chest, my lips parting in surprise.

"W-what are you doing?" I stammer, my heart slamming against my ribcage.

"Proving that I *am* apologetic." He smirks.

20

One moment, we're in the cabin. The next, we're up on a hill, looking down at the village.

Nykander lets me go and I take a step back.

"Where are we?" I frown.

He doesn't answer. Instead, he takes my hand and leads me to a spot a few feet over. My eyes widen when I spot what he wants to show me.

There are a few tools around as well as unfinished pieces of wood. But next to them is a dog house.

A pink dog house.

"What is this?" I whisper.

"PomPom will need to nest when she goes into labor," he explains. "I figured she would be more comfortable here. In pink."

"You... You made this?" I swallow, emotions clogging my throat.

He nods.

"But why?"

He shrugs. "I just did."

He balances from one foot to another in discomfort.

I leave his side and go closer to the dog house to inspect it.

He'd made it a little bigger to fit both PomPom and BonBon, and inside there are two dog beds—both pink.

"Where did you get the materials for this?"

"From the village."

"Pink cushions? *How?*"

He purses his lips.

"I traded in work for them."

His words touch me and they shouldn't.

I continue to examine the house. He built it with his own hands, that much is clear. The details are gorgeous, but as I plop myself on the ground in front of it, I note the engraved writing above the small entrance.

PomPom's villa.

"You shouldn't have," I murmur, my eyes glued to this pink wonder that I have no doubt PomPom will absolutely love.

"Why?"

"I don't like it when you're nice to me, Nykander. In fact, I much prefer it when you're an asshole."

His brows gather together in confusion.

"But I thought you would like it."

"Oh, I do like it. That is not the issue. But when you do things like this, I can't hate you with as much vigor as before."

"Then maybe… Don't hate me?" The question is hopeful. An uncertain smile pulls at his lips.

I shake my head.

"I can't do that. Because if I don't hate you… If I don't have reasons to keep my distance, then…"

"Then what, Barbi?"

"I'll want to be close to you. But being close to you only hurts me, and I really don't want to hurt anymore, Nykander."

"I am sorry." He sighs.

I give him a sad smile.

"Sorry doesn't change our dynamic, does it?"

"But what if it could?"

My brows shoot up in question.

"What if being close to me did not hurt?"

"What are you trying to say?"

He takes a deep breath as he takes a seat on the ground next to me. He takes my hand into his much bigger one and squeezes it lightly.

"I *was* an asshole. But there is a reason for it, Barbs, despite the fact that it's a very poor one."

"Barbs?" I ask in amusement.

"You do not like it?" He blinks.

I shake my head, smiling.

"No one's called me that before. I…like it," I murmur shyly.

He smiles, nodding to himself.

"You were right. I *am* attracted to you. But the mere thought that I would find another female attractive scared me," he admits.

"Why?"

"Because I vowed I would not."

I remain silent as I look at his profile. The moonlight illuminates the high bridge of his nose, making him appear regal, unapproachable. But the mood surrounding us is completely opposite. For the first time, there is a vulnerability to him that calls to me.

And that scares me.

"I will respect your vow, Nykander. I will not attempt anything. Do not worry on my account. But we should continue at least on friendly terms. I forgive you for what you said, but that does not mean I will forget. Your words were cruel."

Guilt pulls at his features.

"That is the issue, Barbs. I have already broken that vow and many others. I do not think this is just the mating bond. I am attracted to you, but more than anything… I want to *spend* time with you."

"You do?" I ask, surprised.

"You're funny and cute and so damn entertaining. I find myself laughing as I have not done in thousands of years. For the first time since Mo died, there is a lightness in my soul when I am in your presence."

My heart pounds in my chest. But my mind refuses to believe his words. After all, I have been burned before.

"What are you trying to say?"

"I have been fighting my growing feelings for you since the moment we met. *Before* the mating bond. In the beginning, I thought you were entertaining because I had been locked up, alone, for so long. But that did not explain why I continued to yearn to be in your presence. After I left you in the woods, I considered walking away. I *tried* to walk away. But I could not. I told myself that I was looking out for you—but when have I looked out for anyone else? From the start, it was an anomaly that I sought to explain even when it was simply unexplainable."

"Yet you pushed me away then too."

"Because I was scared," he admits, tilting his head to gaze at the stars. There is a trace of melancholy in his voice.

"You, scared?" I ask skeptically.

"Me, scared." He chuckles. "Even to my own ears that sounds foreign."

"Then why did you do it? Why were you so mean to me?"

"It was the only way to push you away. The more you smiled at me, the more you made me laugh, and it created a rift in my heart that I was unable to reconcile. One half wanted to continue as I have before: get the artifact, get back to Tartareia, and get my revenge. It seemed easy enough. But the other half wanted…more."

His thumb caresses my wrist before he brings it to his lips

for a soft kiss. Nonetheless, it's one that makes my heart stop in my chest.

"More?"

He simply smiles.

"If I stop running, will you have me?" He turns to me to ask.

I gulp down. The look in his eyes makes me shiver with awareness.

"I—"

"I do not mean right now. I am aware I fucked everything up."

"But what if you decide to run away again? What if…" I pause to gather my composure. "What if you get to Tartareia and you find a way to break our bond. What then?"

He stares at me.

"There is only one way through which I can show you that will not happen."

I raise my brows in question.

"We will consummate our bond so our mating will be complete."

My eyes widen in shock. But before I can process what he just said, he continues.

"Before you, my journey had only one outcome. Death. But with you… Maybe I will get a second chance at life."

My tongue peeks out to wet my lips as I consider his words.

My chest tightens, my heart heavy with emotion. It's everything I've ever wanted to hear, isn't it? But why am I not more…happy? Why am I not throwing myself in his arms already?

The truth is that no matter how much I may yearn for him, there is a small part of me that doubts this—that doubts everything about us.

"Tell me about her," I whisper. "About Mo."

His features tighten, and he looks away.

"If you want this to work, you will have to open up eventually, Nykander. How can I accept you when I know close to nothing about you? About…your love."

Just saying that aloud pains me more than anything. And that is one of the reasons why I doubt this so much.

I don't want to be second best. I don't want him to always think about his past lover and see me only as his consolation prize.

I want…everything.

Maybe it's greedy of me to desire that. But I don't want to be his second chance at life. I want to be his first and only. Too bad one woman already claimed that.

I swallow down against the wave of disappointment that envelops me.

The past is written in stone. I cannot change that. But the future…

"She was my wife," he finally says.

I look at him in surprise.

"In my culture, when males reach their maturity, they will take their first lover, who also serves as their blood donor. It is not uncommon after that for a male to have multiple lovers. Marriage happens much later, when a male is seven to ten thousand years old. There is a group of females in Tartareia —the daughters of Tenebreis—who are specifically reared for the task to be a wife to a male in a position of power. Their breeding is immaculate, and they are raised in complete seclusion to be pure for their future husband and ensure that their children will also have the perfect pedigree. It is an archaic practice, but it is how things are always done within the ranks of the aristocracy."

I nod, urging him to continue.

"I was three thousand years old when I met her. She was…the only person who ever believed in me. Back then, we were at war with Aperion, and I had already seen my fair share of fighting. She was everything the battlefield was not. Pure. Shy. Mischievous." He smiles fondly. "But she was *not* a daughter of Tenebreis. I took her as my wife against my family's wishes. Back then, I was not aware of my brother's plot to kill me. I had always known he did not like me very much since I inherited my teleportation abilities from our mother's side and my dark matter manipulation from our father's. He inherited none. Our conflict began when our father died, a few years after my sister was born. My brother assumed the role of the leader of our clan, but he always saw me as a threat to his power. So one day, he tried to kill me." He stops abruptly, his eyes squeezing shut. "Yet it was not me he killed. It was her. Mo."

A tremble racks his body.

"She died instead of me."

The pain in his voice is unmistakable. It's raw, a wound that is still bleeding.

"Nykander…"

"I could not even say goodbye. Her soul's essence was destroyed, so nothing remained of her. Nothing," he says on a ragged voice.

"I'm so sorry," I whisper.

She might be my opponent in this game of love, but she is also the reason why Nykander is standing here today. With me.

She…saved him.

How can I hate someone like that?

How can I resent someone who saved him so he could find his way to me?

He brings his hand to wipe a tear of blood dripping from the corner of his eye. He looks away from me, not wanting to show me this vulnerable side of him. Yet it's *this* side that makes my heart beat faster in my chest and my soul clamor even more for his.

"It's okay to cry if it hurts, Nykander."

He shakes his head, blinking back more tears.

"Since then, I have been trying to find a way back to avenge her. It was the only thing on my mind until…"

Before I can help myself, I reach for him. I cup his cheeks within my palms and bring his face closer to mine, urging him to look at me. His eyes are a tumultuous gray surrounded by a sea of blood. His eyes bleed just like his soul does, and it breaks my heart despite knowing he bleeds for another—for someone who is *not* me.

"Grieve her. Cry for her. But if you want to come to me, you will have to leave all your baggage behind," I tell him gently. "I like you. I really do. Maybe I more than like you, which, I'll damned if I know why, considering how you've behaved toward me. But there *is* something between us. I will accept that. But I cannot envision spending an eternity with someone who wishes I were another woman. I cannot—*will not*—be with you unless you let her go. I am not asking you to give up your revenge or forget about her—it would be cruel of me to do so. But I am asking you that if you are with me, you are *only* with me. There is no place for a ghost between us, and I would rather spend my life alone than with someone who was hung up on another woman."

He blinks and the blood drops fall down his cheeks. I lean in and lick them with my tongue, tasting the sweetness of his blood.

"What are you doing to me, Barbi?" he asks in a ragged voice. "How is it that you make me forget everything when I am with you?"

He grabs my nape with his hand, bringing me close to him and resting his forehead against mine.

"I have not been with another in seven thousand years," he mutters, his mouth close to my skin. His hot breath fans against my cheek, making me shiver in response. "I have not *looked* at another female in seven thousand years. Until this. Until you."

"Nykan—"

"Let me get it out, Barbi. Words are not my strong suit, and you might find many instances in which I say the wrong things because I cannot articulate the right ones." He swallows. "I was raised in a military household. I trained and fought. After I left Tartareia, I scoured world after world in search of the artifact, doing nothing but scheme, fight, and kill. In all those years, nothing shook my focus. Until you ended up in the same cell with me—until you made me laugh for the first time in forever. I have been fighting this all along, thinking I could not betray Mo's memory. But someone helped me realize that allowing you in would not betray her memory, it would be honoring it."

My lashes flutter in confusion, but he merely smiles.

"I am not a good male, Barbi. I do not have honorable intentions. My plan still stands."

"I don't need you to be good, Nykander. I only need you to be good to *me*."

His hands caress my jaw as he regards me with longing in his eyes. Leaning into me, his lips part over my pulse point as he traces it with his tongue. His fangs elongate, grazing my sensitive flesh.

A low moan erupts from my throat.

In the blink of an eye, I am on my back on the grass, with him looming over me. His features are swathed in darkness. There is only the dim light from the moon that illuminates half of his face, revealing his starved expression.

He brushes his lips over my neck, but he doesn't bite me even though I give him unfettered access.

He moves lower.

His mouth hovers over my breasts, his breath tickling me even through the material of the dress.

My breathing becomes labored as I imagine him touching me there, licking me there…

A shudder travels down my body.

But he is only teasing me.

He slides lower, down my hips.

Pulling on my dress, he lifts it to reveal my naked legs. The cold air of the night caresses my private parts and it dawns on me I'm still not wearing any panties.

"Uhm, Nykander…" I'm about to voice my concern, but the words stop in my throat as he places his mouth on my inner thigh.

He glides his tongue over my skin, kissing his way up. Just as I think I have his trajectory figured out, he surprises me by sinking his fangs into my thigh, feeding directly from my femoral artery.

My back arches as a mix of pain and pleasure shoots through me. Blood flows into his mouth, making me light-headed and entirely at his mercy.

His hands cup my ass as he spreads me further, feasting on me and savoring every drop.

A deep rumble erupts from his chest as he removes his fangs from my flesh, using his mouth instead to lick every bit of blood left until my wound closes.

"Fuck," he mutters in an unrecognizable voice. "So sweet. So…" he trails off as he continues to make his way up, biting into me again.

I thread my fingers through his hair as I urge him to take more, consume me until there's nothing left of me—until every bit of my essence finds its home inside him.

Once more, he leans back to lap at the wound as it's closing, bunching my dress over my hips to reveal my naked sex.

I'm wet. Embarrassingly so.

But he doesn't seem to mind as he inhales me deeply, relishing my scent. His mouth is right on top of my sex, his breath caressing my drenched folds. My body is weeping for him. It doesn't care about anything but fulfillment. It craves that sweet ecstasy that he's flaunting in front of me.

"You smell so good," he rasps, nuzzling his face between my legs. "So fucking sweet."

I gulp down as a wave of embarrassment overtakes me. This is the first time someone has seen me like this, and despite being incredibly attracted to him, something doesn't feel...right.

This is going too fast. I might lust for him with my entire being, but he hasn't even kissed me yet.

"Nykander," I call out, pulling on his hair. He raises his head to look at me. His eyes have the same crazed look as before, his irises almost entirely black. "Stop," I murmur shyly. "This is too soon. Too..."

It takes him a moment to register my words and he suddenly wrenches himself away from me.

He stands up to his full height. He averts his gaze, his chest rising and falling.

"I—" I mumble awkwardly as I get myself into a seating position and pull my dress down to cover myself.

"You do not need to explain yourself to me, Barbi."

"It's not that I don't want to. I do, but..." I bite my lip in uncertainty. "I don't have much experience and we're going too fast."

He whips his head around to stare at me. The intensity of his expression makes the ache between my legs intensity.

My cheeks flame under his perusal, and I squirm around to make myself more presentable while attempting to alleviate some of the discomfort down there.

God, this is the first time I've been this aroused, and I have no idea how to handle it.

"What experience do you have?" The question comes out as a growl as his body tenses.

"Uhm." I peer at him from beneath my lashes. "None?"

His gaze scans me from head to toe before he releases a deep sigh, as if my answer offered him relief.

"And those *guys your age?*" He raises a brow at me.

An awkward smile pulls at my lips.

"There aren't any," I murmur dryly.

Taking a step forward, he drops to one knee in front of me. His palm cups my cheek, his thumb caressing my jaw.

"Good," he purrs. "I will take you back to the cabin now."

I stare at him in confusion.

"W-what?" I blink. That was sudden. "Did I do something wrong? Did you want to…you know? I'm so sorry, Nykander, but I always imagined my first time to be special, and this isn't exactly special." I wave toward the dog house. "Especially since I don't know if I have fully forgiven you just yet. Maybe after we spend more time together? You know, not fighting and with you not being an ass. I know you said you want to consummate the bond but… Can I have some time? That is not to say I don't want to. It's just that I don't know what to expect, really. I've read books and I've seen spicy movies, but that's about it, and I know real life is not fiction so…"

There I go, rambling like a mad woman again.

"Barbi." He smiles. "You do not have to worry about it. We will go at your pace," he assures me.

I give him a tremulous smile.

"Thank you."

"But that is not why I need to take you back," he continues, his voice holding a hint of embarrassment.

My brows go up. In response, he points to his pants.

My eyes travel down his body for the first time and a gasp flies past my lips.

He's hard. Very, very hard. Painfully hard.

"I require some time to fix this problem," he adds apologetically. "And that sweet smell of yours does not make it easy on me."

"Oh."

"Come on, it is late. I will take you back."

He helps me to my feet, ready to go, when I stop him.

"Are you sure you are not mad?" I ask, taking a step back to put some distance between us.

But because I am a clumsy mess who is blushing uncontrollably, I trip backward. Limbs flailing, I almost make contact with the ground when he catches me. He steadies me, his touch burning me through my clothes.

"I am not mad, Barbi. Why should I be? I respect your choices and I will let you take the lead."

I bite my lip.

"Is that painful?" I nod toward the dent in his pants. "Since you know… You haven't had any action in thousands of years. You haven't, right? You said you haven't looked at another woman, but does that mean you also haven't… done *it*?"

"It?" He raises a brow, amused.

"You know what I mean," I mumble awkwardly.

"Yes, that is exactly what it means. I have not been with a female in over seven thousand years."

My lashes flutter.

"That is a long time," I murmur softly.

"Which is why any additional time will not make a difference," he tells me with a gentle smile.

"I see," I reply pensively. "And have you been with many women? How many have you kissed? How many have you been to second base with? What about home run? Were you a playboy? You now know about my experience level, but I don't know about yours. And to make sure things will go smoothly, I need to know what I am up against."

He tilts his head to the side, amused.

"I did not understand half the things you said," he says with a chuckle. "But to answer your first question, the only female I have ever kissed and been with is Mo."

"Oh."

A pang of envy spears through me.

She was his *first*. No wonder he can't forget her. She probably taught him everything.

"Was it...nice?"

"Barbi." He sighs. "What is with all these questions?"

"I am curious."

"I do not think you want to know that. Some things are better left unsaid."

I peer at him surreptitiously.

"You don't have to tell me that then. But what else did you do with her?"

"Barbi," he calls my name in a warning tone.

"Fine, fine. But you said you would f—" I swallow, finding it hard to say the word aloud. "Fuck my ass," I blurt out, immediately reddening in the process. "Did you do that with her too?"

I half turn, palming my cheeks in an attempt to stop my racing heart.

He's right that some things are better left unsaid, but I can't help but be curious. I want to know what I have to measure up against and what I need to do to erase her from his mind until he only sees *me*. And one way I can do that is by having mind-blowing sex with him—so much so he becomes addicted to me.

But the issue remains that I am rather clueless about how to do that.

I should have brought one of my spicy romances with me.

"You are impossible." He shakes his head. "But no. We did not do that."

I whip my head around, my smile widening. I can't say I've given much thought to anal before, but there's a start to everything, no?

"Then I will be your first, too," I declare. "I will have at least one of your firsts," I gush.

He stares at me for moments on end.

"I suppose you are right," he says, his lips curving up. "Assuming you will let me fuck your ass."

I bite my lip as my body becomes even warmer.

"Eventually. We can work our way up to it."

"I cannot believe we are having this conversation." He laughs as he scrubs a hand over his face.

"Why? It's a must-have conversation for new couples. And that is what we are, no? We are a new couple. Not that I have forgiven you just yet. But I am getting there. In the meantime, we are boyfriend and girlfriend," I say as I point at him before pointing at myself.

"A couple, huh? I suppose that is what we are."

"Since intimate relations are important to a couple, I think it's better to lay it all out from the start. This way we will have a much more pleasurable time together," I say confidently.

"And how would you know that?" He raises a brow. "You have no experience."

"Maybe." I shrug. "But that is how I *want* to acquire experience. Transparently. With communication. I want us to be honest with each other. If our souls are in agreement, our bodies will be, too."

His eyes widen at my words and he averts his gaze. His chest moves up and down with every breath.

"You said you wanted your first time to be special. What is special for you?"

"Love," I answer immediately. "I want you to love me. Be so irrevocably in love with me that you cannot envision us being apart even for one moment."

"Love," he repeats, tasting the word on his tongue and finding it foreign.

"Love me, Nykander, and I will give myself wholly to you." I step closer. "Body and soul. I will be yours. Love me, and you will have my unfailing devotion—for an eternity." I raise myself on the tips of my toes and lay a chaste kiss on his neck. "But cheat on me, and I will become your worst nightmare—for eternity and beyond."

He gazes down at me with an inscrutable expression.

"See, I am a rather simple creature. I only require one thing." I smile to make light of the situation.

He doesn't share my amusement.

"You, Barbi, are far from simple, for what you ask is the most invaluable thing in the universe."

21

We walk down the village square hand in hand. He's so big by my side. So protective.

A dreamy sigh escapes me as I nestle closer to his side.

"Come with me. I have something to show you," he says with a wicked gleam in his eyes.

I let him drag me along to one of the village shops. As we make our way inside, the smell of sweets and pastries wafts toward me. I inhale deeply, my mouth already watering.

"Mr. Nykander," the shop keeper addresses him, wiping his hands on his apron. He steps forward with a smile, inviting us to look around.

"Do you have those chocolate truffles I commissioned?"

"Yes, of course," the shopkeeper replies. He goes to the back and in no time, he returns with a tray filled with chocolate truffles.

"We don't have anything to trade in for this." I get up on the tips of my toes to whisper.

"Do not worry about that. They are already paid for," Nykander says with a wink.

The shopkeeper places the truffles in a carton and hands it to him, wishing us a good day.

I lick my lips as I stare at it.

We go out and take a seat on a nearby bench. Before I can try to steal one, he beats me to it. He lifts a truffle to my mouth.

My lashes flutter at his thoughtfulness, and I lean forward, wrapping my lips around the truffle and biting half of it.

He pops the other half into his mouth and I don't think I've ever seen anything more erotic than this.

"You have something here," he murmurs as he comes closer. He brings his thumb to my lower lip, slowly caressing it. His mouth nears mine, and I instinctively close my eyes, waiting for that magical moment.

Yet before his lips can meet mine, a loud bang erupts in the background. I startle back. Nykander does the same, his expression grave. Looking back, I note smoke coming from the western part of the village. Soon, screams accompany it as villagers run for their lives, only to be struck down by an invisible source, cut in two.

Nykander's eyes flash and he immediately places me behind him, his shadows erupting from his body and surrounding me in a protective shell.

"What is it?" I ask as fear grips me like a tight vise.

He doesn't answer, his attention focused in front of him.

As the smoke slowly dissipates, Damien steps forward, followed by Jocelyn and his posse. He's wielding fire lassos as he cuts one terrified villager at a time, killing them without batting an eye.

Jocelyn smirks as she lays her eyes on me, and with a swing of her wrist, she sends a strong gust of wind toward us.

"Stay back, Barbs. I got this," Nykander tells me in a strained voice. Leaving me behind shielded in his dark smoke, he lifts his hand, morphing his shadows into a sword that becomes an extension of his body.

Damien does the same with his flames, containing them within a small blade that destroys everything in its path.

They meet in the middle, their swords clashing just as their energies fight against each other. Nykander's dark shadows meet Damien's scarlet red flames. Their forces seem to relatively match. As one energy gains more ground, the other quickly recovers, driving it back.

My heart beats wildly in my chest. But my focus is shaken as another strong gust of air hits my shield, making it rattle.

Jocelyn appears in front of me.

"You stole my dog," she grits out, sending another blow.

I'm pushed backward, and small cracks appear in the dark shield.

My eyes widen with fear. I can't ask for help, since that would distract Nykander from his battle.

"You didn't deserve him, you two-faced bitch," I yell out.

But my insult only makes her more mad.

She grinds her jaw as she gathers her energy around, shimmery particles erupting from her palms before she throws it at me.

The blow is hard enough that I'm sent flying together with what's left of my shell.

"Barbi!" Nykander shouts my name, glancing back at me. His features are filled with worry as he angles his body toward me, ready to intervene. But that moment of inattention is all it takes for Damien to plunge his blade through his heart—a blade coated with his sire's blood.

"Nykander!" I call out, feeling the pain in my soul.

I startle awake. Sweat covers my entire body.

"Are you all right?" Nykander asks as he bursts into the cabin. "I heard you scream."

"Oh. I am…fine," I mutter.

It was a dream. It was nothing but a dream. I chant to myself in hopes I can get rid of this awful feeling in my chest. It *was* a dream. But it felt so damn real. Down to the taste of the chocolate that still coats my mouth.

"Are you still in pain?" He inquires as he lures the dogs away from me with some food. He drops the morsels into their bowls before he comes to my side, taking a seat on the bed.

"A little." I sigh. "The tincture Mr. Foerie gave me is working, and I'm on the fourth day of my period, so it should end soon."

He grunts.

"It's not really fair that you can mirror all my injuries but you can't feel my period pain," I grumble.

"That is, indeed, quite unfair." He chuckles. "But I have something to hopefully make that better. His smile turns devilish as he reaches into the pocket of his shirt and removes a handkerchief wrapped around some solid items.

Curious, I lean forward and take it from him, slowly unwrapping it to reveal five chocolate truffles.

Just like the ones in my dreams.

I whip my head up in surprise.

"Did you read my mind?"

He shakes his head.

"I do not have that ability, unfortunately."

"Then how did you know I was craving chocolate?" I ask as I inhale the delicious aroma of the truffles.

My mouth waters and I lick my lips as I stare at them longingly.

"You said you liked chocolate a while back. It merely took me a little longer than expected to get them." He smiles ruefully.

"Yes, but *how* did you get them? They don't have any around here."

"I might have spoken with Elijah to allow me to temporarily leave the Sanctuary. I got them from a city called Antwerp in your world. I am told it is the best chocolate available."

I stare at him in wonder.

"You went to my world to get them? But… How if you cannot access the portal?"

"You forget that I have been there before. That allows me to teleport without the use of a portal."

"Oh. So technically you could take me back too if you wanted, no?"

He raises a brow at me.

"*If* I wanted," he replies.

My cheeks heat up and I look away. Since his apology, he's been the consummate gentleman, always looking out for my needs and being there for me to vent if something bothers me. And though I haven't verbally accepted his apology, his behavior has shown me that he is earnest, and that warms my heart.

"Have you heard more about Damien and Jocelyn? What if they follow you here?" I inquire, the pain from my dream still vivid.

"Elijah assured me they will not be able to cross their barriers. The High Priestess herself built them thousands of years ago and so far no one has been able to cross over without an invitation."

I nod slowly, though there is a part of me that is still wary. Damien wouldn't have gone through all the trouble to kidnap Nykander and torture his mind just to give up now. He doesn't strike me as the type to easily accept defeat.

"But what if they find this place?"

"Nothing will happen, Barbi. Trust me. Damien was able to get me before because I was at my weakest. I will not make the same mistake again."

"But he has your sire's blood. Won't that hurt you?"

"Do not worry about it. I will eventually confront Damien, but not here nor now. We are safe in the Sanctuary. And after I get the artifact, it will be even more unlikely that he will be able to defeat me," he adds confidently.

I bite my nails as I consider his words. He knows best, of course. He has fought Damien in the past and he knows what to expect. But still…there is a niggling feeling deep inside me that will not let me be.

"Here," he mentions, taking a truffle and feeding it to me. I bite half of it, and he eats the other half.

This is just like in my dream…

He watches me intently as I chew, bringing his thumb over my lip and swiping the remaining cocoa from my mouth.

"You are so beautiful," he murmurs in a low voice.

I tip my chin down, suddenly shy.

"This is the first time you've told me that."

"Really? My bad. I should tell it to you daily. You are absolutely stunning, Barbs."

My lips pull up in a wide grin. I cannot hide my joy and as I peer at his expression, I note the happiness reflected in his features, too.

I scoot closer to him. Popping another truffle in my mouth, I chew slowly as I throw my hands around his neck, bringing myself at eye level with him.

Errant strands of hair fall across his forehead, making him seem younger, more approachable. I use one hand to push his hair aside, letting my fingers linger on his cheek.

"I forgive you," I whisper. "But don't do it again, okay? You get one more chance, but after this, there will be none."

A strained smile appears on his face before he leans to lay a kiss on my forehead. He doesn't move, simply hovering over my skin, his breath a light caress.

"Thank you," he finally speaks.

"Are you sure Damien will not be able to get here?" I blurt out, ruining the moment.

He threads his fingers through his hair as he releases a heavy sigh.

"I am sure, Barbi. What brought this on?"

"I just had a bad dream." I strain a smile. "It made me a little unsettled."

He frowns.

"What bad dream?"

"That Damien and his group of mages came to the Sanctuary and killed everyone," I confess in a low voice. "He had this fire blade that was coated in your sire's blood and he stabbed you with it."

He narrows his eyes at me.

"Why don't you tell me about this dream from the beginning? It might help to talk about it."

I glance at him from the corner of my eye.

He grabs another truffle and brings it to my mouth.

I slowly bite into it and I recount everything I'd seen in my dream.

He doesn't speak as he listens attentively. And as I eat the last of the truffles, he brings me closer to him, his arms coming around me in a comforting embrace.

"It was just a bad dream, Barbs. Nothing more."

I nod, hugging him tighter.

"I wish I had some powers, too. I felt so useless…"

"You are not useless, and you have me to protect you. Do you trust me, Barbs?"

I peer up at him.

"Yes," I whisper.

"Then trust that I will not fail you."

"If we meet Damien at any point, can you please kill him?"

His brows shoot up in surprise.

"You want me to kill him?"

"I don't want him to get to my world. It might not be the best place, but it's still my world. My parents are there and—"

"I promise you," he interrupts me. "The moment I see him again, he will die by my hand."

His words put me at ease, and I snuggle closer to him as my eyes drift shut once more.

It's sometime later that I'm woken up by a strange noise. I open my eyes to see Nykander pacing up and down the cabin, his expression one of confusion mixed with worry.

"What's wrong?" I frown, rubbing my eyes to chase the sleep away.

"I think PomPom is about to give birth," he states, his eyes full of terror.

I immediately jump out of bed.

"Why didn't you wake me up?"

"You were sleeping and—"

"Nykander! She is my baby. You should have woken me up. Where is she?"

He nods to the bathroom.

I stride there, flinging open the door and finding her nestled inside the pink dog house. She whines in pain, rolling from one side to the other. BonBon is pacing around too, his little barks only making PomPom more anxious.

"Can you please keep BonBon in the room?" I turn to Nykander.

He nods and, taking the dog in his arms, he takes him to the room.

I get down on the floor and slowly massage my baby, murmuring sweet words to her.

"What does she need?" Nykander's voice rings out from the doorway.

I pause for a moment to think.

"Hot towels. Scissors and thread and needle. We will need to cut the umbilical cord and stitch them. At least that's what I saw other people do in videos on YouTube."

He frowns, but he doesn't argue with me. He disappears for a moment before he returns with everything I've asked.

He places the towels on the sink and thoroughly disinfects the scissors and needles.

"What now?" he asks.

I turn to glare at him, but he is as worried as I am.

"Now we wait." I sigh. "She'll let us know when she's ready."

He gives me a tight nod as he sinks to the floor next to me. He surprises me by taking my hand in his and squeezing it.

"It will be all right," he assures me.

"What are we going to do with the puppies, Nykander? How are we going to take care of them? In my world, they would need to go to the vet, get shots, have a wellness exam. There are so many things to think about, like nutrition. Puppies need special food after they're weaned. And they need lots of toys, and—"

"You are getting ahead of yourself, Barbi. We will figure it out together." He gives me a comforting smile.

I know I am getting ahead of myself, but just thinking about those helpless little babies makes my anxiety skyrocket.

PomPom's whines accentuate, and Nykander takes off the roof from the house so we get a better view of her. She's lying on her side, her eyes semi-closed.

I reach out to massage her belly, praying that everything will go smoothly.

"I see something coming out," Nykander exclaims.

"The babies are coming. Oh, Lord!"

I hurry to get the towel and place it under PomPom's bum. I murmur sweet words to her as she struggles to push.

There is a sudden pop and the baby comes out covered in the placenta. Taking the scissors, I look around for the umbilical cord, only to realize it's wrapped around the baby's neck.

"Oh no, Nykander," I murmur, terrified.

I quickly cut the cord and PomPom nuzzles her face against the placenta-covered little pup, licking away and trying to tear it off him. I help her with that, and she finally starts licking at her baby. It's a black male by the sight of it. Except…

He's not breathing.

"Nykander… What are we going to do?" I ask in horror as I turn to look at him.

His jaw twitches as he gazes down at the baby. He doesn't answer me. Instead, he grabs the little pup from PomPom's side, getting the remaining placenta off him and doing some type of CPR on his chest with his fingers.

I swallow hard against the wave of nausea and pain that travels down to my soul.

He presses his forefinger against his tiny chest and establishes a rhythm—up and down.

I bite my lip as I slide closer to him. My shoulder meets his as I watch with trepidation as the seconds go by and yet there is no movement from the baby. He's still not breathing.

"He's…dead," I whisper, and something breaks inside of me. Tears stab at my eyes, rivulets coursing down my cheeks as I cannot contain my anguish.

Nykander shakes his head, a look of pure determination on his face.

"He is not dead. I will not allow him to die," he mutters under his breath, continuing to press on his little body.

But when that doesn't work, he takes him in his hand and brings him to his mouth. Parting the baby's little lips, he blows air into him at the same time as he massages his chest.

He does this for a few seconds before I note the first movement. A leg—he just moved his leg.

Nykander pulls back long enough to notice that the pup is now breathing, so with one last massage, he places him next to PomPom and lets her lick him and give him her motherly heat.

I stare in shock at him.

"Nykander, you… You saved him," I say among sobs.

He barely acknowledges my words as he continues to stare at PomPom with her new pup.

"He will *not* die," he repeats, almost robotically.

I reach for his hand, bringing it against my cheek.

"He will not die." I nod. "Because of you. He will live," I murmur as I continue to stare at him in wonder.

My heart is so full. I don't think I have ever experienced this depth of emotion before. And the fact that he cannot take his eyes off the baby, that he keeps reaching for him to make sure he's all right.

If before I had a crush on him, now it morphed into full-blown love.

"Good girl." He pats PomPom on her head, petting her gently. "You did great."

As we wait for the other babies, I cannot help but be in tune with every little movement he makes, every sigh, every breath.

He gave his breath to the baby. He breathed life into that little pup. I still cannot wrap my mind around it, but I only know that the mark on my chest hums with an unprecedented strength. Yet this time, it's not just surface-level. It reaches deep within to the depths of my soul, caressing my very essence.

I am in awe. Simply, utterly in awe.

And in love.

"I think she only had one baby," he mentions pensively, his eyes glued to her.

I press my hand on her stomach, frowning.

"You might be right. Only one baby. A little miracle," I say as I glance at him. "A miracle you made happen."

"It was nothing," he says gruffly.

"It was everything, Nykander." I smile. "Everything."

He looks away, a flush going up his neck.

I shake my head, but my own heart is still beating like crazy.

We clean PomPom and tie the baby's belly button before we help him search for milk. He nestles close to her nipples, and after a few attempts, he manages to latch.

Nykander and I sigh in relief.

We turn at the same time and our gazes clash. We're both breathing hard.

I lean in at the same time as he does, our lips mere inches apart. I glance up to find him staring at me with an intense expression.

Licking my lips, I close my eyes.

"You're killing me, Barbs," he rasps.

His lips skim the corner of my mouth, moving lower, to my chin and neck. His fangs graze my skin. His arm curls around my waist as he pulls me closer, my body flush against his.

He caresses my pulse point before he sinks his fangs into me.

I moan aloud, twining my arms around his neck and holding him close to me.

"Nykander," I breathe out. "Harder," I urge him as I press against him, feeling the contours of his body.

He complies, angling his mouth to sink his fangs deeper into my flesh.

Pain erupts in that spot, but the pleasure soon follows.

The same spot is gaping open on his neck and, driven by an unknown instinct, I trace my lips down his neck, opening my mouth and drinking in his blood.

The moment stretches forever.

There's only him and the potent taste of his blood. Only him and the pleasure he's giving me with his mouth.

An impossible arousal claims my body and I squirm against him in an effort to find some relief.

He drags himself from my neck, blood dripping down his chin as he stares at me with an odd look in his eyes.

My mind is foggy with desire as I reach for his neck again, licking the last of his blood as his wound closes. I trail my tongue up his face, cupping his cheeks between my hands and licking the drops of blood off his chin.

He grabs my hands, taking them off his face and bringing them to his mouth for a quick kiss.

Our moment is soon ruined, though, as BonBon starts scratching at the door and barking to be let in. He cries and whines the more we ignore him.

Nykander and I look at each other with an amused expression.

"He's already taking the daddy role seriously," I joke.

"Let us reunite him with his family, then," Nykander says.

He gets up and opens the door. BonBon barges in, sniffing his way to PomPom and their baby.

He licks the pup before going to PomPom and licking her everywhere.

A smile pulls at my lips at the pretty picture.

Nykander has the same wistful expression as he glances at the happy family.

We stare at them for a while before we turn at the same time. Our eyes find each other, and slowly, he reaches for my hand, covering it with his own.

He doesn't say anything. But he doesn't have to.

His gentle smile speaks a thousand words. And this time, it's not directed to the dogs.

It's directed toward me.

It dawns on me that the dogs aren't the only family unit here.

I squeeze his hand.

We are a family, too.

22

"**B**ut he's a puppy! His stomach can't digest that," I complain to Mr. Foerie as he gives me a list of foods to give to Ander, our little pup.

"He is already weaned. That means he can start eating hard foods now," he says with a roll of his eyes.

"But… When PomPom was a pup, she had special puppy food that is not available here. Every time she had some chicken, her poop was soft. And it shouldn't be soft. Maybe we can make a paste and dry it? That should help, no? We could at least try and—"

"Miss Barbara. I have tended to my fair share of animals, and they all did fine with meat and rice."

"But my PomPom—"

"Excuse me for saying this, Miss Barbara, but that dog of yours is spoiled. I have never in my eighty years of life seen a dog more pampered, as if it were a person."

I gasp aloud, taking a step back.

"She *is* a person! How dare you suggest otherwise?"

He raises a brow at me, shaking his head.

"You… You…" I stammer. How could he imply that my

PomPom is not a person? She is smart and caring and loyal. She is the *perfect* girl.

"It is quite clear we have a difference of opinions. Please see yourself out," he says, turning his back to me.

I stare at him, flabbergasted.

"You're throwing me out?" I blink.

"I believe that is what I just did," he replies drily. As he steps away from me, he mutters under his breath, "Never seen such an ignorant, empty-headed female before."

His voice was low, his words not meant for my ears. But I heard them anyway.

I blink back tears as I find my voice.

"Why are you calling me empty-headed?" I ask in a small voice. "I just want the best for my dog and I offered some suggestions. Why are you dismissing me like this?"

He stops. Half turning, he glares at me.

"And who is the one with the experience here, Miss Barbara? You asked for my advice and I gave it to you. If you choose to be obstinate, then you can do as you please and leave me alone. I never liked those dogs of yours anyway. Too spoiled," he sneers.

My mouth drops open in shock.

"But… But…"

"Leave, Miss Barbara. You are no longer welcome here."

I am so shocked, I can barely come up with a proper reply. Especially as he goes one step further and pushes me out of his shop, closing the door in my face.

My lashes flutter in disbelief, and for a few moments, I'm unable to move.

He… He kicked me out. He insulted me and my dogs and kicked me out.

I rub my eyes with the back of my hand, though the tears come unbidden.

Am I too sensitive, or was that just downright rude?

Not one to give up, I take a deep breath and stride to the

kitchens. If he isn't going to help me, then I'm going to do everything myself.

More tears fall down my cheeks as I make my way through the village, and it doesn't escape me the way people whisper and speculate for the reason behind them. This might be called the Sanctuary, but who offers a sanctuary to the people inside? Maybe because it's such a small village, but every little thing becomes gossip around here. You could trip and fall in front of your house, and in a matter of minutes, the news spreads throughout the commune. It already happened to me once, and people still gossip about me being the girl with two left feet.

But then again, maybe it is because I am the only human here. To them, I am somewhat of an oddity. I have no abilities save for the healing I borrowed from Nykander. And despite the fact that most females here wish to find a good mate and start a family, they are all knowledgeable in battle and they work side by side with the men.

I try not to mind the way people stare at me as I enter the kitchens. I head straight for the pantry, putting aside a few items that I know are good for puppies—all ingredients PomPom's puppy food had contained.

Cutting them in small bits, I place them in a mortar and start grinding them to a fine paste with a pestle. It's hard work for someone with zero arm strength, but that puppy deserves the best.

Maybe you should have asked Nykander to do it for you.

Maybe. But I did not want to come across as useless—it already happens enough on a daily basis.

In the last weeks, I have embarrassed myself enough with my lack of practical skills that should make Nykander reconsider his stance on dating me. I mean, I wouldn't date myself either. Just imagine that. Two Barbis that have no idea how to survive in the world without modern technology. It would be a disaster!

Maybe Mr. Foerie had a point when he called me empty-headed and ignorant.

A sniffle erupts in the air, and I belatedly realize it's coming from me.

Damn it! Why am I crying again?

He *was* right that I am not very knowledgeable when it comes to a lot of things. But to imply that I would be ignorant about my babies' health is downright insulting.

"I'm not dumb," I whisper to myself. "I really am not..." Another sniffle. "I am a poop master at least," I murmur to myself, a semblance of a smile pulling at my lips. If everything fails, at least I have that. After all, I am the *best* at detecting when my babies are sick just by the color and consistency of their poop.

You're being silly, Barbi.

It is a skill, and one I am proud of—no matter what others might say.

In a way, I'm lucky the fates have decided I would make a good mate for Nykander, since otherwise I would probably be forever alone.

That thought makes me even more desolate.

I wipe my tears away as I focus my efforts on grinding the ingredients for the pup. PomPom no longer has milk. Ander keeps trying to latch to her nipple, but then cries when he cannot get anything to eat.

Nykander had the great idea to get some goat's milk for him, but we need to slowly transition him to solids.

After I'm done with the paste, I spread it evenly on a tray.

A loud bang makes me jump up in surprise as Nykander shows up in front of me.

He regards me with narrowed eyes.

"What happened?" he asks in a low, dangerous voice.

"Oh, why do you think something happened?" I quip in a forced cheery voice. "I was just making something for Ander.

This should help him get used to solids since it's not very hard for him to chew with his little teeth and—"

"Barbi, what happened?" He interrupts me.

"I don't know what you mean," I murmurs.

"Your eyes are red," he grits out as he takes a step toward me.

"That? It's from the onions. You know how they make you cry." I let out a small laugh. "They're strange vegetables, aren't they? I was thinking about what you told me about souls and reincarnations. Could I reincarnate into an onion? Then I would make people cry. Of course, it's sad that I would eventually get eaten, but maybe I could be a mutant onion and give them a stomachache, or maybe food poisoning. Is there such a thing as a poisonous onion?"

"Who made you cry, Barbi?" He stops me from my work, grabbing my hands in his two, much bigger ones.

"No one. I told you—"

"And I do not believe you. Tell me. Who made you cry?"

"It was nothing, Nykander. Really. I was just being particular about Ander's food, and Mr. Foerie and I had a disagreement over it. That is all."

"What did he say to you?" He continues to probe.

"It was just a small disagreement…"

"You cried. That is not small. Tell me," he demands.

I bite my lip as I consider whether I should tell him the truth or lie. I don't want this to turn into a conflict.

"Tell me. And it better be the truth, Barbi. Do not lie to me, or I will find other ways to get the truth."

"Don't do anything, okay? It wasn't a big deal."

"Barbi?" He raises a brow.

"Fine. He said I was empty-headed and that he hated my dogs because they are too spoiled," I say, quickly looking away.

"He said you were empty-headed?"

"And ignorant," I add quietly. "Which isn't entirely false. I know I'm not the brightest..."

He stares at me, his cheek twitching.

"Stop," he suddenly demands.

I close my mouth, glancing warily at him.

"You are not ignorant, Barbi, or empty-headed. How can you believe that?"

"But—"

"I do not like you putting yourself down. It is admirable how much you love your dogs, and you should not let anyone tell you how to care for them. I do not care who they are."

My lips spread into a shy smile.

"Thank you."

"Do not fucking thank me, Barbs. This is not all right. You will not refer to yourself as ignorant again, is that clear?"

"But I am technically ignorant of a lot of things. Before we came here, I had no idea how to cook or do laundry by hand and—"

"And you learned. You did not know, but you put in the effort to learn. No matter how many tries it took, you did it until you perfected it. There is no shame in not knowing something. Recognizing you do not know it and then putting in the work to learn it is a mark of greatness."

He straightens his back as he regards me, his words as unyielding as his countenance.

"Did you call me...great?" I ask tentatively, afraid it was just a figure of speech.

"I did. You are smart, hardworking, humble, and kind. And whoever does not recognize that can go fuck themselves," he states with great conviction.

My heart flutters in my chest.

"No one's ever called me that," I say in a small voice.

He tilts his head to the side, frowning.

"No one?"

I shaky my head.

"Air-headed, ditzy, sometimes delusional. Those are the words people would use to describe me," I murmur, half ashamed.

"Who?"

"Everyone at home. My parents…"

"Your parents?" he asks in horror.

"I do not fit their idea of a perfect daughter. Mainly my mother. But she wants me to be some type of genius when I am not and I have never been," I add with a sigh.

"That is her fault for not recognizing who you are and instead forcing you to be who they want you to be."

"Thank you for saying that."

"It is not a compliment. It is merely the truth."

"Still." I smile. "It's nice to have someone say that. I was feeling pretty shitty before, but now I'm happy," I say in a bright voice.

He watches me intently, a gentle smile curving at his lips.

"Let me help you." He comes over to my aisle and helps me prepare the food for little Ander, following my instructions to a T without voicing any objection.

And as we finish the food and go out, he surprises me with more chocolate truffles.

"I do not like it when you are sad," he mentions awkwardly as we walk back to our cabin. "If anything bothers you, tell me and I will fix it for you."

"I can do it myself, too, Nykander. But I appreciate the sentiment," I tell him with a smile.

He nods and reaches for my hand, cradling it in his bigger one. Warmth spreads through me and I barely contain my glee.

This is the first time he's taken the initiative.

We reach our cabin, and for a short while, we play with the dogs before Nykander tells me to get some rest and he will take them to get some exercise. Despite wanting to disagree for the simple reason that I want to spend more time with him, I relent and go to bed.

"Nykander?" I ask before he's about to go out the door.

"Huh?" He turns toward me, his brows raised.

"Do you think…" I clear my voice, fighting the blush creeping in on my cheeks. "Would you like to sleep on the bed with me at night from now on? You've been sleeping on that hard floor for months now and I worry about your back. Even though you can heal, I'm sure it can't be that comfortable."

"Are you sure you're just worried about my back?" he asks with a knowing smile.

My eyes widen and I avert my gaze.

"*Just* sleeping. Don't go thinking about other stuff. But it's fine if you don't want to. More space for me anyway."

"All right," he answers in a soft voice. "I will join you on the bed from now on."

I slowly glance up at him and our eyes meet. My cheeks are flaming hot. Just picturing him in the same bed with me makes my insides melt—and sends my imagination into overdrive.

His eyes crinkle around the corners, his gaze gentle and affectionate.

My mark heats up across my heart.

"That's it. I'm going to sleep," I suddenly declare, pulling the blanket over my face.

His chuckle echoes in the cabin long before he closes the door after him, and I can't help the giddy squeak that escapes me.

Finally, we will be in close confines. And maybe that proximity might lead to something else. Something of a steamier nature…

I flail my legs under the blanket in excitement. I need to make sure I'm clean-shaven and showered and smelling nice for him before I get into bed. With a smile on my face, I drift off to sleep.

. . .

COLDNESS SEEPS IN MY BONES. Opening my eyes, I realize I am in a dark forest, the wet grass my only cushion.

I'm on my back, staring at the gathering of trees that obstruct the view of the sky.

I jump up, fear creeping down my spine.

Where am I? Just a moment ago, I was in my bed, sleeping.

I look right and left, wondering how the hell I will get back, when I see the semblance of a light in the distance. It must be the village!

I dash toward it, only to find myself at the entrance to a cave. Light streams from inside, together with an echo of voices.

Frowning, I slow my pace as I go inside. Hopefully, I can ask for some guidance.

"Hello? I am no danger. I am lost and in need of help," I declare so that they know I am not an enemy.

No one answers me, and the deeper I go inside the cave, the light shines brighter.

I shield my eyes, blinking to get accustomed to the difference between the darkness outside and the light inside.

"My lady, she has come after the babe," a woman dressed in red mentions.

In the middle of the cave, the room is fully decorated as if it belonged in a palace. There is a king-sized bed, a vanity, and even a luxurious jacuzzi a few steps over.

On the bed, a woman dressed in a white nightdress is lying down, glancing at two newborn babies. Her blond locks obstruct her features, but she's caressing each of their faces with gentleness and love, her hands lingering on their little cheeks.

"Excuse me?" I call out when I'm in the middle of the room. Yet no one turns. It's as if I don't exist.

I go to the lady in red and wave in front of her.

"Can you please help?"

Nothing.

Her attention is focused on the lady in white.

"One more moment, Herwa. I want to commit his features to memory," the lady murmurs.

"Hello? Anyone? I am standing right here!" I call out.

Just like before, no one answers me.

I blink in shock, not knowing what to do. Am I...dead? Is that it? Am I a ghost and they can't see me? But how?

"Lispera." Herwa, the woman in red, sighs. "You do not have to do this."

I move to the side, getting a better look of Lispera. She is stunning. Her blond hair is complemented by a golden complexion, her eyes a deep brown. Her expression exudes warmth and kindness, and I immediately feel an affinity to her.

A sad smile descends upon Lispera's lips as she gazes at the two babies.

"I do. You know I do. Otherwise..." She closes her eyes, a tear slipping down her cheek.

One of the babies starts crying, and she takes him in her arms, swaying him gently and murmuring sweet words in his ears—how much she loves him and how sure she is he will have the best life possible.

"I love you, my baby boy. And I cannot wait to meet you once more. Someday," she says as she lays a kiss on his nose, then on his cheeks and forehead. She keeps him tucked to her side while tears fall down her cheeks.

"You still have time to name him," Herwa mentions as she goes to the bed to pick up the boy.

Lispera shakes her head. She gazes longingly at the baby.

"His new parents will have the perfect name for him."

Herwa lingers for a moment, her expression worried as she takes in Lispera's anguished one.

"Go. Go before I change my mind and cause a disaster," Lispera calls out, averting her eyes.

Herwa nods and retreats out of the room.

When I try to follow her, I find that I cannot. The door she just used to leave will not open for me, effectively keeping me locked inside the room. A sliver of fear courses through me.

"There, my little girl," Lispera speaks again. She cradles the baby to her chest, urging her to latch onto her nipple and feed.

She hums a melody to the baby, her lips trembling with sadness. She tries to smile, but she cannot.

Suddenly, her head whips up, her eyes narrowed.

"You should not be here," she says, staring straight at me.

My lashes flutter in confusion. I take a step forward.

"You can see me?" I ask.

But my question is ignored as the door opens again and Herwa comes inside.

"What about the baby girl? Have you picked a good family for her?"

Lispera shakes her head.

"I do not know what to do, Herwa. I touch her, and I see her future. All the possible versions. If I give her up, she will die. If I keep her by my side, she will die. How can I make a decision when her fate is set in stone? I cannot send my own child to her death," she murmurs in a low, terrified voice.

"You better than anyone know that fate can be cheated, my lady," Herwa says as she takes a seat on the bed.

"No matter what family I give her to, her end will be the same. Her soul will be consumed by a demon and she will be lost to me—forever."

Herwa regards her pensively.

"You have seen the future. But what about the past?"

Lispera frowns, holding tighter onto her baby.

"What do you mean?"

Herwa takes a deep breath.

"You can see her future from *this* point in time. But what if—"

"What you are suggesting is forbidden," Lispera gasps.

"Not any more forbidden than what you have already done, my lady. Shall I remind you who her father is?"

Lispera blushes, glancing away.

"It is because of who her parents are that she will be targeted. She may not be the firstborn, but she is still the daughter of a Supreme and of a half Primordial. That alone will make her a beacon for those wretched demons."

"Take away her powers," Herwa suggests. "Leave only enough to see her through hard times, but take most of her spiritual ability away from her."

Lispera bites her lip as she stares at her baby.

"You know what that does to our kind, Herwa. She will feel the emptiness her entire life."

"But she will be alive."

Lispera spends a few moments debating what to do. With a weary sigh, she places the child on the bed, then removes the cloth wrapped around the baby to reveal her naked flesh. Placing her open palm on her torso, she chants something under her breath. A stark light erupts, a ball of energy coming out from the baby. She maneuvers the energy around, wincing as she tries to control it.

"The jar, Herwa. Give me my jar," she commands.

Herwa rushes to the dresser, rummaging through a few trunks until she finds the jar in question. Grabbing it with both hands, she runs back to Lispera. Once close to the energy source, she opens the jar and Lispera pushes the energy ball inside. They both immediately snap the lid shut and Lispera uses her power to seal it.

But just as she releases a sigh of relief, her eyes go white. Her spine straightens, and she throws her head back.

Tears course down her cheeks and she cries out in anguish.

"My lady!" Herwa shakes her. "Snap out of it."

Seconds pass before Lispera's eyes regain their brown hue.

"It did not work, Herwa. We have not changed her fate at all—merely bought her some more time."

Herwa's features tighten, and she glances down at the chubby baby.

"Then the past is our only option. Depending on how far we go back, no one will know who she is, right?"

"It is worth a try." Lispera nods, bundling her baby against her chest. "Anything as long as she survives until I can meet her again."

I SLOWLY OPEN my eyes to find myself back at the cabin. In my bed. There is a warm body next to me, and as I peek over my shoulder, I note Nykander is fast asleep and hugging me from behind.

My lips stretch into a satisfied smile as I turn to study him.

He has such long lashes for a guy. They're longer than mine!

And his lips. They're so full and thick.

I shaky myself as a blush climbs up my cheeks.

"Are you enjoying the view?" he drawls, slowly opening his eyes.

I squeak aloud as I scramble away. But just as I'm about to fall, he catches me, pulling me on top of his body and cradling me to his chest. The beats of his heart are loud and clear. I hold my breath for a moment, and our heartbeats are fully aligned.

We beat to the same rhythm.

"You are so small," he murmurs in my hair. "You fit perfectly to my side."

"Is that your way of trying to charm me, Nykander?" I

raise a brow as I roll onto my belly. Still on his chest, I place my hands under my chin and watch him with a silly smile on my face.

"Is it working?"

"I don't know. Is it?" I ask mischievously.

"Hmm, what if I try this?" he muses as he leans in, brushing his lips against my forehead.

"I think you need to try more," I murmur breathlessly.

"This?" he asks, kissing my nose.

I giggle at the ticklish feeling, squirming around until I fall to the side. But he wastes no time in pulling me closer to him.

"Did you sleep well while I was gone?"

My brows furrow. Fragments of my unsettling dream come back to me.

"I had a strange dream," I mention.

"Another?"

"This one was even weirder. I was there, but no one could see me. Well, no one except this lady that said *You should not be here*' in an outraged tone."

"What sort of dream was that, Barbi?"

"I honestly don't know." I take a deep breath. "There were two women in the dream. One was named Lispera and one Herwa."

His body freezes.

"Did you say Lispera?"

I nod. "Do you know who that is?"

"Was," he corrects, his eyes wide with shock. "She was the Aperite Supreme who sealed off Tartareia seven thousand years ago."

"But… How would I know about that?"

He shakes his head.

"Precisely. How would *you* know about it?"

"And Herwa?"

"I am not familiar with that name. But Lispera is infamous; or famous, depending on who you ask. She was one of the strongest if not *the* strongest Supreme in generations."

"Did she have kids?"

"Not that I know of. She was unmarried, and Aperites frown upon children born out of wedlock. She was betrothed to another Supreme at some point, though."

"Oh. I wonder why I would dream about her of all things."

"Maybe it is a message."

I raise my brows in question.

"Lispera was the Ananke Supreme. The High Priestess we are looking for was under her direct command."

"If there was a message in there, I'm not sure I understood it," I mutter under my breath.

"Tell me more—" he starts, but before he can finish his words, he's out of bed and looking out the window.

"Get the dogs, Barbs. We need to leave. Now."

"W-what? What are you talking about?" I mumble as I swing my legs over the bed and join him at the window.

My eyes widen in shock as I see the street leading up to the village square filling with angry people. They're coming toward us. Jeya and Elijah are at the front, their bodies humming with energy waiting to be released.

"What's happening?" I ask in confusion.

Nykander presses his lips together.

"It is my fault. I did not think they would find out so soon." He sighs. "I might have..." he trails off, his tendrils already at work to get the dogs next to us and ready to depart.

"You might have what?"

"I might have done something to Mr. Foerie," he mutters, gazing away guiltily.

23

"**N**ykander. What did you do?"

He purses his lips.

"I might have cut his tongue," he mentions casually.

"You might have what?" I blink in shock. "You cut his tongue?"

"He will not be able to insult you from now on," he declares confidently.

"Nykander! We're talking about a person here. You cut someone's tongue?" I repeat, still unable to wrap my mind around it.

He nods, as if he doesn't see anything wrong with it.

"I will protect my mate," he simply states.

"But now we have an entire village on our heads."

"And we shall leave."

"How can we leave when we still need to meet the High Priestess?"

"Barbi—"

"Not one more word, Nykander," I tell him sternly as I fold my arms over my chest. "We are not leaving. We have not worked so hard until now to give up on everything because you can't stop your impulses. I do appreciate you sticking up for me, but in this case, we are going to go out and confront the villagers. You are going to say you are sorry and we will continue with our lives until the High Priestess calls upon us."

"You do not seem to understand that they are coming here with murderous intent," he mutters drily.

"Come," I say as I drag him by the hand and take him outside. "You will say sorry."

"You forget one thing, Barbs. I do *not* apologize." He chuckles. Somehow, though, he lets himself be led outside, going along with my plan.

I raise a brow.

He leans in to breathe into my ear, "Except to you."

My cheeks redden and my heart skips a beat.

"And you would not want me to share my unique apologies that are only reserved to you with everyone else, would you?"

"When you put it like that…" I trail off, shocked at myself for even entertaining his crazy line of thought.

Yet my moralistic side doesn't stop me from being flattered that he would defend me that way. He saw I was upset and he took action. He's just like the swoony romantic hero I've always wanted.

I sigh. Raising my gaze, I peer at him from beneath my lashes.

"You drive a hard bargain, Nykander."

A playful smile tips at his lips.

"Okay, here's how this is going to go," I tell him, urging him to look at me. We don't have much time, so we have to get our story straight. "I will do the talking and say you were defending my honor, all right? You just stand behind me and nod every now and then. Maybe appear brooding. And look at me lovingly. Hmm." I pause. "Maybe look at the villagers threateningly every now and then so they get the picture—if anything happens to me, you're ready to attack."

"That sounds an awful lot like I am your guard dog, Barbi."

"Be thankful you don't have to bark," I joke as I elbow him. "Although a growl every now and then wouldn't hurt."

He raises a brow at me.

"Pretend you're feral about me, okay?" I don't have time to explain how fated mates work in romance books, or how an alpha protects his mate.

"Good thing I do not have to pretend," he adds with a twinkle in his eyes.

"I am not joking about this, Nykander. You want that artifact, so you will have to behave. We won't get anything if we're thrown out of the Sanctuary."

"Got it." He nods. "I will brood, growl, lick your skin, and maybe mark my territory."

I frown.

"Please tell me you will *not* mark your territory with pee." I scrunch my nose in disgust. "We may be mated"—I point toward the two of us—"but I am not into that pee play or whatever. You're not either, I hope?" I narrow my eyes at him.

His lips tremble, threatening to break into a smile.

"No. I am not."

"Good. That makes two of us. It is good to be on the same page when it comes to kinks, you know. That will make for a much better relationship. We've discussed some, but I think we should sit down one day and do one of those questionnaires. You're quite bossy, so I bet you're the dominant type, aren't you? I'm not sure what I am, but I guess I can find out. I like it sometimes when you boss me around, but not when you're being a bossy asshole. There's a difference between the two. But if you call me a good girl and ask me nicely, I can be quite submissive—I think."

"Barbi. I do not think this is the moment to talk about kinks. We are about to be confronted by a mob, remember?"

"Oh, shoot! Yes, you are right," I mumble. "Okay, let's go. I will do the talking and you—"

"Stand back, brood, and growl."

"Exactly." I pat him gently on the shoulder.

We step outside into the chilly night. For all his mischievous mood, Nykander uses his dark shadows to proof our cabin in case the villagers attack us.

Jeya and Elijah stop in front of our cabin. Behind them is a frightened Mr. Foerie, his mouth swollen and bleeding.

"We have been informed of an act of violence against one of our residents," Elijah starts, motioning toward Mr. Foerie.

I take a step forward.

"There is a very reasonable explanation for it. You see, you should be thankful he is still alive."

"Is that so? We should be thankful he is not dead?" Jeya raises a brow.

"Yes, of course. You see, my mate here…" I point toward Nykander. "Now it's time to stare and brood," I whisper under my breath.

He widens his stance, his gaze deadly as he glares at the people surrounding our cabin.

"He was only protecting my honor. He cannot help himself with it. It's our mating bond. It's making him do all sort of things if I am in danger."

"And were you? In danger?"

"Uhm, yes! Mr. Foerie was very rude to me today. He insulted me and my dogs and threw me out of his shop. My mate heard about those insults and he could not let them slide. It's that protective instinct. He cannot help himself, right, dear?" I turn to Nykander, whispering at him to growl.

He growls. A low, deep sound coming from his chest that makes everyone stop in their tracks.

"So there you have it. I was the victim first, and my mate avenged my honor. I would say we are even." I smile, pleased with my speech.

"He cut his tongue out, Miss Barbara. How is that even?"

"And he would have done worse because his insults were really bad and they made me cry. No?" I ask Nykander, motioning for him to brood and growl again. "It must have been payment for my tears."

Another growl.

"I am actually surprised his eyes are intact. You should probably say thank you, Mr. Foerie. Nykander is not the type to let people live. He is a villain who has little regard for others' lives. Except mine. Right, dear? I am the exception. The light to your dark, dark soul."

His lips twitch, but he forces himself to scowl at people.

"You have seen him at the Moon Festival. He is very strong. Are you really going to try something against us when you know he could take all of you out?"

"You have broken the rules. For that, you will be escorted off the premises of the Sanctuary."

My eyes widen in fear. I glance at Nykander, but he doesn't seem too concerned.

Can't he see this will ruin everything? We *need* to be here, otherwise the High Priestess will never give us the artifact.

"You will *not!*" I declare as I take a step forward. I place my hands on my hips and glare at them. "As I mentioned, Mr. Foerie insulted me first, so this is merely an eye for an eye. Well, technically, in this case, it's his insults for his tongue. Very fair, if I do say so myself."

"Miss Barbara, you are not in a position to judge whether this is fair or not." Elijah sighs. "According to our laws, we have to punish your mate for inflicting damage upon Mr. Foerie."

"W-what? No. Of course not. You will not touch him," I burst out, placing myself in front of Nykander with my arms spread out to cover him.

"Barbs, I think we are forgetting who is supposed to be protecting whom," he murmurs in my ear.

"Quiet, Nykander. I am saving your hide," I tell him.

"I can heal, in case you forgot."

"So? You can still feel pain. And I don't want you in pain."

His brows go up. He stares at me, slowly blinking.

"You…do not want me to be in pain?" he repeats slowly.

"That is what I said, so now keep quiet and let me handle this," I say as I straighten my back and turn my gaze toward the crowd. "You will have to go through me first," I declare loudly.

Elijah walks toward us, Jeya right behind him. They are both wielding magic in their hands, so I squeeze my eyes shut and wait for the blow.

"That is enough," Nykander calls out, pulling me against his chest. "I appreciate the sentiment, sweetheart. But what type of mate would I be if I let you protect me? It will always be the other way around."

He presses a soft kiss to my temple.

"What would you have me do?" he asks Elijah and Jeya.

"Instead of being banished out of the Sanctuary, you can be confined to our jail for one year and withstand one hundred lashings," Jeya states.

My eyes flare up.

"Confined? Jail? One hundred lashings? Hell no! What is wrong with you people?" I shout, trying to pull out of Nykander's embrace.

"Those are our rules."

"Let's leave," I whisper. "I'm sorry. We should have left when you said so. I made it worse, didn't I?"

"It's fine, Barbs. One year is not so long," he murmurs softly.

"It might not be for you, but it is for me!" For God's sake, he's already been in that dungeon for years on end. Now he wants to repeat that? No, no. I will not allow it!

"It will be all right—"

"What if I find another man in that time? One year is a

long time. Women have needs too," I say saucily, thinking that might rile him up a little.

His lips twitch in a smile.

"Might I remind you that you are a virgin, Barbs?"

"So? Virgins have needs too," I huff.

"Is that so? And what needs would that be?"

"Uhm, that…" I stammer, blushing furiously.

"Guards, take him," Jeya announces.

Six men stride toward us. Before I can think of something else to say to convince Nykander that getting jailed for one year isn't the way to go, a loud sound erupts in front of us.

Nykander pulls me tighter against his body, shielding me.

As the dust settles, I peek through the tightness of his embrace to see what happened. A newcomer has appeared, and a gasp leaves my mouth when I recognize her.

She's the woman from my dream. Herwa.

Upon seeing her, everyone falls to their knees, bowing deeply to her—including Elijah and Jeya.

"High Priestess." The crowd murmurs the words reverently.

Nykander freezes next to me.

"What happened here?" she asks, looking at Elijah.

"A violation of rules, High Priestess. We have given them the choice to leave the Sanctuary or spend a year in confinement as punishment," he murmurs, his head bent down.

"And what was the rule violation?" She raises a brow.

"He cut the tongue of one of our own, Mr. Foerie."

"He did it to avenge my honor," I blurt out, my voice high-pitched in an effort to talk over Elijah before he smears Nykander's character even more. Okay, so technically he *did* something wrong. But how can I blame him when he was doing it *for me*? Perhaps it was a little bloody and violent, but it's the sentiment behind it that counts. He wanted to punish someone who was mean to me. How can he get even more swoon-worthy than that?

The High Priestess turns to me, her head tilted to the side as she studies me.

"Continue."

"Mr. Foerie insulted me," I start, explaining everything from the beginning. She listens intently, nodding every now and then. When I'm done with my explanation, her gaze slides over to Nykander.

"Is it true? You cut his tongue because he offended your mate?"

"It is true." He inclines his head.

She nods pensively.

"I will personally oversee this case," she addresses the villagers. "You may continue as you were."

"But, High Priestess," Elijah interjects. "What about Mr. Foerie? His tongue is missing!"

Her expression doesn't change.

"I trust that he has learned the concept of holding his tongue, then?" she asks, pinning Mr. Foerie with her gaze.

He's shaking from head to toe, but he nods slowly.

"Good." She takes a step toward us. "Come with me," she tells us.

"What about my dogs? Can they come, too?" I ask eagerly. I am not about to leave them here, especially since Mr. Foerie might think they deserve retribution since they are at the root of the issue.

"You may take them with you," she concedes.

I move to go back to the cabin, but Nykander stops me. Instead, he uses his abilities to bring the dogs to us. I cradle Ander to my chest, fluffy cuteness that he is, while PomPom and BonBon stick by our side.

The High Priestess nods, and with a wave of her hand, she transports us somewhere else.

I blink curiously as the scenery changes. We are now in a sumptuous dining room. A wooden table is in the middle, seating twelve people. A sparkly chandelier descends from the ceiling, hanging low over the table. The walls of the room are gilded, containing bass relief scenes of war.

"You may take a seat," she mentions as she walks to the end of the table.

PomPom and BonBon roam around, sniffing everything, and I tentatively put Ander down, too. He runs away from me, his smile intoxicating as he joins his parents in their exploration of the room.

Nykander draws a chair for me, inviting me to sit while he takes the seat next to me.

"I really hope you can make an exception this one time, High Priestess," I speak. "He was only doing it for me."

Nykander grabs my hand under the table, squeezing it.

"You are quite protective of your mate," she mentions, watching our movements with the eyes of a hawk.

"Well, he protects me and I protect him," I state, pushing my chin up.

"Is that so?" she muses quietly. "Interesting."

"Why have you summoned us here?" Nykander asks.

"You are after the artifact, are you not?" the High Priestess inquires.

"You already know that," Nykander murmurs, his eyes narrowed.

The High Priestess rises from her chair and goes to the back of the room. A door magically appears in front of her, which she opens and heads into a secret room. Moments later, she comes out, carrying an item in both of her hands.

That... I squint to get a better look.

She comes back to the table and deposits a ceramic jar on it.

My eyes widen in disbelief. That's the jar from my dream.

I whip my head up, finding the High Priestess watching me intently.

Two things from my dream have come true. Herwa is a

real person, currently sitting in front of us. And that jar? As far as I remember, it doesn't house any artifact.

"Here," the High Priestess says as she pushes the jar toward us.

Nykander moves to grab it, but she stops him.

"Not you. Her." She nods toward me.

I frown.

"What are you talking about?"

"My orders were to deliver this to you," she says cryptically.

"But he is the one who needs it."

"Yet you are the only one who can open it," she counters.

And to prove her point, she reaches for the jar and attempts to open it. The cap does not move. It does not even rattle.

"You may try as well," she tells Nykander.

He grabs the jar, but it doesn't budge for him either.

"Why me? Why would I be the only one to open it?"

"Open it and you shall see." She smiles.

Nykander pushes the jar in front of me, urging me to give it a try.

I stare at her and gulp down.

In my dream, Lispera placed her daughter's energy in this jar. Could I have been mistaken about it? Could it have been the artifact? Maybe my dream was incorrect…

I reach forward with my hands, cupping the sides of the jar. The moment I touch it, the material vibrates against my palms, a hum that travels down my entire body.

My breathing becomes shallow and my heart pounds in my chest.

"Open it," the High Priestess commands.

With trepidation, I grab the cap, prepared to pull hard on it. But it only takes a limited amount of strength for it to move to the side.

A whoosh of air surrounds me, and I gasp against a sudden breathlessness.

My chest feels tight, my limbs paralyzed.

But that ends just as it starts. I remove the cap and place it on the table next to the jar.

Curious, I lean forward to glance inside.

"It's empty," I blurt out, looking at her in shock. "How can it be empty?"

"What?" Nykander asks as he leans in to take a look as well. He squints in confusion and we both stare at the High Priestess, waiting for an explanation.

A lopsided smile pulls at her mouth. Her gaze skips over me, settling on Nykander.

"The artifact you seek is nothing but a myth," she speaks slowly, confidently. "The Ananke artifact is where it belongs. Within the House of Ananke and guarded by the current High Priestess."

"What about our deal, Priestess?" Nykander stands up, his energy changing.

The High Priestess chuckles.

"I am aware you have been looking for me for thousands of years. But did you never stop to wonder why you found me *now*? Why she came to Akkaya and ended up in the place as you? Why *she* knew the clue when no one else does? Did it never occur to you that the timing of it all is rather…coincidental?"

"What are you talking about? That clue was not that hard. Everyone knows about Akkaya's flower." I frown.

"And yet, no one has been able to find the Sanctuary with that clue. Why would that be?"

Nykander presses his lips together, his stare murderous.

"You lured us in on purpose," he says.

"What?" I look up at him. "Why would she lure us here?"

The High Priestess smiles.

"That is for you to figure out. My task here is done," she

says as she rises from the table, turning her back to us and heading toward the wall with the hidden door.

Nykander clenches his fists by his sides, his anger palpable.

Knowing how much this means to him, I scramble to my feet.

"Stop!" I call out, hoping to deter her from leaving. If she does… I doubt we'll meet her again.

Yet the moment I utter the word, a wave of energy blasts forward, sending the High Priestess flying against the wall.

W-what…

"Barbs," Nykander whispers my name in shock.

"What did you do, Nykander? She's not going to help us if we hurt her," I chastise him.

"Me?" He chuckles. "Oh, that did not come from me. Look down, sweetheart," he murmurs, slowly coming toward me.

I glance down at my body, and my eyes widen in disbelief as I note a lavender mist surrounding me. It's almost like a second layer, creating both a shield and a weapon out of my body.

"What's happening?" I whisper, freaking out. "What did you do, Herwa?" I grit out. Yet the moment my tone goes up, another wave of energy blasts through the room, this time destroying the beautiful carvings and the gilded decorations.

The High Priestess rises to her feet, wiping the blood coming out of her mouth and nose with the back of her hand.

"How lovely. You know my name." She chuckles. "I shouldn't have expected anything less of you." She shakes her head, an amused smile gracing her lips. "She told me once that you would recognize me. I did not believe her. How could you know something like that *without* your powers?" She laughs to herself. "But you know things. Just like *she* did."

"What powers? I don't understand. What the hell is happening?" I ask in frustration. Yet that's another mistake.

The ground shakes under my feet, and it dawns on me

that every outburst of emotion causes waves of energy to disperse around me—*destructive* waves of energy that I don't know how to control.

The High Priestess wobbles on her feet as she comes forward.

"Light purple," she muses quietly as she touches the particles of lavender mist surrounding me. "The mix of both worlds."

"What are you talking about?"

"You are your mother's daughter, Barbi." She smiles. "She would be proud of you—she *will* be proud of you. When you see her, please give her my regards. Tell her… I miss her. And I will see her in another life."

With that, she turns to leave.

"What about the artifact?" Nykander asks in a rough voice.

"There was never any artifact to be found." She half turns. "I may not have given you the artifact, but I have given you something far more powerful."

"You are not making any sense, Priestess. Speak or I will have your head," he grits out.

"My fate is not to die by your hands, demon," she states unflinchingly. "You'd better prize your mate above all, for she is the key to your return home." She pauses, her eyes clouded. "Only essence of the same essence can breach the barrier. It will not destroy the seal, but it will allow you free access to and from Tartareia."

Those are her only words as she disappears from sight.

Nykander blinks slowly before he sets his eyes on me.

My body still shimmers with the same light purple mist, but as I try to calm my heart rate, it slowly dissipates.

"Are you all right?" he asks as he takes a step toward me.

I shake my head.

"No," I whisper. "The jar," I swallow, overwhelmed, as I try to form a coherent sentence. "In my dream, the jar contained the power of Lispera's daughter. She had sealed it so her daughter would not be prey to demons—so she would not die. Then, she hid her somewhere in a different time."

His eyes widen, and I can see him putting two and two together.

"The same essence. *You.*"

I nod.

"I don't know how or why, but... I think Lispera is my mother," I whisper.

24

"But it doesn't make any sense." I sigh in frustration. "How could she be my mother? I know who my parents are, and trust me, my real mom is no goddess."

"I do not understand how this can be either. But your energy does not lie," he says as he comes closer.

His black shadows slither forward, calling forth my lavender shimmering mist.

They merge together until they're one and the same.

"I can feel your power," he whispers, his hand caressing my cheek. "And it is a wondrous thing, Barbs."

I swallow, slowly glancing up at him.

"I can't control it. I don't know *how* to control it. Even now," I murmur, watching the way the shimmer becomes more pronounced, intertwining with his darkness, caressing it and letting it be caressed in return.

"It reacts to your feelings," he says, threading his fingers through mine and holding me close. "It reacts to your moods, just as mine does. But I have had thousands of years to control it. You will learn. I will teach you."

My lips tremble as I attempt a smile.

"I'm scared, Nykander. I… I don't know what to believe anymore." My voice shakes, but I try to control my emotions so I don't cause him any harm.

"Do not be. I am here. With you. I will help you through this, Barbs. I promise you," he murmurs as he brings my hands to his lips for a kiss. "We are together in this."

"I am no longer human, am I?" I ask in a low voice.

"I do not think you were ever human to begin with," he mentions gently. "It was odd from the beginning that my true mate would be human when that is unheard of. I wondered how it could be. Generally, true mates are, if not of the same species, then relatively matched in spiritual energy."

I slowly digest his words.

"You know, when I got to Akkaya, I did not believe it at first. I thought it was all a dream—the culmination of my imagination. Slowly, I started believing that it *is* real. I even started enjoying my adventure in this strange world. But *this*? Now I find out that my parents are *not* really my parents, that I'm the daughter of an ancient goddess who basically planned everything from the start. Lispera could see the future—she could manipulate it. That means everything so far in my life has been the result of her machinations. Did I ever have any free will, or did everything just play according to a script?"

"Barbs…" Nykander glances at me warily.

The layer of energy around my body grows in size, spiking every time my heart rate goes up.

"Fate… It means I never had a choice to begin with, did I? Even liking you… Is that something I did, or something I *had* to do?"

"Fate can only dictate so much," he says. "It is a string of canonical events that are decided by the fate goddesses, but everything in the middle is yours."

"How can that be if no matter what I did I ended up in the same spot?"

"You are thinking of fate in far too negative terms, Barbs.

What about the positives? It brought you here. With me. Does that not count for anything?"

I peer up at him, my heart slamming against my chest in a mix of fear, frustration, and desire.

I look at him through the eyes of a woman in love, but one who is questioning whether that love is even hers.

"You are with me now, sweetheart. Mine. I, for one, thank the fates for that." He smiles.

My eyes widen.

"Were you not cursing the fates for our bond until now? What brought this change?"

"You." One word. One simple word that makes my soul sing. "Against myself and against my past, you wormed your way into my heart. And that is *not* the hand of fate. Fate only brought us together, but *you* made my heart beat again. You with your odd ways and quirky humor. You with your kindness when I least deserved it. You with your patience and forgiveness when I could not forgive myself. That is all *you*, Barbs."

My lashes flutter in surprise at his words. He's never spoken to me like this. The mark on my chest vibrates, but this time, it sends a signal to my volatile energy, making it flash between a light lavender color and a deep purple.

A blush creeps up my cheeks as I stare at him.

"Nykander…" I whisper his name, unable to utter anything else.

His lips curve up, his eyes crinkling around the corners. I've seen him smile before, but never with his full face like this. His energy shifts as well, the darkness of his shadows abating until it becomes a light gray.

His hands cup my cheeks and he leans forward. His breath fans across my lips. The proximity is maddening.

"There was truth in your words when we first met, Barbs," he murmurs. My lips part and I inhale each word. "You are the light to my dark, dark soul."

Slowly, he closes the distance between us. He gives me

enough time to turn my face away should I want to. But how could I when I have been waiting for this moment forever?

His lips touch mine. They're soft but firm. He glides his mouth over mine in a gentle seduction. Each press of his lips is more decadent than the first. Wrapping one arm around my waist, he pulls me close to his body. His heat permeates my body, and our energies merge into one. He parts his lips over mine, coaxing them open so he can taste me better.

A groan vibrates in his chest as he slides his tongue across the seam of my lips.

"Open up for me, Barbs," he murmurs.

I trace the contours of his muscles as I make my way up his arms, gripping him tightly as I allow him access to my mouth.

His tongue slides inside, seeking my own and inviting it to a tantalizing dance that sends a current of electricity down my body and makes my toes curl. I move my hands up, twinning them around his nape. Threading my fingers through his thick hair, I let him deepen the kiss. Our mouths are fused to one another, his breath my breath.

The kiss starts gentle as he eases me into it, but as I urge him on, rubbing against him and opening my mouth wider for his possession, he takes what is freely given.

So lost I am in his embrace that I barely realize that our feet are no longer touching the ground. An otherworldly glow surrounds us as the kiss becomes more urgent. All my inhibitions melt away as I allow him to penetrate every crevice of my soul.

His touch ignites me as I never thought possible—and I have imagined this moment since the first time I saw him.

The heat becomes an incontrollable inferno that burns faster, harder. It opens an abyss of emotion in my heart—one that is pitiless and infinite.

"Barbs," he groans my name against my lips.

We float outside space and time, driven by desire and an ineffable depth of feeling.

Our lips part for a moment, and he pulls at my dress to reveal my glowing mark. He does the same with his shirt, taking my hand and placing it on his naked skin to feel his pulsating mark.

"Feel what you do to me," he whispers. "Feel what fate arranged for us, but that *we* created."

"Nykander…" I whimper.

The glow intensifies.

We are up in the air, breaking through the atmosphere. Dim lights reflect from down below, where the rest of the world resides. But this, now, marks our break from civilization —our coming together as not two, but one.

Us against the world.

The clouds are our only companions as strong gusts of air travel all around us, but it never touches us.

Our energies are in sync. A boundary between us and the rest of the world—the rest of the *universe*.

"Do you feel it, sweetheart?" he asks as he caresses my face.

I lean into his touch, letting it sear itself on my skin. Peering up at him, I note the gentleness with which he regards me.

"Tell me you feel this. Tell me I am not the only one wrapped up in this mad, mad surge of emotion that threatens to consume me from within."

"You're not." I shake my head. "I feel it. Every beat of your heart mirrors mine. Every breath." I pause as I trace his lips with my finger. "Every breath you take is *my* breath."

He swallows hard, his face ravaged by a myriad of emotions.

"I've never felt like this before," he confesses in a thick voice. "Like your lips were perfectly sculpted to fit my own.

Like your curves were made to accommodate every inch of my hardness."

His voice caresses my senses, but it's the meaning behind his words that leaves me breathless.

I stare at him.

He stares at me.

Slowly, a smile curves up his lips.

I smile in return.

And just like that, I know I am fine. Whatever may come our way—whatever the fates may have in store for us—we are fine.

We descend to the ground, landing in the middle of a thick forest. Darkness surrounds us from all sides, but our path is lit up from our merged energy—a light gray with shimmery purple particles.

He uses his teleportation powers to bring the dogs to us and they bark happily when they see us again.

I pet them and give them kisses while Nykander watches me with an amused gleam in his eyes. After I've handed out each of them a small treat from my pocket, I get back to his side.

His hand finds mine and we walk around, wandering aimlessly. The dogs follow close behind.

"Nykander, I have to ask." I gather the courage to speak, knowing bringing up this subject might end our idyllic moment.

"Hm?"

"What about... Mo?"

"I will not lie to you, Barbs. I love Mo. I will always love her. She was my first love and I loved her with the heart of a youth. But she is no longer here. Thousands of years have passed. I am no longer the same youth. I am stronger, wiser, and more weathered. And for the first time, I am ready to open my heart again."

"I will never ask you to forget her," I tell him. "I just do not wish to have her intervene between us."

"She will not." He stops, placing himself in front of me. "Let me have my revenge. Let me have this one goal I have worked so long toward. After that, I will put her to rest. I will be *only* yours—if you will have me."

I smile as I caress his hand.

"I will help you get your revenge, Nykander," I murmur softly. "We will do this together."

"Together. I like the sound of that."

"I think this is one of the perks of having powers," I joke. "You no longer have to treat me with kid gloves. I can finally handle myself."

"*Not* yet." He clicks his tongue against his teeth. "You, sweetheart, are a disaster waiting to be unleashed upon the world. You need to learn to control your powers."

"I'm sure that won't take long with you as a teacher." I flutter my lashes at him.

"Is that so?" He raises a brow, pulling me closer.

"That is not the only thing you will have to teach me," I whisper as I raise myself on the tips of my toes. "There are a lot of things I need to learn. Things that do not require... clothes."

"Sweetheart," he groans. "You just ensured I will not get a wink of sleep until we get to *those* lessons."

I chuckle as I step away from him, winking playfully.

"Patience, my good-looking friend, patience. First, we need to get back to Tartareia."

His features darken and he takes a deep breath.

"We should leave soon. The villagers already took a dislike to us, so there is no point in lingering around."

"You're right," I agree. "But before we go... *How* is

Tartareia? You haven't spoken much about it. I'd like to know what to expect of the so-called original hell."

His features tense, but I glimpse a sliver of longing in his gaze.

"Both beautiful and terrifying. It mirrors its people. We might be descendant from the Seven, but not everyone is... evil. Like with any society, there is good and bad. It just so happens that Tartareians have a greater propensity for the latter. It is primarily due to our abilities to control corrupted souls and turn them into demons. The thirst for power of a few has damned us all." He sighs.

"I'm looking forward to seeing the place you grew up in."

His lips twitch, but sadness descends down his features.

"We should head back and pack. Once we get back to Tartareia, we will need to lie low for some time until I see what has changed since my last time there. And while we do that, we will start your combat lessons. We are heading into dangerous territory and I want you to be prepared for anything," he explains.

"Let's do this then. I'm ready when you are."

He pulls me into his embrace, using his shadowy tentacles to pull the dogs alongside us, and we're back at the cabin.

I take out the few gowns I have and spread them on the bed, using the sheet underneath as a makeshift bag. Nykander hands me his own clothes and the dogs' blankets.

"Stay here. I need to take care of something before we leave," he mentions. I don't get to ask him what before he's gone, leaving me alone with the dogs.

I tend to the dogs, cleaning their little paws from the trek in the woods and making sure their coats are not matted. Since we've been here, I've done my best to care for them to the standards they are used to, but given the rudimentary resources, I've had to improvise.

"You three are the cutest things I've ever seen," I coo at them.

PomPom does a pirouette with BonBon chasing after her tail, while Ander whines that he's not part of the spectacle.

I laugh at their antics and give each a small treat—the last ones we had.

Nykander is back half an hour later.

"I wanted to make sure the road is clear for us to leave since the villagers are still upset with me."

"And?"

"I made peace with Jeya and Elijah. They will not stop us from leaving."

"That is nice of you." I smile. "Although I appreciate you defending my honor, you should have thought about the consequences before."

"But now I have you to be my voice of reason." He winks.

I chuckle. "Speaking of that, we should go to the kitchens and get some food. At least for the dogs," I suggest. Ander in particular needs to eat often since he's a growing pup.

Nykander nods.

After we have all our essentials with us, Nykander lures the dogs inside the pink dog house and locks the door.

"They will be easier to transport this way," he mentions, and I give him a quick kiss on the lips for his thoughtfulness.

He teleports us to the kitchens, and I go through the pantry, taking out some basic items and placing them in a bag.

But just as I'm about to tell him I'm done, a loud bang erupts in the village.

We both freeze. My eyes flare with alarm.

"What was that?" I whisper.

He shakes his head, placing a finger to his lips.

Heading to the window, he pulls the curtain aside to look outside. I follow him.

A devastating fire rages in the western part of the village. At first, we hear the crackling of wood as the flames consume the buildings. The screams of the villagers soon follow. A few run for their lives, only to be struck down by an invisible force, seemingly being cut in two.

"What—" I gasp.

"Stay here," he tells me, and in the next second, he flashes himself out of the room.

He appears in the middle of the road, his expression grave as he awaits something.

Another loud bang erupts in the air, and the High Priestess flies backward, landing next to Nykander. Her clothes are ripped, her body riddled with bleeding wounds. She breathes harshly, barely getting herself back to her feet.

Nykander glances toward her, his eyes narrowed.

She wipes the blood from her mouth and a smirk appears on her face.

"I told you my death will not be by your hands, demon," she murmurs, and somehow I hear her.

I gulp down. It must be these new powers. Yet as her mouth moves again, my ears fail me.

Damn it! I strain to hear but can only make out half words.

Nykander nods at her. His energy shimmers around him, the darkness coming to the surface and forming a shield around him.

The smoke dissipates, and from within its depths, Damien appears. He steps forward, followed by Jocelyn, Arisa, Leoni, and a slew of other magic wielders who are terrorizing the villagers.

Damien swings a fire lasso from his right hand. A villager screams and runs out of the way. But he doesn't stand a chance as Damien cuts him in two, killing him without batting an eye.

My eyes widen. This is too similar to my dream for it to be a coincidence. My instincts kick in and I disobey Nykander's orders, rushing out of the kitchens.

"Barbi, I told you to stay back," his voice booms.

"He has the blood of your sire, Nykander. He will try to stab you with it," I say breathlessly.

He turns to look at me and gives me a brisk nod.

"Stay back now," he decrees and, using his powers, he envelops me in a shield of dark smoke. He directs his attention to Damien, who has now gained more ground. Extending his arm to the side, Nykander morphs a sword from his energy.

Damien raises a daring brow as he emulates his movements, creating a blade from his flames.

They meet in the middle, their swords clashing just as their energies bump one against another—one bright red, one black as midnight. The High Priestess engages with Arisa and Leoni, who are overpowering her.

This… This is *just* like what happened in my dream. With the exception of the presence of the High Priestess, everything is the same.

My fear mounts. But before I can digest what's happening, my eyes connect with Jocelyn. She smirks as she looks at me. With a move of her wrist, she sends a strong gust toward me.

But because of my dream, I am able to anticipate her attack and I move to the side, narrowly evading the blow.

Her eyes widen in surprise, but with a smooth jump, she lands in front of me.

Nykander glances back.

"Barbs," he calls out. But Damien won't give him a moment of rest, brandishing his blade at him. With his eyes on me, Nykander barely dodges the attack and parries it with his own.

"I am fine!" I shout. "Pay attention to your fight," I tell him.

He doesn't seem convinced, but Damien's fighting style is too aggressive. He doesn't give Nykander even one inch, hitting him with blow after blow, even though none of them land on his body. He must be looking to tire him out.

Damien feeds on souls, and since the plague happened, he

must be consuming tens if not hundreds of souls daily. He must be thinking he will have the advantage when it comes to stamina since his power is rechargeable.

I purse my lips.

Somehow, I need to get to Nykander and give him some of my blood. He will need it.

I'm interrupted from my musings when Jocelyn sends another strong wind gust toward me. This time, it rattles the shield Nykander had created for me.

"Nykander, take the shield back!" I yell. He's probably consuming energy trying to maintain it, and if things go according to my dream, it will end up breaking anyway.

"No."

"Please trust me," I whisper, knowing he can hear me. "I know what I'm doing."

His eyes meet mine briefly and he appears at war with himself.

I give him a confident nod and he reluctantly calls his shadows back. The shield dissipates and I slowly let my anger lead me. I might not be able to control these newfound powers. But it seems my emotions can. So I will just lean into them and let them consume me.

Jocelyn smiles smugly when she sees me defenseless, and she readies herself for attack.

"You stole my dog," she grits out. "I'll enjoy stepping over your dead body when I get him back."

She sends another blow my way, but her words only fuel my emotions.

"You stole my dog first, you two-faced bitch," I yell.

At once, the energy around me simmers, enveloping me in a thick purple shield.

Her eyes flare in concern, but she doesn't stop, sending a succession of blows toward me. As they reach me, they dissipate against my shield, and I finally return the smile.

"I don't know what I ever saw in you," I mutter to myself.

"But I will take this opportunity to erase you from my mind once and for all."

She frowns. Of course she doesn't know what I'm talking about—and good thing she doesn't. If she did, she'd laugh in my face at my idiocy. Yet that Barbi seems like a lifetime away.

Since I've come to Akkaya, I've learned more about myself than in twenty-one years of life. And it's all because I finally started living *for* myself instead of trying to emulate someone else. I found my voice while I muted all the other ones telling me I was inconsequential. And I owe that not only to the adversities that have come my way, but also to Nykander, my new partner in crime. He's accepted me with my flaws and told me I was enough.

And that gives me the strength to finally cut this thread loose.

The mere thought that she might get to my dogs provides me with enough anger to channel my energy into a blast that sends her flying through the air. She stabilizes herself with her powers, though, and comes charging toward me again.

Every time she comes, I hit her with a blast. She tries to land blows on me, too, but they lose all strength the moment they encounter my purple shield. Seeing as how none of her attacks work, she comes closer, seeking to hurt me by entering my shield and attacking me from within.

A slow smile pulls at my lips as I allow her to believe she has the upper hand. But the moment she enters my shield, she's trapped.

Panic flares in her features as she realizes she cannot move. She's held immobile by the particles of energy that float around me.

Damien notices too, and he's momentarily distracted, time in which Nykander lands a blow against his stomach, ripping it open. He cuts him from one side to the other, the sound of his sword against Damien's spine reaching my ears.

"You didn't know who you were up to, did you?" I

murmur as I bring my hand around Jocelyn's neck. "Nykander's brother commands you, so I assume he can hear my words, can't he?"

She doesn't answer—she cannot. But I can see the truth reflected in her features.

Leaning in, I whisper, "Hello, Baine. Watch closely how your brother destroys your thrall. I don't know you, but I can already imagine you seething. All those souls—all that power—lost. How does it feel knowing that no matter how dirty you play, your brother still wins?"

JOCELYN'S EYES move wildly in their orbits—the only movement she's capable of. I increase the pressure on her neck, surprised at the ease with which I can make it bend. Alas, it seems my new energy source is not the only power I gained.

My features darken as I stare into her terrified eyes.

"Goodbye, Jocelyn," I murmur. But there is also the unspoken.

Goodbye, Barbi, you aimless fool.

One movement of my wrist and her neck snaps. It slumps to the side, bending at an odd angle. But since I do not know whether she can regenerate or not, I apply some more force and her head becomes detached from her body. It rolls onto the floor, and everything stops as people stare at me in disbelief.

Yet I was so focused on Jocelyn that I didn't notice that the High Priestess had been stabbed in the heart. Arisa is also dead on the ground next to her, and a bleeding Leoni breathes hard as he glares down at her. His body trembles and as he turns to me, he wobbles for a few more steps until he falls to the ground.

In the distance, the other villagers are fighting with

Damien's magic wielder, and little by little, they appear to gain more ground.

There's only Nykander and Damien remaining, their battle tense as Damien calls forth more souls to feed his power.

I don't know if this is another byproduct of my new powers, but my vision has changed. I see the translucent shape of the souls as they travel toward him, becoming a whirlpool of nothingness as they're absorbed into his body.

His flames increase in size with each soul he consumes.

Nykander is holding his own, but I can sense that he is becoming tired. And there is only one way to even out the field.

He needs to feed, too.

"Nykander," I call out. He whips his head to me and I pick up a blade from the ground and slash my left palm. Blood coats the metal. His brows knit in confusion until he sees me throw the knife at him.

He uses one of his tendrils to catch it and he brings it to his mouth, licking every drop of blood from it.

Immediately, his vigor returns.

Yet that one moment of inattention makes it that the events from my dream come to pass.

Damien also coats his blade with blood—the blood of Nykander's sire—and he's ready to strike while Nykander is distracted.

But just as the tip of the blade gets closer to him, I yell loudly.

"No!"

My voice travels to them, morphing into a blow of pure energy that throws Damien off Nykander long enough for my mate to turn that bloody blade to dust.

"I got this," he murmurs in a low voice, his lips curved in a confident smile.

I nod, stepping back and letting him finish the fight.

His strength renewed, he morphs his shadows into two swords, one in each hand, and he strikes at Damien before he has the opportunity to get his bearings together. Nykander slashes his body repeatedly, but unfortunately, each time it regenerates.

I frown.

How can we kill someone who has can channel the souls' energy to heal himself?

Nykander becomes frustrated with that fact too, while Damien is sporting a smug smile on his face every time his flesh mends.

"Not so strong now, are you, brother?" Damien asks, but it is not him who speaks. It is Baine. The voice is deeper, much more sinister than Damien's strangled little tantrums from before.

I bite my lip in worry. The more time goes on, the more energy Nykander will spend and we will be back to the starting point.

Baine appears to be controlling Damien fully now, and in an effort to destroy his brother, he summons forth an army of souls.

Hundreds if not thousands of bright lights fly in the sky, heading straight for Damien's body and charging him with new energy.

Nykander is breathing hard as he takes a step back, his eyes narrowed as he calculates his next movement.

At this rate, Damien will kill us both. The more souls he consumes, the more powerful he will be, and neither Nykander nor I will be a match for him.

Unless...

"Nykander," I call him. While Damien is charging, I rush to Nykander's side and take his hand in mine.

"The only way to defeat him is to stop him from getting more souls," I whisper.

He nods grimly.

"But how? I do not know the spell he used to summon forth all the souls from Akkaya. And with how many he's consuming…"

"What if we try what I did to Jocelyn? Once she was inside my energy field, she could no longer move or summon her powers."

He tilts his head to the side. A bit of blood flows from a wound close to his neck, and I swipe it with my finger, then bring it to my mouth.

"It is worth a try." He nods.

He holds tightly onto my hand as he lets his remaining energy take shape. I inhale deeply as I do the same. The darkness of his essence becomes a light gray as it mixes with my lavender one. And combined, the energies expand to a much wider range.

"Follow my lead," he murmurs, leaning in to lay a kiss on the top of my head.

I nod, and we both turn our attention to Damien.

He's consumed so many souls he no longer looks humanoid. There is a monstrous quality to his form. It's big—and growing larger—bent and misshapen. It's the stuff of nightmares.

Now, if I were the old Barbi—and I promise I'm not…just maybe a little—I would have squeaked and proposed we ran from that boogeyman. But this new Barbi must face her fears head-on.

I glance up at Nykander, admiring his decisive expression and the way he radiates strength even after fighting for so long.

Yes, this new Barbi will not give up.

"Ready, sweetheart?" Nykander smiles at me.

"Yes."

Damien rushes toward us, ready to attack in full force. But as he steps inside our shield, he suddenly becomes immobilized. He snarls at us, his voice hitting me in my eardrums and making me wince. But it's clear that he is trapped.

"Oh my! We did it!"

"Not quite yet," Nykander mentions. "We need to wear him out and kill him *inside* the boundary so he may not consume more souls. Or..." he trails off, turning to look at me.

"Or?"

"I cannot extract the souls out of a demon since I am one myself. But an Aperite deity could."

"You mean...me?" I frown. "But how would I do that?"

"Your mother was a Supreme, Barbs. That means you *have* the ability to extract the souls and save them. And once you do, they will be able to move on."

I blink. He nudges me softly, and I realize he has full confidence in me.

"But how?" I whisper.

I would love nothing more than save those souls and make Nykander proud of me. But no matter my determination, the fact of the matter is that I've only had these powers for a few hours. I don't even know what I'm doing nine times out of ten!

"Focus your energy on him." He nods to Damien, who is currently writhing in agony. "Visualize the energy within him —the *foreign* energy."

Closing my eyes, I push my energy toward Damien. The moment it reaches him, though, I physically recoil from the evil I sense within him. Yet it's not *just* Damien. It's also Baine. Somewhere inside there, Baine's essence also lives, polluting Damien's soul further.

I probe more. There are thick layers of evil and foul intentions. And every time I try to peel a layer, I feel their essence tainting me.

"Breathe, sweetheart. I am here with you," Nykander murmurs in my ear. His lips are on my temple as he pulls me in his arms.

"It's so ugly and vile, Ny," I whisper. "I've never felt such sinister energy before. It makes me feel…dirty."

"You can do this, Barbs. I know you can. Gather all of our energy, mine and yours, and use it as a sword."

"Okay," I whisper.

"Now cut through that malevolent energy."

I do as he says, manifesting a sword in my hands and aiming it at the first layer. I imbue it with my energy, and as I cut, I materialize my intention—not only to destroy the wickedness, but also reform it. The dark, putrid layer begins to dissolve into a white substance, and for the first time, I feel slightly cleaner.

I repeat the same actions all over again. Yet there are so many layers. So many sins and bad deeds. So many wicked intentions.

"That's it, Barbs. That's my girl," Nykander praises me. "He is getting smaller. Keep going, baby."

I cut through more layers until I find the most noxious one. It is so putrid, I barely keep myself from heaving. Disgust and nausea fill me to the brim, but I push past it.

"*Interesting,*" the same malefic voice from before speaks in my head. "*I see Nykander has found himself a little Aperite ally. Who would have thought.*" He laughs. "*I cannot wait to feast on your soul, girl. After I neutralize my brother, I will make you my main course.*"

He makes a slurping noise, and I drag a heavy breath in, forcing myself to keep going.

My knees buckle, but Nykander holds me steady.

He's there, next to me. I can feel the heat of his body. It tethers me, keeping me from getting lost in this sea of monstrosity that is Baine.

I inhale and materialize the sword again, but this time I imagine it to be bigger—stronger. The purple glows from the tip of the sword to the hilt, continuing up my body until I'm one with my weapon.

Raising it high, I use all my strength to bring it down onto that putrid layer, cutting through it and turning it into nothingness. This severs the bond between Baine and Damien, but that doesn't mean my jobs is done.

More layers appear, from all the sins of the souls absorbed in the past. They are easier to get through since I don't think anything can be as vile as Baine.

Slowly, I'm out of layers and I hit a wall.

"There's a wall," I whisper.

"It's all right, Barbs. You are doing so good, baby. Imagine you have a hammer in your hand, and use it to smash the wall to pieces."

I take a deep breath and do as he instructs.

As the wall crumbles to the ground, the same faint lines of energy from before appear—all the souls Damien did not get to fully consume.

"What now?" I ask in a strangled voice.

"Now it's up to you, sweetheart. Wish them free, and they will be free."

I gulp down. Squeezing my eyes shut, I channel my energy into a healing one, letting it spread from soul to soul in an effort to calm them and let them know they are safe—that they can now continue their journey into the afterlife.

A wave of heat develops in my chest and a loud explosion startles me from my trance.

I fall to the ground, but Nykander is there to catch me, cradling my body to his chest.

Pieces of Damien's body are scattered on the ground as Nykander pulls back his shadows.

"Look, Barbs." He nods to the night sky that the thousands of liberated souls lit up. The moment they are out, though, other beings appear. Mechanic and somewhat robotic, they have humanoid appearances, but they do not seem to stray from their script.

"They are messengers," Nykander murmurs. "They are now escorting the souls to P'asala."

"I did it then…" I mutter numbly.

"You did it, Barbs. You did so good. I'm proud of you," he whispers, kissing the tip of my nose.

"I did it," I repeat in disbelief.

Light shimmers around me, and as I look down, I'm startled to see that the previous lavender energy has now changed color.

It is no longer a light purple.

It is pink.

Pink.

Somehow that's fitting.

A smile pulls at my lips, but it's a rather sloppy one as my body fails me.

That's my last thought before my eyes close.

25

"Yes. Eat it all. Just like that, Ander."

Nykander's voice filters through the veil of confusion covering my mind. I slowly open my eyes, and there he is.

He's lying in the grass with Ander in his lap. He's feeding the little pup and praising him every time he eats.

My smile widens.

Nykander whips his head around, his lips curving up. He puts the pup down, urging him to go play with his parents, and he rushes toward me.

"You are awake," he notes, a smile creeping on his face.

I get up. For the first few seconds, I am disoriented as I recall what happened at the Sanctuary.

"Where are we?" I frown as I look around. We are in a forest, but the scenery isn't familiar.

"We are in P'laisa. It is an intermediary realm close to Tartareia. It isn't populated, so I thought we might not stand out too much here."

I nod.

"How are you feeling?" he asks, brushing one hand over my forehead.

My cheeks heat up.

"All things considered, good." I strain a smile.

I don't mention that I still feel the residuals of that putrid essence inside of me. It's almost as if I've been coated in a layer of dirt I cannot shed.

"I am happy to hear that. Here," he says as he gets up and removes a dress from his bag. "There is a river behind those trees. You can wash up and change."

Looking down at myself, I note that I am still covered in blood. My dress is torn, my naked chest on display.

My eyes flare in concern, but as I whip my eyes to his, I note the curve of a smile on his lips.

"I will prepare some food while you wash."

"Thank you," I murmur.

Grabbing the dress, I head in the direction he pointed out. The river is easy to find, the water clean and not too cold. I remove my dirty clothes and step inside.

How I wish I had some soap because no matter how much I scrub, I am unable to erase the taint of evil. It's on my skin, *under* my skin.

It's everywhere.

I take a deep breath and submerge myself under the water.

The seconds trickle by, and I don't resurface.

Eyes closed, I focus on the flowing water that glides over my body in its descent down the stream. I will it to carry with it all the bad experiences and the pure evil that still taints my flesh.

Unable to withstand it much longer, I jump out, taking a deep, big breath.

My limbs are shaking, and a shiver goes down my spine.

As I open my eyes, the water is no longer a crystalline blue. Instead, it's a deep blood red. And as it courses past me, the color sticks to my skin, coating me in blood from head to toe.

Terror rises in my chest and I stumble back, falling once more in the river and swallowing a mouthful of water.

I sputter and flail my hands to reach the surface again.

"Barbs!" His voice is in my ear. His strong arms grip me up, but in my panic, I'm too slow to recognize that he is not my foe—that he is trying to save me not hurt me further.

A loud scream echoes through the forest—*my* scream. And with it, a wave of pure energy is unleashed, blasting everything in its path. Water splashes all around, and the trees in the immediate vicinity are razed to the ground.

I crash down on the shore, barely able to find my breath.

Nykander is a distance away, bloodied and groaning in pain. His limbs are broken and mangled as a result of his proximity to me during the blast.

His bones crack as he aligns them back into place, wincing as he pulls his neck into its proper position.

My eyes are wide with shock, and despite wanting to rush to his side, I find that I am frozen on the spot.

He rises to his feet and comes toward me.

His clothes are a tattered mess, the material clinging to his body.

His features are taut as he rips the dangling strands and throws them to the ground. He strides toward me with precision, his eyes pinning me to the spot.

But his tight expression belies his actions. He drops to his knees in front of me, his fingers on my jaw as he tips my face up so I can look him in the eye.

"Are you all right?" he inquires in a gentle tone. "What happened, Barbs?"

There is no accusation in his gaze. There is no anger.

There is only worry and a desire to understand what prompted my outburst.

Before I can help it, I throw myself into his arms, my tears flowing down my cheeks uncontrollably.

"I can't control it, Nykander," I murmur. "I don't know what I'm doing. I'm so sorry I hurt you…"

"Don't," he grits out. "We will solve this together. What I want to know is why you were so afraid."

I shake my head.

"I'm fine now," I answer weakly.

"You're trembling, Barbs. You are *not* fine."

"Yes, I am. It's all so overwhelming…"

He leans back, his eyes narrowed as he stares at me.

"Are you sure you are telling me the whole truth?"

"W-what do you mean? I'm fine." I force a smile.

He nods slowly, but he doesn't seem convinced.

Helping me to my feet, he turns with his back to me to allow me to dress in peace. Somehow, that small gesture warms my heart.

"We should check on the dogs," I tell him.

As we leave, I glance back at the river.

The water is blue, not red.

You need to get a grip, *Barbi!*

We make it back to our camping spot, and I immediately rush to the dogs. They are all huddled together in the dog house. Ander is squished between PomPom and BonBon.

"They were trying to defend him." I sigh.

"They are good parents." Nykander chuckles. "Come. I found some meat for us to eat. We will sleep here tonight and search for the portal tomorrow."

I follow him, watching as he builds a fire and roasts the meat he'd hunted.

"I have a question," I say after a moment's thought.

Nykander raises his brow at me.

"Why did you not take us straight to Tartareia? You could have teleported there. Why do we need a portal?"

He takes a deep breath.

"I tried. It did not work. I assume it is because you must personally lift the seal."

"And how will I do that?" I frown.

"You will need to channel. Your spiritual signature should open the gate to Tartareia."

"I see."

"Do not worry, Barbs. I will be there to guide you."

My lips tip up.

As he tends to the meat, I take a seat next to him.

"What happened at the Sanctuary after I passed out? Did the High Priestess make it?"

He shakes his head.

"There were a few villagers who made it, but the High Priestess died while fighting the two mages. I suppose she expected that to happen," he muses.

"I wish I had more time with her. There are so many questions running through my mind. She just dropped a bomb on me and…left."

"I am sorry," he murmurs, placing his hand atop mine. "After I kill Baine, we will go to Aperion to find out more about your mother."

"Do you think they will allow us in?"

"Oh, they will. For the mere fact that they will be curious about you. Even now, the Supremes must have found out about the barrage of souls coming into P'asala, and that an unknown Aperite divinity set them free. There are very few with the power to defeat a demon of Damien's level. That alone will make you intriguing to them."

I digest his words. I don't know how I feel about Aperion and being seen as a deity. Me, a goddess? I almost scoff aloud at the thought.

Yet I can't deny there is one part of me that is curious about it—about my elusive birth parents.

"What else do you know about Lispera?"

He thinks about it for a second.

"Not too much. She was a revered Supreme since my time in the army. She was considered a prodigy and she was both feared and respected, even among my kind's ranks. But she never left Aperion, so no one had ever seen her in the flesh. When she sealed off Tartareia, it came as a surprise to everyone since she had never involved herself in the war between the two realms—at least not directly."

"I wonder why the High Priestess told me I would see her again. Do you think she did not die back then?"

He shakes his head.

"With the amount of energy required to seal off Tartareia, it is very unlikely she survived, even for someone as strong as her. Perhaps she meant you might see her in your dreams? Like it happened last time?"

"That's a good point." I nod. "She seemed to see me, too, in the dream. Maybe that's the key to communicating with her."

He smiles at me.

"Once you get better at controlling your powers, you will be able to control what you dream."

The meat is soon ready and I prepare some for the dogs before I resume my seat next to him and we eat in silence.

Tomorrow at this time we might already be in Tartareia, and the concept frightens me. Not because it is considered the literal *hell* of the universe, but because it holds all of Nykander's memories of his precious Mo.

I wrinkle my nose as I glance at him from the corner of my eye.

He might have told me Mo is in the past, but I can't help but be worried.

He hasn't been there in seven thousand years. I fear that as soon as we get there, he's going to be reminded of his time with *her*. It's already enough that his revenge is foremost in his mind, and that is inherently linked to her.

Stop it, Barbi!

I shake myself. I promised him to help, and I will. But despite his assurances, I find myself growing more jealous by the day.

I'm jealous he loved before.

I'm jealous he was with someone before.

I'm jealous of all the time he spent *with* her.

But most of all, I'm jealous of the way he clung to her memory for seven thousand years—the way he still clings to it now, despite not wanting to admit it.

How hypocritical of me. I promised him I was fine with his past, yet all I can think of is him with her. When he touches me, I can't help but wonder if he touched her like that too. If he…

Good Lord! I'm only going to drive myself mad if I continue on like this.

I am his mate, not her. In time, he will love me even more. I'm sure of it.

But are you?

Shut up, inner voice!

"What is the matter?" Nykander suddenly asks.

"W-what?"

"You were frowning just now, and your aura turned a bright pink."

"Oh. I was just thinking about killing Baine for all he's done to you," I lie.

He cracks a smile.

"You are cute." He chuckles, patting my head and ruffling my hair.

Like a child. Like a goddamn child.

And the sad truth is that I *am* a child next to him.

"We should go to sleep. We have a long journey ahead of us," I say as I put away the leftover bones for the dogs.

His brows rise in question, but he doesn't inquire about my sudden shift in disposition. He slowly nods, getting up to put out the fire and arrange our bed for the night. He fills one of the sheets we brought with us with our clothes and places the other on top to cover ourselves with it.

I blink in surprise.

"Only one bed?" I ask slowly.

"I recall you inviting me into your bed," he drawls.

"Ehm. Yes, sure. Why not." I laugh awkwardly.

The dogs are already sleeping in the comfort of their little house.

I pull on my dress nervously and lie down on the makeshift mattress. He slides next to me, the length of his body glued to mine. He covers me with the sheet and leans in to lay a kiss on my forehead.

"Relax, Barbs. I will not do anything to you," he whispers.

"I'm relaxed. I'm *very* relaxed," I mutter anxiously.

"You are anything *but* relaxed." He chuckles.

"You're mistaken," I stammer. "I am not worried about what you will do to me. In fact, I can't wait for it—to do it, I mean."

"To do what?" He raises a brow.

He's resting on his elbow and staring down at me with an amused expression.

"You know what!" I burst out, squeezing my eyes shut.

"I really do not know. I am a little rusty with my old age and all that. You should remind me what *it* is."

"You're making fun of me," I accuse, narrowing my eyes at him.

"You are too cute." He shakes his head.

"I don't want to be cute," I mutter under my breath in annoyance.

"What? Why?"

"Cute is what you'd say to a dog, or a shirt, or I don't know…a child? You don't say that to your mate," I grumble, looking away.

His lips tremble with mirth.

"And what would you prefer then?"

"You know… Beautiful, sexy, seductive…that sort of stuff."

He doesn't reply.

I chance a glance at him, and I note he's staring at me with a gentle smile on his face.

"You have it all wrong, Barbs. Sure, you are beautiful, sexy, alluring, and every synonym in the dictionary. But cute encompasses so much more."

I blink in confusion. "What do you mean?"

"It is a visceral feeling that arises in your chest when you see something that tugs at your heartstrings. It is an itch that cannot be scratched, for if I tried to, I fear I would smother you to death in my embrace."

I stare at him, speechless.

Slowly, I move closer to him, angling my body to better fit his. Wrapping my arms around his waist, I lay my head on his chest.

He appears surprised by my gesture as he remains still.

"That is the sweetest thing you have ever said to me," I whisper. "I think I like cute now."

The tension in his body recedes, and he tentatively places his arms around me.

"Tighter." I chuckle. "You promised to smother me to death. Now you won't deliver, oh, you villainous Dark One?"

His chest rumbles with laughter, but he pulls me tighter against him.

And when he sees I don't object, he holds me even tighter.

"I think I like being smothered to death," I speak softly against his chest.

"But only by me," he adds with a wicked grin.

"Only by you," I agree. "As long as I'm the only one you smother too."

"How did we get to this morbid talk?" He chuckles. "I thought we were talking about *it*."

"Ugh, stop it!" I burrow deeper in his chest to hide my blush.

"You, sweetheart, are far too easy to rile up." He laughs.

"And you love riling me up far too much," I mumble grumpily.

"Why do you think? Because you are so damn cute."

I take his compliment in stride this time, snuggling by his side.

He's warm and comfortable, and despite the fact that my heart races at our proximity, I also feel at peace.

He kisses the top of my head, letting his lips linger there. I wiggle up his body, tipping my head back.

Our eyes meet.

He cups the side of my face with his big hand, and I sigh deeply at the contact.

Leaning in, he kisses my forehead before moving to my nose. Finally, his lips meet mine. The kiss starts slow. Just a languid slide of lips against lips. When he opens his mouth to deepen the kiss, I meet him there, touching my tongue against his.

I whimper softly as I hold on to him, letting him possess my mouth the same way I want him to possess my body.

But he never tries to push for more.

We kiss and kiss until kissing becomes second nature. Until my lips are so inherently connected to his that to keep them apart would mean a death sentence.

We kiss until the entire world fades away. Until there's just his body, my body, and the heat that keeps building between us.

We kiss as if kissing was breathing. Because each touch of his lips breathes life into me.

"You are the sweetest thing I have ever tasted," he murmurs against my mouth. He tugs my lower lip between his teeth, nibbling at it before he peppers light kisses all over my face. "The sweetest and most poisonous."

My eyes widen as I regard him with confusion.

"What do you mean?" I whisper.

"You have the power to end me, Barbs." He gives me a sad smile. "Here." He brings his hand lower, placing it over my chest where the mark we share resides. "One stab here, against your heart, is one stab here, against my heart," he says as he takes my hand and presses it against his mark. "This… us." He takes a deep breath. "I am entrusting you with my heart."

My face lights up at his words. Knowing I can't possibly give him a proper reply, I simply lower myself down his body and press my lips against his chest.

"Your heart is safe with me, Nykander. I will cherish it and take care of it as my most prized possession."

"Nyk," he suddenly says. "Call me Nyk from now on."

I bite my lower lip so I don't dissolve into a crying mess.

"Nyk," I repeat, the word filling me with inexplicable warmth. It feels foreign yet familiar on my tongue. "I will treasure this gift, Nyk."

He smiles at me.

"Sleep, sweetheart. I have you."

Somehow, those words are enough.

In the warmth of his embrace, I let myself succumb to sleep.

He's mine.

I must stop obsessing over Mo. She is gone and I am not.

I am here, with him, and I will be with him for the rest of eternity.

He might have been hers at some point in time, but from now on, he will only ever be mine.

Only ever mine…

26

"How will we find the portal?" I ask as I fold our bedding and place it aside.

Nykander comes behind me, places his hands on my shoulders, and slowly massages them.

"I have been to this realm many times during my time in the military. It was one of our most heavily guarded areas because it leads directly to Tartareia."

"Directly? I thought the portals needed someone native to that world to operate them." I frown.

"Yes and no. There are different types of portals. Even here, there will be the universal portal that can take you anywhere. But the one we are heading for is specifically designed to facilitate travel to and from Tartareia."

I release a soft sigh as I lean further into his touch.

"Then we should have no trouble getting there."

"Yes, but before we leave, I want to teach you something."

I open my eyes to regard him.

"What?"

"Remember how I knew those men in the forest were demons? That is because of their energy signature. Anyone with strong physical abilities can judge another's energy signature. If we go like this, people in Tartareia will be alerted that there is an Aperite deity in their realm."

"So what do we do then?"

"I want to teach you how to hide your energy signature and move around unnoticed. It is a very simple trick, but one that will be very useful in the future."

"Okay." I nod. "Let's do it."

We finish packing our baggage and feed the dogs. As we let them play by themselves around their little pink house, Nykander and I go to a more secluded area of the forest to not disturb the dogs.

He takes a step back, his hands behind his back as he studies me.

"I told you that my kind is considered mature at three thousand years old. But what I failed to mention is that until we reach that milestone, we train nonstop to hone our abilities. It is the same for Aperite deities."

"You…trained for three thousand years?" I gawk at him.

He nods.

"Normally, you would need to train just as much, but since we don't have the luxury of time, I will give you a concise overview of how spiritual ability works and how you can improve."

"Okay…" I murmur.

"A deity is born with a certain amount of spiritual ability that is inherited from both parents. But during your lifetime, you can train and evolve. Generally, you can increase your spiritual ability by fifty to one hundred percent depending on how hard you train."

I blink in surprise. That is…unexpected. And kind of cool.

"But in order to do that, you must first reach your native potential. The first three thousand years are to max out your inherent spiritual ability, after which you start training toward increasing it. In your case, we need to find a way to max out your potential faster."

"You mean cram three thousand years in a few days?" I mutter dryly.

He smirks.

"I never said it was going to be too easy."

"Or feasible. How can you think that's possible?" I frown.

"Because there are ways we can speed up your progress," he adds.

"Okay, I'm listening," I say as I cross my arms over my chest.

"There are nine energy points—you can think of them as gates or checkpoints. Once you have completed all nine, your initial training is finished. In Aperion, despite being a deity by birth, you can only qualify as one after you open all nine checkpoints."

My brows shoot up.

"In Tartareia that's different?"

He smiles.

"We do not bother with those lofty titles, nor do we technically call ourselves deities. We are warriors. You either pass or you do not. And if you do not, you are useless and therefore expendable."

"You mean…"

"Those who do not open their nine checkpoints by the time they reach maturity are demoted and exiled. The Sons of Tenebreis cannot be anything less than perfect. Those who fail are not allowed to identify as one of us. They are still Tartareians, and they can perform other duties within the realm, but they can never erase the shame of having failed to qualify."

"So being a Son of Tenebreis is the highest honor?"

He nods.

"We are the foundation and core of Tartareia."

"I see," I murmur.

"By opening the first gate, you will be able to somewhat control your spiritual ability—at least enough to mask it. But before we plan our attack on Baine, you must open all nine," he continues.

"All nine?" I squeak. "Nyk, I think you're overestimating me. You had three thousand years! This is insane!"

"No, it is not. As long as you open up to your fourth gate on your own, there is one way to quickly advance to the ninth. It is a perilous road that not many survive, but I have trust in you." He purses his lips.

His expression is grave as he regards me, and I can't help but wonder *why* he wants me to open all nine gates at once. It seems ludicrous to even think about it! How can anyone do that in a few days when the norm is thousands of years?

"What are you talking about?"

"There is a lake in Tartareia, Velor—or otherwise called the Lake of Adversity. And just like the name implies, once you step inside, you experience every turbulent emotion; every nightmare materializes—or every dream. You can only come out of it if you defeat your own self and become a master of your emotions. But those who have successfully gone through it have doubled their spiritual ability. In your case, it should help you break through the ninth gate."

"You speak as if you have personal experience with it," I whisper.

A sad smile pulls at his lips.

"I have merely heard tales."

"So you want me to go into that lake?"

"Yes. Going against Baine is not going to be easy, and I will not take any chances with you. The only way I can have some peace of mind is if you are at full strength too."

"Okay." I take a deep breath.

That was a lot to take in, but if it's going to help him, then

I'll do it. I would never want to be a burden to him, and this might be the first time I can prove myself to be useful. To be…strong.

A thrill of excitement goes down my back.

Me, strong. How cool is that?

I can finally be *the* heroine in the story, not just a passive spectator.

"Before you can step inside Velor, you need to open the first four gates. Otherwise, the lake will consume you. So we will start with the basics." He nods.

"And those are?" I ask on a giggle.

He narrows his eyes at me.

"Summon your energy at will and maintain it regardless of the circumstances. That is the first gate. Once you are able to do that, you will also be able to mask your energy signature."

"Oh, okay," I mumble.

We stare at each other for moments on end. Nyk taps his foot restlessly against the ground, his jaw ticking with impatience.

"Well, what are you waiting for? Summon your energy. You know how to do that," he instructs.

My lashes flutter in confusion.

Do I?

Until now, I've summoned it by chance when my emotions were out of control.

"Uhm, how do I do that?" I ask, embarrassed.

He blinks, raising his brows at me. He slowly realizes how overwhelmed I am by all of this because as he speaks again, his voice is softer.

"Focus on your energy and bring that pretty pink shield to the surface, sweetheart."

I take a deep breath and, closing my eyes, I try to focus on the shield.

Moments pass and nothing happens.

I release a sigh of frustration.

"I don't know how!"

"You do," Nykander counters. Taking a step forward, he cups my cheeks and presses a kiss on my lips. Heat travels down my body. A deep blush stains my cheeks.

But just as the kiss starts, it ends.

He backs away from me, a satisfied smile curving up his lips.

"See?" He nods toward me.

I look down at my body to see a pink shimmer surround me, the color slowly intensifying.

"Until you learn how to summon it at will, think of this," he says as he gives me another kiss. "Think of all the ways I want to kiss you. All the ways I have *yet* to kiss you."

"W-what ways?" I whisper.

My heart slams against my ribcage as I find myself utterly lost in those beautiful eyes of his. His pupils dilate, mirroring the desire reflected in my own.

"So many, Barbs." He smirks. "From here"—he lifts his hand and presses his fingers to my tips—"to here…" He trails his fingers down my neck, pausing over my breasts. My nipples are hard and poking against the material of my thin dress. I'm not wearing a bra, and as his eyes zero in on that area, he makes a low, sexy sound deep in his throat. "Then here…" He continues downward, his fingers brushing against my stomach before they settle over my hip bone. He splays his palm over my pubic bone, his fingers achingly close to that place between my thighs that weeps for him.

"And then?" I ask on a breathless whimper.

He gives me a lopsided smile, but he doesn't move, taunting me with that wicked pause.

Feeling my frustration mount, I grab his hand and push it lower until his palm curves around my mound. His touch is scorching hot, even though there are two layers of material separating it from my bare skin. He applies the slightest bit of pressure and I find myself moaning and throwing my head back in reckless abandon. Gripping his shirt in my fingers, I angle my body to give him better access.

"My greedy girl," he drawls, his voice sending shivers down my back. "Go ahead, baby. Take what you need."

My lips tremble as I'm unable to coherently express my desire or my wants. I fist his shirt tighter as I grind against his hand.

"Nyk," I whisper.

He presses his hand deeper between my thighs, cupping my sex and stroking me gently.

My breathing intensifies.

His eyes are on me, watching, waiting.

He applies more pressure on my clit before he moves his hand in slow, languorous circles. My body erupts in goose bumps as the anticipation builds.

His touch is hot and firm. His eyes become hooded as he watches me squirm and move against him.

"Nyk... I..." I whimper.

"Come for me," he murmurs, leaning in to brush his lips against mine. He rubs me faster through my clothes, the roughness of the material providing an additional stimulus. How I wish it were his bare hand, though. How I wish he could sink those thick fingers inside me, stretch me, and claim me until his touch becomes my sole definition for pleasure.

"Just like that, sweetheart. I can see it in your eyes. You're so close," he continues to whisper against my mouth. He slides his tongue over my lips, licking me and showing me the way he'd like to kiss me—*there*.

"I need..." I trail off as my brain short-circuits.

He plays my body like an instrument, and I feel compelled to sing for him. My moans become increasingly louder, the notes higher and higher.

His lips curve in a wicked smile as he continues to assault me with his devilish touch.

He splays his hand over my sex and presses hard. At the same time, he trails his lips over my face, reaching my ear. He nibbles at my earlobe before he commands me in a rough voice.

"Come for me, Barbi. Now!"

There is something in his voice that affects me like never before, as if it's speaking to me on a cellular level. The low bass of his tone caresses my skin, infiltrating into my flesh until it reaches the desired destination.

A fire builds within me the moment his command registers, and my body can do nothing but obey.

My mouth forms an inaudible O as my insides tighten and coil.

One second.

That's all it takes for the orgasm to ravage me. I start trembling uncontrollably as I slump against him, riding on those magnificent throes of pleasure.

"That's my girl," he praises me gently.

I let out a satisfied meowl as I burrow closer against him, leisurely licking his neck. Something pricks at my gums, and I nibble at his flesh in an attempt to alleviate that growing discomfort. His intoxicating scent fills my nostrils, and before I know it, my teeth penetrate his skin. Hot blood floods my mouth and I drink greedily.

He holds me tight, cradling my head as he urges me to drink from him.

I drink my fill, and as I lean back, I note the pink shimmer around me has intensified.

"Just like that, sweetheart. Fuck, you are the hottest thing I've ever seen," he rasps before he crashes his lips to mine.

This kiss is different.

It's urgent, animalistic.

His grip is almost bruising as he pulls me into him.

My mark burns in my chest, the pleasure intensifying with each swipe of his tongue. And it all culminates when he sinks his sharp fangs into my lips, biting me hard enough that blood immediately pools to the surface. In response, his own lips burst open. Our blood mixes together as we continue to kiss, and before I know it, another wave of pleasure hits me.

But this time, I'm not alone.

The shudders racking my body are mirrored by his own. We both tremble as pleasure ripples through us.

He groans and grunts, all sounds that I swallow then echo with my own moans.

It's almost an eternity later that he pulls himself away from me. He's breathing hard, his eyes a deep black that swirls with specks of silver.

"You, Barbi, are a dangerous female." He releases a thick groan as he scrubs a hand over his face.

I blink slowly, unable to catch his meaning.

"W-what?"

His gaze dips lower, and I follow it, my eyes widening as I realize what he means. A dark spot stains the front of his pants.

"You wanted another one of my firsts? You have it," he says with an amused grin. "It is the first time I have spilled my seed clothed."

"Oh," I murmur, my face turning a deep scarlet.

His laughter echoes in the forest as he excuses himself to go clean up.

Maybe before I would have been embarrassed by this. But now there is only an overflowing sense of pride that *I* did that. I made him come without even touching him.

A dreamy sigh slips past my lips as I succumb to the ground. I can't shake the silly smile painted on my face, nor the giddiness that makes me flail my arms and legs.

Of course, when he comes back, I calm down and present myself as the picture of composure.

Yet there is one big development in our training.

Nyk was right.

Now I only need to think of the pleasure he gave me and I can channel my energy to the surface.

"You did it, sweet girl." Nykander claps and praises me when I manage to summon and maintain my shield ten times in a row.

I give him a cheeky wink.

"Now that the first phase is done, it's time we moved to the second."

The second one proves to be a little trickier, though.

"You need to feel your energy around you but imagine it is a thin layer that only you can see or feel," he explains. "Look at me."

He channels his dark shield.

"Do you sense my energy?"

"Is it like a hum under my skin?"

He nods, smiling.

"What about now?" he asks. He keeps his shield visible for my benefit, but I can no longer feel that hum.

"No." I shake my head.

"And now?"

This time, his shield disappears, and I can no longer see nor feel it.

I shake my head again.

"Your turn now. First, summon up your shield."

I do as he asks, and pink shimmery particles appear around the contour of my body.

"Good. Now focus on your shield. This is an extended part of you, Barbs. You are fully in control. You can decide whether I see or feel it."

"Okay. I'll try." I nod, closing my eyes.

I try to make contact with that source of energy I'd tapped earlier. I see it in my mind's eye. It's a swirling mass of pink that seemingly grows in size the more I stare at it.

"You are doing the opposite, Barbs," Nykander tsks.

My eyes flutter open and I immediately see what he means. Instead of hiding my shield, I've made it more conspicuous.

"I can do it," I tell him, closing my eyes once more.

I identify the same source of energy, but this time, instead of watching it grow larger, I tentatively step forward, willing it to become smaller until it can fit in the palm of my hand. Once it's within my reach, I let it wash over me, imagining it's coating me in an invisibility spell.

"Yes. That's it." Nykander's voice echoes in my ear. "I cannot see, nor feel it. You did it, Barbs."

I open my eyes, a wide smile on my face. But the moment my focus rattles, my shield becomes visible again, and the sphere of energy increases in size until I am but a dust speck next to it.

Nykander rushes to my side, his tentacles reaching around me to contain my shield from exploding.

"Almost there." He chuckles.

"Almost," I grumble.

He doesn't seem mad at my failure. On the contrary, he sweeps me off my feet and takes us back to camp, all the while praising me for my efforts.

When we get there, he lays me on the grass next to the dog house.

"You must be starving," he comments. "I will go get food. You rest."

"Is that an order?" I raise a brow.

He shakes his head and laughs.

"You can take it as such."

Smiling, I watch his retreating figure as I barely stop myself from rolling on the grass from too much giddiness.

I guess this is how it feels to be in love.

Ander spots me and runs to my arms, his little teeth

already on my fingers, chewing away. I hold him tight to my chest.

PomPom and BonBon don't even bother with me. They're playing together, almost as if they were in their own little world.

BonBon has a wide smile on his face—well, for a dog—as he chases after PomPom.

It seems I am not the only one who's been hit by the love bug around here. And damn if that doesn't make me even happier.

Nykander returns a few moments later with some meat he'd caught, and he proposes we eat first before we leave.

"We're leaving today? I thought we'd wait a bit longer until I can perfect my technique."

"You will be doing that on the way there. You are already doing so much better than I expected, sweetheart."

I preen under his praise, and because the butterflies in my stomach are so restless, I place Ander on the grass and drag myself closer to Nykander.

He's with his back to me, tending to the fire.

I press and rub myself shamelessly against him.

"What do you think you are doing, you little minx?" His eyes crinkle around the corners as he half-turns to me.

"What am I doing?" I shrug innocently. "I'm merely making myself more comfortable."

"On me?" He raises a brow.

"Well… If you insist, I can find someone else to lean on," I mutter in feigned displeasure.

I move an inch to the side before I find myself on my back, with him looming on top of me.

The warmth in his gaze feeds the butterflies with their much-needed sunlight, and they violently flap their wings in my belly.

I lick my lips.

His gaze dips to my mouth.

But just as he leans in to give me a kiss, PomPom jumps between us, followed by BonBon and Ander.

They sniff and lick us, and without breaking eye contact, both Nykander and I start laughing.

"The kids come first," he whispers playfully.

My lashes flutter in surprise.

He thinks the dogs are our kids?

Swoon!

27

"**A**gain," he demands in a strict voice.

I close my eyes and focus on my energy, doing my best to disguise it. Slowly, the shimmer around me fades.

I gaze up at Nykander, raising my brows in question.

He smiles and nods.

"Good. Let's see how long you can hold it."

"Does that mean we can go now?"

He grunts.

"But"—he raises a finger—"if you cannot hold it until we get to the portal, we will have to stop and do this all over again."

"Nyk." I pout.

"It is not up for debate, Barbs. You need to be able to shield yourself *continuously* once we reach Tartareia. Otherwise, there is no point in hiding. Everyone will be able to find us within moments."

"Fine." I sigh. "We will do it your way."

"Of course. We always do it my way, sweets." He winks at me.

I shake my head at him and return to get the dogs ready.

Leaving some food and water inside their little house, I pack all of our things and wait for Nykander to work his magic.

He grabs the dog house and our baggage with his tentacles, and we are ready to go.

"It's so pretty out today," I quip as we wade through the thick forest.

With how happy I've been in the last few days, I have the urge to skip around, but I don't want Nykander to think me immature—we're already so far apart in age as it is.

So if I can't skip around to my heart's content, then I can at least hum.

Nykander glances at me, his lips tipped up.

"What are you singing?"

"Oh, it's just a Korean song." I wave my hand around.

His brows go up.

"Sing it louder."

My lashes flutter in surprise.

"Uhm, you know I'm not the best singer and—"

"Doesn't matter. Sing to me."

"Fine. But don't you laugh, okay?"

"Me? Never!"

I hike a brow at his exaggerated expression, but I comply and start signing as we walk. I'm not sure if I can do the song justice, since the original is so perfect, but Nykander doesn't seem to be complaining.

He listens attentively when he suddenly stops me.

"What does that mean?"

"Hm? Which part?"

"*Make me go biteul, biteul,*" he repeats, though he butchers the words.

I chuckle at his pronunciation. Going to his side, I raise myself on the tips of my toes and whisper in his ear.

"It means, when I'm with you, you make me so crazy I forget how to walk and every single moment it feels like I'm falling. But even if I *do* fall, I know you'll be there to catch me."

His eyes widen slightly, and his cheeks heat up.

"That is"—he clears his throat—"very expressive."

"It is, isn't it? When we find a place to stay, I'll even show you the dance."

"You will?" he asks, his eyes moving up and down my body. "Without PomPom, I should hope."

"For you, I will make an exception," I murmur.

"Without clothes too." He smirks.

"Now, Mr. Dark One, you are being *too* picky," I chide him playfully.

"Am I? And here I thought it would be easier without clothes. Less restricting... It would do more justice to the moves."

"You haven't even seen the moves to know that," I whisper, lost in his gaze.

"I do not need to see your moves to imagine them, Barbs. You will find that I have quite the rich imagination and whatever you might do, I likely imagined it far ahead of time."

Now it's my turn to blush.

"You...have?" I murmur, averting my gaze.

"Barbs, what do you think seeing you in that drenched, see-through dress did to me? I could not get the picture out of my mind for weeks."

"Oh," I murmur, enjoying having such an effect on him.

"Then it is just as well that I also thought about..." I trail off.

"About?" He raises a brow.

My eyes dip to his pants before I quickly look away.

He chuckles as I furiously blush.

Before I can gather my composure, he whispers in my ear.

"And what did you think about, sweet girl?"

"Well, I... I..." I stammer, unable to find my words. "I..."

"Relax, Barbs." He laughs. "We can continue this conversation later, when we are alone…preferably with a bed nearby," he adds suggestively.

I gulp down.

"But on the bright side, even when you're blushing from head to toe, your shield is still hidden. Well done," he murmurs the praise as he lays a quick kiss on my lips.

We resume our walking, and it's the first time since we've known each other that we have been so at leisure around one another. There is an odd sense of comfort as he listens to me prattle away about my books and my favorite music or movies. And he's not *just* pretending to listen. He muses over my words, asking questions and appearing genuinely interested in what I have to say.

I swear my heart cannot take more of this. How can this man be so perfect?

"And you know, I was very upset when they canceled the show because it was so good! I wish I already had my trust fund as then I could sponsor the show to keep it running and—"

"Shh," Nykander suddenly says as he places a hand up.

He stops, listening closely.

"There is someone coming," he whispers.

"What? But you said this realm wasn't populated."

"So I did." He purses his lips. "He might not be able to sense our energy signature, but he will be able to hear us just as we hear him."

"Him? How do you know?"

"Close your eyes and listen."

I do as he says.

"The steps are punctured, heavy. There is also a rhythm to them that speaks of military training. He knows we are listening and he is making his presence known."

I frown.

"But why?"

"I do not know, but we are about to find out."

"Do we need to fight? I can fight. Well, I might not know how, but I'm sure I can wing it somehow. You don't have to do it all alone. Now I can help you too," I tell him excitedly.

The prospect of being useful and needed is a new one, but I find that I've never been happier.

In the past, I was just part of the decor—whether at home, at school, or with my so-called friends. It made me think that was all I was capable of—to be present but never seen.

Finally, I am important in one way or another.

I might have been mad at the fates initially, but now I'm thankful that they chose me.

"Barbs, quiet," he murmurs.

"Oh, okay, sorry."

He fights a smile as he maintains his concentration.

Lowering the dog house and our luggage to the ground, he retracts his tentacles, making himself look perfectly normal.

My ears perk up. Leaves rattle and twigs break as the stranger continues toward us.

I take a deep breath.

If he attacks, I am ready.

The foliage parts to reveal a tall man dressed in a military uniform—a black linen shirt and trousers covered by a brass armor.

He stops when he sees us, his eyes narrowed.

His features are harsh but beautiful. His jaw is strong and square, his cheekbones high. He appears to have some East Asian ancestry like myself—though I wonder what they call that in other worlds. As I study him, however, it's his eyes that I'm drawn to. They're a beautiful swirling amber, a mix of the lightest honey and red wine.

"Whoa, he's beautiful," I blurt out under my breath.

It's not every day I see someone with his looks. In my

world, he would definitely be an actor or a model, gracing the covers of magazines.

Nykander stiffens next to me, shooting me a harsh look.

"Barbi," he warns softly.

My eyes flare and I realize I misspoke. I certainly wouldn't like it if Nyk called any other woman beautiful.

"Sorry," I mumble.

The newcomer comes closer, his stance that of a warrior ready for battle.

"What brings the two of you here?" he asks, his voice deep and grave. "This is an uninhabited realm."

"We are in passing," Nykander answers in an equally belligerent tone. His body is tense by my side, and I suddenly feel overwhelmed by the testosterone flying in the air.

"We're on a holiday," I hurry to say in an attempt to defuse the situation. "We wanted to take our dogs on a trip." I motion to the dog house and the three dogs currently peeking their heads through the small window.

The man regards us suspiciously.

"This is not a realm where you vacation," he continues, his voice measured. "It is toxic for life, unless..."

"Unless?" I frown, glancing questioningly from him to Nykander.

He hadn't mentioned anything about toxicity. And we have our dogs with us! How could he not tell me that?

"Unless you are immune to it, which would make you either a deity or a demon," the man states. Reaching for the sword sheathed at his waist, I realize he's already determined we must be the enemy.

And based on the fact that he can walk around freely, I assume he is *not* a demon. Then that makes him an Aperite deity.

Nykander tenses.

Oh, no. Don't tell me they are preparing for battle. That's the last thing we need, especially with our dogs here. We might be all right, but they would bear the brunt of the violence.

"Not demons," I blurt out, pressing my palm against Nykander's chest and taking a step forward.

"Barbi? What are you doing?" He grabs my hand, but I shake my head at him.

"We're not demons. I promise," I continue. "In fact, we are *running* away from demons."

The newcomer tilts his head to the side, his expression pensive.

"You are?"

"Yes, yes. You see, we come from a world called Akkaya and there we were chased by this big bad demon called Damien. He was awful. He caused this plague that killed millions of people and he was feeding on their souls to become stronger and—"

The man puts his hand up, silencing me.

"I have heard about that incident. The demon you speak of has been destroyed."

"Oh." I pretend to be surprised. "That is good to hear…" I stammer.

"We do not wish to engage in any conflict," Nykander intervenes. "We are merely trying to find a portal to lead us home."

"Home… And where is that?" the stranger asks.

"Anthropa," Nykander lies.

The man lifts his brows in surprise.

"Then allow me to escort you to the portal." He inclines his head. "It is not safe to be around here."

"I am certain we can find our own way," Nykander states.

Tension crackles in the air as they engage in a staring contest.

"I will escort you," the man repeats. "I also have a few questions about the world you speak of—Akkaya."

"What do you wish to know? I will answer your questions and then we will be on our way," Nykander continues.

The stranger regards us curiously.

I elbow Nykander in the ribs and give him a look. The more he speaks, the more this man is going to suspect we're hiding something.

"Have you seen or heard about a blue dragon in Akkaya?"

"Dragon?" My eyes widen. "They're real?" I whisper to Nykander.

"No, we have not," he replies tersely. "If that is all, we will be on our way."

Nykander lifts the dog house in his arms, nodding for me to take our baggage—though I can barely carry it. Still, we have to maintain a facade of normality. Without another word, we move past the stranger to leave.

But we only make it a few feet before the baggage falls from my hands, the makeshift bag opening and spilling all our clothes.

I immediately drop to my knees to gather them, and the stranger surprisingly joins me, handing me some of the clothes. Our hands accidentally touch, and a spark of electricity runs through my body, but it's a different kind than when Nykander touches me. I pull my hand away, massaging the spot as if I'd been burned by a hot object.

A growl erupts in the air.

"I would appreciate it if you stepped away from my female," Nykander intervenes. He places the dog house on the ground and inserts himself between the stranger and me.

Tension rolls off him in dangerous waves. Just hours before he was teaching me about hiding my energy signature and now he's about to give himself away because of some silly jealousy—though I can't deny that makes my insides mushy.

"Cut it out, Nyk. He was merely trying to help," I murmur.

"*I* can help you. He does not need to concern himself with

us, much less put his finger on you," he grits out. He's staring intently at the man, as if waiting for a reason to strike.

"The dogs are here, Nyk. Please, behave."

He sneers in displeasure. Oh, I can tell he's itching for a fight, but he chose the wrong moment.

"Fine," he mumbles. "But you do *not* touch my female. In fact, I would appreciate it if you took a few steps back. You are far too close as it is," he instructs the stranger, pushing me farther behind him so I'm completely out of sight.

Alas, this would be cuter if this wasn't such a precarious situation. He's been lecturing me up and down about the importance of hiding our identities, but he is ready to risk it all the moment someone looks the wrong way at me.

The stranger does not reply. He's frozen on the spot, staring at the pile of clothes. He wrinkles his nose.

"I smell blood," he mentions in a tight voice.

His cheek twitches as he glances up at Nykander and me.

"*Demon* blood."

He barely finishes his words as he removes his sword from its sheath and sends a blast of energy toward us.

Nykander's shield immediately goes up to obstruct the blow, his dark shadows enveloping both of us.

The stranger's eyes shift color as he regards us with interest.

He smirks as he takes in Nykander's dark energy.

"So I was right," he mutters. "And not just *any* demon. A Son of Tenebreis. Must be my lucky day. You will tell me where Aethon is, demon," he grits out, wielding his sword with deadly precision.

"What? Who's Aethon?" I whisper to Nyk.

He grinds his jaw.

"A general in the Aperite army. He is the blue dragon he is looking for."

"We don't know any Aethon or blue dragon," I call out. "We aren't hurting anyone. Can you just leave us alone?"

"He *must* know. Aethon was last seen chasing after your brethren," the man replies.

"I do not know what brethren you are speaking of, nor do I know anything about Aethon." Nykander squints.

"Nyk, the dogs," I whisper. "I need to get them to safety."

He gives me a tight nod.

His tendrils extend to grab the dog house and move it out of danger. But the stranger mistakes his actions for an offensive, and he strikes out.

My eyes widen in fear. We might heal, but my babies cannot. How dare he put them in danger?

"Leave my dogs out of this!" I shout.

The pink shimmery energy materializes around me, my control slipping from me as I think about anything happening to my babies.

My scream turns into a deadly weapon, the energy rolling off me effortlessly. It takes the shape of a scythe, flying at the stranger with one purpose—to draw blood.

His brows go up in surprise, but with one swish of his sword, he parries my blow.

This gives Nykander enough time to move the dogs out of the danger zone.

"You are not a demon," the man states, his eyes boring into me. "What are you?"

"None of your business, you cretin!" I point my finger at him. "How dare you try to hurt my dogs? You chose the wrong person to anger today, buddy," I say as I cross my arms over my chest. Leaning into Nykander, I whisper, "Make him pay, Nyk. He can't get away after threatening our little ones."

A small smile pulls at Nykander's lips.

"Your wish is my command, sweet thing." He winks at me.

Depositing me aside with one tentacle, he remains in the middle of the clearing, facing the newcomer. With my express approval, he is now more at ease. His expression changes too, and I can tell he enjoys the challenge.

Since the other man is using a sword, Nykander mirrors him, creating his own weapon from his energy.

"You go, Nyk!" I jump up and down, cheering for him. "Kick his ass!"

He rolls his eyes, but I don't miss the small smile pulling at his lips.

The other man is not amused. He glances between the two of us, debating his next move.

"Aethon was following Mideros when he went missing," the man speaks in a low voice. "Tell me where Mideros is and I might let your female live."

"That is the wrong thing to say." Nykander laughs darkly. "Do. Not. Threaten. Her," he utters slowly. "Do not even look at her."

"I see. So she is your weakness," the man muses. "Tell me where Mideros is."

"Mideros is in Tartareia, which is sealed, but you already know that."

"No. He is not. He has been sighted *outside* of Tartareia."

"Impossible! No one can leave Tartareia." Nyk frowns.

The man tilts his head to the side.

"And yet here you are." He smirks. "Nice try."

"He's different," I quip from the sidelines. "He wasn't there when Tartareia was sealed."

"I did not ask for your opinion, female," he states in a deadpan voice, his gaze devoid of any emotion.

"What did I tell you? Do not look at her," Nykander grits out, flashing himself out of sight before appearing in front of the man and striking. The man dodges the blow, a slow, deadly smile pulling at his lips.

"Killing demons is fun. Killing a Son of Tenebreis will be even more entertaining," he mutters under his breath.

So far, he has not summoned his energy to the surface. I still can't detect his energy signature. Despite that, he's able to dodge every attack Nyk sends his way.

He's strong. That much is clear.

He smiles and he rushes toward Nykander.

Their swords clash. They glare at each other, the metal of their blades trembling with tension as they apply more force.

But it seems they are evenly matched.

Specks of energy crackle around them. One moment they're in front of me, sword against sword, the next they're two dots on the horizon, moving at the speed of light. Branches fall, leaves rustle, and trees collapse. They destroy everything in their path as the clash of steel against steel echoes in the stillness of the forest.

The fight stretches for moments on end, and without using their spiritual abilities, they are both becoming exhausted from the back and forth.

The few times I get a better look at them, I note that Nykander's clothes have been slashed, blood staining the material. But the wound has already healed, so his flesh is smooth. The same goes for his opponent. The areas not covered by his brass armor have been cut and shredded, the material hanging loosely on his body. But he, too, does not have any visible injuries.

So he can heal, too.

At this rate, I doubt there will be a winner. One strikes, the other parries. One injures the other, then gets injured in return.

But as they notice the battle stalling, they finally call upon their spiritual energy.

Nykander ditches his sword, letting his dark shadows envelop him. The stranger summons his own energy, a dark magenta with specks of silver.

"Be careful, Nyk," I whisper.

Despite having full confidence in his abilities, I fear for him. He is getting tired and he needs to feed. The stranger, on the other hand, seems to have a strong supply of energy. It's almost like the more Nykander strikes at him, the stronger he becomes.

Damn it!

He must be some type of high-level god. Even Damien with his all-encompassing supply of souls had not been *this* strong.

A loud blast reverberates in the forest before something drops to the ground, creating a deep crater in the soil. Nykander claws his way out, wobbling on his feet. His face is covered in blood and his injuries heal slower than before. God, that must be incredibly painful.

The stranger lands a few feet over, his breathing shallow.

"Where is Mideros?"

"I do not know," Nyk grits out, unleashing his tendrils upon his opponent. While some slither from the front, distracting him, others appear from the back, disguising themselves as the shadows of trees.

While the man fights the ones he can see, the inconspicuous ones curl around his feet, traveling up his legs. He fights them off, using his energy to blast them away, but Nykander reinforces them.

Once he has a good grip on his opponent, Nyk pulls hard on him. He brings him toward him at the same time as he builds a ball of energy in his hands. As the man reaches Nyk's side, he pushes the ball of energy into his gut.

My eyes widen as I see the way the brass armor snaps, shards of it falling to the ground. The energy eats at his flesh until there's a gaping hole in the middle of his torso.

With a feeble blast of energy, the man manages to extricate himself from Nyk's hold, only to collapse a few feet over.

He takes a deep breath as his flesh slowly mends.

Nykander is also breathing hard, his shield flickering in and out and denoting he's close to his limit.

This is it.

I clasp my hands to my front as I watch them breathlessly.

The next clash will denote a winner.

"You can do this, Nyk."

He half-turns toward me, his lips curving in a lopsided smile. Blood drips down his chin. He looks sexy and battered, but still sexy.

He winks at me. But that second of inattention is about to cost him.

"Nyk!" I call out as the man gets to his feet, ready to launch another attack.

Just as they summon their last bit of strength, a loud thud resounds in the forest as someone drops down from the sky.

What the...

28

"Oh my, I really need to work on that landing," the girl who just fell out of the sky mutters. She slowly gets up and dusts her clothes. She's on the taller side, dressed in an off-white regency-style dress. Her bright red hair is gathered atop her head in an elegant bun, with a few curls falling down her forehead.

She blows air upward to move the hair from her eyes. Then she glances around until her eyes find the stranger.

He straightens his spine and brings the back of his hand to his eyes to wipe the blood dripping from a gash in his forehead.

"What are you doing here, Thea?" he asks in a dry, bored tone.

"Do you even have to ask, Cer?" She shakes her head. "You really couldn't choose a more hospitable realm? It took me ages to find you since you know that my navigation system isn't the best. And how do I find you? Bleeding and with a hole in your stomach." Her mouth curls down in disgust. "Aren't you ashamed of yourself? I can see what you had for breakfast." She points to his stomach.

Curious, I glance at his stomach, too, but I can't see what she's referring to. The wound is almost closed by now.

"Is that why you are here, Thea?" He sighs. "To lecture me some more? Could you not have waited until I got home?"

"Good on you to remember you have a home. Don't you know what day is tomorrow?"

He blinks, staring at her, unmoving.

"Oh no, no. Don't you dare tell me you forgot!" She shrieks, launching herself at him.

He extends his arm, his open palm connecting with her forehead as he keeps her at a distance. She flails her arms around, her nails growing in size until they resemble claws as she tries to get a hit on him.

"Thea, if you don't mind, I am in the middle of something," he mutters while holding a squirming Thea at arm's length—literally.

Nykander inches his way toward me, his expression one of confusion that mirrors my own.

"What are we watching?" he asks on a whisper.

"I think it's a lovers' spat," I whisper back. "He probably forgot their anniversary or her birthday," I wager a guess.

"Something?" she repeats, narrowing her eyes as she finally takes note of our presence. "Don't tell me you're fighting over a female!" she exclaims, outraged.

I frown, confused about how she got to that conclusion. But seeing that Nykander is the only one bedraggled in this situation, I can understand her misconception.

"Are you out of your freaking mind, Cer? With all the problems we have, you're now chasing after a female?" She slaps his hand aside and takes a step forward. Despite her being taller than average, she's still much shorter than him. "Have you forgotten about Aethon? What about Wyn? It's her coming out ball tomorrow and you're out here fighting another male over a female!"

"Thea, that is not—"

"How could you do this, Cer? I am so disappointed in you," she continues. "And to make matters worse, while you're out here having your fun, Ze has decided to move into our guest room. That wretched male is corrupting my friend and it is all your fault."

"How is that my fault?" He frowns.

"Because you brought him into our home to begin with! Ugh!" She throws her hands in the air in frustration.

"So let me understand this. I am guilty of everything bad that has ever happened in your life."

"Exactly!" she agrees. Her eyes widen. "Well, it is true. You have singlehandedly ruined everything for me."

"Thea." Cer takes a deep breath. "I think you should go home."

"But—"

"That"—he points to Nykander—"is a Son of Tenebreis. And the female is his. I am not fighting over her. I do not care about her. I am merely performing my duty by interrogating him on the whereabouts of his brethren."

She blinks slowly as she realizes what he's saying. She spares us another glance before she whispers a low, "Oh."

"So you see, I am in the middle of something important. And as a matter of fact, I am searching for Aethon."

"But you did forget about Wyn's ball, didn't you?" She points a finger at him accusatorily.

"No. I did not. I will be there. I promised her the first dance, and I would never renege on that promise."

"Good." She tips her chin up. "It is the least you can do."

He raises a brow at her.

"Why do I feel like we're watching a telenovela?" I whisper to Nykander.

"What is that?"

"It's a TV show where there is plot twist after plot twist and never-ending drama. You know it's terrible, but you can't stop watching."

He nods thoughtfully.

"You are right. This is terrible, but I cannot stop watching."

"Hey!" Thea turns to Nykander, at the same time as Cer pins him with his deathly glare. "How dare you say that? Cer, go win that fight!" she instructs him. "Do you want me to take the female? I have gotten quite good at cat fighting as they call it in the human world. Remember what I did to that foxy lady?" She wiggles her brows up and down.

"Thea. I do not need your help. In fact, please leave. You will only make matters worse."

"Why don't we all agree not to fight?" I chime in. "We can go on our merry way and you can attend that ball or whatever. It's a win-win situation."

"She has a point, Cer. Do you even have a proper suit for tomorrow?" Thea nods, her features grave. "You cannot show up in an old suit. What will people say? That awful Elora already has it out for me. The last thing I need is for the entire court to laugh at me for having an unfashionable brother. They already laugh at me for other things." She sighs. "That's it. You're coming with me. Finish your fight and we're going home so you can get fitted for a new suit."

"Thea—"

"Thea this, Thea that. Do you even know how to say something else?"

"She's right." Nykander and I nod.

"No one asked you." Cer rolls his eyes.

"Look, we battled, no one won, so let us call it a day. The ladies are right. We have better things to do than blow holes through each other."

"But you are a demon," Cer states mechanically.

"Is he, really? He's never turned a soul into a demon. He's quite a good person by those standards, which is ironic considering his nickname is the Dark One. But he is really not that bad. And we have kids together—erm, dogs. Can you really leave my dogs without a father?" I pout.

"You have dogs?" Thea blinks, coming closer.

"Thea. It is not the moment," Cer mentions from behind.

She doesn't mind him, though, shushing him with her hand as she comes toward me.

"Can I see them? I love dogs. My friend has a wagyu cow that she named Belinda, but she'll unfortunately leave soon to better pastures and all that." She waves her hand.

"Greener pastures, Thea," Cer corrects her.

"Same thing."

"You must promise you will not harm them in any shape or form," I add suspiciously.

"Of course! Cer will promise too. You will, won't you, Cer?"

Cer glares at her.

"You will, will you not, my darling Cerenios?" Thea bats her eyes at him.

He mutters something under his breath, which I believe counts as a yes.

"Yes! Can I please see the dogs now?"

Nykander and I glance at each other, and he shakes his head.

"She seems nice," I whisper.

"You are far too naive, Barbi. They are Aperite deities," he grits out.

"Barbi? Your name is Barbi?" The girl nearly topples Nykander over as she places herself in front of me. "That is just like that doll humans play with, no? I used to steal—uhm, buy—some for Wyn when she was younger. She loved them."

"Yes, that is the doll," I mutter, a bit taken aback by her manner. And here I thought I was odd.

"How cute! She's named after a doll, Cer. Isn't that awesome?"

"Thea… This is not the moment."

"The dogs. May I meet the dogs, please?"

She seems genuine, so I convince Nykander to bring the dog house over. When she sees it's pink, she can't stop gushing about how cute it is, but her reaction only gets worse when she meets PomPom, BonBon, and Ander.

"Cer," she cries out—as in, she actually sheds tears. "I need some. You must get me a dog, Cer."

"Thea." He sighs.

"I know the spiel, okay? You are not allowed to behave like this Thea. It is no wonder you remain unmarried in your old age because of this, Thea. You should focus on passing your exams, not on dogs, Thea. Am I missing something?"

"No, I think that covers it all," Cer mutters.

Dressed as she is in that elegant gown, she's now rolling in the grass with the dogs, letting them bite her updo until her hair tumbles down her back.

"Do you think she's stranger than me?" I lean in to whisper to Nykander.

He purses his lips as he thinks for a moment.

"She is strange. But stranger?" He shakes his head. "I think you shall maintain the crown, dear poop master."

I chuckle at our inside joke.

Thea plays with the dogs. Cer scowls by the side. And Nykander and I flirt a few feet over. And just a few moments ago, they were tearing at each other's throats.

"Cer, you must leave these two people alone. How can they be evil if they have such cute dogs?"

"Thea, I am sure there is no correlation between the two."

"Well, I am making it one," she says as she gets up. Her dress is now stained from the grass, but she does not seem to care. "I require a dog too. Even Ze got Luce a cow. What have you ever gotten me?"

"I will not answer that question. Nor will I argue with you further."

"Good. Then we can go home to get you fitted for your suit. And then we can search the universe for a cute dog."

"I will do no such thing."

"Cer." She tilts her head. "We will discuss this further when we get home. We can leave now."

Both Nykander and I stare at them, dumbfounded.

"It was nice meeting you, dolly. You too, bloody man. You have very nice dogs. Take care of them, okay? And don't turn any souls into demons. Then my brother will have to hunt you down and kill you and these cuties will remain without their parents."

"Uhm, thanks?"

She grabs Cer by his shredded shirt and leads him away.

"Thea, you must stop interfering with my work…"

His voice drifts off as they both disappear.

I turn to Nykander.

"What just happened?"

"I think we just got lucky."

"What do you mean?" I frown.

"If I am correct, that male was Cerenios. He is one of the generals in the Aperite army, and he is the protégé of The God Killer."

"The God Killer?"

"The ultimate commander of the Aperite army. He is said to be unmatched in strength. And if that was his protégé, I doubt our fight would have ended anytime soon."

"I suppose it is a good thing he did not question my identity."

He nods.

"But do not think I did not notice you looking at him," Nykander suddenly adds, his eyes narrowing at me. He steps to the side to pick up a clean set of clothes—his last one.

"I was just curious," I reply.

"You also said he was *beautiful*," he continues, making a disgusted face.

"Objectively, he was. But then, so was his sister. They were both a good-looking pair."

Nyk pulls a shirt over his chest and pauses to stare at me.

"More good-looking than *me*?" He raises a brow.

"My, my, are you jealous, oh my dear Dark One?"

He mumbles something under his breath.

"You *are*," I accuse playfully, planting myself in front of him. I arrange the collar of his shirt as an amused smile plays at my lips. "He might have been handsome, but no one compares to you, my good-looking friend. You are the only one whose looks I care about, and the only one I would stare at for an eternity."

He blinks slowly before a flush creeps up his cheeks.

"You…would?" he asks slowly, uncertainly.

"Yes, Mr. Dark One. You are the only good-looking man for me."

He nods, satisfied.

"Now it's your turn," I whisper as I give him a small nudge.

"My turn?" His brows bunch. "For what?"

"Your turn to tell me I am prettier than that girl. Than any girl, for that matter. That I am the prettiest for you in the entire universe."

And to accentuate that I mean the *entire* universe, I extend my arms in an all-encompassing gesture.

He stares at me for a moment, speechless.

"You…are the prettiest?"

"Nyk! Don't just repeat what I said! Didn't you hear the way I phrased my compliment? You must do the same," I tell him.

He scratches the back of his head as he mulls this over.

"You are prettier than that female to me, Barbs—than *any* female. That is not a compliment. It is a reality. I am not one to offer false platitudes, so when I tell you that you are the most beautiful to me, you must believe me."

"Girls like pretty words," I mutter under my breath.

His lips curve up. Tipping my chin, he curves his palm along my jaw.

"Words are meaningless if they are not backed by actions. So let my actions speak for themselves. Let the fact that my eyes see only you be proof enough that no other can measure up to you. Let the fact that I am who I am, *what* I am, because your blood flows through my veins be proof enough that I am, because you are." He takes a deep breath. "Let the fact that my body reacts to you and only you be the only proof you need, sweet thing."

My lashes flutter in surprise. He claims words are meaningless, but then why do his words make my heart flutter? Why does my mark heat up at hearing him speak so prettily?

"You might not think so, but words are also important, Nyk," I whisper, taking his hand and kissing his palm. "The words you speak are the words I hear, the words I replay all over in my head, and the words I carry in my heart. Actions are important, yes. But words are to actions what kisses are to making love. You don't have to kiss to make love, but it's certainly a much more pleasurable activity with it. Same goes for words. You don't need them, but they can enrich everything."

He tilts his head, smiling as he studies me.

"And you are suddenly an expert in making love?"

"No, but I am becoming an expert in kissing," I murmur as I lift myself on the tips of my toes and touch my lips to his. "And I would never give them up for anything in the world. Same for those pretty words."

"Ah, Barbi, Barbi. You win. You will have your kisses and your pretty words," he whispers before he swoops me in his arms and proves it with his actions.

• • •

WE ARRIVE at the portal at dusk. Even with the darkening sky, the portal is a mass of black swirling energy, resembling a black hole.

A shiver of fear and anticipation goes down my back.

This is it. This is the moment he's been waiting for over seven thousand years.

Despite being happy about the prospect of helping him accomplish his revenge, I can't help but be a little apprehensive about what this journey will have in store for us. His home holds so many memories for him—memories of Mo.

Deep down, I am still anxious about his feelings for her, especially when everything around him will remind him of her.

It's okay, Barbi. It's all going to be all right. He will kill his brother and then we will live together happily ever after. It's that simple.

I keep telling myself the same thing over and over again, but seeing the portal in front of me has all these doubts returning with a vengeance.

Nykander places the dog house on the ground and turns to me.

"You must not at any point reveal your energy signature, Barbs. All right? The moment you do, everyone in Tartareia will know there is an Aperite deity in their midst and they will not stop hunting us."

"Okay." I nod. "I can do this."

"I know you can." He smiles as he leans in to kiss my forehead. "And before we cross over, I want you to do something for me."

"What?"

He materializes a knife in his hand and gives it to me.

"Cut my hair."

My eyes widen at his request.

"It will be much easier to avoid attention if I do not look as I used to," he explains.

"Oh, all right."

He takes a seat on the grass in front of me. I thread my fingers through his hair, admiring the silky texture of his locks.

"I think I'll miss you with your long hair," I murmur.

"I can grow it again for you after everything is over," he mentions.

"Good." I chuckle.

It takes me a few tries to cut through his thick hair, especially since I'm using a knife instead of a pair of scissors. He sits patiently, helping me here and there until I'm done. His long locks fall to the ground, his hair now barely above his ears.

"Is this fine?" I ask as I step back.

He ruffles his hand through his hair and nods, satisfied. Despite being so used to his long hair, I have to admit he looks dashing with short hair too. In fact, this new cut gives him an air of danger and mystique that wasn't there before.

He gets up and brushes the remaining hair off his clothes. But as I peek on the ground at the leftover strands, I can't find it in my heart to leave it all behind. Bending down, I grab a thicker strand and braid it.

He looks at me curiously, his eyes widening when he notes what I want to do with it.

"Barbs..."

"It would be a shame if it went to waste," I explain shyly as I tie the newly pleated strands around my wrist like a bracelet.

"That is..." He clears his throat. "I appreciate it."

"Now we can go."

He picks up the dogs and the small baggage and we step forward. The knife is still in my hands and I bring the tip of the blade to the middle of my palm, imbuing my blood with my essence. A few drops fall onto the surface of the portal, and the color immediately changes. From a foreboding black to a welcoming pink.

"It's time." He sighs. A look of pure determination descends upon his features.

Grabbing my hand, we step together inside the portal.

29

Whatever I might have imagined about Tartareia proves to be false.

I had this image of a raging inferno and devil-like creatures running around naked holding pitchforks and chasing the next sin to commit. It is supposed to be the primordial hell, is it not?

Instead, Tartareia is quite…normal.

Well, normal for a realm that does not have a sun. The sky is a reddish color, the only light coming from the four moons hanging over every cardinal point. It is not completely dark, but it is also not overly illuminated.

We arrive at the outskirts of a village, and that scenery lends even less credibility to all those hellish legends. There are houses built of timber, with straw roofs and a little area for livestock. People are going on about their daily tasks, tending to the animals and working the field. Yet that is where the difference starts to become more accentuated.

Due to the lack of sunlight, both the animals and the crops are vastly different from any I've ever seen.

The animals have larger eyes to accommodate for nocturnal vision and the plants are of the variety that require minimal light to thrive. That in turn makes the villagers also exhibit some different features that I am sure could be explained evolutionarily in one way or another. The most striking difference is also in the eyes. Not only are they larger, but their irises have a reddish hue.

"Why don't you have reddish eyes, too?" I ask Nykander as we make our way through the village.

"Tartareians are different from the Sons of Tenebreis for the mere reason that our genetic material is different. These people do not live as long as we do, nor do they have abilities. The Sons of Tenebreis still retain their genetics from the Primordial gods. Tartareians are mortals that moved in the realm thousands upon thousands of years ago, and their biology has changed from generation to generation to better adapt to the environment. Due to the increased lifespan of the Sons of Tenebreis, we do not respond to the same environmental pressures," he explains—quite eruditely I might add.

I gaze at him with a dreamy smile.

Tall, dark, handsome, powerful, *and* smart. Thank you, fates! You really turned my ideal man into reality.

"Wait here," he mentions as he comes to a sudden halt.

I do as he says while he goes to one of the merchant stands by the side of the road. He engages the seller in conversation, and not a few moments later, he returns with some local clothes *and* three small leather harnesses with leashes for the dogs.

I stare at him wide-eyed.

"How..."

"There is a species here that is the size of our dogs. It's called a *pyde* and it is normally used by villagers to hunt the rodents that ruin their crops. I merely asked for the smallest harnesses they have. I hope they will fit them, since carrying the house with us will only attract more attention."

"You're right. You think of everything," I murmur, pleased.

We go to a more secluded corner and get the dogs out of the house, getting them accustomed to the harnesses before placing them on. PomPom is used to one, but it seems BonBon isn't, with Ander even less so. But with the promise of some nice treats, they obey and let us put the harnesses around them.

Building the illusion of a dark smog, Nykander shields us from the rest of the world so we can take the time to put on the clothes he'd bought from the merchant. His is a dark tunic that reaches his calves. It cinches at the waist with a thick leather belt. The design is quite medieval, but it would be hard for him to *not* look good in anything. For me, he'd gotten a simple linen dress in a faded cream color. The irony is that mine is much more conservative than his. It has no belt, or even a string to tie it together at the waist to give my body some shape.

Nope. It's just a sack of potatoes that covers every inch of my skin.

Nykander notices my grumpiness as I glare at my new dress, but he doesn't say anything. Not even a *'you look good, baby, regardless of your clothes.'*

No, he just urges me to get going.

I scoff and trail after him as we get back on the road.

Yet it soon becomes clear that women here do *not* wear sacks of potatoes. In fact, their boobs are hanging out of their bodices, their waists accentuated by a tight belt, and their legs showing from slits cut onto the sides of the skirts.

"Nykander, why is my dress the only one like this?"

"The only one like what?" He has the gall to ask, and I detect a smirk pulling at his lips.

"You know exactly what I mean." I scowl at him. "Look at those girls! They're wearing actual dresses, not an oversized men's shirt."

"I do not care what other females wear." He shrugs. "I care what *my* female wears. And your lovely assets are for my eyes only, sweet thing. I will not have any other male ogle you."

"What if I *want* to be ogled?" I fire back—mostly to rile him up.

He suddenly stops. He turns to me, his eyes blazing.

"Then I feel obliged to show everyone *why* they call me the Dark One. And murdering males right and left is not a good way to maintain our cover. So you either dress like this and I behave myself, or you get an *actual* dress and I leave a trail of bodies in my wake. It is your choice," he declares proudly, folding his arms over his chest.

"Nyk!"

He smiles.

"Yes, sweet thing?" He raises his brows.

"You are impossible! How is that even a choice?"

"You wanted an alternative, so I am giving you one. I might even make a small concession. Instead of killing them, I will just gouge their eyes out. Then you can wear whatever you want."

"But, Nyk," I say in frustration. "It's not like I have any *asset* to put on display. And you're by my side. It's not as if they're going to try something when I'm with you."

"Doesn't matter," he replies flippantly. "I am a greedy male, just like you are my greedy little girl." He smirks. "It does not have to be a rational reaction, or even a sensible one. I am relaying to you what will happen if you decide to wear something else. I will never stop you. But just like that, you cannot stop me from killing whoever sees you either."

"What if it's a female? You're mentioning males, but you have no way of knowing if it's a female into other females," I counter, pushing my chin up in satisfaction when I see an annoyed twitch in his cheek.

"Then I can only thank you for pointing that out. I will

rectify my plan and kill *everyone* who lays eyes on even one inch of your skin. How about that?"

"Good Lord! What is wrong with you?" I exclaim in outrage—well, feigned outrage, since his words make my heart beat a thousand times faster.

He chuckles.

"I am a demon, Barbs. A *greedy* demon. Do not expect me to be good, rational, or upstanding—at least when it comes to you."

I stare at him, speechless.

"Now that we have gotten that out of the way, may we continue? Or will you change your dress and I will shed blood?"

He smiles innocently at me.

I shake my head at him and start walking.

"Let's go," I mumble.

"See, you can be the rational one in this relationship," he calls from behind.

I pretend to ignore him, though my cheeks are flaming hot.

"Oh, and by the way"—he leans in to whisper in my ear —"you have plenty of assets. *Wonderful* assets, though I have yet to explore them all. But that is only for me to know, see, touch, or kiss."

"I see you've taken your job for pretty words quite seriously," I murmur shyly.

"I am doing a good job, I trust?"

"Very." I laugh. "And you'll be doing an even greater job if you tell me where we are going now."

"Based on the geography of the area, I would say we are at the outskirts of the fifth sector. There are six such sectors, and while each has its own ruling city, there is only one capital city in Tartareia—Sattoriya. That is where we are headed. My family resides there—or they did before I left. Nonetheless, my brother should be there to scheme his way to the top."

"Oh, okay."

"We will not enter the city for the time being. Velor is nearby, so we will set camp there for your training. And while you cultivate, I will gather intel about the latest state of affairs."

"Sounds good. Let's do this!" I tell him excitedly. "I can't wait to get better at controlling my abilities."

"You will, Barbs. You most definitely will." He smiles.

We walk out of the village until we reach a more populated area, at which point Nykander stops a carriage taxi and asks the driver to take us to Lake Velor.

At first, I expect the journey to be a regular one. But soon it's clear that taxis in this realm are *not* the regular kind. As we exit the highway, the horses drawing the carriage unfurl their wings and start flying.

"Whaaat?" I let out a squeak of surprise.

Nykander chuckles by my side.

"I forgot to mention that the horses are different here."

"No shit," I mumble.

Once my stomach settles from the sudden flight, I pull aside the curtain to gaze outside.

Lights shine from the ground, with every household illuminated from inside out. And as we climb in altitude, they become bright spots of light that create a beautiful pattern. Despite its dark skies and oddly nocturnal way of life, Tartareia is beautiful. It's not something I would have expected of a demonic realm, but I suppose even the most evil things have a thing of beauty.

The dogs, too, are excited about the scenery, crowding the window for a chance to get the wind to blow in their faces.

Ah, the little rascals. A smile pulls at my lips. At least they aren't scared of the ride. PomPom has never been a good flier, but I suppose flying horses provide a different experience.

"Okay, so let me do a quick recap. Dragons exist, but so do winged horses? What's next? Flying pigs? Cats?"

Nykander laughs at my question.

"Dragons are exceedingly rare. The male Cerenios was looking for is the last blue dragon of his line. Aside from him, there are only a handful of other dragons, most of them in Aperion. They are said to be the species with the purest magic out there, so they were previously hunted to extinction."

"Oh," I murmur. "That's sad."

"As for flying pigs, I am sorry to tell you that I have yet to see one. But I will make sure to keep an eye out for you." He winks at me.

"You're making fun of me again," I grumble.

"Me? Never! But you are so cute when your face lights up with wonder. It makes me want to find a flying pig for you just so you can marvel at its existence."

My lashes flutter as I glance at him.

"Nyk!" I exclaim. "Although you are right. I would love to see one. My mother used the expression 'when pigs fly' so frequently that I would give anything to show her an actual flying pig." I chuckle.

"Then I shall endeavor to find one for you," he murmurs, drawing me closer.

I sigh in happiness as I nestle to his side, my eyes closing as exhaustion finally claims me.

I don't know how long I sleep, but some time later, Nyk shakes me awake, telling me we have arrived. The horses descend from their place high up in the sky, the landing just as startling as the take-off.

Nykander pays the driver and we get out.

"Where did you get the money for that?" I frown.

He shakes his head.

"You do not want to know."

Okay, got it. He stole it.

I bristle at his answer, but I don't get to dwell more on it as my attention is captivated by the scenery around us.

"Wow," I whisper.

The lake is much, much bigger than I would have expected. It stretches across the horizon line, almost like a never-ending sea. There is a pebbled line that divides the shore from the water, and a distance away, a small bridge leads to a lighthouse overlooking the great expanse of water.

But there is one other startling detail about the lake.

It's red.

The water is a deep red.

I recall Nykander telling me that there is no blue sea in Tartareia. Perhaps all bodies of water have an unusual color here as a result of the lack of sunlight.

"Uhm, Nyk?" I ask as I turn to look at him. "If there is no blue water here, then what do you drink?"

"Oh, that." He mentions as he scratches the back of his head. "The only potable water in Tartareia is in Sattoriya. The rest of the population drinks ale."

My mouth drops open.

"That's positively…medieval."

"You will find that regardless of what world you go to, power is distributed the same. A few hold all the resources while the rest battle for their existence."

My lips flatten.

"But enough of that. Come, let me show you where we will be staying for the foreseeable future—or at least until you open your fourth gate."

I'm surprised when Nykander leads me in the direction of the lighthouse.

Built on top of large boulders that seemingly erupt from the water, the lighthouse stands over a hundred feet tall. There are a couple of small windows on the first level, while the top one is entirely made out of floor-to-ceiling ones.

We cross the bridge and arrive at the entrance of the lighthouse. Glancing right and left, I see the water wash against the dark gray stone, staining it with red.

"How deep is the water?" I ask, my eyes affixed to the opaque red surface of the lake.

"Deep," Nykander answers.

A shudder goes down my back as I imagine diving in it. Somehow, that red hue gives me the creeps, and I don't know why. It's not as if it's blood. The color is probably just the result of the plankton living on the bottom of the lake, as well as the lack of light.

"Come in." Nyk's voice startles me from my reverie.

I force a smile as I steer the dogs toward the open door.

As we get inside, Nykander uses his powers to light up the torches on the wall. The inside of the lighthouse lights up, and to say I am not impressed with the result would be an understatement.

"Nyk… How are we going to stay here? It looks like no one has inhabited it in centuries. And considering how long your kind lives, I'd wager *thousands* of years."

Thick layers of dust cover the entirety of the first room. There is a staircase that leads to the superior floors, but the wood is old and decrepit. One step, and it creaks loudly, echoing in the entire lighthouse.

"We will make do," he responds.

I scrunch my nose. The dust is already making me feel itchy and unclean. The dogs, too, sneeze, becoming restless in their leashes.

"It's not good for the dogs either. This is too dirty," I complain.

He gives me a pointed look.

"Wait outside for a while," he says, all but shooing me outside the lighthouse and closing the door in my face.

The dogs are trembling with fear as they stare at the lake just a few steps over. I crouch down in front of them to assure them they are safe and that nothing will happen to them—though I seriously doubt it with the state of our supposed new house.

True to his word, Nykander opens the door a few moments later, inviting us back inside.

I blink in shock.

"You… How?"

"Supernatural speed." He winks.

I get closer and note a dark smudge on his cheek. Smiling, I get up on my tiptoes and wipe it off him.

"Mmm, you are the definition of husband material."

"I aim to please," he mentions, bending in a mock bow.

The dust has been completely cleared, and instead of that old and dusty smell, the tower now smells of flowers and chocolate. That is quite an improvement.

We go up the stairs to the first floor where we find a rudimentary kitchen. It has everything we might need—a table, chairs, a stove, and cupboards as well as a small sink.

I nod my approval. The dogs, too, bark theirs.

Nykander smiles.

"There are two more rooms upstairs. One for the dogs, and one for us," he mentions.

Curious, I follow him to the second floor.

The room is indeed small, but it's safe enough for the little ones to not get into trouble. It even has a door that locks so they can't access the stairs and have an accident—they are quite steep for them.

"Oh, I love this. We can get them a few pillows and toys and put them there." I point to a corner. Walking around, I find a sizable closet. "And here we can train Ander to potty. PomPom and BonBon can also go potty here if it's urgent and we're not available to take them down."

I note that Nykander isn't saying anything, so I close the door to the closet and turn around.

My mouth drops open in shock.

Like I suggested, there are now pillows and toys in the corner. I bend to remove the harnesses from the dogs and they dash toward their new space.

"You're really trying to impress all of us now, aren't you?" I ask him.

He hikes a shoulder up.

"I do not know how much time we will have to spend here, so we might as well make the place comfortable."

I go over to his side and kiss his cheek.

"Show me our room, then," I murmur.

He inclines his head.

We leave the dogs behind and close the door so they don't venture out. Going up the stairs, we reach the last level—the one where the walls are entirely made of windows.

The redness of the lake is emphasized by the dim light of the moon shining from up above. There is a beauty to this scenery that takes my breath away, regardless of how dangerous and morbid it is.

"Wow," I whisper. "This view is everything," I say as I go directly to the windows. I trace my fingers over the glass. I barely dare to glance down, though. The fall is steep. One wrong step, and the red abyss will swallow you.

I back away, my smile trembling.

"Barbs," Nyk calls out.

I swivel.

A king-sized bed is in the middle of the room. The mattress, sheets, and pillows are all fresh and new. The smell of clean cotton fills my nostrils and I sigh in satisfaction.

There are a few other items around—a wardrobe, a small table and two chairs. But I barely glance at them as I hurl myself on the bed.

The soft mattress gives way under the weight of my body, bouncing with me.

I release a loud giggle.

"This feels so good, Nyk! Thank you!"

He doesn't join me. He's staring at me from the end of the bed with an odd expression on his face. It's a split second later that he remembers to smile.

"I have filled the wardrobe with clothes too."

Before he can finish his words, I jump up and hurry to the wardrobe.

"They are not fancy since you will use them to train."

"Oh," I murmur when I note the nondescript linen dresses he'd gotten for me. But hey, at least they're pink—sort of. It's a darker shade than I would have chosen for myself, but I appreciate his effort. After all, color is influenced by light, and Tartareia lacks that.

"Thank you. I appreciate it."

He nods.

"There is also a bathroom in the back. It is not very spacious, but it should suffice."

The bathroom has a standing shower, a toilet, and a sink.

"What type of water is this?" I ask as I tentatively reach inside the shower to turn on the water. Surprisingly, though, it's not red. It's a greenish color. I hold my hand under the stream for a few moments, satisfied when it doesn't stain my skin.

"It comes from the mainland. The lighthouse was used by soldiers a long time ago. It was a surveillance point for those who decided to go into the lake to increase their spiritual energy."

"Why did they abandon it? If the lake is such a precious resource, why not continue using it?"

A barely detectable twitch appears above his upper lip.

"Because most people who went inside the lake never came out," he replies in a deadpan voice.

30

"Clear your mind, Barbs," he instructs. "Now picture your shield expanding."

I do as he says, focusing on the energy shimmering around me but also making sure I keep its signature hidden. Easier said than done, though. Within moments, I crash to the ground, sweat dripping down my face as I heave uncontrollably.

"Almost there, sweet thing," Nyk says as he leans down to pat my hair. "You've already done better than anyone I know."

"But I've only reached the second gate," I say in between harsh puffs of air. "It's going to take me forever to get to the fourth."

He smiles.

"You will do it. I know you will."

"I appreciate your confidence in me, but I'm tired," I complain as I slump down. I lie on my back on the grass and stare at the semi-dark sky.

We've been here two weeks now and the lack of light has certainly taken a toll on my body. I laugh less, I smile less, I do everything less except for sleep. When it comes to sleep, I'd just sleep the days away. But with Nykander waking me up every single day to train, it's nearly impossible to get a moment to myself.

He does everything.

He cooks. He cleans. He takes care of the dogs. In return, all I have to do is train.

And I'm so damn tired of it.

"Can I have a break?" I glance up at him, batting my lashes flirtatiously.

He tilts his head to the side and lifts one brow.

"Open your third gate and we will talk."

"But… How?" I cry out in frustration, flailing my limbs around.

"It's all in here, Barbs," he says as he takes a seat on the grass next to me and points at my head. "Clear your mind and let go of all your doubts. Trust yourself and your abilities. Now enough rolling on the grass. I want you to hit those targets with your energy." He points toward a few wooden sticks a distance away.

"What?"

"As I said before. Picture your shield as an unlimited resource that you can draw from. Take a piece of it and aim it at the target."

And with that, he gets up and leaves, going to spend time with the dogs.

I want to spend time with them, but I barely have time to sleep and eat.

Grumbling a few curses under my breath, I get up and position myself in front of the targets.

Closing my eyes, I picture my energy shield in my mind. Pink particles shimmer around me, surrounding me from head to toe.

Initially, it's only a few inches thick. But I do as Nyk instructed and I push against it, willing it to become wider.

The first few tries result in failure—as the hundreds of times before it.

The shape and size of my shield does not budge. It remains steady. And when I feel like I am about to lose control of my cloaking spell, I stop altogether.

I release a deep breath as I rest my hands on top of my knees. I might not channel enough energy to hit the targets, but the mere exercise of summoning my shield while cloaking it is entirely exhausting.

Not one to give up, though, I take a five-minute break before I try again. And again. For hours on end.

Unfortunately, each exercise ends in utter failure.

Tired, sweaty, and barely in control of my own body, I slowly make my way back inside the lighthouse. I haven't seen Nykander in a few hours, so I assume he's inside with the dogs.

The moment I open the door to the lighthouse, a delicious smell of roast meat wafts toward me, making me salivate.

I am on autopilot as my feet lead me to the kitchen on the first floor where Nykander is arranging the dinner table with a variety of dishes. There are bowls filled with soup, roasted meat, and vegetables as well as warm bread.

"Come eat," he says when he sees me stare at the food.

"Damn it, I am ravenous, Nyk," I blurt out as I take a seat. I don't even wait for him as I dig in, eating a mouthful of meat and washing it with soup. I take a little of each, stuffing my mouth as if this is the last meal I'm ever going to have. But with the way my body has been consuming energy recently, I doubt this will be enough.

"Easy, Barbs." Nykander chuckles.

"You spend an entire day training and then eat slowly," I mutter in between bites.

"How did the last round go?"

"The same."

"Do not worry too much. It will happen," he mentions as he pats me gently on the shoulder.

I glare at him, but it only serves to amuse him further.

My portion is not enough, and I finish everything within minutes. Nykander gives me seconds, then thirds.

"You certainly worked an appetite," he jokes when he pours the last of the soup in my bowl.

"I've never eaten so much in my life," I say, my mouth filled with food. I am the least ladylike woman in this moment, and if my mother saw me, she would have a fit. But if I am training like a soldier, then maybe I am allowed a respite from those socially constructed standards.

"I have dessert, too," Nyk says.

"Chocolate?"

He shakes his head.

Taking the dishes from the table, he uses his tentacles to wash them in the sink while he extends his arm toward me.

"Feed, Barbs. You need it."

I gulp down. Not only do I need it, but I *crave* it.

With how grueling the training has been lately, Nykander has fed me his blood daily. He rarely takes more than a few drops from me a day, saying I need all the energy to work.

Although his blood works wonders on my stamina, refreshing both my mind and body, the fact that he hasn't fed directly from my neck in so long has put a damper on our growing intimacy.

We sleep together. We sometimes kiss. But we haven't done more than that. Of course, the moment I hit the pillow, my eyes are closed, so it's hard to muster up the energy for bedroom activities. Still, somehow I'd hoped that when we got here, we'd be able to move things along a bit faster.

Though I had been the one to suggest we take things slow, now I am the one who is impatient.

"You should go shower. I have already fed and walked the dogs. I even got Ander a new toy to chew on when I went into town," he mentions with a smile. "I shall finish cleaning up and I will join you in bed."

With that, he turns his back to me, effectively dismissing me.

I am too tired to pick a fight with him for his lack of attention. Dear Lord, but I'm becoming as needy as Ander, requiring words of affirmation every five seconds to know I am loved.

Speaking of love. Has Nykander ever said the words to me before?

My brows draw together as I try to remember.

I slowly walk up the stairs, wobbling every now and then from the ache in my muscles. When I reach the third floor and get inside the bathroom, I still have not found an answer to that question.

He has mentioned time and time again that he feels something for me, but has he defined that something?

I discard my sweaty clothes and throw them in the laundry bag. Turning on the shower, I step inside. There is a slightly sweet smell that accompanies the jet of hot green water. You'd think I would have gotten used to it by now, but these odd features never fail to startle me.

I scrub my skin clean, after which I apply some of the lotion Nykander had gotten for me.

How the hell can I doubt him or be mad at him when he's so thoughtful?

Half the day he spends with me, training. The other half he goes into nearby towns to buy food, clothes, and any other items I or the dogs might need. Although the main purpose is to gather intel, he has never come home without a small gift—which always warms my heart.

As I get out of the bathroom, sure enough, I spot a little package on the bed.

Chocolate. Or, at least, the Tartarian version, which is more bitter.

My lips curve up in a smile.

"Thank you, Nyk," I whisper, knowing he can hear me.

I eat the chocolate and nestle between the clean sheets.

"I am happy you like today's surprise," he murmurs from the doorway. He's leaning against the wall, dressed in a pair of loose dark pants and a white shirt that emphasizes his striking looks.

The gray of his eyes is different in this lighting, the color more like a silver white.

He steps inside the room, closing the door behind him.

"Come." I pat the empty spot next to me on the bed.

He pulls his shirt over his head, making it vanish before he kicks his pants, remaining only in his boxer briefs.

Sliding under the blanket, he draws me to his chest and holds me close.

"Sleep, sweet thing," he whispers, laying a kiss on my forehead.

"So tired," I mumble, my eyes already closing. "But, Nyk… Do you not want me anymore?" I ask sleepily.

"What?"

"You…" I yawn. "You never try to take things further than a kiss. Is it the lighting in this place? Do I look worse?"

"Barbs," he starts in a stern voice.

My eyes flutter open, worry filling me.

"You are absolutely stunning in any lighting, and in any world. And I want you. Very, very much," he confirms, taking my hand and sliding it over the bulge in his underpants. "But I would never make *any* demands of you when your body is already at its limit. We have an eternity for lovemaking, sweets."

I blush furiously and snatch my hand back.

"You said lovemaking," I mumble dreamily, burrowing closer into him and wrapping my arms around his waist. "That means you love me, no? Because I love you, Nyk. I love you so, so, so much."

There's a pause before he replies.

"Of course I do, sweet thing," he says in a gentle voice.

That is enough to lull me into a sense of comfort and security.

Closing my eyes once more, I let his warmth be the only cover I'll ever need in the cold of the night.

THE PSYCHOLOGICAL STRAIN of the training is getting to me. Failure after failure has shot my confidence down until all I can expect *is* failure.

I take a deep breath as I plop myself on the ground.

Nykander is gone. Again.

He said he went to gather intel from the capital, but when I offered to go with him, he told me to focus on my training.

And I am… But it all seems to be in vain.

Tired, hungry, and annoyed at myself, I decide to take a break and play with the dogs. It's been a while since we've spent time together, and I miss them terribly.

Going inside the lighthouse, I place the harnesses on their backs and take them out for a run. The moment they see me, they jump up and down in excitement and rush to lick every inch of me.

"I missed you too, babies," I murmur lovingly. "I promise I will make up for all the lost time."

We walk alongside the shore of the lake. The sky is a reddish gray color, but it's not yet entirely dark. The two moons provide plenty of light so we can take a longer walk before returning to the lighthouse.

The dogs are excited, and that means my happiness level has immediately gone up.

Yet I can't deny that I feel weary and tired. While I understand Nykander's concerns, I can't help but feel he has been pushing me too much. I know he needs me to open my fourth gate soon, but his training has been far too grueling considering I've never before done any of this. It just makes me wonder what the hurry is.

Before, he was ready to take on Baine by himself—he certainly did not need my assistance. Aside from helping him get to Tartareia, my role was supposed to be minimal. Now, though, he needs me to perfect my abilities in such a short period of time when he's had thousands of years to do so.

He's just worried about you, my inner voice chides.

A spark of warmth erupts in my chest. He is, isn't he? Despite having insane standards when it comes to my training, he's been supportive throughout the entire process. It's just that I wish he were a little more…affectionate?

Ugh! Why am I out here overthinking things when I'm supposed to be enjoying some time with the dogs?

Getting to my knees, I remove the leash from their harnesses and let them play around. And when they jump on me, nibbling on my hands, I can't do anything to stop them.

"You cuties. I've missed you so much. Come give me some love!" I coo.

And oh but they do. They cuddle with me and lick my face and bite my clothes—all part of their love language. PomPom and BonBon are the first ones to retreat, going to play by themselves a distance over and leaving me alone with little Ander.

"You've grown so much, baby," I murmur as I thread my fingers through his thick baby coat. It's so soft and black, I want to bury my face in it and kiss him all over his little body.

He grabs the hem of my shirt with his little teeth and pulls on it, mistaking it for his toy.

I giggle at his lousy attempts, but I don't stop him.

"You're a playful little man, aren't you? Oh, you cutie pie!"

He releases a soft whine, jumping up and down before finding another part of me to bite on.

I shake my head in amusement.

Nykander needs to buy them more toys.

But as I play with Ander, a foreign sound echoes in my ears. I place him down and urge him to go to his parents while I get up and go to investigate the source of the sound.

The sound of thudding steps becomes louder and louder in my ears. I frown.

Who can it be? Nykander mentioned no one comes by this place any longer.

As the sound intensifies, so does my fear.

"Babies, come here!" I call out, grabbing the three of them and running back to the lighthouse with them.

I push the door open and dash to their room, placing them inside. After I make sure they have food and water, I lock the door and go up to the third floor to survey the area.

My eyes widen in shock as I spot a group of men coming in the direction of the lighthouse.

By my count, there are about ten or twelve.

But what would they be looking for here?

I continue to watch them with trepidation, hoping they'll change their direction at the last moment. But as the seconds trickle by, it's clear they're coming directly for the lighthouse.

Did I make a mistake? Did I accidentally reveal my energy signature while I was practicing?

My body tenses as I mentally go over everything I did today. I trained hard, it's true. But not harder than in the past.

It doesn't make sense.

The strange men continue to get closer.

Without Nykander here, I don't know how I'm going to manage, so the only recourse I have is to call him back. But in a world where there are no mobile phones, there is only one way I can reach him.

I rush down the stairs to the kitchen in search of a knife. Pressing the tip of the blade on the surface of my forearm, I trace the word *help*. I wince at the pain, grinding my teeth to push through it. The word takes shape on my skin, but in mere seconds, my skin starts healing and it's gone.

Signal for help sent, I get back to monitoring the situation. Moving a chair to the kitchen window, I climb on it and watch what's happening outside while I wait with bated breath for Nykander to return.

"Please hurry," I whisper, even though I know he cannot hear me.

My eyes widen, though, as I realize that the people outside *could* hear me. I don't know what their abilities are. If they are strong individually, then in a group of almost a dozen people they will be no match for me.

Nyk had mentioned there are people in Tartareia without abilities, but they are unlikely to be dressed in military uniforms or move in a rehearsed formation as those people are.

My pulse quickens as the minutes go by and Nykander doesn't come.

Another glance outside reveals the men almost at the entrance of the lighthouse.

Damn it!

I cannot allow them to come inside. I don't know their intentions and I'm not about to let them hurt the dogs. The only way to keep them safe is to get the men away from here.

I squeeze my eyes shut.

I am *not* ready for this. Good Lord, I have no idea what I'm supposed to do.

Before, I'd had Nykander by my side and that had given me confidence. I could channel my energy *because* he was there, having my back.

But now?

Where are you, Nyk? Why are you not here?

Yet waiting more time for him means potentially placing the dogs in danger, and I can't afford that.

I take a few steadying breaths, calming my racing heart and clearing my mind.

I can do this. To protect my babies, I can do it.

After giving myself a much-needed pep talk, I straighten my back and head downstairs.

I can hear them.

They're right outside, talking amongst themselves—laughing.

They're making bawdy jokes about their plans tonight at a brothel and how many hours with a prostitute this job will buy them.

Gross.

But that reveals something about them. They are doing a job, which means they were sent here by *someone*.

I can work with that.

Pulling the door open, I stare them right in the eye.

"What brings you here?" I ask in a fake sweet voice.

But as I regard the group of men, I realize that my initial estimates were way off. It's not ten or twelve, but close to twenty. Where the hell had the rest come from?

I do my best to keep my poker face so they don't see how intimidated I am. But a woman alone with a group of men? When is that not absolutely terrifying?

"Who are you and what are you doing here?" One of the men steps forward, narrowing his eyes at me.

I note the weapons peeking through their clothes.

"What?" I smile.

"The lighthouse is property of the House of Jubal of Sattoriya. You are trespassing."

"Oh, really? I am so sorry. I did not know," I say in a sweet voice. "I thought it was an abandoned place. But no worries, I will gather my things and leave."

With another smile, I take a step back, closing the door.

A booted foot blocks it.

"You must identify yourself. Trespassing on the property of the House of Jubal is a crime."

"Oh, maybe you can overlook it this one time?" I bat my lashes at them. "You have no idea what I've been through." I let out a quiet sob. "I was just trying to get to my grandmother who's severely sick and—"

"We have received a report that you have run away from your husband, which is against the law," the same man says, interrupting me. "We are here to retrieve you so you can be judged accordingly."

My eyes flare in shock. I gawk at them, slowly digesting these outrageous accusations.

What?

They received a report? About me?

What the hell? And the report said I ran away from my husband? This must be a mistake. Maybe there was another woman who fled from her husband in the area, and now they decided to pin this on me. Otherwise, nothing makes sense.

"You are under arrest and will stand trial at the House of Jubal for trespassing, after which you will be moved to the Public House of Sattoriya for abandonment of the marital home," he continues in a robotic tone. "You are required to tell us your name and your affiliation so we can identify your husband. He will need to be present for the trial."

"What are you talking about?" I frown.

He stares at me blankly.

Before I know what's happening, he pushes the door open and instructs two men to hold me.

"W-what are you doing?" I stammer when I note him removing a device from his pouch. It resembles a pair of cuffs, but there is something odd about them. They are made from a golden material, but there is an unusual green glow to them. As it nears me, the glow intensifies, and specks of foreign energy float around the metal.

It must be a magical device of sorts. And if they put that on me, I don't know what might happen.

Panic swells in my breast and I start flailing my arms and legs.

I struggle to get the men off me, but they are much stronger and within seconds, they subdue me, pushing me against the wall and pulling my hands behind my back.

A scorching heat envelops my body as the cuffs make contact with my skin.

31

"Search the house," the man commands.

No, no, no! Who knows what they will do if they find the dogs. Oh, Lord! They can't get their hands on my babies!

Right as the cuffs are about to click around my wrists, I let out a loud scream that brings my energy to the surface.

The blast from my scream sends the entrance door and everyone in my vicinity flying away from me.

I slowly turn around.

The men are groaning in pain on the ground. But before I can get my bearings together, they get up and channel their own energies, preparing to strike.

I gulp down.

Where the hell are you, Nyk?

Letting my energy surface, I watch as the pink glow envelops me, creating a powerful shield. And as the first men send blows my way, I focus on deflecting them. Their energies are dark, similar to Nykander's, but there is another layer of foulness that reminds me of Baine's putrid influence over Damien.

I rush out of the lighthouse, worried any blow might harm

the structure and in turn hurt the dogs. The men, seeing me flee, follow me. I run toward the shore, my pulse pounding in my temples as I try to remember what I learned in the last few weeks. If Nykander isn't here to help, then the only thing I can do is help myself.

The men assemble in a triangular formation, uniting their powers into one huge cloud of energy. Like a cannonball, they aim it toward me and fire. A ball of dark, dangerous energy heads my way, and I turn just in time to reinforce my shields to deflect it.

Yet this time it's too powerful.

I'm thrown back, spinning in the air before I tumble to the ground.

My shield disintegrates.

Bones crack and snap, the sounds drowning among the battle cries of the soldiers rushing toward me. My tibia breaks through the surface of my skin, the bone broken in half. One part is sticking out, shattered from the impact.

My breathing turns harsh as a ringing echoes in my ear.

The soldiers eat the distance in seconds.

Stumbling to my feet, I bring my fist against my lower leg, pushing the bone inside. The pain is astounding. But the fear of what might happen to me if they catch me is stronger.

Once the soldiers are close enough, they resume their formation. It strikes me that this is the only way they can channel enough power as independently their blows had been mild. That means the key to getting out of this situation alive is to eliminate them one by one in order to ruin their formation.

While they merge their energies together, I close my eyes, willing my shield to take shape—but this time stronger, more durable.

The pink mist surrounds me, the shield thicker than before. From a shimmery shadow, it turns more opaque as if I were enveloped by a border. To bolster it, I imagine the layer expanding, becoming broader. Slowly, it bleeds into the space around me.

What had Nyk said? The moment it becomes thick enough, I should pull from it and mold it to my will. The goal is to create a weapon of pure energy as he'd done with his sword.

The darkness around the soldiers increases, becoming more opaque too. The triangle becomes filled with a black mass that seemingly morphs and moves as if it has a life of its own. Out of that dark pit, a creature of a sorts takes shape.

It has a head, arms, and legs. But its interior is entirely black. The same putrid stench comes from it, filling my nostrils and threatening to make me sick.

The dark creature stands tall above the triangle until it's fully formed. Stepping outside of the formation, it presses its heavy feet on the ground, which results in a slight quake—enough for the lake to become unsettled and water to spill over the pebbled shore.

The soldiers move in tandem to avoid contact with the water. I do as well, knowing one touch might prove fatal at this time. But the creature doesn't. It remains unmoving even as drops of that cursed water wash over its dark surface.

Despite having no eyes, it follows my movements with its head, orientating itself toward me and releasing a loud roar.

Damn it!

"Where are you, Nyk?" I ask for the thousand time.

The commotion makes the dogs agitated, and I can hear their little terrified barks as they scratch at the locked door.

My eyes flare in panic. Good Lord, they must be in such distress to behave like this that it breaks my heart.

I need to end this quickly.

Extending my arms to my side, I focus on my energy, morphing it into two boomerangs.

Another loud noise breaks my concentration as the creature dashes toward me.

It's over eight feet tall, and every time it steps onto the ground, a quake ensues. His steps are powerful and merciless.

Seeing as how the creature is following me, I run farther away from the lighthouse, using one boomerang to probe at its dark surface. But my boomerang doesn't even make contact with the creature. As it flies toward it, it seemingly melts into its dark body. At the same time, a sickening sensation overtakes me. The creature swallows my energy. Despite not hurting me physically, a stain forms in my soul—similar to what had happened when I'd confronted Baine's demon.

I bite my lip in uncertainty. If I can't strike the creature, then what can I do?

My eyes move across the field, and I spot the soldiers' formation. They are still chanting together. Above the triangle, the dark surface from which the creature had been born is continuously shifting and morphing. There are waves on its surface as they channel more energy and infuse it into the creature.

If I can't cause any damage to the creature, then maybe hitting the formation might help.

As I run from the creature, I take a deep breath, willing my powers to obey me for once. Using the boomerang I have left, I throw it toward the creature. But instead of willing my weapon to hit it, I command it to circle him.

The creature might be huge, but it's quite slow.

As the boomerang flies around its frame, it struggles to catch it in his humongous hands. I maintain my focus, willing the boomerang to do a few spins around the creature and distract it long enough so I can plan my attack on the soldiers.

Just as the creature reaches for the boomerang again, seemingly capturing it in its dark fist, my weapon dips low, barely escaping the creature's grasp. My eyes are on the boomerang as I use my hands to dictate its next movements. Flying low around the creature, I command it to slip between its legs and head for the soldiers at maximum speed.

By the time the creature tries to grab the boomerang again, it's already on its way to the formation.

This is it.

I inhale deeply, keeping my focus sharp.

The boomerang flies with increased speed, aiming straight for the head of the triangular formation.

The soldiers recognize the incoming attack, but as the creature turns around to protect them, it's too late. The boomerang hits the first man, cutting through his flesh until his torso becomes separated from his lower body.

"Yes," I whisper. "Go on."

It doesn't stop at the first man. It flies farther within the formation, injuring a few more. Unfortunately, the momentum dies, and before the creature can swallow my energy up, I absorb it back into my shield.

The formation wobbles as the soldiers hurry to resume a triangular shape without the man who died. The injured ones are still alive, the wounds minor. Yet there is one sign that tells me to continue.

As soon as the formation shrinks, the creature does too. It becomes smaller by almost a head.

My eyes widen, and hope blossoms in my chest.

It will be impossible to deal with the creature directly, so I will have to attack the soldiers instead. But now that they've seen my strategy, they command their creature to stick by their side to protect them. Instead of taking the offensive, now the creature is on the defensive. And with it eating up my energy every time it swallows it up, I can't afford to waste my attacks.

The chants of the formation change, and the creature places its hands together, weaving some of its darkness into a ball of energy that it shoots my way. Different from the first time, though, this one chases me around, hitting my shield time and time again until cracks appear over the surface.

What...

My eyes widen in shock, and one second of inattention is

enough to give the creature an advantage. I'm flung backward, and as I land on the ground, my shield shatters around me. Shards of pinkish colored glass are strewn all around me, a physical manifestation of my weakness.

Bringing my hand to my nose, I wipe away drops of blood that drip down my mouth and chin.

I'm breathing hard.

My body hurts, both from the impact and from the energy I used up.

Yet I can't give up.

The whines of the dogs are loud in my ears. PomPom's sharp cry followed by BonBon's howl and Ander's whimpers of uncertainty cause a rift inside my soul.

They won't hurt my babies. Even if it's the last thing I will do, I will make sure my babies are safe.

Sniffling and wiping the blood from my face, I get to my feet. Feet apart, I assume the posture Nykander taught me. Closing my eyes, I visualize my shield taking shape again. I channel my energy to the surface, but this time ten times stronger.

More blood pours from my nose as I force the power out of me. My ears are ringing, and the veins in my temples throb from the effort. But I don't let the overwhelming sensation of pain stop me.

"You will not win," I mutter. First, it's a whisper. But as my energy spills forth from deep within me, my words become a loud cry—a weapon that spears right through the soldiers' formation.

They hold steady, ordering the creature to move in front of them and absorb the blow. But I take advantage of the creature's lack of speed to run around in circles, releasing shout after shout until my throat is raw from screaming. Each vocalization is a blow.

My voice is my weapon, and as I slowly learn how to use

it, I dig deep within my soul, ransacking all those conflicting emotions and bringing them to the surface to fuel my rage.

The creature runs with me, trying to keep up. But even at my normal pace, I'm faster than it.

The wave of energy my voice produces causes ripples in the formation. And as the formation wobbles, so does the creature, losing some of its balance. I take advantage of that to channel my energy into boomerangs again.

I destabilize them with my screams, and before they can gather their bearings, I unleash my boomerangs.

It's hard to control both weapons at the same time.

My voice is easier since it comes naturally. But the boomerangs require precision and aim.

My vision becomes a tunnel, and the target is the light at the end.

The boomerangs circle around the creature while I rattle the formation some more. While the creature chases after one of the boomerangs, the other heads straight for the bottom of the triangular formation where most of the soldiers are gathered together. As it reaches close to them, I pull all my remaining energy and imbue it into that weapon. The boomerang grows in size exponentially, and by the time it hits the target, it's the size of the entire line-up of soldiers, cutting them all in one go. As it moves farther into the triangle, it loses some of the momentum, but it still manages to kill another row.

My knees buckle and I collapse to the floor.

There are around six soldiers left alive, out of which most are already injured.

The dark veil covering their foundation dissipates, and with it, so does the creature, melting seemingly into the ground.

I breathe harshly. My throat aches, and I can't even swallow the excess saliva coating my mouth.

More blood flows from my nose and ears. My eyes, too,

are bleeding tears of blood. Every orifice in my body is suddenly assaulted by uncontrollable hemorrhage. My energy flickers in and out around me, close to disappearing.

The remaining soldiers assess the damage with horror in their eyes. But soon, that horror turns to anger and they turn their attention toward me. Unsheathing their swords, they rush toward me with a cry of war.

I startle back, wobbling to my feet. My legs tremble, and I'm barely able to move from the weakness that settles in my bones.

I'm too slow for them, and before I know it, they're in front of me, waving their swords in blinding motions until each blade cuts me in a different spot.

More blood gushes from my flesh, the cuts so deep, they aren't even healing anymore.

And as one sword penetrates my midriff, I choke on the blood rushing up my throat.

I cough uncontrollably, all the while flailing my arms and legs in an attempt to move away from them.

Dizziness overtakes me.

"Nyk," I whisper. "Where are you?"

My voice is barely audible from the damage to my throat. Pain unlike any I've ever felt sears itself in my soul, as well as the anguish at being abandoned like this.

He was supposed to be by my side. He was supposed to protect me. So where is he? Where is he when my flesh is being torn from me? When blow after blow cuts me so deep, I cannot verbalize the pain any longer.

My attempts to invoke my shield are useless. It materializes for a few seconds before it disappears. The pain is too great for me to focus on anything other than the puncture wounds.

I crumble to the ground, unable to move, or fight, or even speak.

As they see me down and defeated, they don't stop. At once, the six of them raise their swords high and aim them for my chest. The sharp tips sink in my skin, eliciting a muted groan of pain. My mouth is wide open, my mind screaming, yet only silence greets me.

The soldiers laugh at my pain, kicking me with their feet and spitting on me in derision. I turn my head to the side, closing my eyes so I don't see their mocking expressions or the promise of more pain reflected in their gazes.

Yet throughout this entire ordeal, there is only one pervasive thought.

Nyk… Where are you?

I refuse to believe he would abandon me like this in my time of need. I refuse to believe he wouldn't come once my wounds mirrored on his body. And if he's not here, then there is only one explanation.

He's hurt too.

He's somewhere out there, hurting as much as I am—perhaps more.

I'm sorry, Nyk…

My lashes are heavy with a mix of salty tears and thick blood, clogging my sight.

Pain is everywhere.

My awareness dims by the second, but it's not before I hear more laughter, accompanied by a, *'we have to make her pay for killing our brothers.'* But if that had been all, I would have been fine. Yet right as they remove their swords out of my body, the suggestions change. No longer is the punishment for killing their brother's death. No, it is something far worse.

I blink against the dried blood holding my lids together. They barely creep open, my lashes ripping with the effort. My sight is hazy, but I can make out the circle they've made around me. They snicker and kick at me. But not before long, the taunts turn from violent to sexual. One of the men reaches for the fastening of his trousers, pulling his dick out.

Terror grips me from deep within, but I am too weak to move—too weak to even vocalize a protest.

Warm, foul liquid sprays over me as he relieves himself on my battered body.

The jokes continue, calling me a whore who cheated her husband of his property. And there is only one lesson for one such as me.

The others follow the man's lead, opening their trousers and peeing on me.

It takes everything in me to move my head to the side so they don't aim at my face.

If it had ended with this humiliation, I could have lived with myself. But as they kneel next to me, pulling at my pants, I know that what awaits me is a fate worse than death.

Nyk… Where are you when I need you, Nyk?

A lone tear rolls down my cheek before I close my eyes. If this is going to happen, then at least I want no memory of it— of their dirty touches.

A wild cry permeates the air, and before the men can touch me, they're thrown off me. They land a distance away on the shore, and right as they try to get up and fight, they are turned into dust.

Nyk…

He's here.

My lips tremble in a failed attempt at a smile.

I don't think I've ever been happier in my life.

He crouches next to me, his features as ravaged by pain as mine. He lifts a hand to my face, caressing me lightly.

"Drink," he whispers, bringing his wrist to my mouth and urging me to bite him.

I can barely open my mouth wide enough to grasp at his skin. My gums tingle, and my fangs slowly extend. The process in itself is arduous as I can hardly control my body. My fangs graze his skin and a few drops of blood hit my tongue.

That is enough to help expedite my healing and allow me to bite into his flesh more thoroughly.

His blood flows into my mouth, and as I gain more strength, I pull his hand closer, wrapping my lips around his wrist and drinking greedily.

He stares at me with an odd look in his eyes. There's anguish but also something else.

"Where...were...you?" I ask once my throat has healed enough that I can speak. "I waited...for you...Nyk. I waited..."

"I am here now, Barbs," he murmurs.

"Why... Why did you not come to me?" I swallow down against the wave of pain that hits me—yet this time it's not physical. As my body starts to mend, the pain that remains behind is entirely on the inside. "I called...for you," I croak.

"I came as soon as I could, Barbs." His lips flatten.

"I called for you," I repeat, breaking down in sobs as I curl into a fetal position.

He stares at me, his Adam's apple bobbing up and down.

"I was at the Jubal palace and they have runes around the place that inhibit powers. I am so sorry, Barbs," he explains, his voice tinged with regret.

I avert my gaze, shutting my eyes as a shudder goes down my back.

"If you hadn't come..." I whisper. "If you'd been a few minutes late, they would have..." My voice breaks as I imagine what could have happened. "And I was powerless to stop them. They would have raped me and I couldn't even move to defend myself," I cry out.

"Barbs," he murmurs my name in a soft voice. "I am so sorry, sweet thing. I am so fucking sorry."

"You weren't here, Nyk," I continue. "You promised me... You promised you would protect me and..." I choke on my sobs as I bring my hands to shield my face.

I feel dirty, tired, and utterly heartbroken for an ineffable reason.

He couldn't come. I understand that. But it doesn't make

the heartache any less. It doesn't take away from my pain, my terror, and my now-dying expectations of him.

"I waited for you…" I whisper like a broken record.

Guilt flashes across his face and he leans in to lay a kiss on my forehead.

"I will make it up to you, I swear," he says.

"I don't think you can…" I slowly look up, regarding him with the broken shards of my innocence.

32

He doesn't speak as he gathers me in his arms and treks across the grassland to the lighthouse. He walks slowly, taking one stair at a time until he reaches the third floor of the lighthouse.

"The dogs…" I croak.

"They are fine. *You*, are not," he states in a tight voice.

I don't have the energy to argue, so I let him take me to our room.

He pushes the door open, but instead of placing me on the bed, he takes me to the bathroom, closing the door behind us. He deposits me on the floor of the shower stall. Discarding his clothes until he remains in his underpants, he steps inside the stall with me and crouches down in front of me.

"Barbs," he murmurs my name softly.

I bring my knees to my chest, trembling from the residual adrenaline. My physical wounds have healed. The ones that cut me deep in my soul, however, are bleeding invisible blood.

"May I undress you?"

I slowly glance up, meeting his gaze.

I wonder what he sees. Blood stains my exposed skin. My clothes are in tatters, torn and slashed in the same pattern as my now healed injuries. My face is streaked with blood and tears and an indescribable feeling of loss. I am quite the sight, am I not?

I give him a tentative nod.

He reaches for the hem of my shirt, gently pulling it up. I lift my hands to aid him, and he throws it on the bathroom floor.

A shiver goes down my back as he takes in the streaks of blood on my chest. I'm not wearing a bra, and this is the first time he's ever seen me naked.

My cheeks heat up as I cross my arm over my chest to shield my breasts.

His hands move to the band of my pants, his gaze meeting mine as he waits for my approval.

I lift my butt, wiggling from side to side to allow him to slide my pants and my panties down my legs.

He throws them outside the stall, too.

Now, I am completely bare before him.

I hug my knees and look away.

"Barbi," he calls softly. "You are safe with me, sweet thing. I will not hurt you. Do you understand that?"

He tips my chin up, forcing me to meet his gaze.

"Do you understand?"

I nod.

"Good. I will clean you up now, sweetie. May I touch you?"

Another nod.

He takes the shower head and tests the temperature of the water. Satisfied when it's not too hot nor too cold, he glides the jet over my body. The green water mixes with the red of my blood, and I stare down at the dark yellow water that accumulates around my body.

"They…" I swallow. "They peed on me."

The shower head drops from his hand to the ground. He stares at me, his eyes swirling a dark gray. His nostrils flare as he inhales and exhales, all the while never taking his eyes off me.

"Come here," he says as he pulls me into his arms.

He holds me close, skin to skin, his fingers gliding down my back in a soothing gesture.

"I am so incredibly sorry, sweet thing," he whispers. "You cannot imagine how sorry I am."

I flatten my lips, holding in a sob as I tighten my arms around him.

"Let me wash you," he murmurs. "Let me wipe everything away."

HE TURNS ME AROUND, bringing the shower over my head and wetting my hair. His touch is soft and gentle as he washes the dirt away. He massages my scalp with slow, deliberate movements, and I let out a sigh of relief as I lean into him.

"You are doing great, sweetie," he murmurs approvingly in my ear. My eyes close as I let him take over.

He rinses my hair thoroughly before he lathers soap onto his palms and brings them to my body. He works the soap into my skin, cleansing every bit of those men's touch away.

Slowly, my fear dissipates until I feel comfortable letting go. My body relaxes, slumping against him as I allow him to touch every inch of my skin.

Despite the intimate way in which he is touching me, there is no discomfort. He does his best to put me at ease, keeping his touches clinical. He's seeing me fully naked for the first time, but I find no disconcerting lust in his eyes, only worry and affection. He handles me like a prized possession, and my heart silently weeps, thankful for him but still shaken by his absence.

Yet despite my disappointment, I want to understand why he couldn't come. I want to know what happened to him and why he wasn't there when I needed him—why he didn't answer my calls.

The soap foams all over my body, the yellow water slowly becoming green again as the blood floats away. He rinses my body gently before he wraps me in his arms and takes me out of the shower. Grabbing a towel, he wraps it around me, drying me off before swathing me in it so I am warm and comfortable. Only then does he do the same to his own body.

Wrapped tightly in the towel, he carries me to the bed. He pulls the covers and places me gently on the clean sheets.

"Are you thirsty? Hungry?" he asks as he watches me with worry in his gaze.

"Water, please," I whisper.

He nods. In a matter of seconds, he's back with a jug of water. He takes a seat on the bed next to me and brings the jug to my lips, helping me drink. I gulp down greedily, my thirst seemingly uncontrollable.

I am hungry, too. But I don't think I can eat just yet. Not when the images from before continue to play in my head, threatening to make me sick.

"What else do you need? Say the word and I'll give it to you."

I purse my lips, slowly shaking my head.

"Please, Barbs. You are breaking my heart, sweetie. Tell me what I can do to help."

I don't know what kind of answer he wants, but it is not one I can provide.

Placing the empty jug by the bed, he shuffles closer to me. His palm curves along my cheek, his thumb caressing my skin softly.

"Look at me, Barbs. Look at me, baby," he whispers in an anguished voice.

I bite my lip as I gaze up.

His features are tight and wrought with pain. But how can I ease his pain when mine is ready to spill over?

He leans in, pressing his forehead to mine and breathing me in deeply.

"I am sorry," he apologizes again. "I am so, so sorry."

His lips brush against my nose and cheeks before he aims for my mouth. Something in me rebels and I turn around, avoiding the contact.

He freezes.

I take a deep breath and push him away.

"I would like to go to sleep," I whisper.

He stares at me numbly before slowly nodding.

I lie down and pull the covers over my body.

Nyk stands up, still watching me with befuddlement. When I don't give him attention, he goes around the bed and slides in, sticking to his side.

Silence descends between us.

There's nothing more I wish than to have him hug me and tell me that everything will be all right—that it will all be okay. But it's not. And I don't know how to make sense of this.

Moments on end pass. My eyes are closed as I seek that elusive sleep. It beckons me, only to shut the door in my face when my mind replays the horrific images from before.

Tears cling to my lashes and I desperately blink them away, not wanting Nykander to see or hear my sobs.

"You are shutting me out, Barbs, and I do not like it," he says in a gruff voice.

A frisson goes down my back at the emotion echoing in those words.

"Tell me," I speak softly. "Tell me everything, Nyk. Why did you not come when I called?"

He takes a deep breath. The seconds in which he does not speak are seconds in which the gulf between us widens. A chasm opens in my heart as I wait with bated breath for him to justify himself and his actions.

I want—*need*—him to give me a reason. Otherwise, I will go crazy with all these maddening thoughts and suppositions.

"I did not mean to be away for so long," he starts, his tone weary. "I found a way inside the Jubal palace. That palace is one of the most guarded places in Tartareia and I could not miss the chance."

"The soldiers mentioned the House of Jubal too; that this is their territory and I was trespassing."

"That is correct. The lighthouse *is* under their jurisdiction. The House of Jubal owns the entire land in northern Sattoriya and vast parts of the realm. Together with three other houses, they are the direct descendants of the Seven and the current ruling power of the Tartareia," he explains.

"But why would you go there? You said you were investigating your family and—"

"The House of Jubal *is* my family," he cuts me off.

I frown. Why am I only hearing about this now?

"But that... That makes you... Tartareian royalty?" I swallow.

He grunts.

"I do not have a title since I am the second born. My brother currently holds the title of Duke of v'Kyro. The House of Jubal has several branches, and a few of them have royal titles. In Tartareia, the most important position you could have is a royal title, which is why people have been fighting for them from the creation of the Sons of Tenebreis."

"Oh," I murmur.

Why am I only hearing about this now?

"The Jubal palace is not a residence," he continues. "It is an official building from wherein the House of Jubal conducts its affairs. It is the place where all the extended branches of the house come together to discuss matters of policy and hegemony. Because of that, it is close to impossible to get near it, which is what I have been trying to achieve for the past weeks. I found a way in by disguising myself as a merchant, but I could not stay long. The palace not only has runes in place that inhibit the use of powers, but it also has top-notch surveillance. The moment I stepped inside the palace, Barbs…"

He takes a deep breath. "I had no control over my abilities. I couldn't feel your call. I couldn't even feel your injuries. But as soon as I realized you were in danger, I rushed to your side. Please believe me."

I digest his words, hugging the pillow to my chest.

It's not his fault, is it? He did not know—he couldn't have known. But though the logical side of me understands this information, there is another part of me, a primal one, that continues to be wrecked by a deep disappointment.

"Did you find anything?" I eventually ask.

"I did." He nods. "The House of Jubal is hosting a ball next week at the palace. For my sister's engagement," he adds in a tight voice.

"Oh, Nyk…"

"It is her second one, it seems. Her first husband died under mysterious circumstances a few thousand years ago and she has just come out of her mourning period. It appears my brother did not waste any time in finding her another husband," he adds angrily.

"What do you plan on doing?" I turn around to regard him, sliding closer and reveling in the heat emanating from his body.

"I will go to the ball," he states staunchly. "It is a masquerade-themed ball, so I should be able to get around undetected. The only issue is that because it is an official affair, the runes on that day will be more powerful than ever to prevent any unwanted incidents."

"Unwanted incidents?" I frown.

A wry smile tips at his lips.

"This is Tartareia, Barbs. The land of the wicked. Just because we are family does not mean we do not kill each other. In the name of power, everyone betrays everyone. It is why the palace is considered neutral ground for such events."

"I see." I nod. "I will come with you," I declare.

"You do not have to come." He shakes his head. "After what happened today…"

"After what happened today more than ever. I will not stay behind anymore, Nyk. Just thinking about calling out to you and waiting for you with no response fills me with dread. Where you go, I go," I tell him confidently.

He stares at me. A slow smile appears on his face.

"Where I go, you go. I like the sound of that."

"If no one is allowed to use their powers, then I will be far safer there," I continue to make my case. "And maybe I can be of some help too."

He nods pensively.

"I might need a distraction while I go in search of my brother."

"Do you plan on killing him there? With no powers?"

"Tempting, but no." He chuckles. "I would never take the easy way out. When I kill him, I want everyone to see I did it on my own. No tricks. I merely want to gather some information. It has been seven thousand years. The brother I know is bound to have changed somewhat."

"I see." I nod. "I will help you as much as I can. They don't know who I am anyway."

"How are you so sweet?" he murmurs as he reaches for me. "I failed you and you still offer to help me." He smiles. "You have a beautiful soul, Barbs. Far more beautiful than I deserve."

He cups my cheek in his big hand, and I nestle closer, closing my eyes and breathing him in.

"I cannot help it," I whisper, tears trickling down my cheeks. "You are my weakness, Nyk. I don't know what that says about me, but I could forgive you anything."

"Anything?" he asks, raising his brow.

"Anything."

He studies me for a moment, an odd expression

descending upon his features. Leaning in, he presses his lips to my cheeks, catching those errant tears with his tongue. His mouth seeks my own, and this time, I give in to the kiss, allowing him to pull me to his chest. His tongue delves deep into my mouth, meeting mine and beginning a mating dance as old as time.

I cling to him, digging my nails into his shoulder.

"Let me erase everything," he whispers. "Let me replace the bad memories with good ones."

I don't know what he's asking exactly, but I find myself nodding.

He trails his lips down my chin, sucking my skin in his mouth. His fangs graze the sensitive skin of my neck in his exploration, but he doesn't bite me. He draws only a few drops of blood, and he licks them languidly off my skin.

In one smooth move, he splays me on my back, kicking the covers aside and looming over me. With one hand, he unknots my towel, leaving me bare to his sight.

The wind brushes against my naked skin, and a shiver goes down my back.

"Let me see you," he murmurs.

I look uncertainly in his eyes. They're the darkest black, signaling his lust—his need for me.

My pulse quickens. My breathing hitches in anticipation of his next move.

He trails his gaze all over my body, smiling appreciatively.

"You are so beautiful. So perfect for me," he says as he leans in to lay a kiss on my mark.

A scorching heat envelops me, and I tremble at the feel of his lips atop my chest.

"*My* beautiful girl," he continues. Slowly, he glides his lips over my breasts, opening his mouth and dragging one nipple between his teeth.

My back arches and a gasp of surprise escapes me.

"Nyk…"

He swirls his tongue around my nipple, and the sensation shoots straight to my core. I squirm against him as shivers of awareness spread through me.

"That's my girl. You feel it, don't you? The way your body craves mine," he whispers as he moves to my other breast. He lavishes the same attention on it, kissing, sucking, nibbling.

I'm a mess of sensations as I cradle his head to my chest, willing him to never stop.

"My greedy girl." He chuckles, blowing hot air over my nipples.

My cheeks turn red at his words, but I can't stop the grin that pulls at my lips.

He moves lower. He slides his tongue down the valley of my breasts, kissing my stomach before he sucks my skin in his mouth, leaving red marks behind. Alas, they quickly fade as they heal, but that only incentivizes him to mark me further.

There is not one inch of skin that remains untouched by his lips, unmarked by his possessive bite.

But then he's there.

His mouth hovers over my sex, his hot breath caressing my drenched folds.

A wave of embarrassment crashes over me and I attempt to lock my legs together.

He chuckles and, bringing his finger down my stomach, he follows the slope of my mound until he reaches that place between my thighs.

At first, he only dips one finger between my folds, coating it in moisture.

"Ah, Barbs," he groans, bringing his finger to his mouth and sucking on it. "You are killing me, sweetie."

I smile and look away.

"So shy. So beautifully innocent. And all mine," he murmurs lovingly.

Using the same finger, he traces my sex, teasing me until I become comfortable enough to part my legs for him to settle between my thighs. With a wicked smile, he places my legs on his shoulders and he leans in, his mouth at the same level as my sex.

"Nyk... Uhm..." I mumble, utterly embarrassed.

"Do not hide from me, Barbs. You are my mate. That means this is mine, is that not so?" he asks shamelessly as he presses his finger against my clit.

I shudder.

He moves lower, circling my entrance and gathering all the moisture gushing from inside of me.

"Look how wet you are for me. Fucking hell, Barbs." He closes his eyes and inhales me deeply.

I squirm against him. His tentative touches are threatening to kill me.

"Ah, there is my greedy girl." He smirks. "And your cunt is just as greedy for me, isn't it?"

My eyes flare in shock at his words, and I grab a pillow and place it over my face in embarrassment.

"Do not!" he commands, and the pillow flies from my hands. "I want to see you, Barbs. I want to see the pleasure on your face. I want to see your every damn reaction."

I lick my lips and I give him a tentative nod.

He smiles, and he turns his attention back to my aching sex.

He pushes his finger inside me, probing at my entrance.

I tense. That stings.

"Fuck me. You are so damn tight," he mutters to himself.

I don't have time to think about that, however, as he leans in and gives me a slow lick just as he pushes his thick finger farther inside me. It's a tight fit, and he's only using one finger.

He lays the flat of his tongue against my clit as he thrusts his finger in and out of me.

My toes curl against the mattress. I arch my back and release a soft moan.

Threading my fingers through his hair, I hold him in

place. If a moment ago I was uncertain about this, now I can only urge him forward, beg him to devour me and bring me closer to that ineffable pleasure.

He smiles against me and blows hot air over my clit. He drags his tongue all along my slit, and with each new tease, I get wetter, more aroused. He takes his time to elicit every sensation possible out of my body, yet it's all a tease as he brings me to the peak, only to pull me back, tricking me with the promise of that delicious fulfillment.

"You taste so sweet, baby. Just like I knew you would," he purrs, burrowing his face between my thighs. "You have been taunting me with the smell of this sweet cunt for months. And here I am. Too weak to fucking resist you," he says as he sucks my clit between his lips, the vibrations from his throat sending me into overdrive. He works his finger in and out of me until he hits a spot that has me spasming.

"Nyk… Almost there… I'm almost…"

"Just like that, sweet girl. Come for me," he commands, biting hard on my clit. His fangs penetrate my flesh, drawing blood at the same time as my orgasm grips me.

I dig my heels into the mattress, clamping my thighs around his head. He continues to lick the mix of arousal and blood.

My eyes snap shut and I can barely cling to sanity as I ride wave after wave. The mark on my chest too, vibrates, enhancing the pleasure until I'm not sure anymore whether I'm on a physical plane or a metaphysical one.

My lips part until the only sounds I make are a succession of gasps and moans. The more he teases my sex, the more the aftershocks affect me, and I tumble into another orgasm.

The waves are never-ending.

They ripple and they form again, seemingly one stronger than the other. And as he digs his fangs into my inner thigh, drawing more blood, I scream out his name. So loud, the earth shakes. So loud, the walls around us quake, the glass windows cracking from the high voltage.

"Nyk, Nyk, Nyk," I chant his name all over again.

I don't know what's going on anymore.

There's only the weight of his body on top of mine as he continues to kiss his way up my chest. I'm still caught in the throes of the orgasm when he lays his lips on top of mine, letting me taste myself on his tongue.

"You are *mine*," he rasps against my lips. "Only mine. Only *ever* mine."

The fog that's laid claim over my mind suddenly dissipates when I feel a strong pressure at my entrance. Tears burn behind my retina as my eyes flare open in shock. He's there, trying to push inside of me.

He's staring at me with a savage expression—one that's both claimed by lust but also something else. A calculating look that scares me to my core.

"Nyk, no," I finally find my voice as I push at his shoulders. "Not now. I'm not ready," I tell him.

He stares at me unflinchingly and he doesn't stop.

The head of his thick cock slips a little inside of me, stretching me painfully.

"Nyk, stop it!" I repeat, trying to get him off me.

It's almost as if he's a different person. He regards me with a total lack of empathy, his expression cold and apathetic. Yet in a flash, that dangerous look is gone. He's back to being my Nyk and he pulls back. A stinging pain echoes at my entrance.

I scramble away from him, blinking repeatedly in shock.

"I got carried away." He gives me a tight smile. "Sorry."

I breathe in and out. The euphoria from before is all but gone as I try to reconcile the Nyk I know to the one I just witnessed.

Wrapping the towel around me, I get out of bed and head to the window in an attempt to put some distance between us.

A throbbing headache assails me, and more pain flares

between my legs. Glancing down, I note a few drops of pink flowing down my inner thighs.

"Barbs?" Nyk's voice startles me. He's behind me.

"If I say no, you need to stop." I turn to tell him.

"I lost control. I am sorry," he murmurs, leaning down to press a kiss against my temple.

"I appreciate you trying to comfort me, but I almost got raped today," I tell him sternly. "Do you think I'd want to lose my virginity right after such a traumatic event?"

"I know, I'm sorry." He embraces me from behind. "But look on the bright side. You opened your fourth gate today. You are almost there."

I freeze. A cold feeling of dread spreads down my spine.

What the hell?

<h1 style="text-align:center">33</h1>

That odd moment is quickly forgotten as we continue with my training for the remainder of the week while also planning for our presence at the masquerade ball.

"I have managed to find the list of attendees," Nyk says as I take a break from my training. "I have already taken care of some inconsequential ones, and we will go to the ball in their stead."

"Are you sure we will not get caught?" I frown.

He smiles.

"I have everything planned out, Barbs. We will be in and out. I only need to gather some information on my family's state of affairs to know where to strike next."

"Oh. So there won't be any confrontation at the ball?"

"No. This is just reconnaissance. Once I have the necessary information, we can make our exit, and we can focus on your descent into the lake. Although you have opened the fourth gate, I want to personally test you to make sure you are ready," he adds.

"Okay. You know best."

He seems pleased with my words.

"Come. Let me show you what I got us for the masquerade."

He leads me upstairs to our room. On the bed, a large pink box awaits me, with a smaller white one next to it.

Giddiness erupts inside of me as I hurry forward.

Nykander leans against the doorframe, watching me with satisfaction in his eyes.

I all but rip the cover of the first box, my breath leaving my lungs as I stare at the most gorgeous dusty shade of pink I've ever seen. Taking out the dress from the box, I lay it over the bed, marveling at the rich details and the flattering silhouette.

"Wow, Nyk! I have no words. Where did you get this? It's absolutely gorgeous!"

"I knew you'd like it," he mentions as he comes in. "Put it on. I want to see you in it."

I quickly kick off my training gear and put the dress on. Nyk helps me tie the corset at the back and snap all the buttons in place.

The dress is a regency-style one with a high empire waist and a flowing silky skirt made out of multiple layers of the softest material I've ever felt. The bodice has embroidery all over the chest area, depicting a bucolic hunting scene in different shades of pink. But what's even more impressive is the fact that there are three small dogs embroidered on it—*our* dogs.

"You had this custom made, didn't you?"

He smiles, and that's confirmation enough.

The next box contains the shoes. They are a satin pink with a three-inch heel and a similar embroidery on the front of the shoe. I put them on and immediately I feel like a princess who's just stepped into a real-life fairy tale.

"This is wonderful, Nyk. Absolutely wonderful! Thank you so much. It's the best gift someone's ever given me!" I tell him as I twirl around the room, letting my happiness spill forward.

"There is something more," he adds.

Moving to the bed, I realize there is one more small box. Opening it, he removes a black and pink lace mask from within. He places it over my face and moves behind me to tie it off at the back of my head.

"You are beautiful, Barbs," he murmurs, leaning in to lay a gentle kiss on my shoulder.

That night, I go to sleep filled with happiness and hope.

Although that incident last week had left a sour taste in my mouth, Nyk had more than made it up to me. He's been thoughtful and attentive, and the amount of detail he'd put into this dress alone speaks of the fact that he knows me.

He knows and loves me.

A dreamy sigh escapes me as I succumb to sleep. And despite my initial reservations, I am ready for the masquerade.

The following day, we spend hours getting ready and going over every potential thing that might go wrong.

Nyk gives me a quick lesson on some of the most important guests I should avoid and a short overview of the Jubal palace and the main area where the party will be conducted.

I do my makeup and put the dress and mask on while Nykander puts on a dashing velvet red suit accompanied by a similar mask that covers two thirds of his face.

"Shall we?" he asks as he takes my arm.

"Is it bad that I'm a bit excited about it? Especially since it's a masquerade. How fun is that!" I gush.

He smiles and shakes his head.

Leading me out of the lighthouse, I'm surprised to see a carriage with flying horses waiting for us out front.

Nyk opens the door for me to climb and then joins me.

It doesn't take long for us to reach Jubal palace. We land a small distance away, and the horses continue on a canter forward.

There is a long line of carriages leading up to the palace gates.

Due to the number of guests, the line moves slowly, during which time Nykander reminds me once more of the protocol at the party.

"Try to speak as little as possible," he advises. "You might speak the same language, but there are certain tells that will give you away. Do not engage with other males. While I am gone, stick to a corner and pretend to eat or drink something."

"My, but you should have given me a list. This is too much for my feeble brain," I add playfully.

"Barbi," he adds in a warning tone. "I am serious. This is a very important event and we cannot be found out. I am not ready for Tartareia to know I have returned."

"All right, all right. I will behave."

He grunts.

Our carriage moves forward, finally stopping at the palace gates for the guards to check our identities.

Nykander places his arm over me.

"Lord and Lady Garos," he states.

The guards stare at us intently for moments on end before they nod, ticking off the names on their list.

"What just happened?" I ask on a whisper.

"Let's just say our aura matched that of Lord and Lady Garos," he adds in a tight voice.

Before I can question how that is possible, we've made it past the palace gates. Immediately, I feel a shift within me and I lose all contact with my source of energy.

Suddenly, I feel…bereft.

A gasp escapes me, but Nyk grabs my hand and squeezes it—a sign he needs me to keep quiet.

I've only had my abilities for a while, but the sudden absence cuts me to my core.

"You will get used to it," Nyk whispers. "It is always harder the first time."

"But—"

"We have arrived," he states as the carriage comes to a halt.

He helps me out and leads me toward the sumptuous entrance of the palace. Gilded marble shadowed by a blood-red sky. Despite my first impression of a fairy tale, it is quite clear I am in hell.

As we step through the arched entrance, we go down a long corridor that is decorated with skulls, bones, and other artifacts. There is a line of people ahead of us, and they all stop to admire the objects on display.

"What are those?"

"Dead Aperite Supremes," Nykander mentions. "Each House proudly displays their spoils of war, and the House of Jubal has one of the most impressive collections of Supreme memorabilia."

My mouth drops open in shock.

We walk slowly, following the rest of the guests, but I can't help the way my gaze is drawn to the barbaric display. Especially now knowing that those are *my* people. Are any relatives of mine there too? People that my mother would have known? A feeling of disgust settles in my stomach—and we haven't even reached the ballroom.

All the other guests are wearing masks concealing most of their features. But there seems to be an unspoken rule that everyone knows everyone by the way they interact with each other. It makes me wary about our ruse being discovered before Nyk gets the information he needs.

"Chin up, Barbi. You cannot let them know you are afraid," Nyk murmurs in my ear.

I gulp down in uncertainty, but I nod my assent, doing as he says.

After a long meandering through the hallway full of war spoils, we finally reach the main ballroom. My mouth drops open in shock. The ceiling must be twenty feet tall. The walls are painted a dark red, which is complemented by gilded accessories. Six huge chandeliers hung from the ceiling, their brilliance enveloping the entire room in a bright light.

The floor is a hard wood accompanied by the occasional blood red carpet.

On all sides of the ballroom, there are tables with food and drink, but there are no seating arrangements, suggesting this is a standing event not a sitting one.

The ballroom quickly fills up. By my estimations, there must be a couple hundred people in here.

With everyone busy greeting each other, Nykander leads me in the back to one of the refreshment tables. Handing me a glass, he pretends to make conversation while he surreptitiously studies his surroundings.

"Do you see your family?" I whisper.

He shakes his head. "Not yet. I assume they will arrive later since they are from the bride's side."

I NOD. "Do you know anyone else here?"

HIS LIPS CURVE UP. "I know *everyone* here. Which is why I cannot be seen or recognized."

"Even with the mask…?"

"I will not take any chances," he mutters, not looking at me. "Stay here. Nurse your drink. Grab a bite to eat. But most importantly, do *not* talk to people. I will be back shortly. Is that clear?"

"You are already leaving?" My eyes widen.

"I need to finish this fast," he mentions as he leans in to kiss me on the cheek. "I will come back for you here, so do not wander too much."

With that, he turns his back to me and leaves. I follow his retreating figure until I lose him amid the sea of guests.

A shudder of discomfort goes down my back.

I knew what to expect, but I did not anticipate I would feel so out of place.

Taking his advice, I turn to the table and study the offerings. I grab a plate and fill it with some food that looks remotely familiar—meat, eggs, and a few snacks—after which I grab a glass of wine.

"Pelopia is so lucky that Armand wants to marry her," a voice speaks. A group of girls gathers close to the refreshments table and fills their plates with food.

"Right? I cannot believe he will overlook her widow status. It's positively scandalous."

"Why do you think that is, Mia?" Another girl rolls her eyes. "He wants the v'Kyro connection. He is playing the long game. He knows the *thantor* will return and he wants to make sure he's on the right side when he does."

"It's been too long. Do you really think he is going to return? We've all been stuck here for thousands of years."

"The Council is close to finding a way out. Have you forgotten about Elias and the Chalice? He's on our side now. It won't be long before the realm's doors will open for good. Rumor has it that the Chalice is *here*, at the palace."

"I don't know. Even with the Chalice, the Sons of Tenebreis that can go outside can only do so for a limited amount of time before they're yanked back by the seal. I doubt the *thantor* can do anything."

"We shall see," the girl huffs.

I'm not entirely sure what their conversation is about, but before they can spot me and God forbid, ask me who I am, I quickly sneak away with my food. Nyk said I should stick by the refreshments table, but surely he won't mind if I go onto the balcony. After all, I'll draw far less attention there than in the ballroom. If he wanted me not to stand out, maybe he shouldn't have gotten me such a pretty ensemble. Not that everyone else isn't beautifully dressed. But my pink dress is one of a kind if I do say so myself.

Smiling to myself, I head out the double doors that lead onto a small balcony.

A light breeze brushes against my cheek and I take a deep breath. This feels nice.

There is a table and two chairs a little farther inside the balcony, and I take a seat, placing my food and drink on the table.

I eat slowly.

Music blares from inside the ballroom, and the party begins in full swing.

I sip my wine. It's quite nice. It has a sweet, cherry undertone to it. I take another sip.

Minutes pass, and boredom ensues.

But right as I'm about to get up and go back to the refreshments table in case Nyk is searching for me, a woman plops herself in the other seat. She releases a loud sigh and downs the remainder liquid from her glass.

I stare at her. I should leave…

I stand up and slowly step away, but her hand reaches out and she pulls on my skirt, stopping me.

"You do not have to leave," she slurs. "It is my fault I intruded," she murmurs. Her eyes are unfocused, her body slumped over the table as if she can barely stop herself from falling asleep.

With the protective runes in place, I assume that people are more susceptible to getting drunk and sick. And despite knowing I shouldn't interact with anyone, I can't leave her like this.

"Are you all right?" I ask as I pat her back. "Do you want me to call someone?"

She releases a laugh that turns into a snort.

"My future husband. But he will not care much. There is also my mother. But she would get mad at me for ruining the party, so please no." She wrinkles her nose, her expression pensive. "There is also my brother. But he is currently negotiating a business deal with an important guest... I forgot his name." She burps. "Oops, I'm sorry." She giggles.

"It's all right." I smile.

"There is my other brother too." She frowns. "He would have cared. But he is not here. He is loooong gone."

"I'm sorry," I murmur.

"Oh, he is not dead, though sometimes I wish he were," she continues.

I frown. That does not make much sense, does it?

"You're probably wondering who this crazy lady is." She laughs. "Trust me, I wonder about that all the time too."

With her free hand, she wrenches her mask away, regarding me expectantly as if waiting for me to recognize her.

Shit!

I mask my features and plaster a polite smile on my face.

"I know what you're thinking. Why would the bride-to-be get so drunk at her own engagement party?"

"I'm sure it's none of my business..."

"I *hate* him. That wretched Armand. I hate, hate, hate, hate, hate. Did I say I hate him? Because I do. He is a wimp and a half, and I'd rather die than marry him. But I don't even have the luxury of dying," she grits out, smashing her glass to the ground.

"Erm..."

Okay, so this is Nyk's sister. They don't look alike at all. She's a petite blonde with blue eyes while he's a giant and a half.

"If only Nykander were here." She sighs. "He would put an end to this farce."

"I'm sorry," I whisper again, not knowing what else to say to comfort her.

"He would have probably killed that wimpy Armand for even daring to look at me," she continues. "But then again, it's been a lifetime since I've seen him. I doubt he would even recognize me now."

"Maybe I should leave." I smile. "And you can have a moment to yourself away from the party."

"I always thought I would have what he and Mo did," she slurs out as she rests her head on the table. "He never looked at another. Even to my young eyes that was impressive. That dolt Armand has eleven mistresses. Eleven! When does he even have the time to be with them? It's outrageous! Damn it! I hope his dick falls off," she murmurs sleepily.

A moment later, her snores echo in my ears.

My lips purse.

Why do I have to be reminded of that goddamn Mo at every turn?

"Ugh," I grit aloud as I stomp out of the balcony and back to the ballroom.

Making my way back to the refreshments table, I spot Nykander looking frantically for me. His eyes widen when he spots me, and without a word, he grabs my arm and leads me toward the exit.

"What's going on?" I frown.

"We need to leave. Now."

"But—"

"Later, Barbi. It is imperative we leave *now*."

I go along with him. As we reach the hallway with the spoils of war, he stops in front of one of the skulls. Reaching behind it, he presses a button that opens a small doorway. He drags me inside and closes the door.

Loud footsteps echo outside the moment we're inside.

"Come," he says, pulling me farther down the small corridor. It's almost pitch-black, but he appears to know where we're going.

We walk for what feels like forever before we come to a wall. He pushes me behind him as he throws his entire body weight against the wall until it gives way. And when it does, we're outside, far away from the city or the palace.

"Hold on to me. I'll teleport us back to the lighthouse."

He doesn't give me time to speak as he wraps me in his arms. The next time I open my eyes, we're back in our room.

He releases a harsh breath as he throws his mask to the bed and drags his fingers through his hair.

"What happened?"

"I must have triggered an alarm or something," he says, muttering a string of curses under his breath. "But it is all right now. We made it out and they don't know it was me who triggered the alarm."

There's something odd about him.

He seems on edge. Tense.

"I met your sister," I mention, though it doesn't seem to be the right thing to say.

He narrows his eyes at me.

"I told you not to talk to anyone."

"*She* talked to me." I shrug. "She was drunk and sad because she hates her fiancé."

"Doesn't surprise me. He is a fucking loser."

"That's what she said, too." I giggle.

"What else did she say?" he asks, staring at me intently.

"She mentioned you, actually," I start. He freezes, and a twitch appears in his cheek.

"Is that so?" he asks slowly.

"She said she wanted what you and Mo had. That you were so devoted to her you never looked at another woman."

His shoulders relax.

"Barbs. We have talked about this before. Mo was in the past. You are my present."

"Is it going to be like this every time, then? When I meet someone from your past, are they all going to mention how much you loved Mo? How good you were together?"

"Barbs…"

"It's always Mo this, Mo that. How can I compete with a ghost, Nyk?"

"You are blowing this out of proportion. I assured you she would not come between us."

"You did. But sometimes I can't help but wonder. You said you will always love her, and I can accept that, but... Do you love her *more* than me?"

"Barbs, please." He takes a step back.

"Please tell me," I beg. "I want to hear it from your lips."

He presses his lips together.

"No," he speaks slowly. "I do not love her more than you. Does that answer your question?"

I stare at him.

Slowly, I nod.

"Good. Now come here," he murmurs, spreading his arms open.

I run into his embrace, letting the warmth from his body soak into my own.

"No more doubts, Barbs. Promise me," he whispers against my hair.

"No more doubts. I just... I want to be the only one you love."

"You are the only female in my life, sweet thing," he says gently, seeking my lips with his own.

I wrap my arms around his neck and let him lead me to the bed, slowly lowering me onto the mattress and blanketing my body with his.

"Be mine, Barbi," he murmurs huskily as he peppers kisses all over my face. "I need you, sweetheart. I need to feel you, own you, sink myself into you until you crave me as much as I crave you."

I swallow hard, his deep voice sending a shiver down my spine.

"Nyk..."

"Please say yes, sweet thing," he continues, raising himself slightly to look into my eyes.

His irises swirl into a mercury silver shade as he regards me.

"Tell me you are ready for me. Tell me you want me as much as I want you; that you yearn for my touch as much as I yearn for yours," he whispers softly.

I bite my lip as I give him a slight nod.

"I do. I want you. I do, but——"

"No buts," he cuts me off. "It's just us. Me and you, Barbs. Me and you against the world. And I need you more than I need my next breath."

I bring my hand to his cheek and he leans into my touch, closing his eyes and releasing a deep breath.

"You love me, do you not?" He asks as he presses a kiss to the center of my palm.

I nod.

"I love you more than anything," I confirm.

His lips curl up.

"Show me. Show me how much you love me, Barbs. Let your body be the medium through which you show me what words fail to," he murmurs.

My lashes flutter, simulating the way the butterflies in my stomach flap their wings at his sweet words.

"I am on fire for you, sweet thing. Feel this," he says as he takes my hand and presses it against his chest. The beat of his heart reverberates against my palm, and as he slides my hand upward, I feel the searing pulsation of our bonding mark.

If we do this… If we give in to this insane compulsion, the bonding mark will become a mating one.

We will be mated.

For all eternity.

Suddenly, I feel ready.

For him. For us. For the life that awaits us—together.

"Do you feel it, Barbs? Do you feel what you do to me?"

Before I can answer, he slides my hand lower, over the hard planes of his chest. He doesn't stop. My fingers graze his belt before he places my open palm over the hardness pushing against the fabric of his trousers.

My breath hitches.

"This is how much I need you," he rasps. "I need to fuck you. Claim you. Mark you. I need to own your body just like I know I own your soul."

My pulse speeds up with every word he utters.

Heat pools low in my belly, desire unlike I have ever experienced poking its head through the surface and drowning me in a sea of emotions. It's overwhelming. It's absolutely breathtaking. As breathtaking as his dark gaze is as it engulfs me into its depths.

I wet my lips.

"I don't want you to fuck me," I start. His eyes widen and his body tenses. "Not now."

His gaze darkens as he braces himself for my refusal.

I smile. "I want you to make love to me, Nyk. You can fuck me later all you want. Now I just want to feel you."

An odd look crosses his face before his lips slowly curve up.

"Ah, sweetheart. I will make love to you until you melt in my arms. That is a promise," he says with a wicked smile.

Pulling back, he undoes the buttons of his shirt, throwing it to the floor.

I greedily take him in. His skin glows in the dim lighting offered to us by the twin moons. His muscles bulge and flex with every movement, emphasizing his strong built and filling me with a sense of safety. In his arms, I am at home. Safe. Protected.

I trail my fingers over the ridges of his abdominals, feeling him strain against my touch.

He's a wonderful male specimen. So beautiful, sometimes it hurts to look at him.

And he's all mine.

The fates decreed he would be mine, and now, in this moment, he will irrevocably become mine.

"Let me see you," he rasps. With expert fingers, he gently undoes the opening of my dress, sliding it down my body until I'm left only in my underthings.

I get the momentary urge to cover myself, but I fight against it.

It's him. Nykander. My love. My mate. There is nothing to fear when I am in his care—nothing at all.

He presses his hand against my throat in a possessive grip before he trails his fingers down my body, slowly caressing me. Before I know it, he takes my bra off and throws it to the floor. I arch my back, thrusting my breasts forward. My mind becomes blank until the only thing I can think of is his hands on my body and his mouth on my skin.

"So beautiful," he whispers, but he doesn't indulge me immediately.

He stares at my body in awe, his eyes dripping with desire.

With one finger, he trails a scorching path between my breasts, teasing me mercilessly.

"Nyk," I call out his name, my voice breathy and needy.

34

"There she is." He smirks. "There's my girl."

His girl. That's all I want to be. His.

I want to belong to him wholly until we are no longer two people, just one. Until my heart matches the beat of his heart.

"Yours," I whisper. "I've been yours from the beginning."

He lowers his mouth to my breasts, his hot breath caressing my skin. His lips trail over my flesh before he lays a kiss over my bonding mark. Slowly, he travels lower, wrapping his lips around one nipple and sucking on it.

A wave of electricity travels through me. I let out a breathy moan as his tongue circles around the erect bud, nibbling on the sensitive flesh.

"Nyk," I whimper, thrashing my head from side to side.

His body blankets mine, his heat transferring into me and providing me with warmth where I didn't know I was cold.

"I love you," I whisper. "So, so much."

He hums deep in his throat as he sucks on my nipple. Moving to the other breasts, he repeats the ministrations.

His hot mouth slides lower to my stomach, and he lays wet, open-mouthed kisses all over my flesh.

"You like that," he murmurs, the vibrations echoing into my skin. "You like my mouth on you, don't you, Barbs?"

"Yes," I nod. "Please…"

I don't know what I'm asking him to do. There's only this overwhelming need to feel him closer; to have him touch me everywhere.

He smiles, nuzzling his face against my stomach. The sharp tips of his fangs graze against my skin, and a spark of electricity erupts within me. His big hands cup my breasts, pleasuring me gently while he teases me with the promise of pain.

A moan slips past my lips when his fangs penetrate my skin. Blood flows into his mouth, splattering over my stomach. The same spot on his stomach rips apart, gushing more blood, staining both of our bodies in a combination of our essences.

He licks a fiery path from under my breasts to my hip bone, where he nibbles on my flesh. It's slow and playful at first before he lodges his fangs into my skin.

I cry out.

He drags his fangs lower, creating a gash in my flesh that gushes out blood.

The pain is intense. But so is the pleasure of his touch and the wetness of his mouth as he flicks his tongue over the wound.

It's hot. It's primal, animalistic and hot.

His own flesh rips apart, mirroring my own wounds, and more blood flows between our bodies, lubricating our movements and staining the entire bed red.

His tongue laps greedily at my blood, not letting any drop go to waste.

And as he moves lower, tension knots in my belly as I await for him to touch me where I need him the most—where my blood and arousal meet and await for him to feast.

My light pink panties are drenched and dripping red. His

nostrils flare as he lays his nose against my mound, sniffing me.

"So damn sweet." He groans, squeezing his eyes shut. "Your sweet cunt is weeping for me, isn't that right, Barbs?"

I nod eagerly.

"This is mine," he murmurs. "This sweet spot between your legs that no one's ever touched before—that only I know what it tastes like."

"Yes, only yours. Now please…"

I can barely form any coherent thoughts as he dips one finger between my legs, following the contour of my sex through my soaked panties. There's only a scrap of fabric separating us, and I wiggle against him as I urge him to remove that last barrier and touch me.

"Nyk… I need…"

"I know what you need." He winks at me.

The tip of his finger stops over my clit, and he gives it a soft flick that has me digging my heels in the mattress.

But Nykander doesn't play fair.

His mouth hovers over my aching sex as he teases me with the promise of sweet fulfillment. But suddenly, he stops. He raises his head just enough to give me a bloody smirk before he flips me on my belly.

A startled cry escapes me.

"Do you know," he starts as he lays the flat of his tongue over my ass cheek, "I have been watching you shake this ass in front of me for months and I have been imagining all the ways I would take you—all the ways I would claim this tight body of yours."

My breath hitches.

"Hard. Fast. Rough…" He pauses. "But also slow and gentle, taking my time with you until you beg me for more. Until you beg me to take you like the animal that I am."

He drags his fangs over my ass, gripping my flesh tightly before he bites it.

"Nyk," I moan aloud.

The sting of pain immediately gives way to immense pleasure, especially as he grabs on the sides of my underwear and tugs. The material rips, and as he discards it aside, he now has direct access to my most intimate spot.

I thrust my ass towards him, arching my back as I seek more of his touch.

"Please…"

"Please what? Say the words, Barbi. Tell me what you want me to do."

"Touch me," I whimper. "Put me out of my misery, please."

"Like this?" He asks as he dips one finger between my ass cheeks, sliding it lower until he encounters my wetness. He circles my hole, playing with my arousal.

I squirm against him.

"Yes… Oh, yes!"

He probes my entrance, pushing his finger inside me and stroking my inner walls. I clench around his digit, my breath coming in short spurts as my anticipation builds.

He trails his mouth all over my ass cheeks, biting and nibbling and occasionally sinking his fangs into me, all the while pumping his finger in and out of me.

"So wet," he murmurs appreciatively. "So fucking wet for me."

I feel his hot breath against my wetness, his mouth moving lower until his tongue replaces his finger. He presses his tongue deep inside me, tasting me, drinking me in.

I pull at the sheets, my fingers wrapped around the material.

His big palms cup my ass cheeks, kneading my flesh while his face is buried between them. He licks and kisses me as if he can't get enough, and the sensation of his tongue alone is enough to send me into overdrive.

His touch is fire, but one I would willingly allow to consume me.

Trailing his tongue lower, he wraps his mouth around my clit, sucking on it. I almost shoot off the bed at the sudden burst of electricity that moves through my body..

"Hold onto the railing," he commands.

I do as he says, wrapping my fingers around the metal railing of the bed and holding tight.

He nuzzled his face between my legs, and I feel him smile against my most intimate place before he resumes his ministrations. He flicks his tongue across my clit in rapid motions. My muscles tense, knots forming in my belly as my body prepares itself for the impending release.

But then he stops. Again.

"Nyk," I call out on a frustrated moan. "I need…"

"I know sweet thing." He chuckles, blowing air against my dampness. "I know exactly what you need. And you will get it. When the time is right."

"You wicked demon!" I retort, my voice breathy.

I bury my head in the sheets as he continues his torture, licking, nibbling and biting until he drives me crazy with want only to stop when I'm about to come.

Sweat builds up on my forehead, and tears stab at my eyes as I feel myself right at the edge of the precipice but unable to jump.

His sharp fangs graze my clit as he sucks in it, drawing blood.

The mix of pain and pleasure makes me spasm, an echo of an orgasm building inside of me. Just as tension builds inside of me again, ready to be released, he flips me onto my back.

I let out a surprised cry.

He chuckles, a dark look descending upon his features as he stares at my naked sex.

His lips and chin are stained red. A few drops of blood cling to his fangs, slowly transferring onto his lips.

I lean forward, pressing my lips against his own and capturing those errant drops. I suck his lower lip in my mouth, tasting myself on him.

His eyes widen in surprise at my initiative. His mouth curves up as he licks my lips before biting me in return. Blood flows between us. I bleed, he bleeds.

He wraps his hand around my throat and pulls me back, his eyes a cloudy silver that swirls with uncertainty. His tongue peeks out to lick the residual blood before he pushes me on the mattress and looms over me.

My wounds are already healed, but as he leans forward and captures my lips anew, he bites me so hard, I twitch in pain. His fangs penetrate my lower lip, and they lodge deeply in my flesh. Closing his mouth over my lower lip, he plays with it with his tongue, sucking all the blood flowing from my wound. And just as it threatens to close again, he increases the pressure, his bite even stronger.

His fingers are tightly wound around my neck and he has me trapped. The hold is not unbearable, but it is one step away from being suffocating. The pain from my lip makes me lightheaded, but as he reaches between our bodies with his other hand, he finds my damp sex and applies pressure in the right spot to make me buck against him.

He slips two fingers inside me—a delicious stretch. He pumps them in and out with increasing rapidity until I can't help the sounds that I make—the moans that he swallows and steals from me.

His thumb is on my clit as he pistons his fingers in and out of me.

"N-n-n-y-y-k…" I struggle to speak.

"Fuck you're hot. So damn hot," he says as he pulls his fangs from my lip. More blood flows between our mouths, down our chins and chests and covering us in red. He laps every drop off me as he continues to assault me with his fingers until I can't bear it anymore—until I scream at the top of my lungs as my release claims me.

Yet if I thought that was the end, I am about to be sorely mistaken.

My mind is fogged up by desire and the aftermath of my orgasm. I barely feel him release his hold on my neck and move down my body. But in no time he has my legs over his shoulders, his face buried between my thighs.

"Oh my God!" I yell as he flicks his tongue over my already sensitive flesh.

"Not God." He pauses, raising those stormy grey eyes to meet mine. "There is no god in this room other than me, sweet thing. Say my name," he commands.

My chest moves up and down, my breathing shallow.

"My name, Barbs. Say my name!"

"Nykander… Nyk…"

His lips twitch.

"Good girl," he murmurs.

He lays open-mouthed kisses all over my sex, teasing my clit with his teeth before sucking it in his mouth. He hums in the back of his throat, and the vibrations travel through me, intensifying all of his movements.

Despite being incredibly sensitive, I can't stop myself from coming again.

"Oh my—"

"My name, Barbs. I want to hear my name!" He interrupts me as I arch my back in the throes of my climax. I grasp onto the tangled sheets, my eyes squeezed shut as tears fall down my cheeks.

"Nyk," I moan. "My Nyk."

"That's my girl." He chuckles.

He gives me one last lick before he climbs up my body again, cleaning up the rest of the blood.

It takes me a moment to compose myself. And as I open my eyes, I come face to face with him.

He's so beautiful.

My heart thuds in my chest, threatening to poke a hole through it.

He's all wild locks and bloody lips, and when he looks at me with those stormy eyes of his, I feel like I've died and gone to heaven. It's the only explanation for this—for how lucky I am that the fates have paired us together.

"You're beautiful," I whisper, cupping his cheek.

He lays a kiss to the center of my palm.

"Not as beautiful as you," he murmurs. "You are perfect. Perfect for me," he continues, nibbling on my fingers. "Sweet. Innocent. *Untouched*. You are mine. Just mine. As it was meant to be."

I blink at his odd words, but I don't dwell on them.

Smiling, I push him off me, reversing our positions so that he's now on his back and I'm on top of him.

He raises a lazy brow, watching me with interest.

"My turn," I add shyly.

"Hmm, is that so?" He asks. "And what did you have in mind?" He places his arms under his head, gazing at me with droopy eyes.

"Well…" I bite my lip as I scan his strong chest. My gaze drops to his half undone belt and the hardness straining against the material of his pants. "First, you are wearing far too many clothes," I say as a shiver of anticipation goes down my back.

"Then you should do something about it," he challenges.

I swallow.

Letting him take the lead was much easier since he didn't give me the time to get lost in my head. But this… Do I dare?

One glance at him strengthens my resolve.

With careful fingers, I grab onto his belt and undo it before moving to the buttons of his pants.

Butterflies dance in my stomach, anxious ones, but also excited ones.

I might not know what I'm doing, but I've read enough to do a decent job—I think.

I take a deep breath as the last button pops free. Tugging on the waist band, I urge him to help me take his pants off.

A wicked smile pulls at his lips as he complies.

Throwing the pair of pants on the floor, he's now wearing only a pair of briefs.

"And…this?" I ask breathlessly.

He nods. "Go ahead."

Right. I can do this.

I nibble on my lower lip as I bring my hands to his briefs, slowly tugging them off.

His laughter echoes in the room as he stops me. My eyes fly to his. But in no time, he pulls his underwear off and he's naked before me—truly naked.

Good Lord!

This is the first time I've seen him fully naked. Heat travels up my neck, and my cheeks must be stained red—in addition to the blood stains.

I get the urge to fan myself, and also fangirl in a corner for a moment. But it wouldn't do to behave thusly when we're about to get down and dirty.

I stare intently at that hard part of him, unable to believe my eyes.

I'd felt it before. I'd also touched it through his pants. But I never realized it would look so…threatening?

I gulp down warily.

Glancing up, I find him watching me daringly, his handsome brow raised in an overt challenge.

"You have gone quiet," he notes, his voice dripping with amusement. "Do I not please you, sweetheart?"

"It does. I mean, you do," I stammer, forcing a smile. "It's a nice…appendage," I say, making a fool of myself—again.

Damn it! We just had an awesome sensual interlude just moments ago and here I go ruining it with my idiotic comments.

Appendage! Who the hell says that?

Well, me apparently.

"Appendage?" He repeats, the hint of a smile on his face.

"Uhm, yes. It is a nice package you got there." I laugh nervously. And to prove I'm not afraid of it—though I totally am—I touch it gently with one finger.

It twitches.

My eyes widen and I pull back.

"Barbs?" He calls my name, his head tilted to the side as he studies me.

"I'm fine, I'm fine," I repeat like a moron. "I'm *not* fine!" I eventually cry out, pointing out at his…thing. "That is too big, Nykander! You're going to split me into two. Why didn't you warn me?"

"Warn you?" He laughs. "And pray tell me, how should I have warned you?"

"I don't know. You could have told me that you have a monster in your pants? I could have at least mentally and spiritually prepared myself for it. But now…"

"Now?"

"You forget that the most I've had inside me are your two fingers—which are pretty big too, by the way. I don't know how that's gonna go in without tearing me in half."

"Sweetheart, I think you are getting ahead of yourself and—"

"Look," I say as I get closer to it. "It's literally the size of my forearm." I place my forearm next to his gigantic erection. They match. In fact, his might be thicker.

His shaft is straining against his stomach, angry veins scattered along its surface. The tip is a darker shade, spurting drops of white liquid. It's quite possibly the most beautiful dick I've ever seen—well, it's the only one I've ever seen in real life. But how will that translate to the actual *act*? I may heal, but... Oh my, will he feel it too? When he puts that thing inside of me, will he feel the pain of it too?

Well, he should! Why are women always on the painful receiving end of things?

The more I stare at it, especially as it twitches some more in my direction, the more my anxiety skyrockets.

Good Lord! This is how I'm going to die. Impaled on a gigantic demon dick.

And here I was laughing when the heroine in my romance novels was making a ruckus about the hero's dick. I mean, even in porn, I don't think I've ever seen a man sporting something the size of Nyk's dick.

"Barbs, you have gone silent again," he notes. But this time, as I look up, all traces of amusement are gone, his features tight with worry. "Are you all right?"

"Yes, of course," I mutter, leaning further in to inspect it. "I am just trying to get used to the thought of that thing going inside of me," I add absentmindedly.

"Cock," he says huskily.

"Huh?" I blink.

"It is not a thing, Barbs. It is a cock."

"Oh, okay."

"Say it," he demands.

I wet my lips. I am face to face with his...cock. It's even bigger up-close.

"Cock," I whisper. I touch the tips of my fingers to the shaft. Oh, it's soft. And warm. "This feels nice," I nod to myself. "But I still don't think it's going to fit very well. Look, it doesn't even fit in my mouth." As I say this, I pull his shaft towards me and fit my mouth over the tip. My jaw strains to accommodate his size, and though it's uncomfortable, I manage to stick at least the tip inside.

"Barbs." He groans, throwing his head back.

"What?" My voice is muffled, and I forget that I have very

sensitive flesh in my mouth. My teeth make contact with his shaft, and blood spurts inside my mouth.

My eyes widen.

"I-I a-am s-s-sorry," I stammer, but in my attempt to apologize, I bite down again. And this time, because the taste of blood is already fresh in my mouth, my fangs decide to make an impromptu appearance, nicking a vein.

Good Lord! I'm now going to drown in the blood from his dick!

I gag on the sudden flow of liquid, but surprisingly, instead of pulling me off him, Nyk grabs the back of my head and pushes me further down his shaft, feeding me a few more inches of his cock until it hits the back of my throat. My fangs graze more of his shaft due to the motion, but he doesn't seem to mind. Instead, he tightens his hold in my hair, his hips lifting off the mattress as he starts thrusting in and out of my mouth.

His head is thrown back, his mouth open as low moans of pleasure echo in my ears.

Oh. I must be doing something good. And to my surprise, I don't mind being choked on his cock. In fact, it's rather… pleasant. Especially as I watch his reactions and the way he's about to lose control.

His dark shadows seep out, surrounding us in a tight cocoon.

The blood overflows, dripping out of my mouth and down my chin.

His movements gain speed.

"Fuck. Just like that. Bite me," he rasps out.

I do as he asks, my fangs grazing up and down his cock before biting down hard.

He lets out a loud groan. He holds me down, thrusting into my mouth until he sticks the entire length of his monstrous cock down my throat. How he does it, I don't know, but I guess I'm here for the ride.

I breathe through my nose, slowly getting used to his intensity.

Maybe I should have asked him to fuck me from the get go. I'm kind of digging this forceful action he has going on. It's hot, not going to lie. Even as I'm choking and sputtering and my eyes tear from the intensity of it, it's hot.

Okay, that alleviates some of my concerns. If having his cock slammed down my throat is this hot, then having it slammed some other places might be even hotter.

My thoughts are interrupted when he pushes inside me all the way. My lips meet the base of his shaft when he stops, holding me in place. My jaw hurts. My lips are stretched around his thickness.

"That's a good girl," he rasps as he leans forward to watch me—us.

He holds me still against the base of his cock for a moment before he starts rocking slightly, pushing more of his length inside me.

Arousal drips out of me as I note the look of pure ecstasy on his face.

"Fuck. You have no idea what seeing you like this does to me," he mumbles, his voice barely coherent. His eyes are glazed, his irises a darker shade.

His nostrils flare.

"Ah." He smiles. "It makes you wet, too. You love being fucked like this, don't you?"

I nod eagerly. Yes, please fuck me some more. In fact, let's forget I asked about slow and gentle and give me hard and fast. Except I don't say this—I can't. The few mumbled words that come out result in more blood flooding my mouth.

He moans and rocks harder against me.

A few seconds later, the blood is accompanied by his hot seed. They mix in my mouth before going down my throat. He thrusts a few more times before he pulls me off him. His hand around my neck, he tips my head up to look at him.

"Swallow," he orders. "Swallow it all."

I do as he says.

His thumb caresses my lips, prying them open to inspect that I have, indeed, swallowed.

"Good girl," he whispers with a wink.

"You…liked it?" I ask in a low voice, needing more validation—needing to know he enjoyed it as much as I did.

"I fucking loved it. If I didn't know, I would have never thought this was your first time." He pauses. "It is, isn't it?" He narrows his eyes.

I nod.

"Of course it is," I huff aloud, rolling my eyes. "I've never even seen a…cock in person before today."

"Good." He nods, satisfied. "That is good. You are *mine*, Barbi. This body is mine and only mine, understood?"

"Yes. I am yours. Only yours."

A smile curves up his lips as he flips me on my back, pushing my legs open and sliding between them.

"So soon?" My eyes widen. "Don't you need time to…you know…recover?"

He smirks.

"You forget what I am, Barbs," he murmurs. "I am a wicked demon who is about to have his way with you."

As my eyes dip to his cock, I see that he is hard once more, blood staining his shaft and balls. He grips himself tightly as he rubs the tip of his cock against my entrance. He traces the outline of my sex, finding me even more drenched than before.

He lets out a low hum of approval.

"Fuck, you are so hot," he mutters under his breath as he mixes our juices together.

He slides his cock along the seam of my lips, eliciting low mewling sounds from me.

The fear from before is all but gone. He can split me in two all he wants as long as he takes me, ruts me, fucks me, does anything he wants with me. I don't even know where all these thoughts are coming from, but there is something inside of me that craves everything he has to give me.

"Do it," I tell him. "Take me."

I don't say it aloud, but he knows it.

Give me the pleasure and the pain!

"Patience." He chuckles.

He strokes me lightly, his thumb on my clit as he aligns the head of his cock to my entrance. Slowly, he pushes in.

My pulse quickens.

The mark on my chest heats up, creating an ungodly glow, one that's mirrored by his own mark.

There's a stinging sensation as he stretches me, inching his way inside as he continues to pet my clit.

I squirm against him. The pain is there, but it's not nearly as bad as I thought it would be. I am more annoyed at his slowness.

"Nyk, please," I whimper as I cant my hips so he can slide inside me faster.

"Tell me when it hurts," he grits out, his features strained.

"It's fine. Please…"

He pushes further in, filling me slowly. Despite my assurances, he takes his time. And when he's sheathed to the hilt, he stops, giving me time to accommodate to his girth.

The feeling of him inside of me is…wondrous. A dreamy sigh escapes me.

"Oh, Nykander," I murmur, beckoning him towards me. "Do you feel this?" I lay my hand flat on his chest, right on top of the mating mark.

It glows a deep red, its heat seeping into my palm and traveling through my body all the way to *my* mating mark. Through the simple act of touching, of having him inside me like this, the individual marks become one too. They morph under my very gaze, the symbols moving and turning until they settle on a shared combination—one that's now a dark red as opposed to the previous jet black.

"I do," he groans. His voice is thick and heavy, and as he looks into my eyes, I note the moisture clinging to his lashes.

He's…crying?

"Nyk…"

He squeezes his eyes shut and a teardrop falls down his cheek.

Digging his fingers into my hip bones, he withdraws all the way before he slams himself back inside of me, the power of his thrust making me reel. I hold onto him, grabbing onto his biceps as he lowers his mouth to mine, claiming it as he claims my body.

I'm wet enough that he slides easily in and out. Once the initial discomfort gives way, he moves smoothly, his length caressing my inner walls.

I wrap my legs around him, holding him close to me.

Each thrust is more powerful than the last. His mouth, too, emulates those movements as his tongue spars with mine, invading my mouth like he is invading my body—savagely but lovingly.

I clench my muscles around him and he groans against my mouth.

"Fuck. I don't think I'm going to last," he mutters in a low voice. "So tight. Been too long… I…" Before he can finish his sentence, his mouth seeks my neck and he bites me hard just as his cock starts spasming inside of me, filling me with his release.

I caress him gently down his back while he feeds, holding him deep inside of me until the last of his tremors have subsided.

When he's done, he laps gently at the wound until it closes, but he doesn't move.

His head on my chest, his cock still inside of me, he falls asleep in my embrace.

35

A pleasant smile pulls at my lips as I stretch awake. Nyk is next to me, the heat from his body seeping into my own and warming me to my core.

"Hello there," I murmur as I roll on top of him.

He blinks awake. His hair is mussed, stray locks draping down his forehead. There are still stains of red from last night's activities marring his flawless flesh.

I trace his lips with my finger, leaning down to lay a kiss at the corner of his mouth.

He mumbles something under his breath, his eyes suddenly opening.

"What are you doing?" He asks in a raspy voice.

I smile conspiratorially. "What do you think I am doing?"

I straddle him, my hands finding his hard flesh and stroking him lightly.

His brows go up in surprise.

"I remember saying you could fuck me after the first time," I murmur seductively.

His eyes flash at me.

"Is that so?"

I shrug, slowly raising myself and positioning him at my entrance.

He watches me intently.

Although it's still a tight fit, I take him in far easier than the night before. And as he nestles inside me fully, I release a throaty moan at being filled like this.

"Nyk…" I call his name.

I can feel my energy going wild around us, a pink mist emanating from my body as I start riding him.

"That's it," he encourages me, settling his hands on my hips and guiding me. "Take me. Take all of me, Barbs."

"Yes," I breathe out.

"Fuck yourself on my cock," he rasps. "Just like that."

His groans fill my ears as I close my eyes and throw my head back, focusing on this feeling of completion that is so much greater than I could have ever imagined.

I slide my hands lower down his chest, resting one palm against his mark while placing my other hand on my mark. The symbols heat up at once, the pleasure intensifying with each stroke of his cock inside me.

"I love you," I whisper, grabbing his hand and placing it on top of my mark so he can feel this too. "I love you so damn much, Nyk."

As I'm waiting to hear back the words, however, the pink mist around us intensifies and grows out of control. My eyes snap open, an unimaginable heat claiming my body as I make eye contact with him.

His features drip with indifference.

One split second is all it takes for his mask to drop.

Confusion swirls in my mind. I dig my nails into his mark, drawing blood.

My mouth opens and closes as a different picture forms before my eyes.

I blink and find myself in a dark cave. There is only one

stream of light coming from an opening in the right side of the ceiling. Yet as I look down, I realize it's not my body.

It's Nykander's.

My consciousness is here, but I am not in control. I am only a spectator.

"I have done what you asked of me," Nykander's voice calls out. There is a deep revulsion behind those words, but no reply is forthcoming.

Nykander lets his senses drift through every crevice of the cave. She is there. He can sense her.

"Show yourself!" he shouts.

Seconds trickle by and her steps resound in the cave.

She stops right under the beam of light, letting it illuminate her features. Her dark hair flows down her back, her face hidden beneath a thin veil.

"You would go this far for your revenge?" She tilts her head to the side as she assesses him.

"I am not required to give you an explanation," he grinds out. "I did as you asked. I apologized and she believes I want to be with her."

"And you do not regret lying to her? She is your true mate, after all."

His nostrils flare.

"It does not matter."

"See, but it does. I am curious, Nykander v'Kyró. You would forsake your true mate, the only being made just for you in the entire universe, to fulfill a revenge for someone who is long gone?"

"I require you to keep *your* side of the bargain, Priestess."

"I will call upon you in due time. That which you want will be yours once I am convinced you have fully played your part." She inclines her head.

Nykander nods and turns to leave.

Shock reverberates within me. He… He was pretending? But why? For what?

Realization dawns on me, the treachery of his actions stabbing my very soul.

The artifact.

He was bargaining for the artifact.

"You might fight it, but you *are* drawn to her. And when you fall for her as I know you will, what will you do if she finds out about your deception?" The High Priestess continues.

"I will *not* fall for her. There is only *one* female for me, and she is gone. Anything I do now is to honor her as I have vowed."

"And yet…" She clicks her tongue against her teeth. "You forget that I can see things invisible to the naked eye. You *will* fall, Nykander. I just pray when you do it will not be too late."

Nykander strides out of the cave, not bothering to look back.

Yet her words affect him, echoing in his ears and blaring louder and louder despite the increasing distance.

A foul taste coats his mouth—my mouth—the result of all the lies he spewed. But he is ready to pay any price for his revenge.

But I don't get to witness more as the scenery changes.

Nyk is in front of me, staring at me with an odd expression in his eyes while I fold our clothes to leave the Sanctuary.

"Stay here. I need to take care of something before we leave," he says, though the words come out of my mouth.

I remember exactly what moment this was—when he'd claimed he went to patch things up with Jeya and Elijah.

My presence remains in his psyche, yet there is still a barrier that does not allow me to read his thoughts in their entirety. I can only see what he sees—a spectator, not an active participant.

He teleports himself out of our cabin and into the woods nearby.

"You are late," a voice calls from behind.

Nyk turns.

Shock fills me to the brim when I see who the owner of that voice is.

Damien.

"She is Lispera's daughter. I was correct," he says in a tight voice. "Did you find what I asked you to?"

Damien walks around with his hands in his pockets.

"And if I did? What is in it for me?"

"I have already given you plenty of souls to consume, Damien. Cut the bullshit and tell me what you found."

Damien chuckles.

"Sure, master," he replies in a mocking tone as he half-bows.

Nykander scowls.

"The Seer confirmed that Mo's essence will be able to take over Barbi's body once she enters Lake Velor."

Nykander narrows his eyes.

"And the terms? What are the terms for this exchange to happen?"

Damien tilts his head to the side, silent for a moment.

"Speak or I will take away all those precious souls you store within your essence," Nykander thunders.

Damien grits his teeth, not responding well to the threat.

"You can channel her essence into the body of your female only once she's strong enough to withstand it. She will need to open her fourth gate."

"And?"

Another silence. Nykander uses grips tightly onto the master-slave bond he has with Damien to pry the words out of his mouth.

"You cannot claim her until she has opened the fourth gate. After she does, you must fulfill the mating bond. She cannot enter the lake while the bond is only half-fulfilled." The words flow out of Damien's mouth but he suddenly halts, his body trembling as he forces himself to clamp his mouth shut.

"Do not think to trick me, demon. What else? Tell. Me," Nykander warns.

"The female will need to wear something Mo prized— something that can call to her essence."

"Is that all?"

"Indeed, master." Damien nods.

Nykander considers his answer.

"Vow it on your existence."

Damien's nostrils flare.

"I vow it on my existence, master," the demon complies.

"I see. Thank you," Nykander mutters, deep in thought. "You may continue with what we have planned."

"As you say, master." Damien smirks, stepping back and retreating into the shadows.

Nykander waits for him to leave before he withdraws the red ruby ring from his pocket—the same one I thought he'd traded in the village. He touches the ring reverently before bringing it to his lips.

"Soon, Mo. You will be mine again."

His words echo in my ear as I am jolted back into the present.

Eyes wide, heart pounding in my chest, I push myself off him, stumbling on the far end of the bed. His absence inside me is marked, but the betrayal that stings at my soul eclipses every positive feeling I might have ever had for him.

"Barbs?" He frowns. "What is wrong?"

"Stay away from me," I say, my voice trembling with pain.

"Barbs—"

"Don't touch me!" I slap his hands aside as he tries to reach for me.

In my struggle to get away from him, I fall off the bed. And as he comes closer, I continue to retreat, my expression one of horror as I look into the face of the man I love—the man I gave myself to—and find a stranger.

"This was all a lie," I whisper. "Everything was a lie." I

shake my head in one last attempt at denial. But how can I deny what's in front of me. All at once, his features morph. He no longer sports the sweet, loving look he used to. Now his mouth is set in a grim line, his beautiful eyes hollow and empty. Indifference replaces what I had previously interpreted as love.

"You saw something," he comments in a bored voice. "What did you see, Barbi?"

"Everything," I whisper. "I saw everything… You've been using me all along, pretending to care about me when in fact…" I trail off as a sob racks my body. "My God, but you had me fooled. You had me wholly and utterly fooled. How you must have laughed at me," I add bitterly.

His cheek twitches. He stands up, unabashed about his nudity as he walks casually toward me.

"You were not supposed to find out like this." He sighs.

"No? And how was I supposed to find out? When my soul left my body so that your beloved can replace me? When my entire essence gets destroyed so your darling Mo can claim my body? When, Nykander? When?" I shout, the windows of the lighthouse shattering at my anger.

His lips flatten in annoyance—the only genuine emotion he appears to be capable of when it comes to me.

"Calm down, Barbi and we will discuss it. You likely only saw snippets out of context," he says.

"Oh, what was out of context? The fact that *you* caused the plague? Or that Damien was *your* thrall? Tell me, when he attacked the Sanctuary, it wasn't your brother controlling him, was it? It was you."

His silence speaks a thousand words.

I let out a dry laugh. Cracks slowly form around my heart, and with every second, I'm closer than ever to my breaking point.

"You killed millions of people. *Millions.*"

"I did what I had to do," he grits out. "You have no idea

what I have been through or the sacrifices I have had to make."

"Right. Go ahead and justify mass murder," I spit out.

He shrugs. And that tells me everything there is to know about him.

He is a monster.

"At least tell me something. When did you decide to use *me* in your plan?

His eyes glint dangerously. He takes another step forward.

I move back, stepping on broken glass that cuts into the soles of my feet just as the truth cuts into my heart.

"You are hurting yourself," he mentions, his tendrils seeping out of his body and moving wildly around, ready to strike. "Let us talk about this calmly."

"When, Nykander?" I demand again.

He tilts his head to the side.

I can't stop comparing the Nykander in front of me to the one I used to know. They are both equally beautiful, but where one was warm, the other is…horrifyingly cold. There is no empathy in his gaze, no compassion. There is only a cold, calculative look that chills me to my core.

He is…frightening in his indifference.

"When you arrived in Kiya," he answers. "You were supposed to lead me and my army of demons to Anthropa, but as it happened, I got lucky." He lets out a dry laugh.

"W-what?" I blink.

He takes another step forward.

"Why do you think I needed all those souls, Barbi?" He raises a brow. "They were not for me, nor were they to feed my legion of thralls, though they certainly got their due. A soul is the purest energy in the universe. And with enough of them, I would have been able to craft a new body for Mo. But as it happens, you fell into my lap and made my job so much easier," he smirks.

"But how… How could you have known what I was? How could you…"

He throws back his head and laughs.

"You are so awfully ignorant, sweetheart," he drawls.

"Don't call me that," I snap.

He merely chuckles.

"A true mating only happens within the same species. When the mating mark appeared, I knew you could not be *just* a human. You must have some divine energy within you. Whether that was Tartareian or Aperite…" he shrugs. "It was only a matter of finding what you are and how I could use that best, and…" he trails off with a smile. "You certainly did not disappoint. The daughter of the great Lispera herself."

It dawns on me that this *is* who he is. Until now, he's just been playing a role. He needed me, so he made himself into my ideal man, saying and doing all the things he *knew* would make me fall for him.

"You are vile," I whisper. "All those lies…"

"How is it my fault that you are so gullible? You are cute, Barbi and quite endearing. I must say, this was fun while it lasted."

My mouth opens and closes in shock.

Fun? This was…fun?

My energy simmers around me, my heartbreak fueling my anger. I'll show him fun! I'll fucking show him…

His dark tendrils surround me, extinguishing my emerging powers. He has me surrounded as he holds me in a tight grip, yet he's not touching me. I try to summon my shield, but I fail miserably.

"You are powerful, I will give you that. But you are no match to me." He laughs at my struggles.

"Fuck. You!" I grit out and spit in his face.

He wipes the moisture from his cheek before he curls his hand around my throat, lifting me in the air. His fingers dig into my airways, and I flail my limbs around in an attempt to get him off me.

"It really was not supposed to end this way."

He glances at me, his expression inscrutable.

"If only you had remained ignorant until the end… You would have gone into that lake, as I told you to, and all this mess would have been avoided. Now…" His lips pull up in a sad smile.

He carries me over to the broken window, dangling me over the edge.

I glance down, terror engulfing me.

The lake is unsettled, the red of the water rippling all around the lighthouse and forming a whirlpool of misery—*my* misery.

At once, I know that these are my last moments alive.

"Stop," I cry out. I attempt to hold onto him with all my might as my stomach drops just looking at the steep fall.

"I am sorry, Barbs. I really am." He smiles as he tucks a strand of hair behind my ear. "I do care about you, you know." He leans to whisper in my ear. "But I can never love you. My heart will be forever with her."

"Nyk, please," I stammer as he takes a step over the edge of the window. He floats in the air while I hold onto him for dear life. My powers are useless. No matter how much I summon my energy to the surface, I cannot. The shield he's placed over me inhibits my abilities, rendering me useless.

I can only stare into his hauntingly beautiful face as he sends me to my death.

Thud. Thud. Thud.

My heart beats louder and louder in my chest. The mating mark burns a hole through me, echoing this ineffable anguish that is wrecking my soul.

"Goodbye, Barbi," he murmurs softly as he lays a chaste kiss on my lips and wraps the necklace with his ring around my neck. "I will remember you fondly for your sacrifice."

Sacrifice? What sacrifice? This is *murder*, plain and simple.

He is…killing me. After all we shared, after all we have been through. He is killing me.

None of it was real.

Even my love that sprung from the deepest corners of my soul was not real.

I loved an illusion.

Once more, I fell in love with a character, not a person.

His cold gaze is the last thing I see as he pushes me off him.

My eyes flare in shock. I am unable to muster any strength to fight for my life. Disappointment and despair are my two companions as gravity pulls me down into the abyss. My mark consumes my flesh as pain consumes my soul.

Still, I watch him, wanting to remember this heartbreak forever. Even if my soul somehow dies, and even if Mo takes over my body, I want this pain to become ingrained in my flesh and every atom of my being.

"I hate you, Nykander v'Kyro," I whisper. And as I get close to the water, I close my eyes, readying myself for my demise.

The red water swallows me.

There is no more consciousness. No more awareness.

Just the emptiness of *not* being.

TO BE CONTINUED

For more epic romance set in the same fantastical universe, check out Of Ice and Villains and Fairydale!

BONUS CONTENT

Scan the code below for **FREE** bonus content!
Or visit www.veronicalancet.com/bonus-content

ALSO BY VERONICA LANCET

Barbi & the Villain Trilogy

Barbi & The Villain

House of Cryos Trilogy

Of Ice and Villains

Morally Ambiguous Duet

The Cute Psycho

His Hell Girl

Standalones

Fairydale

Frivolous

Morally Corrupt

War of Sins Series

The Taste of Revenge

The Foiled Plan

The Counterfeit Lover

The Sins of Noelle

The Moral Dilemma